Scaley Tales

G F Brogan

Kind regards
Gerry Brogan
xx

SWAN PUBLISHING
BEXLEY • KENT

First published in Great Britain in 2004 by
SWAN PUBLISHING
73 High Street
Bexley
Kent
DA5 1AA

ISBN 0-9547612-0-0

Produced and printed by members of
THE GUILD OF MASTER CRAFTSMEN

Book Design and Typesetting by Cecil Smith
Typeset in Galliard

Cover design and illustration by Stephen Coles

Printed and bound in Great Britain by
RPM PRINT & DESIGN
2-3 Spur Road, Quarry Lane, Chichester, West Sussex PO19 8PR

Dedication

This book is dedicated firstly to Auntie Ann who has tried to make sure that all sentences have a verb in them, secondly to my friend Brian who shortened this work by taking out most of the swear words, and finally to all those coppers who have been screwed by the system.

Contents

Introduction

This is a story about policemen and their daily 'doings' in the sixties and seventies. It is a blend of fact and fiction; which is which is for me to know and you to wonder about. I was not pursued by demons of conscience to write this account, far from it. In fact I have no view one way or the other about the wrongdoings or otherwise of the 'old bill'. All I am really saying is, this is the way it was, and some of this happened to me. It strikes me quite forcibly that the difference today with yesterday is that yesterday the villains were apprehensive and the coppers were confident. It is now the other way round with an extra complication of senior officers being bilingual in 'bollockese'.

This account was born out of a cardiac seizure. Whilst recovering from a heart attack, and in deep depression, a good friend of mine and fellow freemason encouraged me to write down all those, sometimes, funny stories which were trotted out so readily at the bar after a lodge meeting. The following is what evolved which I hope you, the reader, will find amusing in places and maybe thought provoking in others. This is as good a point as any to lay the ghost of 'freemasonry' which seems to have loomed large lately in the media. During the period covered by these scribblings I was not a freemason. I only joined some twenty years later as a good friend introduced me to the fraternity. I was impressed by the members and the work for charity and I joined and have enjoyed it immensely ever since. At the time covered by this journal freemasonry was not the route to the top in the Police Force. That was the province of a Guild of a religious denomination. It was amazing how many conversions on the road to Damascus there were, and how many careers blossomed by equal amounts with religious zeal. It just goes to show

I suppose that if some ambitious young man works out that his boss is a freemason, lay preacher, Bush Baptist, coarse fisher, or whatever, his career may be accelerated upwards by joining the same organisation to which his boss belongs.

The title 'Scaleys' refers to Aids (not a modern medical term) to CID and young Detectives, who have not yet made their bones, usually shortened to 'Scaley'. The scaley's office or, more properly, the aids office was almost always referred to as the 'Snake Pit'.

As to corruption, that in the story may shock some readers and, for shaking them out of their comfortable rose-tinted world, I apologise. However, I come from the back streets of London, and have seen corruption since my earliest days and am not the slightest bit surprised by any of it, preferring to regard it as an integral part of human nature. I do well remember as an eleven year old at a primary school in Chelsea watching the son of one of the officers of the Guards Regiment at the Chelsea Barracks taking his eleven plus examination twice, having failed the first time and getting loads of assistance on the second occasion. I think that the main things to be considered about corruption are opportunity and motive. Also, it is not always money that causes the rules to be bent, although little brown envelopes seem be in vogue with politicians recently. Some Public Relations Agencies study closely the aspirations and dreams of those who influence the game. As one instructor at the Detective Training School put it, "anything below a hundred pounds is a bribe, above that it is encouragement." This view was stated some thirty plus years ago, therefore inflation has probably altered the amounts. Within the Police Force corruption takes on yet another face, that of unbridled ambition. Some of the officers who were originally posted to the new A10 (later CIB2) were definitely of the poacher turned gamekeeper variety, and would, and did, sell their souls to fit up brother officers, easily encompassing the fact within their elastic consciences, A10 being an assured path to higher rank.

The violence depicted in the book may seem strange to most readers, as it contains none of the stylised nonsense trotted out on the television. One of the best pieces of advice given to me as a young copper was, "Remember who you are and where you are, don't fight unless you have to and don't fight unless you are going to win." Looking back down the years as I am now doing, I feel qualified to add one little gem extra, "Never fight to impress a woman." It follows that if we got involved in violence it was unavoidable. Our dealing with that threat was quick and ruthless, as there is no point in lying in the gutter taking a kicking from some tuppenny halfpenny villain who has got lucky on the fact that you have given him the opportunity.

The characters in the tale are based on real people but, of course, the names have been changed to protect the guilty. Rodney Road Police Station where Briggs and Jones are stationed does not exist. There was a Police Station there until the end of the Second World War, after which it became a store, and is now a builder's yard. The scope of the story is supported in many respects by my official detective diaries. These by rule should have been handed in when complete, and a new one issued. Indeed they were handed in, only I stole them back from the store after they had been filed. The stealing of my diaries was not done in an effort to afford material for these scribblings, but to foil the activities of the Complaints Investigation Branch. I will explain. On receipt of a complaint from a member of the public about the behaviour of a Detective Officer, one of the first actions by A10, or CIB(2) as it later became known, was to seize current and previous diaries of the suspect officer. These seized diaries were scrutinised to discover any evidence of wrongdoing, not necessarily in connection with the complaint under investigation. So by taking them back into my custody I was merely saving a future complaints officer lots of work.

I do hope you enjoy this book and find it entertaining. I have thought of punching a hole in the right hand corner, so that if it was found to be boring, it could be hung up in the toilet and therefore not absolutely useless.

Day Dreaming

Briggs woke, his mind scrambled with a mixture of dreams and reality. He lay on his right side looking at the wall of his bed space cubicle. The notice board that should have displayed photographs of his family and other mementoes was bare. The only thing that remained was a newspaper photograph of his trial Judge. Briggs had taken to addressing this photograph in aggressive terms when the mood took him. Briggs smiled at the likeness of the trial Judge, it had been reported the day previous that his wife had divorced him for 'unreasonable behaviour', "I know how she felt," thought Briggs.

Down each side of the notice board was a string of dates which Briggs had noted during his prison sentence. Each Wednesday he had written the date, another Wednesday, another week done, another week nearer to being with his family. The two columns of dates were there, but the photographs were missing.

"Some bastards nicked my photos," thought Briggs swinging his legs out of bed. A strange theft, for in prison one of the many odd taboos was interfering with an inmate's photographs or other bits from home.

His mind cleared itself of sleep, and the mildly erotic dream he had been experiencing. "I wonder if nurses in uniform ever get up to such things," thought Briggs, shocked that he could indulge in such goings on, even in a dream.

"Of course, I am on the out today, all my gear, including my photographs are over at reception waiting for me to join them." Briggs smiled happily at the thought.

"Oi, oi, sarge, last cup of tea." Hero plonked the mug down on

Briggs' cabinet. "I shall miss you mate. Even though you are ex old bill." Hero was almost misty eyed. Briggs smiled and nodded. He picked up the mug, sipped the tea, and pondered the events that had led him to the prison gate.

"Ere keep your hands to yourself, you some sort of nonce?" The Southwark matron barked the enquiry at Briggs' attempt at common courtesy.

"Just helping you off the bus my dear, that's all", Briggs surprised that anyone could take offence at his attempts at courtesy.

"I don't need no help, specially from an old bill," the old lady snapped with venom and feeling, exercising that inbuilt supernatural sixth sense which warns of the presence of 'old bill' even out of uniform.

Briggs shrugged, looked and felt perplexed. "How did she know?" he thought. He turned and walked away towards Stones End, the name derived from where the cobbles ended after Southwark Bridge. He marched rather than walked, as this was the high point of his career – so far. His brand new Marks and Sparks suit and non-leather black shoes screamed his superiority. He was on his way, ready to shape the world and its events according to his views and beliefs. He climbed the front steps of the Police Station and entered the front office where a Sergeant was holding court in front of two Constables. The Constables were paying rapt attention to every word of the Sergeant. He being their shift supervisor, he could exact revenge at will if he felt his jokes did not receive the correct amount of applause.

"Er excuse me," Briggs trying earnestly to get into the conversation without upsetting the Sergeant. But he was studiously ignored as an in-depth discussion on some event that had occurred on night duty was in full flood. The Sergeant expanded his chest.

"Yes, when I was at Peckham, we had one gink try exactly the same thing, brother did he get a kicking for his trouble." The Constables nodded dutifully.

Briggs broke the reverie. "Er Sergeant excuse me, I am DC Briggs, newly posted in, to see the Detective Chief Super. Could you tell me where his office is – please?" Briggs added the 'Please' with an almost wail of servility.

The Sergeant stared at Briggs, dumbstruck that a mere DC, had the temerity to break into his conversation in his front office. After a pause he said, "Are you now, how very interesting. Brand new is it?" The Sergeant inclined his head with the question; Briggs nodded his vigorously. "Now then no more out in the cold for you my son." The Sergeant smiled the smile that old sweats reserve for callow rookies.

"Yes that's correct Sergeant." Briggs was careful to avoid the use of 'Sarge' or 'Skip' for fear of upsetting this king of the front office and his two princelings. "Made up to Detective today." Briggs said it as it though he was about to be congratulated.

"Detective, you a Detective, you couldn't detect your dick unaided," the Sergeant sneered. The Constables giggled as on cue. "Up those stairs to the right, marked Divisional CID." The Sergeant nodded curtly towards the stairs outside the front office, and turned his back on Briggs.

Briggs didn't feel this was the time to exercise his renowned temper. He turned on his heels and left the office. The waves of laughter rose around him. His plastic shoes squeaked their derision of him.

Briggs found the described office. He knocked on the door and entered without waiting for a response. A civilian clerk and a typist stared him an unspoken question. Briggs still smarting from his front office treatment stared back, coldly.

"Detective Constable Briggs to see the guvnor." Briggs almost barked the words, in compensation for his failure to handle the front office skipper.

The civilian clerk spoke sharply, "Not 'the Guvnor', it's Detective Chief Superintendent Bolton. Bear that in mind and you will go a long way."

"Yes all the way to Rodney Road," thought Briggs, but said nothing.

The civilian continued, "My name is French by the way, I am Divisional CID Office Manager." French stood up pulled himself to his full height, which was a bit of a pantomime as French in these days of political correctness could only be described as vertically challenged, or in the vernacular of the day a 'shortarse'.

Briggs studied this dwarf before him, and was amused, but said, "So nice to meet you."

French continued, "Mr. Bolton is busy at the moment, but if you wait outside his office down the hall I'll call you when he's free."

French waved his hand towards the door, dismissing Briggs.

Briggs nodded and left the office. He ambled down the hall and found the door marked "Detective Chief Superintendent' and parked himself alongside it.

The usual day-to-day sounds and smells of a Police Station surrounded him. To his left and on a lower level was the canteen. He could tell this from the smell of boiled cabbage that emanated from that end. No matter what meal was being prepared it always seemed as though boiled cabbage was on the menu. He heard slamming doors from his right. Loud, banging, cell doors, overnight prisoners being chivvied on their way into the prison van and onward to the Magistrates' Court. He could hear the custody sergeant roundly cursing them into acceleration. A girl came out of an office down the corridor, carrying papers. Had she been a boat she would have been termed 'well timbered', with huge breasts and hips, both of which (when she saw Briggs) began to swing like John Wayne's saddlebags. Starkly blonde from a bottle, she swished her way down the hall past Briggs, licking her lips to make them shine. Briggs could hear her stockings rubbing together as she walked. She passed him and went on. She looked over her shoulder at him to make sure he was paying attention to this strange behaviour, which he was, short of heavy breathing, but definitely paying attention.

"I bet she's seen some late night action," thought Briggs.

The great man's door opened. The dwarf French stood in the opening. "Did he dematerialise in his office and do the reverse in the guvnor's?" thought Briggs but realised that a connecting door must be the answer.

"Mr. Bolton will see you now D.C. Briggs." The clerk ushered Briggs into the office. The great one sat behind a standard issue desk on which rested a slim glass jar with a single rose in it.

"Maybe the blonde boiler in the hall gave it to him," wondered Briggs.

There was also a photograph of his family, all grouped together and grinning at Daddy.

Bolton was staring at a file on his desk. Without looking up he said, "Stand at ease Briggs." Briggs not feeling that he was 'on parade', promptly slammed to attention to bring himself so, and then complied with the order of 'stand at ease' in true standard stupid

British Army tradition. Bolton looked up startled, no doubt, by all the noise. French stood behind the desk slightly to right of his hero; his hands clasped in front of him wearing that smile which is never sincere.

"Briggs isn't it?" asked Bolton still studying the file.

"I wonder if he knows," thought Briggs, "but he really has got terminal dandruff and his head seems to be poking a hole in his thatch" but decided against mentioning it and confined himself to "Yes sir."

"I am studying your personal file Briggs and am wondering why you took so long to get here?" Bolton looked up at Briggs.

"Well sir I caught a bus at Rodney Road and it got held up round the Elephant." Briggs wondered why Bolton should be worried over his travelling arrangements.

"Not the bus ride, but here, where you are now, a Detective Constable" Bolton snapped.

"I am not sure that I follow you sir," Briggs looking down at Bolton. He noticed that Bolton was wearing a wristwatch also a watch chain was slung across his waistcoat. "Was he obsessed by time, or just an over-dressed prick" thought Briggs, but waited in silence.

"Well, put it this way." Bolton said it as though explaining something very basic to a child. "I am four years older than you. At your age I was Detective Inspector on the squad. Here I am a Detective Chief Superintendent and you are only a Detective Constable, why is that?"

Briggs looked at the admiring French and thought he was going to break into raptures of applause. "Well sir, apart from the obvious, I did six years army service before joining the Met, then three years uniform, followed by five years aiding and here we are."

Bolton screwed his face up into what he thought made him look deep and intense. "Please state the obvious I do not follow." Bolton removed a handkerchief from his sleeve, blew his nose into it, and replaced it up his sleeve.

"He's poking snot up his sleeve" thought Briggs. Briggs then noticed that Bolton had another handkerchief in his top pocket, red silk, or something very close to it. There were about four inches of handkerchief hanging out of his pocket. The shade of the tie exactly matched that of the handkerchief, which was close to the red of

Bolton's hair. "He looks like an outbreak of acne," thought Briggs.

Clearing his mind Briggs said, "The obvious Sir is, with all due respect, that you are obviously a much more able and erudite man than me. It is therefore right that you should ascend the ladder of life quicker than the likes of me." Briggs felt that it was better to state as the truth what this ginger haired prick thought of himself and perhaps get on to the next bit. He thought of ending his little speech with, "Don't pull the chain sir, I'll eat it." Or perhaps in true Dickensian style, "Oh sir I am ever so 'umble, and would be pleased to lick your boots" but contented himself with the combined look of admiration from Bolton and French.

French muttered, "Hear hear."

"That is all cogent and true, but don't forget, there is room for us all in this great job of ours." Bolton beamed with self-satisfaction and seemed to be mounting some well-used hobbyhorse.

"I do hope he doesn't give me the bit about the Field Marshal's baton being in every common soldier's haversack," Briggs thought fervently.

Bolton coughed to clear his throat. "I have been examining your records Briggs. It discloses that you served in the Army for six years, but does not state which arm. Where were you for six years?" Bolton looked up at him.

Briggs had been in this position once before. As a matter of experience, he had found it better to follow the official line and then cave in to mounting pressure.

"Er, sorry sir, that's classified information, can't tell you." Briggs smiled apologetically, but well knew what was coming next.

Bolton seemed nonplussed. "I am your Chief Superintendent, I am entitled to know, tell me now." Bolton punched the question at Briggs.

"Can't sir, Official Secrets Act and all that." Briggs smiled knowing what was coming next.

"But I am your Chief Superintendent, I am entitled to know, now stop prevaricating and tell me." Bolton seemed peeved that he was being excluded from this now not vital information. Both he and French regarded Briggs with almost suspicion, feeling maybe that he was winding them up. Briggs felt that he should heighten the tension by saying something like, "Shaken not stirred maybe."

"But I have signed the Official Secrets Act, so has Mr. French here. Further, I don't like mysteries; where were you?" Bolton snapped the question in exasperation.

The time had come for Briggs to give in gracefully, well as graceful as ever Briggs could be.

"Special Air Service sir, first year and a half with the Royal Engineers and then four and a half years with the SAS."

French looked startled by this glamorous news. In recognition of this, Briggs treated French to his standard 'hard man's stare' and was gratified to note that French could not hold his stare. Bolton was searching for something to say that would re-establish his superiority in this encounter, but failed. Instead he said, "I see."

Bolton changed the subject with a cough. "Mr. French, I think we have a vacancy at Rodney Road is that correct?" Bolton looked sideways at his dwarf.

French straightened himself into his regular soldier pose. "Quite right sir."

Briggs was relieved that he was being sent to Rodney Road as he had parked his car there this morning. Once again, the grapevine had been correct. "Oh that will suit me fine sir, a nice active ground," Briggs trying to give the impression of being an eager beaver.

"Yes Rodney Road." Bolton paused as though the words had some secret portent. "Rodney Road, more villains per square mile than anywhere else in the Met. You'll have your work cut out there."

"Oh yes sir, I think so sir." Briggs said it because it was expected.

Bolton continued. "A few do's and don'ts to be going on with. Firstly no getting involved with bunging. Any villain tries to bung you; you report it straight away to your Detective Inspector who will take the appropriate action. Understand?"

"Oh yes sir." Briggs responded all earnest and honest. He had seen this 'appropriate action' at his previous nick, which seemed to be that the Detective Inspector took your place in the proceedings.

Bolton continued. "Some places I want you to keep away from. The Duke of Clarence in East Street, that place is run by two strong villains. You go in there and you will be walking into trouble, got it?"

Briggs took out his official notebook and made a note. "Got it sir, Duke of Clarence."

"Further, keep away from scrap metal dealers, the regular calls under the Scrap Metal Dealers Act will be made by Sub Divisional Inspectors, right?"

"Yes sir," Briggs making another note in his pocket book.

"You get any information on scrap metal dealers you report it to your Detective Inspector first. It may be that he already has the matter in hand."

Briggs smiled to himself, but carried on writing. The way the Detective Inspectors at his last nick had 'minded' the scrap metal dealers, it was obvious there was some form of vested interest. Briggs was surprised that it ascended to Bolton's elevated position.

"Finally Manor Place Baths on boxing nights, definitely a no-go area unless you are with colleagues and friends who can ensure your safety. Otherwise keep out."

"Of course sir." Briggs made the required note. Later in his career he had actually attended a boxing match at Manor Place Baths, and had not been surprised to see the Chief Superintendent at the ringside, accompanied by a number of fawning 'faces' (strong villains).

Bolton finished that part of his lecture and turned his attention to Briggs' file. "Finally I am not at all happy with your discipline record as an aid, too many complaints, far too many. Violence, verbals, fitting up, not heeding to words of advice from senior uniform officers." Bolton made a face to show his distaste; on cue, French followed suit. Briggs considered the list of alleged misdemeanors to be a fine record that recommended him as an active detective.

Briggs allowed himself to bristle just a touch as he felt this was expected. "Those aren't discipline matters sir, they are complaints made against me by members of the public. They have been investigated and I was exonerated in each case." Briggs allowed a trace of anger to creep into his voice.

Bolton looked down at the file grimacing. "I agree you have been lucky, but it does show system. Look at this one Briggs, you broke a man's jaw." Bolton looked pained at the distasteful prospect of the actual application of the law. French adopted the look.

"But sir, he was a heavy breaker. We had a fight during arrest, he could have broken my jaw. Anyway, the Judge highly commended me for my actions," Briggs stating the support of a High Court Judge as his excuse.

Bolton sighed. "Yes I know Judges say strange things at times. However I do not feel that just because a Judge commends you, it entitles you to go around breaking people's jaws, so let's have some self-discipline and restraint – yes?" Bolton punched the question at Briggs.

Briggs sprang to attention. "Yes sir, of course sir."

"Right then off you go, let me hear good things of you," Bolton pleased and relieved that he got through his script even with Briggs' help

Briggs left the office and went down the stairs towards the exit into Borough High Street, pleased to be out of the company of the guvnor and his ditto man. The front office skipper stood in the foyer outside his office. Briggs approached him. The sergeant turned, his face becoming the sneer that Briggs expected.

"Er excuse me Sergeant, do you find your gums bleed once a month?" Briggs giving a concerned smile.

The sergeant looked puzzled. "No why?" And fell into Briggs' trap.

"Well you certainly talk like one." Briggs left the Sergeant to figure it out, by which time he would be well on his way to Rodney Road. Should he ever be questioned about this incident he would of course deny it, there being no witnesses either way.

Rodney Road

Ever since the Assistant Commissioner (Crime) had told him that Detective Officers should wear a hat at all times, Detective Chief Inspector Jack Parris, who was almost universally known as 'Jack the Hat', rarely removed his. He now sat behind his desk in shirtsleeves, red armbands and braces but with brown trilby hat on his head. He glowered at the Scaley before him – Briggsy.

"Briggs?" Jack the Hat barked.

"Yes sir," Briggs straightening himself, trying to assess this odd senior officer. At the same time Jack the Hat was trying to do the same thing to Briggs but with the benefit of exalted rank.

"You seen the guvnor?" Jack the Hat toyed with a file on his desk.

"Mr. Bolton at Southwark, yes sir." Briggs nodded.

"Did he tell you how good he is, and how fast he came up the steam pipe?" Jack the Hat grinning well knowing that Bolton just could not give up the possibility of blowing his own trumpet on such an occasion.

"Yes sir, he did enlarge on that subject," said Briggs warily, not sure where this conversation was heading.

"The guvnor does tend to go on about how he came up the ladder quickly. However he is a very good detective, even if he does lack a bit of time in the saddle so to speak." Jack the Hat leaned back in his chair studying Briggs under his hat brim.

"Oh yes sir," Briggs relieved at being indicated the party line. "I read about his efforts on the Black Country kidnap job" proving that maybe he had done his homework.

Jack the Hat grinned at Briggs, knowing bullshit for exactly what it was. "I know your former D.I. He says you're full of bullshit, which you have just shown me but that your saving grace is that you can do the job. Well just make sure you do and don't piss me about, got it?"

The words hit Briggs like a bucket of cold water. "Yes sir, of course sir" he stammered.

"And it's guv or boss, whatever you like, but never sir, right?" Jack the Hat stared at Briggs almost trying to see the fall of his words on Briggsy's brain

"Yes er guv," Briggs with the wind entirely out of his sails.

"You are shrewd enough to know that there are, shall we say, commercial opportunities in our game," Jack the Hat noting Briggs' puzzled expression. "Put it this way, they can have as much help as they like, payment after conviction, but no outers, you let 'em go and I will bounce you back to the big hat so fast it will give your cobblers travel sickness, got it?"

"Yes guv." Briggs was a bit chastened by this brazen approach about that which most of the time remained unspoken.

"Further you earn a bit out of help, don't forget your insurance premium to your guvnor. You go in for a bit of private enterprise and I will cut you off at the knees," Jack the Hat punching the words at Briggs. This caused Briggs to smile inwardly. He never could see what he would get for the guvnor's share. At his last nick he remembered the D.I. saying on such an occasion, "You will not lose by this my son." Briggs smiled as he remembered his thoughts on the subject. "Neither will I gain very much either."

"Right then, that's sorted. I am putting you with Jones," said Jack the Hat studying Briggs closely. "He's been here about three weeks and still finding his feet." Jack the Hat pulled a Gold Flake from the packet on the desk and lit it. Briggs didn't think he intentionally blew the smoke his way, but it had that effect, more like a destroyer laying smoke. "I hope you're up on your Bible. Jones is a lay preacher or something in the Methodist Chapel, takes it very seriously, apparently."

Momentarily a picture of a young Briggs and friend on a bombsite in immediate post war Central London came up in his brain. They were tearing pages out of a bible to use as cigarette papers. "I shall take his religious views into account guv," Briggs not relishing sermons on late turn or anything like it.

"I am sure you will Briggsy, that's what they call you isn't it, Briggsy?" Jack the Hat nodding the question to the answer.

"Yes guv, ever since I joined the job it's always been Briggsy, sometimes something ruder, depending on the rank involved." Briggs grinned cheekily.

"Funny you should mention that, I have had a Desk Sergeant on to me, he apparently alleges you were more than a little rude to him?" Jack the Hat treated Briggs to his version of an enigmatic smile. "I don't know what he's talking about guv," Briggs deadpan prepared to brass it out.

"Yes he did say that there were no witnesses old son. Anyway." Jack the Hat dismissing the sergeant's hurt feelings to the unprovable domain of gossip. "Your overall supervisor is Sid Mills. He is one nice man – don't turn him into a nasty one. Your immediate supervisor is Winkle Smith."

"Winkle guv?" Briggs mystified by the nickname.

"Yes Winkle, it comes from his habit of singing the cockney winkle song when he's pissed." Jack the Hat stared into Briggs' puzzled expression. "Don't worry if you ain't heard it you ain't missed much. Now go and find your buck and chase some villains about the ground, and most important of all don't get caught, and if you do don't call me."

Briggs, thus dismissed, left the boss's office and walked down the corridor to the main office. He stood just inside the doorway and surveyed the office. "That must be my space," he thought as he noticed an empty desk at the end of the office. There were no files on the desk, just a few bits in the 'in' tray. There were four or five officers sitting at their desks. They ignored him. Two were doing that daily task of writing up their diaries. Briggs wondered how many officers, by their own hand, had been sunk by their handwritten entries in their diaries. He remembered one memorable occasion when an officer had made up evidence from a telephone tap. The telephone tap could not be given in evidence. However some smart barrister called his diary into question in Court, and proved that the officer was either lying in his diary or lying in the pocket book, they could not both be true. The officer was precluded from disclosing the existence of the telephone tap and ended up with seven years imprisonment for his keenness.

Briggs walked over to the apparently empty desk and sat down. The chair wobbled under his weight. "I bet that was swapped before I got here." Briggs peered round at the faulty chair. He opened the desk drawer from which it would appear that his predecessor had lead an interesting life. A packet of three French letters containing just one, three or four whisky bottle caps. "I wonder if he had the scotch before, after or during," thought Briggs. He examined the few pieces of correspondence in the 'in' tray – a transmission report awaiting signature. A couple of Criminal Record Files minus court results.

"You Briggs?" The flat Wiltshire drawl grated on Briggs who squirmed around on his rickety chair to see a florid faced man looming over him. Briggs gauged him to be about the same age as him, maybe a little older.

"Yes that's me." Briggs noted he wore the same matching tie and handkerchief set he had seen Bolton sporting. "And you are?" Briggs not making the effort to shake hands or be polite until he established who he was talking to, might be the office cleaner for all he knew, or perhaps from the way he was dressed, the local pox doctor's clerk.

"John Barking, top Detective at this nick." The big man stroked his lapel as though admiring himself. Briggs felt like laughing but didn't. Instead he said, "Really, how nice to meet you." He extended his hand in greeting. Barking ignored it.

"Yes, I am the man," he continued, looking past Briggs out of the open window, in the manner of Stewart Grainger staring heroically into the distance. Briggs was amused, but didn't show it. This one was obviously suffering from some form of dementia. "All the decent bodies in this office are down to me mate. I am the man."

Barking spoke with the emphasis of Muhammad Ali. "Perhaps he is trying to convince himself," thought Briggs but instead said, "I see, how very interesting, what's the point?" Briggs asking but not really interested.

"Point? Point? I don't need to make a point with you, I am the main man." Barking preened himself. Something about Barking's manner twigged Briggs that he was more than likely a homosexual.

Briggs smiled and adopted as friendly a manner as possible. "Listen dear, if it makes you happy, just book it down that you told me, and, for what it's worth book it also that I am most definitely impressed – yes?" Briggs nodding and Barking following suit. "Now fuck off and leave me alone, sweetheart." Briggs patted Barking on the cheek and blew him a kiss.

Barking was startled. "I would be careful sunshine, life could get painful for you." Barking flexed his large shoulders in the manner of a public house bouncer.

"You make an appointment shithead, I would hate to be out when you call." Briggs grinned cheekily. Barking went red in the face.

"You're obviously the new man in, most pleased to meet you." said a middle aged greying man. "I am Sid Mills, First Class Skipper. I see you have already met our John." Sid clapped Barking on the shoulder. "John's a great one for wind-ups, but it's all in fun," which was contrary to Briggs' view of the man, but Sid was making the rough passions subside. Barking retreated scowling, leaving Briggs with the impression that he had not made a friend. "Get yourself sorted and I will show you round the nick." Briggs was grateful for Sid's intercession and immediately warmed to the First Class Sergeant.

Briggs settled himself into his new surroundings and was installing his pens and rulers etc. when a hand was placed on his shoulder. Briggs scowled, still a little irritated at Barking. "Don't tell me you're the second best Detective in this nick – right?"

"Wrong, the name's Jones, Ron Jones," said with the lilt of the Rhondda but with the inflection of 007. Briggs had often come across the accent when playing rugby, and couldn't understand it then. He concentrated hard. "We are bucks I understand."

After a pause, during which he considered various versions of what could have been said Briggs replied, "Yes so I understand," hoping that he had got it right. Eventually, after some weeks, Briggs had no trouble understanding Jones.

Briggs studied his buck closely perhaps looking for a weakness. Briggs later found that Ron suffered from selective messianic fervour. Sober he could be pedantic and bigoted on the scriptures, with a couple of pints inside him he would get up and fuck the crack of dawn if it had fur around it. Later, sober, after such endeavours he almost always suffered from severe bouts of conscience of the lapsed holiness variety. "Come on I'll get you a cuppa," said Briggs. They left the office for the canteen where the first of many conversations was held over a cup of tea.

Walking with Ron

Life in harness alongside Ron was a never ending source of amusement, frustration and sometimes fury to Briggsy. Whether he was a religious bigot or a rapacious womaniser depended largely on the time of day and whether he had had a drink or not. Briggs often considered Ron's over active libido and came to the conclusion that it was all down to the shortage of attractive woman in Wales (maybe), however eventually Briggsy met up with Audrey and all was explained.

Ron had been born and lived his life, up to joining the Met that is, in Pontardawe, a small Welsh village carved out of the side of a hill. Ron's father had been the Vicar of the local Methodist Chapel, which probably explained Ron's constant bouts of anguish and conscience when he fell off the horse of rectitude. Ron often quoted from the Bible in the canteen, and at the drop of knickers would preach too. He kept little tracts of Bible quotes about his person, always ready to press one into someone's hand.

Before joining the Met Ron had been employed in an insurance office in Cardiff. This he informed everyone was not exciting enough. On the contrary, it was rumoured that he had made one of his co-workers pregnant. Hopefully this person was female. Ron on the other hand always denied that he had had any unlawful sexual intercourse – maybe this pregnancy was a further bout of virgin birth. For the unknowing, Unlawful Sexual Intercourse is that congress which takes place outside the bounds of marriage. There doesn't seem to be a penalty attached to this activity. The offence itself comes from Canon Law – so not binding on most of us, but surely must have weighed heavily on Ron.

Ron's dress and attitude was garnered from his insurance company employment. He almost invariably wore a dark grey suit, and adopted the attitude of the 'The Man from the Pru' in the forties. In winter he took to wearing a suede trilby, but gave this up when the guvnor, Jack the Hat, commented that he stood out like a 'pork chop in a synagogue'. The suede titfer was not seen again.

After some months in harness together, Briggs eventually invited Jones and his wife Audrey for Sunday afternoon tea, and regretted it. Jones' Audrey turned out to be very Welsh and terminally ugly, which probably explained Jones' compulsion to have sex when drunk with anything that was remotely female and more attractive than Audrey. Briggs noted that Audrey was in dire need of a shave across her top lip, further, on the side of her chin she had a mole with a veritable bush growing out of it. Briggs was fascinated by this mole and could hardly take his eyes off it. It was almost like the case when you are in the company of someone who is wearing an awful wig, your eyes are constantly drawn to it. Like Jones she tended to punctuate her conversation with passages from the Bible, which didn't endear her to anyone on Briggs' side. Their two children, boys about four and six seemed in comparison to Briggs' unruly brood to be sullen and subdued. Briggs suggested that he and the boys should go into the garden and play 'World Cup Football'. To Briggs' lot this meant roaring around the garden with a football somewhere in the general vicinity, eventually getting Dad down and kicking the lights out of him. All this orchestrated by a barking cocker spaniel who, in excitement, would take to nipping the participants. This they proceeded to do. The Jones boys stood and stared and seemed unsure as to what they should be doing. "Oh, we don't let them get involved in rough games you see, we think it might make them into brutes," Audrey the Hairy Mole trying to explain her sons' confusion and offending Maggie Briggs at the same time.

By judicious questioning it eventually emerged that the union with Audrey the Hairy Mole was prompted by Jones' father. Audrey was a Sunday School teacher at the little Methodist Chapel in the valley. Briggs surmised that Jones senior had sized her up as a likely consort and pushed Ron into her ugly path. The thinking being that she was well versed in the scriptures and too ugly to get involved in original sin. Although to be fair, Jones must have indulged at least twice which would account for the presence of the two little consciences.

In return for their hospitality, Jones invited Briggs and tribe to a meeting in the Bromley Methodist Chapel, with the attractive prospect of tea with Ron, Audrey and the goody two shoes afterwards. Briggs made an excuse that weekends were more than often taken up with visiting relatives and the like. But at heart Briggs knew that his two boys could not hold good behaviour for the length of a religious service. But the most pressing reason for stepping sideways out of the invitation was that Maggie Briggs could not abide Jones and his patronising Welsh wife.

One of the favourite watering holes of the Dynamic Duo, as they became known, was a notorious gay pub. Briggs steered Jones towards this particular pub on the basis that he was fervently heterosexual and unlikely to get into any trouble. This ploy worked very well. They would stand at the bar and sink a couple of pints and watch the drag artists perform. Then exit and on with the constant white hot war against crime in South London. Except that one particular night there was what appeared to be a young woman in the bar to whom Jones was drawn like a moth to flame. She/he/it fluttered her eyelids at the bold Welsh hero. More beer flowed and Jones became even more interested, and engaged in kissing in the corner, tongues and all. Disgusting to behold. When he surfaced for air Briggs said, "I would be careful there Ron, could be a bloke in drag," hoping to dampen his ardour with common sense. "Not a chance mate, I have had a feel see." Jones demonstrated his technique for fondling female breasts. Seeing that Jones was rampant and on the scent of illicit sex Briggs left him to it and went home.

Some weeks later Briggs and Jones were in the local Magistrates' Court waiting for their prisoner to be put up. The overnight drunks were dealt with first. The last drunk was Jones' conquest in the gay bar, charged with drunk and disorderly but still wearing the party dress. 'He, she or it' looked over and saw Ron and waved by raising her hand and flexing her fingers in what he/she thought was a cute way. Ron blushed. The drunken transvestite was then formally charged in a fellow's name. Briggs whispered to Jones, "So you were positive were you?" The other coppers in court picked up the embarrassment and sniggered. One commented in a stage whisper, "Marginally better than sheep shagging, but not much."

Eventually they became settled in their roles as partners. Briggsy had to overcome his dislike, hatred almost, of all things Welsh. He had been evacuated as child during the war and with his brother had been very badly treated, hungry most of the time with regular beatings, one incidentally for not understanding the Welsh language. This situation was not improved by the Welsh superiority in the sixties and seventies at rugby, Briggs' chosen blood sport. It always appeared that the English traipsed down to Cardiff each year to get a ritual bashing. Looking at it in hindsight the amusing offshoot was that anyone with a Welsh sounding name would wander around singing 'Bread of Heaven' and 'Saucepan Bach' and talk almost knowledgeably about the 'front five' and half back play etc, most of them never having been on the pitch, let alone see some fast flanker coming towards them with evil intent. Briggs would be pleased that in the new millennium things have changed. The visiting English team cause silence at what used to be Cardiff Arms Park. They are still not admired but feared. The blokes with the Welsh sounding names now profess, "Oh I don't like rugby you see, such a barbaric game. I much prefer poetry and going to the Eisteddford." But all things considered Briggs and Jones accepted each other's faults and got on with the game of catching crooks.

Charlie's Hoard

Sometimes the careful planning, the ultra intelligent collation of facts and the scientific forensic studies would be as nothing without the simple added ingredient – luck. I remember an old copper at Bromley who received a high commendation from the Commissioner for the apprehension of a shop burglar. He had been present when the burglar had thrown his loot over the back wall of a shop closely followed by his body, and was promptly nicked. What was never revealed or considered was 'What was he doing there in the first place?' Of course the answer to this would never be truthful. However I feel that the truth can now be printed, the copper was there to have an illicit fag and relieve his bladder. Right place right time = Commissioner's commendation.

The Aylesbury Estate. The name conjures up dreams of green fields, pleasant yeoman people, hearty laughter, buxom women, sunshine and roses, which is probably what the planner intended when he chose the name for the abortion of concrete and tarmac lying between Walworth Road and the Old Kent Road in South London. It was the planner's proud claim that the pedestrian could walk from Walworth Road to the Old Kent Road completely on elevated walkways. Perhaps he should have added that the same pedestrian would have been out of touch of the patrolling copper at ground level and in a police car. This fact alone probably accounted for most of the muggings committed on the estate, i.e. the firm knowledge that the offender was safe from the attentions of the old bill.

Early evening, dark and raining, Briggs and Jones in the middle of Aylesbury Estate, if not quite lost at least not able to find the location of Mulberry Villas. The large blocks of flats crowded above them, shiny wet and threatening. Briggs studied the council supplied map. "About as much use as a French letter with a hole in it." Briggs studied the map closely.

"Not shown then?" Ron peered over Briggs' shoulder.

"Well if it is I can't find it." Briggs threw the map over the seat into the back. "Here what about him, he looks as if he's local, ask him the way." Briggs indicated an elderly man carrying a holdall making his way against the driving rain, his raincoat shiny, water drizzling off the bottom, his flat cap pulled down against the wind and rain.

"Er excuse me sir," Jones called to the man, who stopped and looked at Jones and the car. "Could you please tell me the way to Mulberry Villas?" The elderly man looked as if Ron was the reincarnation of Count Dracula and endeavoured to run off, but age had slowed him and he just shuffled quickly.

Jones looked at Briggs. "What do you make of that then, a bit rude I thought." Ron startled at the actions of the elderly man.

"I make it that he he's probably got something in the holdall, how would you like to catch him and find out." Briggs pushed Jones out of the car. Jones ran after the old man. Briggs turned the CID car around and followed. In short order Jones had caught the man and was questioning him over the open holdall.

"Here Tel what about this then?" Ron showing Tel the open holdall. Briggs peered inside with the aid of a pocket torch. In the thin glare he saw some stainless steel bowls, about ten long playing records, and two brand new electric drills.

"They're a present from a friend," volunteered the old man, his voice shaking. Briggs noted that his hands were trembling, not surprising, the old man was terrified.

"If that's true why run away?" Jones asked, holding the old man by his arm.

The old man screwed his face up. "You frightened me didn't yer, I thought you was going to mug me didn't I," adding as though a pearl of wisdom, "There's been a lot of mugging around here you know."

"Yes I do know that" said Briggs patiently, "but most of those muggers are black and as you can see we are white. You ran because you knew we are old bill and you had bent gear in the holdall." Briggs held the bag open before him. "Come on Pops give your name and address," Briggs said gently.

"Sod off, I know my rights I don't have to say nuffink, do I, and don't call me pops." The old man stuck his hands deep into his raincoat pockets almost as resistance to Ron holding his arm.

"You're right of course." Briggs responded getting his pocket book out, "but that does not stop us from arresting you on reasonable suspicion that you're dishonestly handling this gear. Then we get your name and address at the nick when we search you and everyone will know you have not been helpful, including the magistrate at court, and of course you are in custody while awaiting court as someone with no name." Briggs raised his voice slightly and with affected menace, "Now stop fucking us about and let's have your name and address." The old man flinched at the change of mood.

"Alright, no need to be heavy or nuffink. Charlie Moffat, 164, Arnhem House, just over there." He indicated a block of flats in the corner of a playground on the same side of the road.

"Do you live with anyone?" asked Briggs with pen poised over pocket book.

"Only the trouble (trouble and strife = wife) the kids have left home." Charlie resigned to his fate.

"Well let's go and have a look at home shall we?" Ron helping Charlie along by the elbow. All three made their way towards the block of flats.

"You going to nick the old lady as well?" Charlie looking earnestly into Jones' face.

"No reason to if she has nothing to do with it is there." Jones answered stating the obvious.

"Only she's been ill this last year, not bedridden or anything like, but you know women's problems, and it would upset her if she got her collar felt as well, know what I mean?"

"Well let's see how we get on." Briggs leaned on the lift operating button.

They entered the lift and, in common with most council house lifts, found that it doubled as the tenants' urinal. "Fuck me there are some dirty bastards about, what a pen and ink," Briggs complained dodging the waves of yellow fluid that surged around as the lift got under way.

"It's the kids what do it." Charlie Moffat said as though this was an explanation. "It's the parents I blame." All three were very careful where they placed their feet.

The lift stopped on the seventh floor, they exited on to the landing. No 164 was to the left and one of four flats on this landing. Charlie opened the door with his latch key and called out, "Only me dear." Briggs felt he was bracing himself for the confrontation to come, and because of this Briggs felt himself tense. As they went through the door Briggs noted that either side of the hallway there were cardboard boxes stacked floor to ceiling, leaving only enough room for them to inch down the hall sideways. They turned left into the sitting room in convoy. This again was stacked floor to ceiling with boxes. It later transpired that the whole flat was in a similar state. In the centre of this store of boxes sat a middle aged woman, a running television in front of her. She glared a question at them.

Briggs felt impelled to speak as he sensed Charlie was unable. "Sorry to trouble you my dear, but I am afraid we have arrested Charlie here for receiving stolen gear." It all came out in a burst of nervous speech. Briggs had used the old time description of the offence as receiving rather than dishonestly handling stolen property, it being probably more instantly recognised by Mrs. Moffatt. She was quiet for an instant, as though mulling over options.

"I knew it, I fucking knew it." She exploded from the chair and almost fell over the full boxes stacked around her. "How many times have I told you not to get involved with buying bent gear, but you wouldn't be told, not you, always knew better." Charlie's head went down, and Briggs recognised the familiar position of a married man who has got it wrong and it is come-uppance time. "Well you're doing the job, what chance of bail?" direct and to the point. "We've got form but it's a long time ago, during the war, black market and all that you know, nothing since then." She raised an eyebrow to reinforce the question.

Jones looked to Briggs expectantly who on cue said, "Well it's a bit early to talk about bail, it looks to me as though all the gear here is subject to investigation and while those enquiries are going on we couldn't possibly release Charlie as he might hinder them." Briggs spoke slowly spelling out the situation. Mrs. Moffatt paid rapt attention nodding her head in assent.

At the end of Briggs' little speech she said, "Right, we'll soon sort this out, everything in the flat is nicked, apart from the kitchen stuff, the armchair, telly and the bed, apart from that it's all hookey, been bought bent at some time or other." Briggs was startled by her candid treatment of the situation, "Really" Jones expressed surprised. "Yes really." She continued her diatribe, "it's like a disease with him he can't leave it alone, he's got a little bit of money, and what he does he buys a little bit of gear, then he sells part of that parcel and gets his money back and he's off again buying. The profit he stores here." She waved her arms around her with a theatrical gesture.

Briggs caught Jones' attention and nodded to the bedroom. Once in the bedroom he found he could not close the door as the boxes were in the way. "Ron," Briggs spoke quietly. "Get on to Rodney Road and get them to send a van and a couple of uniforms to assist if possible."

Ron was amazed, or perhaps frightened by the prospect of hard work. "What are we going to seize it all?"

"What option do we have, his missus has done it, she's admitted that it's bent, now we have to seize it." Ron left dejected by the prospect of heavy lifting, I won't say heavy humping as this would probably have lifted his spirits. Ron cheered up immensely as when the job was finished they both got commended by the court for 'Outstanding Detective Ability'.

Briggs with Charlie in attendance began to look through various boxes, one contained British Homes Stores sheets and pillowcases still wrapped in their original cellophane; another box had shoes in various sizes, the pair on the top looked as though they were hunting boots of a sort of about size 16. "I'd hate to meet the guy they were made for."

Charlie smiled grimly. "I was had over on that deal, if you look closely you will see that all those shoes are specials, surgical some of them, I had no chance from the beginning," said Charlie shaking his head. "You have to be so careful there are some right villains about."

"I suppose that's true, I really would not know." Briggs amused but managing to control laughter.

The uniform officers arrived with Ron in tow. Under Briggs' and

Ron's instruction they began to load the boxes onto a trolley and transport it down to the waiting van. This was now surrounded by interested spectators. 'Nosey bastards' as Charlie called them.

The scale and variety of the property seized amazed both the CID and uniform alike. It included five or six electric sewing machines, numerous cutlery sets, onyx table lamps and tables, clothing, shoes, sheets and pillow cases, bathroom scales, and a crate which contained hundreds, if not thousands, of quality pens, pencils, ballpoint pens and presentation sets in leather bound cases, although the exact amount contained in the crate became the subject of artistic licence later. Although he had not had time to make a detailed inventory Briggs admonished the van driver and his helpers, "I shall know if anything is missing gents," he said tapping his pocket book knowingly, The uniform or woodentops as they are affectionately known, for their part knew this to be CID bullshit and sorted themselves various presents along the way, nothing too big just a memento of the occasion.

Ron and Briggsy stood in the flat and supervised the removal of the gear together with Mrs. Moffat. A tall blonde young woman walked in through the door. Expensively dressed, camel hair coat which hung open to show an expensive off white silk blouse with gold necklace tastefully under the collar and around her neck, this ensemble accentuated by brown leather accessories. Briggs wondered as to the origin of these high fashion items. Immediately Ron paid attention to the young lady, but thankfully as he had not been drinking she was quite safe. Briggs thought she was the epitome of Knightsbridge class and whispered to Ron, "Close your mouth Ron there's a train coming." Ron closed with a gulp but his interest was obvious as was the fact that he was most definitely impressed until this woman addressed Mrs. Moffat.

"Hello mum what's the filth doing here?" She almost spat the words at Briggs who gained the impression that she possibly did not like him very much.

"It's alright my dear, father has got his collar felt, and Mr. Briggs here is going to try and get him bail, well almost straight away, isn't that nice of him?" Trying to get the expensively attired daughter to see it her way. "Oh, right, I'll get Jimmy to attend the nick shall I?" She nodded the question at Briggs.

"Oh yes alright but later we have lots to do. If he rings me I will let him know exactly what surety is required."

Her expensively plucked eyebrows arched and she became red in the face. "We don't need to be told a bleeding amount, whatever it is we can afford it."

"Flash as fuck," thought Briggs but said, "Oh I see, suit yourself then." He turned his back and went further into the flat.

They carried on loading and counting until all that was thought to be bent had been safely transferred to Rodney Road where it filled the property store and five cells. Charlie's flat was reduced to a skeleton, the armchair and the television remained, the double bed, the kitchen stove and most of the utensils, even the Persian carpets had been taken on Mrs. Moffatt's insistence and, with such an amount, no attempt could be made at this stage to make a comprehensive list of all items seized. Whilst checking the last load in the yard, the Moffat daughter came down and got into a flash Lotus Cortina. As she started the car she sneered at Briggs and said something like 'Anchor' though why she should be advertising New Zealand butter was completely beyond Briggs. Briggs spoke softly "Ron write this down on the corner of the sheet Kilo Kilo Papa 438 Foxtrot – got it? Repeat it." Ron dutifully sang the index number back. Briggs smiled, "I think we shall have to find out a bit more about her."

Later that evening Charlie found himself sitting, or rather slumped on a chair in the interview room, staring fixedly at the floor. "Are you going to charge me now?"

"Shortly after we have had a chat Charlie," said Ron shuffling the papers on the bench before him. "One thing at a time old son." Charlie grunted his assent. "Perhaps the best thing for you to do is to make a statement. Put it all down on paper, clear your slate," Ron suggested, arranging his pens for the kill.

"No reason not to is there. She has already put my hands up for me hasn't she?"

Ron wrote the statement out for Charlie. It included, on Briggs' insistence, the fact that Charlie had got started on this terrible road to ruin by buying and selling gear during the war and that now he didn't need to do it he carried on nevertheless, as it was now some sort of compulsion and in fact he had become a magpie, hoarding property against a fictitious day of want. Charlie felt that the inclusion of this statement was a great favour by Briggs, but it was probably nearer the truth than anything else that had been said about Charlie.

At the end of the statement Charlie signed it after completing the certificate.

After being charged Charlie was bailed in his own recognizance of £500 and one surety of £1000. The surety arrived some ten minutes later. A large florid man in a flashy suit and expensive shoes. He spoke with the usual South London accent. "You the old bill in charge?" He almost flung the words at Briggs.

"Only of this little case." Briggs trod warily as he knew he was dealing with a 'face', the South London term for a heavy villain.

"My old man needs a bit of help on this one." The son shrugged his shoulders in the accepted manner. "I mean we don't need no bird, know what I mean.

"Not exactly old son I don't," Briggs replied, seemingly unconcerned. Jones stood behind Ginger and gesticulated his nervousness. "Listen mate your old man has put his hands up, he's got to plead now."

Ginger's face fell. "I don't believe it, Dad would never plead. We don't do that, same as we never grass."

Briggs thought he was going to add, "Cos I'm hard." but he didn't. "Well mate there are two things you can do firstly sign up as your Dad's surety in the sum of one thousand pounds." Ginger put his hand into his inside pocket and got out a large brown paper envelope. Briggs smiled, "No mate you only have to sign, if your Dad doesn't turn up on the 15th then you owe Her Majesty one grand." Ginger seemed confused, he was obviously used to different set of rules. "And the other thing," Briggs continued. "Get your Dad a decent brief, one that can tell the wood from the trees – click?" Ginger brightened with understanding.

"Oh yes of course, any particular brief you have in mind?" Briggs made as if pondering the question. "Yes there is one who might help," Briggs accentuated the 'help', "That is Mr. Beamish of Beamish and Beamish, he doesn't take legal aid and will want some up front, but he does know what he is on about, got it?"

Ginger nodded, "Yes and thanks for talking to us, I'll get on to

Mr. Beamish in the morning. No doubt he can talk to you?" Briggs nodded. Ginger left the nick with his Dad in tow.

Briggs and Jones spent the next few days happily logging all the property and transferring it to a railway arch at the back of the nick. Their enquiries as to the origin of the property led them nowhere as some of it was over twenty years old, and although in most cases they knew the manufacturer no-one could state where and if anything had gone missing.

Whilst Briggs was engaged alone one morning still logging endless quantities of sheets and pillowcases he was graced by the appearance of Jack the Hat. "Morning guv," Briggs looking up and standing, well almost to attention. Jack the Hat grunted a reply of sorts. He continued to wander around the store picking up odd articles and examining them. Eventually, after an eternity, he said,

"The guvnor has heard of this job you know, very impressed he is too." Jack the Hat was turning over expensive pens in the crate. Briggs watched him mesmerised by the pens and glitter.

"Is he guv, that's nice. Mr. Bolton at Southwark guv."

Jack the Hat nodded sagely, "However," he spoke slowly., "he does not feel you are showing the correct amount of respect." Jack the Hat peered at Briggs from beneath his trilby.

"I am afraid I don't understand guv," said Briggs mystified.

"Well let's put it this way," said Jack the Hat, speaking as though he was about to begin a fairy story for a very young child, but still fiddling with the pens. "Mr. Bolton signs your expenses every week and he has only got the issue biro to do it with."

"And you think it would be much better if he had something more in keeping with his senior position like a Schaeffer pen set for example, replied Briggs, catching on at the speed of light. "Exactly Tel, exactly." Jack the Hat's change in voice showing pleasure that his errand had been achieved.

Together they sorted through the pens and found a gold plated set which Briggs thought fitted the bill. "Oh yes very nice, he will be pleased with that, and his wife would obviously appreciate the Schaeffer lady set," Jack the Hat said as he placed Mr. Bolton's set in his pocket, "and his daughter's just off to a new school." Exit another pen set. "And of course me being your guvnor, you wouldn't dream of leaving me out would you," Jack the Hat pocketing yet another pen set.

"Just one problem guv, what about the Property Register sheets?" Briggs seeing himself saddled with a huge bill to replace missing expensive pens. "No problem young Tel," Jack the Hat pulled a sheaf of property forms from the inside pocket of his jacket. "But if I might make a suggestion I wouldn't fill those in until after the job has been completed." Jack the Hat winked and left the store.

In the ensuing weeks Jones and Briggs received so many requests for pens and pen sets that it was necessary to compile a rank structure. That is, Chief Inspectors and above got the complete pen set, Inspectors pen and ball point, Sergeants and Constables either ball point pen or pen but not both. Briggs subsequently found himself in the humorous position of arguing the toss with a Detective Inspector who was pressing his suit for the complete set on the basis that he was acting Chief Inspector at East Dulwich and therefore entitled. But basically everyone got something. Charlie's wife was also pleased she got a clear flat for the first time in years. Charlie was pleased as well as he received three years' probation for basically a first offence, whether this lesson was a lasting one only time would tell.

Briggs and Jones never did find Mulberry Villas.

The Likely Lad

The lady who sits forever on the top of the Old Bailey demonstrates that British Justice is blind, it being dispensed with the same level on all who come under its scrutiny, be they beggar or rich man, without fear or favour. Likewise, he who seeks justice will be patiently heard and although 'it is better that a thousand guilty men go free than one innocent man be incarcerated' the truly guilty will be punished with the full force of the law. – Bollocks.

The drill buzzed through Briggs' brain as well as his rotten tooth. He stared hard at the ceiling trying to exclude what was happening, in the manner of those ladies who 'laid back and thought of England.' Briggs always reckoned that they enjoyed it really but were too prim to say. This was not the case in hand; this hurt. In the large lampshade above him he could see a reflection of what was happening. His face contorted to give access to the drill.

"Wasn't that a strange thing that happened next door to me?" enquired the dentist Mr. Budden, making small talk.

"I don't know Mr. Budden, what was that?" is what Briggs meant to say but it came out distorted and almost a foreign language. However Mr. Budden was used to conversing in a strange language.

"The other day, Tuesday, some of your chaps attended, didn't you hear?" Mr. Budden punctuated his question with a gouging motion of the drill which made Briggs clench his hands and feet.

"No I've been on night duty observations this last month, what happened?"

Mr. Budden stopped drilling. "Well," he said hanging his drill on its perch whilst Briggs' tongue explored the hole in his molar.

"I hope he doesn't forget to fill that crater after this war story."

thought Briggs.

"Well I was in the kitchen at my house in Farmer's Lane, you know, where I live." Briggs nodded. "Well anyway I saw this chap in next door's garden and as I knew they were out I went round to challenge him. As I went into their garden he was trying to force the back door with a screwdriver. I shouted at him and as he went to run past me, I took him down with the old rugby tackle, Saracens you know, first team and all that." His eyes became dreamy in memory, but he shook himself out of his reverie. "Anyway we had a fight, nothing too serious, he struck me as bit of big girl. He was yelling 'Oh please let me go, let me go,' but I wouldn't and we scrambled about in the flower beds. Eventually he kneed me in the downstairs regions got up and ran off."

"Oh yes, very interesting, and you called the Police?" Briggs asked but without paying much attention to the words but imagining the portly dentist scrabbling with a breaker.

"Not quite, I did call the Police but then I got into my car and went off up the back road in the direction I thought he might have taken. At the top of the road I turned left and there he was! Well I went for him and gave him what for. I'm sure I gave him a black eye, left one I think. Anyway he caught me a fourpenny one and ran off again. The Police found me and I told them all about it but they didn't seem very interested although I gave them a good description and told them where he could be arrested. They still didn't seem very interested. That Detective Constable Barking from your office was most rude I thought."

Briggs became interested at the prospect of an arrest. "Are you saying Mr. Budden that you know where this man can be arrested?" Briggs waited with baited breath and holey tooth.

"That's right," answered Mr. Budden, with the tone of one who has been trying very hard to get his point across.

"And where would that be sir?" Briggs asked whilst trying to fish out his pocket book being still in the chair and covered with a baby's bib. Budden waited whilst Briggs arranged himself in relation to his pocket book and pen. "He eats most lunchtimes in the Chinese Restaurant down the road, he's most distinctive. He's got sandy unkempt hair and wears big horn rimmed glasses. He's about six foot tall and I should say he's fairly fit. Oh yes I noticed he was wearing this sweatshirt with UCLA on the front and underneath it says 'Legalise pot' He was wearing that when I tried to apprehend him."

Briggs scribbled the description in his book. "Well sir the next time you see him perhaps you would be kind enough to ring me at the Station. It would give me great pleasure to entertain him at the nick for a while," said Briggs putting his pocket book away. "And now sir perhaps you would be so kind as to fill this hole in my tooth," said Briggs opening his mouth and indicating the holey fang.

Budden laughed, "Of course I forgot in the heat of telling about my fisticuffs and all that." Briggs laid back and thought of England.

Briggs entered the CID office and went to his desk. There were a number of messages stuck under the blotter. He picked them up and read them. Nothing too urgent, and placed them back under the blotter. "You alright Tel?" Ron asked from the other side of the desk. "Yeah fine, but I could do without half of my face being numb." Briggs slurred his speech.

"Take heart old son, street people pay fortunes for a similar experience." Tony Richards spoke up, ex of the Drugs Squad and therefore should have knowledge about the subject.

"The only difference being they don't have large holes dug in their teeth at the same time," said Briggs rubbing his jaw and feeling nothing. "Mind you this stuff must be blinding in a punch up, you'd never feel anything"

"I suppose so, but I bet it hurts when it wears off," laughed Jones, inevitably writing in his diary.

The telephone in the middle of the desk rang. Jones picked it up, saying in his almost non Welsh telephone voice, "CID Rodney Road, how can I help?"

"Oh very American," thought Briggs. "I would love to hear him end up with "Have a nice day, y'hear."

"Yes sir, I will get him for you," Jones said putting his hand over the mouthpiece. "Tel, it's Mr. Budden for you."

Briggs took the telephone and placed a piece of rough paper on his blotter. "Yes Mr. Budden sorry about the voice, but it's your fault anyway."

"Not a problem, I can understand you – just. It's about the man we were talking about, the breaker, the one I had a fight with, well two actually and lost them both." Budden gave a nervous laugh.

"Yes I do remember of course," Briggs getting his 'Moffat' pen out ready.

"Well he's in the Chinese Restaurant now."

Briggs wrote the message on automatic. "Come on Ron, we've a body to nick." and they both left as though their backsides were alight.

Briggs screeched the CID car to halt outside the restaurant. Budden was standing outside peering into the restaurant with his hands shielding his eyes. He turned towards them as they got out of the car. "He's in there, Mr. Briggs, in the chair in the corner. He's on his pudding now." Budden hopped from one foot to the other in excitement.

"Right, Mr. Budden you stay here and Ron and I will go in and question him." They both entered the restaurant. "Ron count the number of customers in here."

"Count the customers?" repeated Jones, surprised.

"It proves how strong the ID was. Do it while I speak to chummy." Ron stood in the centre of the room and counted heads. Briggs walked over to the corner where the identified sandy haired felon sat crouched over his pudding. Briggs stood close to him and said in a quiet voice, "Er excuse me sir, I am a CID officer from Rodney Road Police Station and I have good reason to believe that you were involved in an offence of burglary on Tuesday of last week. Will you please step outside with me?" The man looked up at Briggs and methodically put down his spoon, at which time Briggs was joined by Jones. "Please sir." Briggs softly just in case this was not the wanted man.

The man leaned back in his chair and seemed to Briggs to be examining him or perhaps weighing him up. "Now look here officer, you're making a terrible mistake you know." Briggs was stunned by the upper crust drawl, completely out of place in Camberwell, but responded still in quiet tones but with less tolerance in his voice. "Well that's our problem isn't it, now come along Sir."

The man looked down at this pudding plate. Briggs thought, "I bet he doesn't call it that, it's either sweet or dessert, but not pudding and definitely not afters."

"No," said the man considering his dessert. "I shall finish my meal first, now go away and leave me alone." Briggs looked across at Jones and nodded to the man and the door. Jones grabbed the man's elbow, Briggs getting hold of his side and together they lifted the man out of his chair and across the table and through his pudding remains and towards the door.

"Witnesses, witnesses," the man screeched, "I'm being kidnapped by the Gestapo."

"They're old bill. they are not Ges... whatever it was he said, they're old bill from Rodney Road." A male customer announced their identity to the whole shop. Another voice said, "Old bill, definitely old bill." This double pronouncement was accepted without question and they returned to their meals.

They dragged Ginger outside the shop to a confrontation with Mr. Budden. Briggs sensed that Budden was nervous, and felt like placating him by announcing that the prisoner would not could get to him, but didn't. "Mr Budden is this the man, who, you say tried to break into your neighbour's house?" Briggs asked, holding the breaker with one hand and indicating him with the other.

Budden responded, stepping back. "It most certainly is officer, I have no doubt whatsoever. He is the man. I would recognise him anywhere. Look he's even got a black eye, I said that didn't I."

Briggs turned to the breaker and said officiously, "I am arresting you on reasonable suspicion that you have committed the offence of burglary, you're not obliged to say anything unless you wish to do so but what you say may be put into writing and given in evidence, do you understand?"

"Absolutely old boy," the plummy accent grated with Briggs. "Absolutely, but I must say that you and your friend here have a bizarre approach to career planning."

Briggs ignored him and turned to the dentist "Mr. Budden we will meet you at the Police Station for the purpose of you giving a statement, are you available for that?" Budden nodded his assent and scuttled off.

At which time the breaker began to struggle against Jones and began shouting, "Let me go. Let me go you have no right. I will not be arrested." Briggs let go of the man which made Jones hang on like a man possessed. Once free, Briggs elbowed this upper class prisoner in the ribs, not hard enough to break anything but hard enough to wind. The prisoner winced, and held his side. "You will be sorry officer, I promise you you will be sorry."

"I am already sorry, sorry that you tried to break into the house, sorry that you were ever born in fact, and if you don't shut the fuck up, I am going to make you ever so sorry you upset me, do you understand me?" The prisoner's head went down and he nodded without speaking, an attitude which was of immense relief to Briggs.

Jones sat in the back of the CID car with the prisoner and they drove in sullen silence to the nick.

Standing in the charge room, while Ron fetched the station sergeant, the prisoner spoke to Briggs with the air of one who is used to gaining precedence by the use of a name. "You don't know who I am do you?" He smiled tolerantly as he spoke. Briggs stared him straight in the eye and spoke slowly and with almost menace.

"No, I don't old son, but I have this strange feeling that given time you just might tell me. I have your name recorded but that is not what you mean, am I right?"

"No Constable that isn't it at all. My name is Peter de la Mare, does that name mean anything to you at all?"

"No" responded Briggs, "I am afraid it doesn't, apart from the poet, are you related to him?"

de la Mare laughed. "Only very distantly, I can't write beautiful prose or anything like that."

"Neither can I," said Briggs "There you are we do have something in common." Briggs dug de la Mare in the ribs and noted that he shrunk from the contact,

The portly Station Sergeant entered with a self-important swagger, he placed the blank charge sheet and backing folder down on the bench in front of the prisoner and his escort. "Right who do we have here then?" the Sergeant alternating his gaze between the prisoner and Briggs, but clearly addressing himself to Briggs.

"Peter de la Mare, Jones and I have nicked him for burglary. There is an independent witness, who is waiting outside for a statement to be taken, after which Mr. de la Mare will be charged. Jones and I request that he be detained pending those enquiries."

"How long do you reckon?" asked the Sergeant, busily writing on the charge sheet.

"A good couple of hours, by the time we have interviewed the witness, then him." Briggs indicated the prisoner with a nod. "Two to two and a half hours I should think."

de la Mare looked pained, "I say look here Sergeant, when do I get my say, these two ruffians have spoilt my lunch on the say so of a scruffy pleb. I am here but I am not going to stay against my will." de la Mare was flushed and angry, and almost to the foot stamping stage.

"Mr. de la Mare, you have been arrested on reasonable suspicion that you have committed the offence of burglary and you will be detained whilst these officers complete their enquiries, do you understand?" The Sergeant looked intently into the face of de la Mare. de la Mare hesitated, no doubt feeling in spite of his exalted social status just a little out numbered.

"Yes Sergeant I do understand but could you please inform my father," de la Mare now with a pleading tone. "He would like to be informed and it may be that he can help me and you in this predicament." de la Mare's plummy accent rang round the charge room.

The Sergeant straightened and pulled himself up to his full height. "Sir you are an adult, you can inform him yourself after you have been charged if that is what these officers decide to do." The Sergeant gathered the papers off the bench and strode out of the charge room with a curt nod to Briggs.

Briggs watched the Sergeant on his way out, continued his conversation, "Make it the main topic of your evening chat, he'll enjoy that. That is of course depending on whether we give you bail or not, and you won't get bail calling us ruffians. Mr. Jones here is a lay preacher with the Bromley Methodist Chapel I'll have you know, a veritable pillar of the community and, although I have ruffianish tendencies, they are being brought under control by the calming influence of Mr. Jones here. So in the meantime," Briggs continuing with a raised voice, "Cut the crap and get in that cell." He caught hold of the scruff of de la Mare's coat and hurled him through he open cell door.

De la Mare stood in the centre of the cell and whined, "Once my father hears about this you will be sorry, I mean really sorry that you ever set eyes on me."

Briggs felt that de la Mare was close to tears.

"Tell me about it when it happens." Briggs kicked the cell door shut with his foot, checking at the same time the lock indicated that it had secured.

Jones and Briggs then adjourned to the interview room where Mr. Budden awaited them. Briggs wrote out the statement much as Mr. Budden had told him the story and, at the end read the statement back to him and said, "Have I got everything down as it happened?"

Mr. Budden stared coldly at Briggs. "As far as it goes yes, but what about Detective Constable Barking, he wasn't as efficient as Mr. Jones and you, was he? It is only right and proper to state that I originally complained to Mr. Barking and that all I got from him was rudeness and facetiousness."

Briggs paused. However much he disliked Barking he felt a sort of loyalty to him and would not do him down unless it was absolutely necessary. Faced with this quandary Briggs spoke as he wrote, "I shall put in here that you reported the matter to Detective Constable Barking of Rodney Road Police Station during the evening of the offence and you have yet to hear the result of his enquiries."

Budden smiled, "Before me I see the operation of the old pals act, blood thicker than water is that it?"

Briggs was on the spot. Jones was looking out of the window studiously observing two pigeons engaged in sexual wrestling and, obviously, did not intend to offer any help to either side in this minor confrontation. Briggs continued, "Well Mr. Budden, what you say about Mr. Barking's rudeness isn't evidence as such. However if you would like to make a formal complaint I can arrange for you to make it to the Duty Inspector. Alternatively you could mention it when giving evidence, whichever you prefer."

Budden, recognising Briggs' problem, closed the subject quietly by saying. "I'll leave it as it is for the time being." Briggs gratefully handed him the statement and having read it signed where indicated by Briggs.

"Now sir, just a few formalities. Have you any dates to avoid for court, holidays, hospital appointments, dentists perhaps?" Briggs grinned.

Budden laughed, "I don't trust another dentist with my teeth, they are a bunch of ruffians." Budden reached inside his coat and fished out his diary, he opened and studied it. "On holiday first two weeks in July and nothing after until the end of the year. He's unlikely to come up at Christmas is he."

Briggs laughed, "I don't think so. Now sir what religion are you?" Budden did not reply and Briggs looked up. "For the oath sir, the one you take before you give evidence."

Budden smiled, "Oh I see, I am a Jehovah's Witness." Briggs paused and made a note. Jones coughed, embarrassed, Briggs could see that he wanted to say something but Briggs decided not to give him the chance.

"Well that will be all sir, we'll ring you at the surgery as and when we have something to impart, court dates and the like. If you have anything to else to tell us please do not hesitate to call us, and thank you for assisting us in this matter."

Budden got up and shook hands with Briggs. Jones made it impossible for the dentist to do any such thing to him. Budden and Jones merely stared at each other with the beginnings of animosity growing between them. Budden left the Police Station, being shown out by Briggs.

Briggs found Jones in the canteen, sitting behind a cup of tea, staring into it as though trying to define some sense from it. "What the hell's the matter with you Ron? Why did you give old Budden the bum's rush?"

Ron replied like a sulky child. "I was alright, just didn't feel the need to—, to get too pally that's all," still staring into his cup.

"You were not alright to him, you made it obvious that you didn't like him, you refused to shake his hand." Briggs leaned over the table at Jones, Ron refused to meet Briggs' stare, but said in a feeble tone.

"Well it's his religion really, Jehovah's Witness, all that, can't stand it you know."

Briggs showing his temper, "Ron as far as I can see his religion has got sod all to do with you or me, so what's your problem?"

Ron, now fidgeting and obviously ill at ease with his bias, "Well you know, they don't allow their children to have blood transfusions, and their teachings about the Bible are all boss-eyed, very odd you see." Jones looked up at Briggs pleading for understanding.

"I can't see that it matters over much, they believe in something different from you, just leave it at that, I believe in absolutely nothing, where does that leave me in your reckoning?"

"Oh well you being a primitive, that's alright as you don't know any better," said Ron brightly. "When you get to the Pearly Gates St Peter will treat you kindly as you are a friend of mine." Ron said it as though absolving this sinner from all blame.

"Ron you're a prick, I don't know why you get involved in all this shit, it strikes me there is just enough religion in the world for men to hate each other and not enough so that they will understand and maybe forgive."

Jones beginning to recover himself faced Briggs and laughingly asked, "That's a very sophisticated view, even for you, are you planning to go on the telly with Malcolm Muggeridge and show this new found tolerance to the world? I bet if you ever go to confession, the priest who takes it will be able to write a best seller."

Briggs keeping his temper in check, shrugged his shoulders, stood up to leave and said by way of drawing the conversation to an end, "Just try and to be a bit more understanding, that's all, he probably thinks that the strict chapel Methodists from South Wales are all sheep shaggers anyway. Come on, let's go and interview old de la wotsit." Ron followed Briggs as always but pleased to be away from this subject which made him confused and uncomfortable.

Being Connected

The skill in interrogation is not giving a good hiding to a prisoner in an effort to wheedle the truth from him. It is all about uncertainty, the thought that you might beat the living daylights out of him is much better than actually doing it, or as one expert interrogator put it, 'Climb into his brain and unlock some certainties, and play on that insecurity'. We never went as far as the American Intelligence Services in Vietnam, where they took suspects, one who knew everything and was well connected to the Viet Cong, and another who was an also ran. They took them both up in a helicopter and at a great height enquired on the also ran, "Tell me about the Ho Chi Min Trail." The also ran would plead that he knew nothing and was promptly thrown out of the helicopter to his certain death as parachutes were an unlikely extra. Then the interrogator turned to the other one, the main man who knew everything and said, "Now you tell me about the Ho Chi Min trail and anything else you think might interest us." It would take a very strong man to resist such persuasive methods. The introduction of the Police and Criminal Evidence Act has curtailed the more colourful activities of Detective Officers, whether this is a good thing remains to be seen.

"Er, skip," Briggs standing before the First Class's desk. "Jones and I have a body. We think he needs a bit of goody and baddy, and he knows both of us."

The amiable Sid looked up, smiled the rhetorical question, 'You think I can unlock the truth from him, yes?"

"Well skip I think a change of pace would help, if you know what I mean, also he thinks he's a bit special – connected and all that."

Sid laughed, "He's one of those, right, consider it done old son, where are you gong to be?" Sid stood up and straightened his desk.

"In the main CID office, they're all out or gone home."

Briggs left the skipper, went downstairs and got de la Mare from the cells. He was leading him upstairs to the CID office when de la Mare whined, "Oh God this is such a bore, when am I going to be released, this is encroaching on my civil liberties?"

The upper class drawl grated on Briggs' nerves. "You will be released when I say so, till then behave yourself." de la Mare tried to squirm away from Briggs' firm grip. Briggs released him and squared up. "Come on you high class ponce, you want it." Briggs was ready to give de la Mare a short course in unconsciousness. de la Mare showed fear in his eyes, his lower lip trembled.

Briggs felt a little ashamed and said, "Now come on and don't fuck about – right?" de la Mare nodded quietly, and then continued upstairs together.

They entered the CID office where Ron was sitting at his desk. Pocket book on blotter ready to start taking notes. Ron rarely questioned, partly because South London villains usually had difficulty with Ron's accent, but also because he was content to let Briggs play the main part and collect half the credit at the end of the job, on the reverse if there was any grief to come it was Briggs'. Briggs pulled a chair over for de la Mare. "I do not want to sit down, I want to go home," snapped de la Mare almost to the foot stamping stage.

"Come on Peter, be a bit friendly, sit down we have lots of questions to put to you." Briggs indicated the vacant chair with his open hand.

"I do not wish to be friendly with you two, I do not even like you, you're horrible and nasty." Briggs now thought he detected an element of gay campishness in de la Mare's speech which in turn ruffled the bigotry in Briggs' character.

"Oh I see, you're obviously an ex public schoolboy, yes?"

De la Mare straightened himself. "Yes of course," and slyly added,"I can tell at a glance neither of you are."

Briggs laughed, content to give de la Mare the moment. "It's that obvious is it?" responding in like manner. "I would have thought our Ron here could have been taken for a well educated, possibly public schoolboy, but you say no?"

De la Mare, feeling confident, "Definitely not with that accent." Ron looked up, offended.

Just then the office door burst open and Sid Mills bustled in, both Ron and Briggs stood rigidly to attention. "Where the fuck is everyone?" roared Sid.

"Either gone home, or out on enquiries, Sah," Briggs roared as though on parade.

"Right I'll see to them in the morning, not bloody having this." Mills grumbled as he looked through the crime and duty books. In mock anger he ripped some blank pages out of the back of the crime book and tore them into little pieces. "Rubbish absolute fucking rubbish," roared Sid, "who's in charge of investigations in this office?"

Briggs spoke softly as though in awe of the speaker. "Well sir the first class is Sergeant Mills and the Chief Inspector is Mr. Parris – sir."

Sid paused as though thinking. "Right tell both of them to report to my office up the Yard in the morning and to bring their diaries with them, and you," Sid indicated Jones, "Stand up straight you're like a hairpin with a bend in the middle." Ron straightened himself. "Who the hell is this?" Sid continued without a pause indicating de la Mare. de la Mare started to answer. "Keep quiet shithead, I am talking to a Detective Officer." Sid glared at de la Mare, who almost flinched at the expected tirade.

Briggs again in a soft tone "He is Peter de la Mare sir, in for suspected burglary, independent witness has identified and given a statement. The witness is in fact a dentist, a professional man of good standing." Briggs still rigidly to attention.

Sid patted de la Mare on the cheek. de la Mare leaned away from the contact. "So our little Peter hasn't a chance in the world?" Sid cocked his head to the side in questioning.

"Well no sir, not really, he says he wants to go home sir."

de la Mare began to say something. "Shut up, don't you understand me you little maggot," to which de la Mare fell silent. Sid turned to Briggs. "Wants to go home does he? Right then Briggs should you fail to unlock the truth from this article, I will take personal interest in this case together with my chauffeur of course." Sid glared at de la Mare his face contorted with fake rage. "Think on shithead, life could get painful, or even terminal." Sid then stormed out slamming the office door behind him.

Briggs and Jones slumped in their chairs and Briggs waved de la Mare to follow suit. "Trust that dickhead to turn up, at the wrong time too." Jones nodded agreement, both looked crestfallen.

Puzzled and shaken by the confrontation de la Mare said. "Just who is he?"

"Deputy Assistant Commissioner Raglan that's who, top Detective in the Met, one hard no good shit. His methods came more from the Gestapo than the Salvation Army, and that chauffeur, well he's a muscle bound goon. He's really Raglan's minder and will do anything he's ordered to." Briggs emphasised the 'anything'. de la Mare gulped and looked worried.

"Right then where were we, ah yes, we were about to discuss Mr. Budden's allegations against you," Briggs said indicating Budden's statement. de la Mare nodded as Briggs continued, "Ah yes here we go, Mr. Budden says he caught you at the back of a house in Farmer's Lane. Is that the truth?"

de la Mare stared fixedly at the floor. "Yes that's true," he said quietly.

"And Mr. Budden says you were trying to jemmy the kitchen door. Is that true too?" Briggs continued quietly, not wanting to change the mood.

"Yes that's true as well." de la Mare stared fixedly at the floor.

Briggs smiled at de la Mare. "Mr. Budden says he had two fights with you, one in the garden and one up the road, is that true as well?" de la Mare nodded.

"Yes that's right he gave me a black eye." de la Mare indicated his left eye which was swollen and black. "But you also jabbed me in the ribs." de la Mare looked petulant.

Briggs trying to get back on the track where things had been going his way said, "I am ever so sorry about that Peter, but you must admit we were not getting on so well were we?"

"No we were not." de la Mare said it slowly and emphatically.

Briggs stared at de la Mare, trying almost to ascertain the function of his brain, or rather how much he understood. "Now Peter" said Briggs breezily. "What were you going to do inside the house?" Briggs raised his eyebrows to punctuate the question. Ron scribbled furiously.

"Well I was going to steal something, cash if it was there. I could see a woman's handbag on the kitchen table, they've usually got something in them."

Briggs prompted de la Mare into the right direction. "And you were going to steal it, the handbag that it?" de la Mare hesitated, Briggs felt that the whole truth had not been told, or maybe they had misunderstood.

"Well no only the money. I also have a problem." de la Mare looked down at the floor as he spoke. "I can't stand women, so I tend to do something, you know against them."

"You've done this before, is that what you are saying? If you have now's the time to tell us. Remember we can find out in all sorts of strange ways." said Briggs while de la Mare fiddled with the edge of the blotter.

"Well yes I have, I like to get their handbags, take the money, and do something in the handbag," de la Mare stressed the something and looked embarrassed.

"Do you mean you shit in their handbags?" Briggs was incredulous and wanted to laugh.

"Yes. if I can't manage that I pee in it," de la Mare in a rush and pleading for understanding and not surprisingly failing to get it.

Briggs was off balance. "Let's get this right, you break into houses where a handbag is visible, take the money and shit or piss in the handbag, is that right?" Ron was writing furiously making faces at the same time.

"Yes that's about it." de la Mare was shamefaced. A moment later he added, "I would like to say I'm sorry."

"Peter how many times have you done this?" Briggs paused expectantly sincerely hoping that de la Mare was not going to admit hundreds offences and cause him hours and hours of hard work.

"About six in all. I suppose." de la Mare looked up at the ceiling as though the answer to questions were written there. "Most of them around here. I also did a couple in Greenwich."

"When were these offences committed?" Briggs' mind was racing ahead.

"Oh during the last eighteen months certainly." de la Mare now anxious to help the kind officer.

Briggs nodded to Jones. "Peter I shall be out for a moment, you stay here and discuss theology with my colleague."

Briggs found the station collator in his office, inevitably doing his filing. "Tom how are you going, alright?" and without waiting for an answer, "Good. Listen have you had any break ins where the offender has pissed or shit in a handbag on the premises?"

Tom laughed. "An amazing idea, but as it happens we've had about three of them, small amounts of money taken and as he leaves he shits in the handbag, you do get some kinky bastards, don't you?"

"Ron and I have nicked him, he's upstairs in the CID office. See if you can dig out those crime reports and give us a ring, also he says he's done a couple in Greenwich. See if you can find those as well, the full bit mind, when how, where and how much was nicked." Briggs made for the door. Stephens was nettled. "You don't have to tell me, I know what I am doing," he almost yelled at Briggs' retreating back.

Briggs re-entered the CID office. de la Mare was staring fixedly at the floor. He looked up as Briggs came in. "Right then Peter do you want to make a statement about all this? Put it all down on paper, how you do things. The sooner you have done this the sooner you can go home."

de la Mare looked up, there were the beginnings of tears in his eyes. "Yes I suppose so, Nanny will be so disappointed with me, that's who I live with, she looks after me."

Briggs felt the beginnings of misgivings. "Peter how old are you?" Briggs asked quietly.

"I shall be twenty nine next birthday." de la Mare was now pouting like a spoilt child. "Why do you want to know?"

"Oh just form you know." Briggs was gradually coming to the opinion that all was not well with this breaker. "And where exactly do you live?" Ron's pen was poised.

"122 Carnforth Mansions, Knightsbridge, it's an apartment, Daddy has had it for years, he lets Nanny and me live there," de la Mare smiling at the memory.

"Does Nanny do everything for you?" Briggs asked quietly.

"Yes she does, she has been my Nanny as long as I can

remember." de la Mare looked puzzled. 'Why do you ask?"

"Just wondered who you lived with that's all, does Nanny take you to the doctors or the hospital when you need to go?" Ron's pen was streaking across the page.

"Yes she does. I said she does everything for me." de la Mare was peering like a schoolboy at Ron's notes.

"And when was the last time you went to see the doctor?" Briggs was looking at de la Mare closely.

"Last Wednesday, yes last Wednesday," said de la Mare brightly. "We go every Wednesday afternoon to see Doctor Sutherland, he's a psychiatrist you know," added de la Mare as though imparting some really useful piece of information.

"And why do you go and see Doctor Sutherland?" asked Briggs pressing on but really having a shrewd idea of the likely answer.

de la Mare spoke in a strange clipped manner as though repeating his medical notes "Because I keep losing my identity and going, well, strange. He says I'm not mad, but just confused."

"Do you hear voices that tell you to do things, voices that do not come from anyone?" Briggs was quite getting into the Freudian aspect of police work.

"Yes I do, why, do you get them as well?" de la Mare asked excitedly.

"No I don't, but I have heard of it." Briggs paused thinking. Ron looked at him as though trying to say something. Briggs didn't give him the opportunity. "Peter do you wish to make a statement?"

"About the thing with handbag and all that?" de la Mare seemed almost excited by the prospect as though writing about it he would experience the thrill of defecating in handbags.

Briggs limited himself to, "Yes it would be your opportunity to put your side of it." Briggs smiled helpfully.

"Er Tel, I think you should sign the certificate," Ron interjected as he pushed a sheet of paper towards Briggs. Briggs picked it up and read the message, 'He's barking mad why bother with a statement? Call the Police Surgeon and have him deemed'. Briggs signed what de la Mare thought was his signature at the bottom of the sheet of paper but was really 'get stuffed'.

"Thank you for reminding me Mr. Jones, now we shall get on

with the statement?" Ron huffed and puffed at his advice being ignored, but in any case began to take a statement at Briggs' dictation. At the conclusion Briggs got de la Mare to write the certificate and sign where indicated.

Once the statement had been topped and tailed, they took de la Mare to the charge room and awaited the presence of the duty sergeant. Once the Sergeant hustled in Briggs explained the charge he wished to prefer. The Sergeant wrote it down and rearranged it on the charge sheet. He then called de la Mare from the bench where he was lounging. "Oi you, come here and stand before the bench. This is an important moment in British legal history. Stand up straight you are going to be charged with attempt housebreaking." de la Mare was jolted back to reality from where he had been.

"Are we going to see nanny now?" he cried in a high pitched voice.

"Just as soon as you have been charged," Briggs said trying to allay his fears.

The Duty Sergeant looked searchingly at Briggs. "Briggsy are you sure about this?"

Briggs fixed the Sergeant with his best 'This is the law' stare and said, "Sergeant we have a statement from an independent witness who puts de la Mare at the scene of an attempted burglary, and he himself admits breaking into the same house and fighting with the witness. What we really have is something for the court to decide."

The Sergeant looked down at the charge sheet pondering. Eventually he said, "I am constrained to agree." The sergeant turned to de la Mare, "Oi you listen up the charge against you is... The sergeant recited the charge in the time honoured manner and cautioned de la Mare at the end. de la Mare looked completely mystified by the proceedings and said nothing. "No reply." intoned the Sergeant. Briggs indicated where de la Mare should sign the charge sheet and also how to complete the own recognizance bail form.

Briggs took de la Mare by the arm. "Come on now Peter we will take you home to Nanny." de la Mare brightened. "Oh good, Nanny will make us cocoa and sandwiches, she really is very nice, when you get to know her."

Briggs and Jones stood outside 122, Carnforth Mansions, with de la Mare between them. The door was opened by a lady in late middle age, dressed in a nurses' uniform, except for the comfortable slippers.

"Why Master Peter, where have you been and who are these two people? Are they new friends, you know your father's rule on new friends don't you?" She wrung her hands together in a worried manner.

Briggs interceded for the sake of regularity. "Madam we are not friends of Peter's. We are Police Officers from Rodney Road and we have arrested Peter for offences of burglary. He has been charged and we are now going to search his room for corroboration of the evidence we have secured so far." Briggs dragged de la Mare into the hallway.

Nanny seemed to be confused. "Master Peter whatever will your father say, whatever shall I do? Shall I ring your father now? What shall I do?" She spoke more to herself than anyone else as she hopped from one foot to another.

"Madam." Briggs' voice seemed to bring Nanny back to reality. "You may do as you wish, but first direct us to Master Peter's room so we can get on."

Nanny nodded vigorously "Of course, of course." she muttered and led them down the hall. Briggs noticed, in passing, that the lounge was sumptuously furnished; the television was on, there was a bottle of gin, and another of tonic on the side table next to an ice bucket. Nanny apparently had it made. They opened the door of a side room indicated by Nanny.

Briggs with de la Mare beside him began searching in a large chest of drawers. Professional he searched from bottom to top, thereby saving the time of closing the drawers. In the second drawer from the bottom he found a yellow sweatshirt with a large round emblem on the front and 'UCLA' underneath. Beneath that were the words 'legalise pot.'

"This yours?" Briggs holding the sweatshirt up to de la Mare.

"Yes of course it is, it's in my clothes chest."

Nanny got into the act. "I have only just washed it, it was ever so grubby, I don't know what he does with his clothes." Briggs put the sweatshirt in a polythene bag and sealed it.

"I am seizing this as evidence." Ron was standing doing nothing. "You finished Ron?"

"Yes the only things I found in there were a couple of grubby handbags."

Briggs grunted, "Seize them," hoping that Ron would fall in and he would not have to embarrass him.

"Seize them why? they're only old handbags?" Ron, as usual, arguing the point of no action.

Briggs spoke slowly, "They might be connected to an offence." Briggs noting that Ron was still confused said, "Ron for fuck sake where does he like to have a crap?"

"Oh right got it," and Ron sealed the handbags in polythene. Jones and Briggs left Peter with Nanny clucking over his welfare, and real and imagined hurts.

A Day In Court

Briggs was in the CID office quietly writing. Jones was opposite studying the duty sheet, working out which weekend would be his and which the chapel's. Jack the Hat stood in the office door and bellowed "Who's nicked one Peter de la Mare?" Jack the Hat was staring down at a piece of paper. "Come on own up who is it?"

Briggs stood up. "Er it's Jones and me guv, nicked him yesterday," offered Briggs. "Why is something wrong?" Jones' attention was caught. Jack the Hat nodded back into his office.

"Into my office you two, Sid you come as well," Jack the Hat continued and nodded in the direction of Sid Mills.

They all crowded into Jack the Hat's office. "Right come in and sit down, find yourself a space somewhere." Briggs perched himself on the arm of the chair into which Sid had subsided.

"Right now what's this all about? You seem switched on Briggs, tell me the story, the unofficial one as well." Briggs opened the case file and recounted the events of the day before. He omitted to mention Sid's walk on speaking part as DAC (Crime), but the rest was laid before Jack the Hat much as it happened, including Budden's statement, de la Mare's admission and the discovery of the sweatshirt and handbags at Nanny's flat.

Jack the Hat read the statement of de la Mare. "Mm, seems to be a very strong case against the young man. However questions have been asked from on high about this one. It would appear that our Peter is the son of the ex Mayor and as such is well connected and does not expect to be nicked, especially not by the likes of you two. Anyway the guvnor wants to know what can be done." Jack the Hat looked expectantly at all three. "Well?"

Jones paled and groaned "The Mayor."

Mills ignored Jones and said, "Nothing at all guv, as far as I can see, Briggs and Jones have done a good job and I cannot see outers anywhere. Further I don't see why we should contemplate it either," Sid added, jaw jutting and moustache quivering.

"Well for what it's worth they will have outers, and it's being approached on the basis that he's nutty as fruit cake and should not have been charged in the first place." Jack the Hat leaned back in his chair studying the trio before him.

Briggs responded. "I did consider that last night guv, didn't take advice or anything, but it is our view that" Ron nearly fell off his perch at his sudden inclusion in all this grief, "the decision as to whether he is crackers or not should not be taken by police, but by the Magistrate dealing, and then only after he has had the benefit of mental and medical reports. I think Archbolds states that the police are not possessed of magisterial powers." Briggs was not certain of the quotation or the source but from the look on the faces of all concerned he could see that they didn't know any different.

"You might have a point there Briggs. However I have been told to tell you both that the lot at the top will have outers for their little chap, further if you two state that you made a mistake your careers will not suffer."

"And we will not suffer?" Briggs snorted. "Come on guv they will be all over us like a rash. They can't even lie straight in bed never mind keep a promise."

Jack the Hat laughed "You've seen too much my old son. It's just that powerful people will have the chap free of charge so to speak, whatever we say. What do you think?"

Sid spoke giving this approach the kiss of death. "It just isn't going to run guv, he's been charged, we can't do anything without the D of PP's permission. I'm sorry guv I can't see it." Jack the Hat paused, really trying to think how else to approach this matter.

"Well it won't end there chaps, you know that?" Jack the Hat was apologetic.

"Right then chaps put in a legal aid report. Let's get some help at court for what that is worth. Needless to say I'll back you," said Jack the Hat, signalling the interview was over by picking up a report from the pile in his in tray and beginning to read it.

They all got up and left.

"I said we should have called the Police Surgeon for his opinion. I said that didn't I," Jones mumbled morosely, also seeing his prospects of promotion receding. Briggs' patience was wearing thin. "And I told you that it would make no difference. The Police Surgeon does not make decisions as to whether someone is charged or not, we do and we did didn't we?"

"Yes I suppose so," replied Jones, unhappy.

"Just you remember that, also that Sid was never there, right?" Briggs leaned forward and stressed the message.

"Alright, I won't, I've never let anyone down, have I?" Jones was defiant.

"Well don't make this your first time, okay," Briggs walking away to his desk.

The intervening two weeks between arrest and court appearance passed fairly quietly, apart from sly comments about 'Miscarriage of Justice'. and how the 'big guns' were being primed for the dynamic duo. Briggs was accosted by the Station Deputy a Superintendent in the cell corridor. The Superintendent, in an effort to cover his painful shyness, had effected the phrase 'Alright', with or without a question mark. On this occasion he said, "Alright Briggs, it might be that you and Jones have made a terrible mistake – alright."

Briggs, caught unawares, said, "I shall bear it in mind guv." The super scuttled off his mission accomplished. It was not at all uncommon for Senior Officers to adopt catchphrases, usually done to hide their real or imagined inability to cope with leadership; one used the phrase 'in point of fact' constantly, so much so that when he was in charge of a briefing, the audience would run a book on how many times the phrase was used.

On the day of the court hearing both Jones and Briggs attended together with Mr. Budden. They waited outside for their case to be called. Briggs as officer in charge of the case, entered the court and approached the solicitor sitting on the Prosecution side of the court. "Morning guv, you for the Police against de la Mare?" The thin grey haired man looked up from his papers, Briggs noticed he was wearing the old boys' tie of a very well known public school and thought, "He'll be in good company with this lot, probably specially selected."

"Yes I am," with the same high class whine effected by de la Mare.

"Witnesses are all here, Mr. Budden, D.C. Jones and myself," said Briggs laying his case file down on the bench.

"If all goes to plan, we should not need any of you." The brief spoke off handedly still looking at his file, in the manner somewhat of doctors who don't look up when you enter their surgery.

"What's going on, are we going for a remand then?" Briggs puzzled by this development.

"No we are not going for a remand."

Briggs felt he wanted to add, "You unclean oaf." Briggs felt the hairs on the back of his neck begin to rise, however he managed to speak calmly, "Well what then? What surprises are the old pals going to rally round and produce today?"

The brief squirmed at Briggs' insult but with forced dignity the brief replied, "An alternative charge which will result in him being bound over."

"A bind over for burglary! You must be joking surely." But Briggs knew the brief wasn't. "Listen to me carefully, very carefully, I am the officer in charge of this case and you are supposed to be working for me not the other way around. How is it I didn't know about this alternative charge?"

The brief got up and held his hands up in a defensive manner "There is no need to shout officer, it has all been arranged with your Detective Chief Superintendent, I think he outranks you as officer in charge of this case – just." The brief smirked with the cool sarcasm of the establishment.

Briggs let the news of Bolton's involvement settle in his brain. Jones was approaching, agitated and attracted by the noise of Briggs' raised voice. Briggs waved him away. "And what is this alternative charge?" Briggs asked quietly and slowly.

"Being unlawfully in the back garden of a house in Farmer's Lane contrary to the Justice Of the Peace Act 1361" The brief handed Briggs a summons as he spoke. "and I shall be requiring you to serve a summons on de la Mare to that effect."

Briggs read the alternative charge and spat out, "1361, I don't believe it, you lot have really scraped the barrel this time. Fuck me, 1361, I don't think I have ever heard of that one being used before."

Briggs' words did not have any effect on the snooty brief. "Well in any case you have the summons please serve it. He's through there." The brief indicated a side door from the court.

Briggs read the summons. Sure enough, it read "To show cause why you Peter de la Mare should not be bound over in the sum of thirty pounds for a period of three years to be of good behaviour." Briggs carried on and read the issue date and the signature of the magistrate who signed it.

The brief waited whilst Briggs finished reading. "Now if you don't mind officer, I should be obliged if you would serve it on de la Mare." demanded the brief with the all the confidence that the officer class exhibit when pushing the other ranks into line.

Briggs smiled, the beginnings of a small amount of revenge creeping into his brain. "I expect you would sir." Briggs spoke quietly and evenly. "However I am unable to accede to your request." The brief looked startled.

"You don't seem to understand officer, this isn't a request, it is an order. You will do it because your Detective Chief Superintendent says so and I endorse that order." The brief waved his hand in a scooping manner to indicate that he no longer wished to be involved with this unclean article.

Briggs stood firm in spite of the withering gaze of the brief. "If I might enquire, as I am entitled to, when was the information laid in respect of this summons?"

"The information? This morning why?" The brief was puzzled. Briggs felt like he was delivering a grand slam at bridge.

"Well sir, if I understand the Magistrates Courts Act 1952 there should be an interval of seven days between the laying of an information and the issue of a summons. As there hasn't been, the law would appear not to have been adhered to and therefore, it may be said that this summons is an illegal document and therefore I am not going to serve it, sir." Briggs handed back the disputed document.

"But officer, your Detective Chief Superintendent has said that it will be served and I agree with that view." The brief was beginning to feel that Briggs may have something to say here, and was almost pleading with him.

"Well sir, with as much respect as I can muster, serve it yourself, or better still get the Detective Chief Superintendent to serve it, for one thing's for sure old son I ain't going to. Got it?" Briggs could see that his words had an angering effect on the brief and he continued, "So sir, whilst you" (he emphasised the 'you') "sort out the service of the summons, I will go and inform our witnesses how it is that we have managed to conspire to pervert the course of justice and get away with it. All because we have funny names, plenty of dough, and have all been to public school where they teach sodomy as an extra subject. You ought to be ashamed of yourself, but I don't expect you are, as you look as though you're specially selected." Briggs stormed out of court and joined up with Budden and Jones. A heated discussion took place.

"Call Peter de la Mare." The call was repeated again at the bottom of the dock steps. After a short while de la Mare's head appeared over the parapet of the dock.

"Are you Peter de la Mare?" the Magistrates' clerk asked. de la Mare nodded his head. The clerk then intoned the main charge and the alliterative summons. "How do you plead?" Surprised de la Mare said, "Where's Nanny, I want my Nanny." Briggs thought, "I bet he's been rehearsed at that."

The lady magistrate was known to all at Rodney Road as 'Mrs. Twin Set and Pearls' as this is what she always wore, together with pointy end glasses and a sharp manner. Winkle had previously opined, "I know what she needs, but I really can't see anyone obliging her, a blind man maybe, but even then you'd be put off by the voice." The lady magistrate looked down at the assembled lawyers and clerks.

The barrister for the defence, the dreaded John Boyne QC, who Briggs knew by reputation only, got to his feet. "I appear for the defence your worship and would say that we hotly dispute the burglary charge, but in all honesty I cannot show cause why my client should not be bound over in the sum of thirty pounds for a period of three years."

The lady conferred with her colleagues and said, "Well Mr. Sharples what do you think?"

Sharples rose to his feet, "Yes your worships, I am obliged to Mr. Boyne for his kind assistance in this matter. In all the circumstances, I can see that the prosecution would be hard put to to secure a conviction on the burglary charge. In the circumstances I ask that de la Mare be bound over for a period of three years in the sum of thirty pounds.

"This is a travesty of British justice," bellowed Budden from the public gallery. "You are all engaged in a conspiracy to pervert the course of common justice. This man was caught by me breaking into my neighbour's house and he admitted his felonious intent to officer Briggs. He even signed a statement to that effect."

Twin set and pearls, startled by the outburst, again conferred with her colleagues, then to the court inspector, "Officer remove that man from this court."

Budden kept up a stream of abuse whilst being removed. As he was excluded he was yelling, "Perjurers, perjurers the Jehovah's wrath shall be on you come Armageddon." Briggs smiled at his success at rehearsing a witness.

De la Mare was then bound over for three years as planned. At the end of his sentencing de la Mare said, "Can I see my Nanny now?"

The Magistrates' clerk said, "Next case please."

Whilst the next case was being put up Briggs sauntered over to the court reporter of the local rag and said in a loud stage whisper, "Let's see you do a nice spread on this one, perhaps sell it to the tabloids maybe, or are you connected as well?" He strolled out of court and noticed that Mr. Budden was receiving words of advice as to his recent and future conduct. No surprise to Briggs the case got about three lines in the local rag, and no mention whatever in the National Dailies where the ex Mayor would have made good copy.

Briggs and Jones entered the CID office like whipped dogs, well puppies really. The sight of the establishment protecting its own had had a very sobering effect on Ron. "I just don't believe they could do such a thing. I just don't believe it." He was shocked, all his values were under threat, the cast iron standards that he believed in, like truth and justice were crumbling.

"Strange thing Ron, I have always believed they could and would do such a thing, shall I tell you what the next move is?"

Ron still looked sullen and beaten, but said, "Go on then sharpie, tell me."

Briggs smiled at Jones' predicament "Us mate, they'll come

looking for us."

Ron looked shocked as if his whole life was coming apart. "But why, we've only done our jobs. We've done nothing wrong."

Briggs laughed at this confusion. "It's not a matter of right or wrong, the establishment will always want to get its own back," Ron did not answer but sat looking at the case file, "and because it's about to go boss-eyed I think the time is right to take out some insurance, give us the file here." Briggs took the file and went through it, he pulled out some documents and put them in an envelope, he sealed them and signed across the flap. "Right I am going to have a drink with a friend." Briggs put the envelope in his inside pocket and started to leave.

"I'll come with you I could really do with a drink." Ron was getting up and about to put his jacket on.

But Briggs said quietly "No not this time Ron, it's a matter of what you don't know." Briggs left the office.

Confronting it

Briggs and Jones stood before Jack the Hat's desk, both sort of to attention in deference to the 'beasting' about to be delivered or rather expected. "Put the file on my desk." Jack the Hat indicated a space in front of his blotter. "It's all there is it?" Jack the Hat was in an unsmiling mood.

"Yes guv." Briggs answered to save Jones burdening himself with a lie.

"Right then." Jack the Hat breathed deeply. "This afternoon 2.30pm both of you at the guvnor's office Southwark, and before you ask I don't know what's going to happen, but I can tell you they are gunning for you both. Briggsy that roasting you gave to the brief from the yard was, well at the best ill advised, but I would have loved to have heard it." Jack the Hat almost smiled in contemplation.

"Has a complaint been made?" Briggs hoped that this was the case. A complaint has to be investigated within parameters and in this case Briggs felt he could carry the day, that is, if they played almost fairly.

Jack the Hat laughed. "I think you will find that they'll do away with such niceties, but the bottom line is, I don't know. I offered to castigate the pair of you and leave it at that, but they wouldn't have it." Briggs looked at Ron, tears didn't seem very far away.

"The joke is guv, if this was one of the unemployed dross his feet wouldn't touch, and as for that bollocks of him being so nutty we couldn't contemplate a charge, well, does that apply across the board – I don't think so." Briggs glared at Jack the Hat.

"Briggsy you turned philosopher have, you? Well catch this, we have to deal with things the way they are not as we would wish."

Briggs nodded, "I suppose so guv, but it does needle as being unfair."

Jack the Hat replied "I know what you mean but there it is, best advice is don't make an issue and perhaps they will let it pass, and for fucks sake forget that bollocks about it being unfair, you'll have me in tears." Jack the Hat grinned. "Now get out of my sight,." They left the office.

They adjourned as in all times of stress and strain to the canteen. Briggs got the teas in and they went to their corner plot where they hoped they couldn't be overheard.

"What the hell are we going to do? It's all your fault Briggsy, I should never have got involved in all this." Ron wailed his concern for his fast retreating career.

"Too late for that old son, we have to think for ourselves, damage limitation I think it's called." Briggs was not unaffected by the prospects of severe aggravation but still managed to be amused by Ron's hysterical outburst.

"What now?" moaned Ron with his head in his hands. "What will they do to me?" Briggs noted that there was no consideration of 'we' in Ron's thinking.

"Well Ron put it this way, they can't eat you, kill you, or make you pregnant, they can fuck you but they can't make you pregnant, well – if they do make you pregnant they can't make you love the little shit. So they haven't got a lot going for them have they?" Briggs beamed at this sparkling logic.

Ron looked up bemused. "Is that it, the sum total of your thoughts on damage limitation as you call it. God help us." Ron looked to the ceiling for inspiration.

"I am pleased you brought him into the equation, and as you have got a sort of trade discount with the almighty I wonder if you could give him a ring, tell him that it has all gone boss-eyed, not down to you of course, but because you got involved with this primitive." Briggs laughed at Ron's sad countenance. He continued, "Seriously Ron, here's what we do, say nothing let me do the talking, that way they get no conflict on which to play, keep mum and stum. Whatever happens say nothing, agreed?"

"What have I got to lose, agreed." Ron resigned himself to be blown about in the coming storm.

They spent the intervening four hours until the dreaded hour going through their desks, weeding out that which could prove embarrassing in the event of a 'bin spin', that inspection usually carried out in your absence by the 1st Class Sergeant or the Detective Chief Inspector, which could disclose correspondence which hadn't been attended to, enquiries requested by other forces, property not returned after conclusion of cases and of course illegal bottles of booze. The Detective Chief Inspector usually imposed a fine of one bottle of gin, plus of course the contraband, not a bad system from the guvnor's point of view. Ron was really going to town, paper and dust were everywhere.

"Ron slow down old son, if they were going to bounce our desks they would have done it by now. If I were you Ron I would top it all out with a nicely written suicide note, something simple written in your blood, you know – "goodbye cruel world," Briggs easing his concerns by playing on Jones' apprehension.

Ron moaned, exasperated. "It's alright for you, nothing hangs on it, if you fall your life will still be the same," Ron flicking dust over to Briggs' side.

"Ron my old mate, what you really mean is that my friends couldn't care less if I am a copper or not, in fact a bent copper or not, the only thing that concerns them is whether I get caught or not and I don't intend to be, not on this old son." Ron stopped his Mrs. Mopp routine and studied Briggs as if for the first time.

"Don't you worry about publicity, about your standing in the community, about what others think of you?" Ron was incredulous and interested.

"Not really, mind over matter is it." Ron looked querulous. "Those who mind don't matter and the other way round. So long as the family is OK, I have no worries. I really can't get worked up about what some sky pilot thinks about me, or what I have done." Out of the corner of his eye Briggs saw John Barking approaching and inwardly groaned.

"You two are for the high jump. then." John sneered, looking at the rubbish being shuffled on the desks.

"That's right is it? You've heard?" Briggs non-committal but inwardly cursing the station gossips. Barking continued "S'right, one of my snouts came up with it, it's back to uniform for both of you, hello, hello pointed hat brigade here come two right wallies." Briggs held his temper, which was something he allowed vent to with regard to Barking later. "Oh really, in that case I think we had better clear the slate before we go. What do you think Ron, shall we go all Serpico and tell the truth?"

Ron for once in his present predicament smiled. "Oh I think we should Tel, you never know it might be logged on our records when we get up there." Ron indicated the heavens.

"In that case John I think we should mention about the deal you and Winkle had with Philly Cousins, something about five hundred for bail and two grand for outers." Briggs studied Barking and felt that his face said that the truth had been spoken. "Now that came to me from a real snout, not one pulled out of the telephone directory."

Barking had gone extremely pale. "Only larking about Tel, just a wind-up, nothing meant. How did you know about Phil Cousins?"

Briggs feeling it was better to have Barking off balance all the time said, "That's for me to know and you to wonder about old son, but John you really must learn to control yourself. I am sorry I must mention this incident to the guvnor when we have our conference this afternoon."

Barking was puzzled. "Conference, what do you mean I was told you were going up there to get your arses kicked and a posting back to the big hat department."

"John you really should get some decent snouts. That about being sent back to uniform is just a cover, we're really going over there for a briefing." Briggs lowered his voice so that only John could hear.

"Briefing? What about?"

Briggs looked up and down the office then whispered, "We are going underground."

Barking exploded realising maybe that Briggs was winding him. "Underground you two, where are you going on the District Line? Fuck off." Barking was back in sneering mode.

Briggs shrugged "OK John you believe what you want, but don't spread it OK." Barking was unsure and showed it.

"Ok I'll keep mum."

"Mr. Bolton will see you now." French ushered Briggs and Jones into the presence. Bolton sat as always, in front of a single rose in a specimen jar and a photo of his assembled offspring grinning up at him. They both stood in front of his desk, feet on the edge of the carpet. Bolton was looking down at a report. After a dramatic pause Bolton said, "Right then," and looked up. "You both know why you are here don't you?" Jones nodded his head vigorously.

Briggs said, "No sir we do not."

"I know that Mr. Parris has already prepared the ground for me so to speak." Briggs still shook his head. As though explaining Bolton said, "It's about this de la Mare debacle at court." Bolton wore the grim expression expected of a Detective Chief Superintendent about to deliver a mega bollocking and sentence the miscreants to whatever.

"I don't know sir, I thought your lot handled it very well." Briggs chirpy in the face of so much high ranking opposition. French stood as always behind the great man's chair and shook his head.

"Whatever do you mean Briggs?" Bolton asked hotly continuing, "Under the circumstances there wasn't much else that could be done, you and your partner had soured the waters for any sensible solution."

"Sensible solution?" Briggs was livid, or at least gave the impression he was. "As I see it sir, we have done nothing other than our job, no more no less." Briggs leaned forward, and Bolton paid him the compliment of leaning back.

"Don't you adopt that attitude with me Briggs, plain unadulterated over zealousness that's what this was. You should have at least taken a Senior Officer's advice with regard to his unbalanced state. Only a Senior Officer should have taken such a decision to proceed." Briggs stared at Bolton across the desk, Jones nudged Briggs to shut up.

"Sir, you have my record, you will see that I am qualified for promotion."

Bolton looked down and said, "Yes you are."

Briggs continued, "You will also note that I passed out top of the Detective Training School course for Detectives." Bolton again looked down at Briggs' record.

"Why yes you did." Bolton looked as though it was the first time he had ever heard of such a thing and was impressed.

"From all the instruction and studying I have done I have never disclosed anything which says or infers that we have to consult a

Senior Officer with regard to a charge of this nature. My understanding is that it is up to the court to decide all things, including mental stability or otherwise, sir." Briggs left a short pause before the 'sir'.

Bolton was speechless, and cast around for an answer, and as though coming across it by accident, said "Common sense, that's it common sense prevails, your common sense should have told you to consult with a Senior Officer."

Briggs stared down at Bolton, "Sir, would you please ask Mr. French to retire?" French was startled and showed It.

Bolton was emphatic, "No I will not, Mr. French is my office manager and I want him here, now you listen to me."

Briggs cut across him, "No sir for a change you listen to me, I am not going to have this. Now before this matter becomes a matter of national comment ask your lackey to retire. Don't do it and I promise you will not believe it while it is happening." Bolton paused, Jack the Hat had described Briggs as a bullshit artist but also that he was a good detective.

Bolton eventually decided to dismiss French and listen to what Briggs thought was of interest nationally. He spoke directly to French. "Mr. French would you be so kind as to leave the room for a short while."

French looked pained. "As you order it sir of course." French made it sound as though he was off to wipe Royalty's arses. French left with what remnant of dignity he had left.

After the door closed behind French, Bolton said, "Right what is so important that it can't be said in front of my most trusted man."

"It's sad sir that you only have a civilian to describe in such a manner." Briggs continued, "Now sir, if I, or Jones hear one more word of criticism about this job, we are both going to resign," Briggs glanced at Jones who seemed to have something stuck in his throat,"and publish what has happened in the national dailies or, more to the point, the tabloids. Now do you understand, we are not standing for this, is that clear – sir?"

Bolton was struggling to find something to say. "You can't." He spluttered. "Official Secrets and all that."

Briggs was ready and had already thought it out. "Official Secrets does not apply sir. This matter has already been in the public domain.

The court has already heard the case. In any case the press will publish and risk the flak later. As for us we would rather resign than continue to be crucified for doing our duty when all the establishment is doing is closing ranks around one of their own, who in any case should be locked away for disgusting acts of filth and theft. So as for publicity we couldn't give a shit could we Ron?"

Jones did not appear nearly so confident but managed a croaky "No."

Whilst Bolton endeavoured to recover control of this turbulent conversation he said, "Anyway we are talking about top people here, special people you know with weight."

Briggs snorted, "And because we haven't funny names and no dough we have to stand for this shit do we? Is that what you are telling me, that the Theft Act applies only to the grubby horde, not to the 'Special people'? I do not agree sir, and I feel the editors of the national dailies will see it my way, as good copy and also, as it happens, the truth."

Bolton realising the folly of speaking of hoping that Briggs would fall into line just because he was a senior officer pondered for while. "Ah yes," he said brightly. "You don't have the original statements, without those you are talking about gossip, pure gossip." Bolton beamed self-satisfaction.

Briggs spoke evenly and quietly, just in case French was listening at the door. "I don't think so, if you check with Mr. Parris you will find he has everything but the originals. I have those and they are locked away," Briggs said impassively.

Bolton got up, obviously shaken. Briggs thought for an instant that he was about to launch himself across the desk at Briggs. Bolton paused. "Wait here," he said, and stumbled out of the office.

In Bolton's absence Ron said, "You're mad Briggsy, stark staring fucking mad. I'll never work with you again, that's it never no more." And where did you get this shit about resigning?" Briggs assumed that Jones was a little upset.

"Well I thought it sounded very dramatic like, you know very Burt Lancasterish. Anyway it's a lot better than that, "I am ever so sorry sir, and I will enjoy it in uniform bollocks." Briggs spoke rubbing his hands with glee. "He's gone to speak with Jack the Hat who'll go ballistic when he finds he hasn't got the originals."

"The trouble with you Briggsy is that you thrive on all this aggravation, love it you do." Jones was red faced and almost in tears.

"Listen mate stand with me, ok? Don't let 'em push you into uniform, this way we'll either get the sack or be back at dear old Rodney Road with enhanced reputations." Briggs searched Jones' face for a reaction "Okay?"

Jones resigned to his fate. "Yes okay, it's too late to do anything else, sod you Briggsy." And gave a weak smile.

The door flung open and a rather red faced angry Bolton entered. "Right, you pair of bastards I'll have those originals, now, where are they?!" Bolton spat the words, almost to the floor stamping stage.

"Funny," thought Briggs, "I never sussed him as a big mary but he obviously is." Jones was silently looking at the floor for inspiration.

"Sorry guv, we are not parting with them ever, insurance if you like, but rest assured they will not be used – so long as we are happy." Briggs left the last part to sink in. Bolton sat down shaken. "I am your boss, I am entitled to your respect and obedience, this is treachery of the most foul kind, I demand to know where they are." Bolton made the effort to keep his temper in check.

Briggs spoke quietly and appeared confident. "Now listen carefully guv." Bolton was paying attention. "The job will never see these statements again unless of course it decides it wants to sacrifice us for the benefit of the establishment. Further, any later act of revenge by you or one of your lackeys will be seen in the same light, got it?"

Bolton protested. "You can't do this to me I am your guvnor, I have never done you any harm," he whined plaintively.

Briggs nodded "That is quite true sir, you haven't but that is only because we got in first. The other thing you have got to weigh up is that the court never dealt with the seven other offences which were to be dealt with by way of TIC (Taken into Consideration), some were on our ground, but there were a couple on R Division at Greenwich."

Bolton treated Briggs to a cold stare. "Obviously they are the result of duress, he admitted them due to duress."

Briggs could see that Bolton was in a fix about all of this. "Look guv, let it be and nothing will happen, go after us and we will do the business that you lot would do to us. It's that simple."

Bolton got up and wandered around the office. "What is to be done, what would my father do?" What is to be done?" He could almost see his illustrious career falling to pieces.

"If I might make a suggestion sir," and without waiting to be asked, "What we do is this, we first forget that de la Mare ever happened. We go back to Rodney Road after, say, two weeks on a special squad and you do not mention to whoever is after our blood exactly how you sorted this out." Briggs said with huge self-satisfaction.

"Briggs I follow most things, why the special squad?" Bolton said showing that he was paying attention to this cocksure cockney lad who might just have the answer to his problems.

"Well sir, there is no Special Squad, we sit at home, not booked on anywhere, the heat dies down, they forget about us, feeling that their version of justice has taken place, after two weeks we slink back into Rodney Road, hows about that then?" Briggs felt like the television magician.

Bolton was still thinking it through. "I am supposed to send you two back to uniform, but if I do that you will resign and blow the gaff right?"

They both nodded. Briggs as ever said, "Absolutely correct sir."

"Right then do it, go home and I will contact you in two weeks' time." Bolton waved them away completely defeated. Briggs and Jones marched out of the office.

On the way down the corridor they passed French. Briggs could not control himself and as he passed Briggs said, "Arsehole." French recoiled but said nothing.

The Rings

"Sid have you any idea where the special squad is working out of?"
John Barking was lounging in Jones' chair idly riffling through the
contents of Ron's filing trays and of course his diary.

"John, I haven't got a clue, the only one who's got half an idea
would be Bolton, and he's not saying. To be fair I don't think he
knows too much, just a contact phone and a time to ring that's the
usual." Sid spoke from his desk in the corner where he was auditing
the property register. Sid did not think it was strange that he was
doing it with his 'Moffat' pen.

"Only," continued John, wistfully dreaming of himself in combat
fatigues chasing nubile women, or men about the place, "It would be
a help to talk about something like that on a promotion board, you
know secret squirrel operations and the like," said John fantasising.

"The thing about secret squirrel jobs is that you are not supposed
to talk about them, you do 'em and forget 'em. If a nosey guvnor
asks you about it you blank it and don't know what he's on about.
That's the way it's supposed to be," responded Sid, not taking his
eyes of the register and suddenly bellowing, "Richards get your arse
here now." Richards put his pen down and said as he got up warily,
"What? Is it my turn in the barrel Sid?"

Sid laughed, "It might be better for you if it was, this gear from
the breaking in East Lane, if it was any older we'd give it to the
British Museum as being the same age as the dead sea scrolls – get
rid of it."

"Can I help you gentlemen?" John directed the question to two
mean looking men in combat jackets jeans and heavy work boots.
Large sunglasses hid most of their faces. The normal office hustle and

67

bustle was stilled by the presence of these two 'special operations' types.

"You can start by getting out of my chair and leaving my corres (correspondence) alone," Ron giving his all as Dirty Harry.

"Ron is that you, Ron?" Barking was amazed at the change. "You both look as though have been out on the edge." Barking moved out of the chair without taking his eyes off Jones and Briggs.

"Yes, been on the edge a few times recently." Jones said enigmatically thinking of the roof repairs he'd carried out at home and the one time when he had slipped off the bungalow roof and onto the coal shed. "Yes, came off once, was saved by coal, Polish coal."

Barking's mouth fell open like a cross channel ferry. "Ron, shut up, we gave our words – no showboating, that's the rule," said Briggs sharply, "You're endangering good men who are still there."

Ron replied as he was taking his sunglasses off, relieved as he had impaired vision with them on, "Sorry Tel just thinking aloud you know. I suppose really I am just pleased to be back in my little desk, pleased that we didn't get caught when they came for us. Oops sorry Tel." Ron was enjoying playing Barking along, and maybe repaying him for the months of scorn and jibes about religion etc.

"Ron shut the fuck up, if you carry on like this they won't consider you on the new squad." Briggs riffling through the outstanding messages on his desk, but really waiting for the Barking fish to bite.

"A new squad?" Barking became very intense and interested. "Did you say a new squad? I could be well interested in that."

Briggs looked across the desk at Barking. Barking looked hopeful. "Could you now John? You realise you have to be recommended don't you? It's not that easy, you depend on others, they depend on you, lives in hands that sort of thing, got to be bottle unlimited, think you can cope?" Briggs was playing his fish into shallow water.

"Cope? Of course I can cope, no problem." Barking said with bated breath. "Where's the squad to be based?" Briggs paused and looked up and down the office, and noticed that a number of them were leaning forward in their chairs expectantly.

Briggs stage whispered "Mozambique."

"Mozambique!" John almost bellowed the word. "Fucking Mozambique."

Briggs spoke quietly into Barking's ear, "Not so loud John, just keep it to yourself. If it comes off, we're only there for a few days, do the job and leave quietly. The only development there could be is a plain clothes incursion into Chad, but hopefully we'll beat the clock." Barking looked worried, concerned even. "Shall I put your name in the frame then John?" Briggs got his Charlie issue pen out ready.

"Er, not for the moment Tel. thanks, but I have a lot on my plate at the moment, you know my Mum and the kids and all that." Barking looked down at his blotter for inspiration "and of course my mum's not been well lately, bit worried about her I am." It was poor but it was the best that Barking could manage at short notice.

"Oh that's a shame John, I would have thought you would have been ideally suited to our brand of special ops, but there you are, if you can't volunteer, you can't." Briggs said it as though very disappointed. "We will just have to do without you, won't we Ron?" Briggs nodded to Ron.

"S'right Tel, shame it is." Ron looked down to avoid seeing Barking's face and laughing.

"Anyway we are only here for few minutes to get sorted. We'll be back on full duty tomorrow, properly dressed of course." Briggs sat down and examined the litter on his desk.

The office door burst open and Jack the Hat entered, "Briggs" he bellowed, "What the hell are you doing dressed like that, you look like a Bulgarian pirate who has been frightened by a pox doctor?" Briggs stood embarrassed stripped of pretence.

"Just popped in from seconded duty guv, we'll be back on full duty tomorrow."

Jack the Hat noticed Ron dressed as Rambo's cousin. "The lay preacher too? Will he ever be the same?"

Ron stunned into silence let Briggs answer for him. "I don't know guv, but I think being close to danger has reinforced his faith – sort of."

"Another dollop of Briggs' bullshit," said Jack the Hat amused but not smiling. "Which reminds me Briggs into my office, we have something to sort."

Briggs walked along the office and into Jack the Hat's office. Jack the Hat positioned himself behind his desk, slowly lit a cigarette and stared coldly at Briggs. After exhaling smoke across his little office

Jack the Hat said, "Now tell me how it is that you said that all the documents were in the de la Mare file, when the important ones were not? Did you get Jones to invoke divine inspiration on your behalf, or was it straightforward double dealing?"

Briggs was almost embarrassed, but ready, as he thought that Jack the Hat would not let his subterfuge go unmentioned. "Double dealing guv," Briggs admitting what Jack the Hat knew. "I am sorry guv, but it was them or us, and where survival is concerned I tend to make sure it's us – sorry." And meant it.

"Another situation like this and I will not accept your word you know that." Briggs was relieved that Jack the Hat was not going to make an issue out of it, but maybe he thought that Briggs might invoke the publication of the statements in retribution.

"Of course guv, I quite understand." Briggs said it as though he was forgiving the guvnor for doubting his word.

"Don't you patronise me you flash little git. I don't know what game you played with Bolton and I don't want to, but you step out of line with me and I will make your head spin. Got it?"

Briggs, abashed, said "Yes guv."

"Now get out my sight and be here tomorrow morning and be properly dressed."

Briggs again, "Yes guv." And marched out relieved that Jack the Hat was treating it as a straightforward bollocking which would be forgotten in the morning.

On return to normal duty, Jones and Briggs sculled around the ground trying to cause terminal diarrhoea amongst the criminal classes. They investigated burglaries, robberies, rapes anything that came into their path. The facade of being once removed from the SAS kept coming up and the dynamic duo did nothing to deflate it. Almost every time they entered a canteen Briggs could feel that they were being pointed out. As a result they both developed the deadpan expression and slight swagger that is the badge of cloak and dagger exponents, which in most cases is developed to hide an acute embarrassment at being exactly what they are.

One of the offences that troubled Briggs and Jones at this time was a young man who stole rings from jewellers' shops. He achieved the theft by posing as a customer and asking to see a tray of rings from the window. Having achieved the presence of a tray of rings on the counter, he then asked to see another, and if the assistant was not shrewd enough to take the first one away and put it back in stock, the young man obliged them by putting it in his own stock, decamping from the shop at high speed. He had hit the jackpot at least seven times, there being twenty rings to a tray, that should make his personal stock some 140 rings – various designs but all gold.

Jones and Briggs had come very close to capturing 'Ronny the Rings' as they came to call him, when they were called on an emergency basis to a jeweller's shop in the Old Kent Road, where the manager had a customer who was performing exactly like Ronnie the Ring. Briggs and Jones rushed in through one door and Ronnie rushed out of the other. Jones and Briggs gave chase with Briggs in the lead, they were actually gaining on Ronnie when turning a corner Briggs ran into a 'No waiting' sign and fell dazed to the ground. He was overtaken by Jones who did the best he could but lost the culprit when he jumped on a bus going to Camberwell. Jones returned to Briggs who was just getting up rubbing his tender bits. "You alright Tel?" Ron helped him up.

"I will be in a minute, you lost him obviously." Briggs spat out his disappointment. "One thing's for sure he can gallop along, that ought to be part of Olympic training didn't it?"

"What?" Ron puzzled.

"Well if the old sprinters are not up to scratch, put a swift old bill behind them and if they get caught they have to do twelve moon. That would sharpen their attitudes a bit." With Briggs hobbling they returned to the jeweller's shop.

"Well who's going to pay for the rings?" the manager asked pugnaciously. "You had him in your sights and you let him go? How much did he pay you?"

Briggs eyed the red faced manager and although it seemed that 'fuck you' would save an awful lot of time and temper he said, "Now come along guv there's no need to be that way, he gave us nothing, I told you we just couldn't catch him." Briggs was holding back his infamous bad temper in an effort to take steps to allay a sense of grievance as it said in General Orders and to get this irate manager to see that they did try, but were unsuccessful.

"And why couldn't you catch him? Are you both lame or something? What was he a fucking surperman? Did he leap over buildings or what?" The tirade continued as the manager became more and more hysterical.

"Calm down sir, we have ideas, we think we know where he lives, or the area where he comes from at least," Briggs trying to take the steam out of confrontation.

"If you can't catch him in straight contest how can you catch him otherwise?" the shop manager was red faced and angry. "I rang you and told you he was at it and he still got away with it. What am I supposed to do now, wait until he passes this way again? I think the only answer is that I must complain about your inefficiency, about how you let him go and all that." Briggs stared at his feet as eye contact seemed to inflame the situation. Jones coughed quietly to remind all and sundry that he was still about.

"Just give us a few days to see if we can catch the bugger guv, be fair now." Briggs pleaded hoping to hit the kinder, more charitable side of the manager's nature.

"Give you a chance?" The manager snorted. "The same sort of chance you gave ginger is that what you want?" The manager blew up in everyone's face.

"Oi, hold, on be fair now, behave. All I'm asking is the return of a favour that's all." The manager became calmer, well calmish,

"Exactly what favour do I owe you officer?" This time the manager spoke quietly, but there was an implied menace in his voice and with as much dignity as his previous temper would allow.

"Well that burglar we nicked the other month, he sold you some gear. We wrote it down as you believing it to be straight, but really it should have been decided by a magistrate or jury." The mood was broken and we were back in the midst of bad temper.

"Don't you lean on me officer, I told the truth and, as it was the truth I wasn't charged as God is my judge." The manager began smoothing down his jacket as if wiping something off – guilt maybe.

Briggs could see it was pointless and knew they were both going to collect a complaint on this one so it might as well be for a sheep as for a lamb. "Well sod you you soapy bastard." Briggs erupted into the manager's face. The manager cowered as he thought Briggs was about to hit him. "Complain if you like. By the way does your wife know about what goes on after closing with Shirley Temple over there?" repeating a rumour he had heard from the uniform recently and deciding to take a jump in the dark.

"Out, out, get out," screamed the manager and his assistant promptly cherried up a nice shade of pink.

"Come on Ron." Briggs turned and walked out.

As they left Ron asked, "Tel, why the hell do you have to do it? Now he'll complain about that as well. Don't forget I am on board for skipper later this year and I could do without this shit in the fan." Ron was angry that his future career could be affected.

"Why worry Ron, you never passed the first, and by the time you get the second I promise you that you will be as pure as driven snow." A wrong and strangely prophetic statement.

They reached the CID car and got in. Pausing to collect his thoughts before driving off Ron said, "Is that true about him and that girl assistant, dirty old sod."

"As I understand it, he has been spied in the middle of sexual gymnastics with the poor young thing." Briggs laughed at the imagined event, "I bet that's something to behold, old fatty there, getting all red faced, while he climbs aboard Miss Skinny Ribs."

They returned to the nick and immediately camped out in the collator's office, going over files, index cards, crime intelligence reports, dragging out details of suspects who answered the description of the youth they had chased, ginger hair and being a teenager being the commanding factors. They ended up with a mixed bunch of ten, five from Camberwell Peckham and Walworth the remainder being from Bermondsey and Rotherhithe.

They decided to have tea and then go on a foray around the various manors, knocking at doors and patrolling streets hoping to dredge up the right man. Tea was consumed in silence, the impending complaint by the shop manager souring their usual evening's conversation. They finished and left the Police Station booking themselves out as 'Enquiries re jewellery thefts back conc'.

They started their saga on Peckham's manor, calling at two suspects' addresses to find their man had moved away in both cases and in which the parents could be awarded the title 'Couldn't give a shit'. On the way back towards Camberwell as they were travelling along Peckham Rye towards Peckham they stopped at traffic lights. As the lights turned green, a young man dashed across the road in front of traffic moving off. Horns blared and swearwords uttered but the young man seemed oblivious and went on his way. "That's him." Ron said, first with suspicion then, excitedly, and with conviction "Tel, that's him I tell you – turn left."

Briggs was caught unawares. "Are you sure Ron?" he asked but pulled across the traffic just in case and parked in the side of the road. They watched the youth swagger his way towards Dog Kennel Hill. "He must be wearing about ten rings per hand. I think we can safely say that we have our man in sight." Ron was making as though to get out of the car.

"Hang fire Ron, we know he can motor. You try and take him on foot he'll be off like a long dog."

Briggs took Jones' elbow. "How about we get a bit closer by car and then I'll trail him on foot and take him out?"

Which is what they did. Ron took over the driving and they drove within twenty yards of 'Ronny the Rings'. Briggs got out and walked along the pavement, keeping close to the shop windows, dodging quickly in and out of the shop doorway, so that if Ronny turned around he possibly wouldn't see Briggs. Briggs carried on on this stalking routine until he was only a few yards behind Ronny. He then burst out of a shop doorway and took Ronny around the legs, these being the parts which caused him to avoid arrest last time. They crashed to the floor, Briggs still holding on and on top of Ronny. "Ere what's your game gerroff," shrieked Ronny, getting quite upset and kicking his legs out and struggling. Briggs said nothing but changed his grip and pinioned Ronny on the arms. He then took out his handcuffs and cuffed Ronny to himself.

"Now if you can leg it now you prick – good luck."

Ron was out of the car and standing next to them. "Alright Tel?" Ron assisted to get Ronny to the vertical.

"I am arresting you on reasonable suspicion that you have stolen these rings." Briggs held up one of Ronny's hands which were covered in rings – various. Briggs cautioned Ronny, that he was not obliged to say anything etc.

At that moment Briggs felt a blow across his shoulders, accompanied by the shrill screech of, "Let him go you oafs, this is London not New York." Without loosening their hold on Ronny, Briggs and Jones turned. Before them was Miss Freedom Fighter, replete in cheesecloth dress, open-toed sandals and raffia shopping bag, which had been used to clump Briggs.

"We are Police Officers my dear and we have arrested this man for theft. Now will you please go about your business. I shall ignore the assault on Police providing that you go away." Briggs said it with that deep brown copper's voice that made people stop and think, even when he did not know what he was talking about.

"I don't care, you have violated this poor man's civil liberties, and I for one am protesting. Take those handcuffs off this minute," Miss Freedom Fighter demanded whilst endeavouring to get the cuffs off herself. She succeeded in tightening them. Ronny screamed, not at all pleased with the intervention of Miss Freedom Fighter.

"Oi, leave off, they're too tight now you soppy cow. No don't move them please. Fuck me me does that hurt or what?"

"Ron, nick her, she's pissed as a fart, I'll dump wonder boy here in the motor and get a uniform lot to take her in." Ron took hold of Miss Freedom Fighter by the arm and also the hair, a move always certain to suppress the violence of a belligerent woman. "And no getting on intimate terms now." Jones made a face and Briggs took Ronny over to the car and pushed him on to the back seat, he undid the painful shackles. Ronny immediately edged over to the opposite door and tried to undo it, but couldn't. "The child locks are on my side old son, I personally wouldn't advise running for it, as this time I will kick the shit out of you." Briggs spoke as he leaned over the back seat. Ronny nodded and looked to the floor of the car for inspiration. Ron had now walked Miss Freedom Fighter over to the car.

Briggs used the radio and called up assistance from any other Police vehicle. There was no response but this was not unusual for the uniform at Peckham had a very poor opinion of their own CID and the Flying Squad who also made regular forays onto the ground.

"Right cuff her to our bold Ronny here and we'll take her in," Briggs said using the handcuffs again and aiming her towards the back seat of the car.

"Help, help," she screeched. These men are trying to abduct me for an immoral purpose, they are going to rape me," Miss Freedom Fighter giving vent to her fantasies.

"If you don't shut up you soppy cow." Briggs pushed her into the back seat of the car and handcuffed her to Ronny, "our Ron here will shag you with the rough end of a pineapple," which caused her to giggle and settle down. The sickly aroma of best bitter surrounded them.

As they drove along, the action of the car had an unfortunate effect on the digestive system of Miss Freedom Fighter causing her to break wind noisily, which she did by lifting her leg to punctuate the emission. The car filled with an extreme lavatorial aroma. "Here fuck me does she stink or what? For Christ's sake open that window, I'm being bleeding well gassed," called Ronny the Rings, being very upset.

"Are you going to put your hands up to nicking the rings? If so I'll open both front windows. If not you will have to suffer the consequences of your own stubbornness," Briggs offered, amused at Ronny's discomfort but secretly hoping he would quickly make up his mind as the smell was beginning to creep into the front of the car with strength.

"To get away from that I'd admit to witchcraft. Yes yes book it all down to me." At which the windows were opened in the front of the car. Ronny breathed deeply "Ah is that better or what?"

On arrival at Rodney Road both prisoners were booked in, Miss Freedom Fighter was left in the tender care of the Matron, a lady who not only looked like a Tiger tank but with attitude to match. When searched, Miss Freedom Fighter was found in possession of five round pieces of brown substance which, on analysis, turned out to be cannabis. This was subsequently added to the charge.

On interviewing Ronny the Ring, it very soon became evident that he was mentally unstable and that he stole the rings to assist his grandmother who, coincidentally, had died a year before. However, she was always with him now and it was to her that he spoke at great length most of the time. Ronny and his grandmother readily admitted the thefts of the rings. He was of course also identified by Briggs, Jones, the irate shop manager and his assistant/sexual partner.

"As he's as nutty as fruitcake, we'd better take advice from a senior officer," said Briggs writing details in the antecedent form. "What for, he's going to be charged, they'll sort him out at court won't they?"

Jones was mystified. "Well Bolton did say about de la Mare that we should have taken the advice of a Senior Officer that is together with all the other bullshit they dished us up with." Briggs showing his delight at Jones squirming. "Down to you Briggsy, down to you."

Briggs shrugged. "Wasn't it ever thus my old son." He picked up the telephone and dialled a number.

"Southwark Police" responded the female tele-op. "Detective Chief Superintendent Bolton please love," asked Briggs, with Jones already flinching at the expected onslaught of aggravation.

"Hello Detective Chief Superintendent Bolton," said the answering voice. Briggs thought it a bit of a mouthful he could have said "Bolton," or maybe "Chief Superintendent."

"Er Briggs here sir, Detective Constable Briggs. I have a problem and I think the situation would benefit from your advice, based on your experience."

"Well it really should be your Chief Inspector, but go ahead, if I can help I will." Bolton didn't sound cautious at all, which if the situation had been the other way round Briggs would have told him to put it in writing and rung off.

"Well sir, we have arrested a man for theft and he appears to be mentally disturbed and, bearing in mind your criticism on the de la Mare case sir, I appeal to you for advice on the matter." There was a prolonged silence, eventually Briggs said "Sir?"

Bolton snapped, "Charge him Briggs and stop taking the piss." The line went dead.

Ronny was remanded for mental and medical reports and was later sentenced to two years' probation with the condition that he attend a psychiatric clinic.

Tulips From Amsterdam

"Office meeting tonight, don't tell Barking." The words were dropped quietly into Briggs' ear. "Tell the preacher and be there at 8.30pm." Briggs accepted the instructions without comment, but with an acknowledging nod. Why it should be that an office meeting should be clothed in such cloak and dagger measures mystified Briggs. Such meetings were usually called to discuss children's Christmas parties or perhaps to discuss the united view on the new duty roster, none of which could be described as 'Secret Squirrel'. Briggs told Jones who commented that it was an odd time to have an office meeting, such gatherings were usually around 12.30pm so that after they could adjourn for lunch and bitch and whinge about what went on.

"Right you lot, come to order," Sid called down the main office, banging his large ruler on his desk. "Governor in the chair, me first class as Secretary and taking minutes. Eyes down look in."

Jack the Hat cleared his throat and spoke to the assembled throng. "Three items on the agenda, first you have all seen the modified duty roster which has come down from the big house? I do not agree with it, how about you lot?" to which there was a concerted "No way guv."

"Right then, Sid put that down as unanimously against. The next thing is the venue for the Divisional Ball. As usual Fairfield Halls at Croydon has been suggested. What do you think? Any against?" Response was silence.

"Okay Sid put that down as unanimously in favour." Jack the Hat leaned back in his chair and surveyed his massed force of irregular troops. "The final and most important item on the agenda

78

is our John Barking." There were puzzled looks all round as he went on. "I understand that he's become an irritating influence in the office, indulging in silly wind-ups etc, and generally playing the prick. Anybody any comment on that?"

"Well guv, John does have a remorseless sense of humour, but I am sure there is no harm in him," Sid, ever the nice man, trying to save one of his little chicks as he referred to them.

Jack the Hat put this view to bed with, "I am sure that is a correct assessment of our John, Sid. However he has over-indulged his privilege of wind ups in the last three or four months and is running out of control. I think it might do the young man a favour to bring him back to reality." Jack the Hat grinned the grin of a truly wicked man.

Sid could now see the point, "Oh I see guv, you aren't proposing discipline or anything like that, something which would have a permanent effect like." Everyone in the room could see that Sid was relieved.

"Not at all Sid, what I suggest is an atomic grade wind-up, something which would stop him once and for all. Let's face it, he does go on and on, and become intensely irritating. Eventually someone is going to bang him, then the shit will definitely go fanwise." Jack the Hat, still leaning back in his chair, assessed his pack. "Any suggestions?"

"Sir I will, if I may, restate our objectives in this matter." Sergeant Williams spoke as he was polishing his glasses and practicing to become a Chief Constable (which in effect he did later achieve.) "Barking has become an irritating event in our lives, and you are suggesting that we tame his errant humour once and for all by us indulging in a similar wind-up that he might use? Hoist him on his own petard – so to speak?" All could see that Williams loved the sound of his own voice.

Jack the Hat reclaimed the stage with, "I thought that was what I said Sergeant. It's just that you said it with a much more educated tone; in fact it might be said Sergeant that you suffer from irritable vowel syndrome." The meeting erupted in loud laughter at the come-uppance of one very unpopular Sergeant. Jack the Hat was unable to not to show his dislike of Williams, but at the same time he was aware that, because of his high connections and posh background, it would not be a good idea to upset Williams' rocketing career. "Now before we descend to discussing 'terms of reference and engagement," Jack the Hat was unable to resist a dig at Williams who had written a very impressive paper entitled just that, the underlying feeling being that Williams never wrote it, but that it came from someone at one of the universities, "let's get on. What I propose is this, if we all think and watch, he must come upon something which we can develop as a monumental wind-up. Has anyone any immediate ideas?"

"His dress, we must not forget his dress, the colours are all wrong, they fight each other." Simon Bernstein flicked his blonde hair in disgust, and most of those present became aware, if they weren't already, of Simon's confused sexuality. Briggs had been tempted to mention his suspicion that Barking could be what is known now as bisexual, but didn't, not wanting to offend Simon.

"Well bear it in mind chaps, it's obvious from this short conference that he has not endeared himself to you at all and that in the fullness of time, if we are vigilant, an opportunity will arise for us to set him right and put him on the road to fulfilment – ours that is." This last statement caused a chorus of laughter.

"Only vague things, guv, more like character traits like." Charlie Parsons spoke more to the floor than to anyone in particular. "Things that might come in handy see, like he's flash as hell."

"And he thinks no bird can resist him," Billy Samuels added, still smarting from Barking's attempt at pulling his wife at a recent social function. It wasn't so much that he tried to pull his wife which upset Billy so much, as in most men's company such things are regarded as a compliment, but Barking's assertion that he was really doing Billy a favour as he wasn't man enough etc, etc. Billy's friends had to hold him back and vengeance still smouldered in Billy's heart.

The meeting adjourned to the Temple Bar where John Barking's irritating humour was discussed into the night. Briggs, while Jones was in full chat up mode of a lady in the bar, approached Sid Mills who was on his own in a corner. "What's John done to upset Jack the Hat Sid? I mean this seems a bit OTT (Over the Top)" Sid nodded sagely peering into his beer for inspiration. Sid was not a drinker and had had more than enough.

"Well Briggsy he's trod on Jack the Hat's corns rather heavily."

Briggs was puzzled, "How do you mean Sid?"

Sid smiled. "You being a kind soul Briggsy, well almost, you haven't noticed that your bold hero goes missing every Thursday afternoon, early closing day."

"Well no Sid, I can't say I have." Briggs waited for Sid to take a sip of his beer "And?" Briggs prodded him on his way.

"Well when Jack the Hat was here as a Sergeant he formed a liaison with a lady who was then a sales person in the chemists in the High Street. Well she is now the manageress and the arrangement has continued. I think the guvnor would like to knock it on the head, but the lady will have none of it." Briggs wondered at the prospect of Jack the Hat getting his bits seen to.

"Did he take his hat off?" he wondered. Shaking himself back to reality he said, "So what's this got to do with our John?" Briggs persisted with the half drunk Sid.

"Well he's taken to ringing up the trysting post and asking to speak to Chief Inspector Parris, when Jack comes to the phone he rings off."

Briggs, although not liking Barking, could see that he might be able to get him out of the mire. "So it could be anyone couldn't it Sid not just John?"

Sid chuckled, "Could be yes, except that the lady in question comes from Wiltshire, although now she has killed her accent, however she states that not only is the caller from Wiltshire he is also from Devizes, got to be John hasn't it?"

Briggs nodded sagely, "Only a Monmouth jury would acquit Sid."

Sid slid off the bar stool and nearly fell over. Briggs grabbed him. "Anyway Briggsy keep it to yourself."

"I certainly shall not tell Jonesy, he will be praying and splashing holy water about on the event of unlawful carnal knowledge."

Sid straightened himself, "Yes Jones, he does know it's hypocrisy does he? Look at him now." Sid indicated Jones now in late night conference with the lady, disgustingly tongue in ear. Briggs shuddered at the prospect.

"Ah yes, but he will be full of remorse in the morning."

Some weeks later Briggs and Jones, having finished their evening enquiries, happened to call into the London Park Hotel, a large building very close to the Elephant and Castle. This hotel had at one time been a reception centre, or doss house, where the homeless could obtain a night's board for a few shillings. It had been converted to an Inner London Tourist Hotel with very little alteration to achieve this transformation, a situation which Briggs found amusing. Over the time that Briggs had been at Rodney Road, the London Park Hotel had become a favourite haunt of detectives of 'M' division, mainly as the tourists rarely got pissed and got into fights thus the detectives could be assured of a bit of peace and quiet. This particular night only John Barking was present when they walked in and, although Briggs was unwilling to drink with Barking, had little choice.

"Wotcha John, on observations again I see." Briggs commented on Barking's interest in two female continental tourists sitting together in the corner of the bar.

"Oh right, yeah well, they've been eyeing me all evening, obvious they fancy me init?" John straightened himself and preened himself in the bar back mirror.

"More like they can't believe their eyes. They probably think you're going to a fancy dress party or something. Where the hell do you get these strange clothes, are they left over from some theatrical production or what?" Briggs flicked the large fluffy ruff on the front of John's shirt.

"Your trouble is that you have no savoir-faire, know what I mean?"

Jones and Briggs both laughed. "Yes I suppose I do," and catching the barman's eye, "Two, light and bitters please mate."

The Italian looking barman inclined his head, "In the same glass sir?" blandly taking the piss. Briggs nodded, he couldn't be bothered to bite.

Barking answered for him, quick to get a pointed remark in. "In a bucket if you like, you see my friends are completely without class." The swarthy barman smiled, amused at Barking's comments.

Briggs broke the spell. "If you two are anything to go by, I'd rather be without thanks. Now mince across and get us those beers, you poof." The barman's smile disappeared and he went down the bar as though electrified.

"Do you have to be so offensive Tel, after all everyone wants to be loved don't they?" Barking was talking to Briggs but still staring at the continental girls who Briggs could see were now almost openly laughing at Briggs.

"John if you're all that impressed, why don't you go over and give them a tug? They can only say no." Briggs was really hoping for Barking to make a fool of himself, at the same time leaving himself and Jones to have a peaceful drink.

"I might just do that, they won't say no though, after all how could they resist a top detective, full blown sexual animal and all that. Truth be known I would probably completely overwhelm them, too much, too much." John was breathing into his palm checking for bad breath as he spoke. "Right ready for action, which of you wants the excess?" Jones and Briggs looked blank and puzzled. "The one that loses the fight for my body" explained John.

"Not for me thanks mate, not my style, you know, lay preacher and all that." Jones threw in quickly, "Holiness equals celibacy, see?"

Briggs was pleased to see Jones was beginning to be able to laugh at himself, and put this down to the continual piss taking that went on, particularly with Ron as the butt of all jokes. Barking looked questioningly at Briggs.

"Definitely not my scene, I'm far too ugly. I was lucky to be taken off the shelf by my old lady. Count your blessings and all that."

Barking shrugged his shoulders in the accepted hard man fashion "Right then I'd best show you how it's done."

He put his glass on the counter and approached the girls who Briggs, from their chatter, took to be Dutch. John spoke to the girl on the left, who appeared slightly more blowsy than the other. She shook her head in a negative manner. John then turned to the other one and she shook her head also. John then fished a visiting card from his wallet and gave one to each girl. Briggs remembered Barking having had these printed some months ago and seemed to recall they stated that John Barking, ace investigator, was top detective, not just at Rodney Road station but all over the Metropolitan Police.

"I bet they are impressed with that." said Briggs talking to Jones from behind his beer.

"Look he's got a knock back," said Jones gleefully at Barking's failure in the department of sexual overtures.

Barking rejoined them at the bar. "Got a blank then John, there's nasty see, sorry about that boyo." Jones was pleasant and patronising.

"Me, draw a blank? You must be joking, you sheep shagger, the younger one's got the hots for it. She's going to ring me tomorrow." Barking hissed the words from injured pride as he picked his beer up from the bar.

Jones was about to retaliate when Briggs jabbed him in the ribs and said to Barking, "Well anyway John, what's the arrangement, you going for a meal or what?"

Barking red faced and thinking quickly, "I'll play it by ear when she rings."

Jones was puzzled by Briggs' kind interest, where usually he served up Barking silent scorn. Furthermore Briggs was quiet and thoughtful for the remainder of the evening, grunting replies at Barking's attempts at wind-ups.

The next morning as usual Jones and Briggs assembled in the canteen before their daily assault on the crime figures. After the ritual of morning tea, Briggs nodded to Jones and indicated that he should leave. They walked out of the canteen, into the main entrance to the nick and then into the telephone operators' room, where the busty Joyce was making valiant attempts at running communications with an extremely antiquated switchboard. "Briggsy how nice to see you, I haven't seen you since we got together at that posting party, do you remember?" She grinned wickedly at his discomfort and squirmed for a further invitation to dance.

"Yes, Joyce I do remember, very well." The memory of heaving bodies and moaned explicit sexual instructions swam before his mind. "Very nice too, but Ron and I are here to ask for a favour, a very special favour." Joyce leered at them like a Cobra examining two mice.

"Be my special pleasure," she said breathing her Marilyn Monroe impersonation.

"No, not like that Joyce, well not this time anyway. Can you speak Dutch?" Briggs asked, hopeful in the extreme.

"Dutch! You want me to speak bleeding Dutch?" Joyce asked astounded by this latest request.

"Well not exactly. Can you make it sound like Dutch, I mean

English but with a strange accent?" Briggs explaining with difficulty.

"What is it something operational?" Joyce being a touch wary for such a bold girl.

"Er not exactly, it's a wind-up we're trying to put over on John Barking." Briggs asked hopefully at Joyce, knowing full well that Joyce hated Barking, mainly because she was sure he was a closet homosexual.

"Oh zee Barking, 1, how would zay, love to engage in zee vind up on old big head," Joyce giving a fair impression of something continental mainly French but could be Dutch.

"Oh lovely darling, he's such a shithead he'll fall full tilt for that." Joyce grinned at Briggs' fulsome praise at what she had said. Briggs continued, "Now what we want done is this...." thereafter followed an in depth briefing on the way the conversation should take place. Joyce made notes. "Are you happy with that love?" Briggs enquired earnestly. "Are you sure you can get away with it?"

" Absolutely," breathed the Marilyn impersonation. "By the time I am finished with him he will have a hard on fit to hang a Union Jack on."

"Right then shall we do it now?" Briggs suggested excitedly. Jones, as in all cases of difficulty or danger which might require some decision, remained silent.

"Yes, let's go for it." Joyce was red faced and getting quite a buzz from all this chat about hard ons etc. Briggs ruefully hoped that this incident would not necessitate a further bout of catch as catch can wrestling in the back of Joyce's car, but if it did he was prepared to sacrifice himself on the altar of winding up John Barking.

"Right then, ring him up and make out you're the Dutch girl he met last night, that your name is Tulip and guess where you come from?" Briggs was already laughing at the expected reply.

"Amsterdam" cried Joyce, giggling girlishly, purely from memory of course.

"Best put that in later on, the Amsterdam bit, put both parts together and he's bound to cotton on." Briggs was being cautious. "Mind you he's as thick as a Ghurka's foreskin, so maybe not. Ron and I will listen in on the extension. If you're in difficulty, make out you don't understand and I'll write down what I want you to say OK?" Joyce nodded and gave the spare headset to Briggs. She then connected Barking's extension to the switchboard.

"Hello Rodney Road CID, can I help?" the harsh Wiltshire nasal tone grated on everyone's ear.

"Ja, er 'ello mistair, I am, how you say vishing to speak with Mistair Barking the top detective, please sir," Joyce said struggling with her straight face and therefore straight acting.

"This is Barking here. Who is calling?" Barking spoke very slowly realising that he was speaking to a foreigner who might not understand.

"Iz zat you Jan? Iz zat really you, you sounded much bigger in the hotel last night, you give ze, er how you card, ze card, to me last night." Joyce paused, waiting for the fall of shot.

Barking sounded cautious. "The Dutch young lady, the one sitting with her friend in the corner?" Barking asked brightly at a fish jumping on to his particular hook, Barking spoke quickly in case this particular fish jumped off again. "Yes I do remember, which one are you?"

"I am ze young one, the uzzer one is sister, she in charge, but I find money and ring you." Joyce paused and made what she thought was sexy heavy breathing, but to Briggs sounded like a steam locomotive starting up.

Whatever, Barking seemed impressed. "That is very thoughtful of you, we're both attracted to each other." Barking tentatively feeling his way.

"Oh yes, oh yes." exploded Joyce.

"And," continued Barking "I was wondering what you are doing tonight, could we meet perhaps?" Briggs thought Barking sounded as though he was not at all sure of himself or the caller, had he sussed it?

"Only meet, how you say, no more than meet?" Joyce sounded puzzled. "Could you come to the same hotel, my room is there?" There was a pause and when he replied Barking sounded as though his tie was too tight for him, or perhaps something had become wedged somewhere.

"Yes, yes of course, how about 8 o'clock?" John definitely sounding as though in receipt of a strangulated erection.

"Earlier, much earlier, I want to spend so much time wiz you, zeven make it zeven," Joyce responded breathless and panting.

"What is your name?" John sounded almost dreamy with suppressed passion as he asked the question.

"I have, how you say a family name, but my real name is Tulip. Say it John say it now, so I can keep it wiz me all afternoon." John sounded off the boil or going that way. "Zay my name, zay it pleez."

There was a pause and Barking replied, "Tulip." slowly and with what he thought was feeling. Briggs had to gag Jones who was sharing the headset with him.

"Zat is lovely, Jan, you're voice is so dark and sex," Joyce giving the handset plenty of heavy breathing.

"Till seven then" Barking left a pause. "Tonight at seven Tulip, I shall be there." John spoke quietly as though straining to hold back some dark passion, which was probably true.

"Oh Jan, Jan tonight at seven don't be late. I look for you." Joyce rang off and turned to Briggs. "Well what do you fink Tel?"

Briggs gave Joyce a big brother peck on the cheek and said, "Joyce that was fantastic. It had me going and our Ron is looking very seedy with passion, I expect our John is upstairs now with steam coming out of his ears."

Jones and Briggs left Joyce in her little office and returned upstairs to the CID Office, where the usual morning clamour of getting off to court and making arrangements for crimes to be investigated were being made. Barking was standing by his desk. If Briggs was right and an erection was present this was probably the most comfortable position. His face was flushed with something, expectation maybe, leading forth to Richards and Winkle on the subject of his male supremacy. Catching sight of Jones he called, "There you are, what did I tell you, the young one is arching for it." Jones looked blank "Sorry John don't follow you, young one what young one?" Jones was poker faced as he picked up a new file on his desk.

"The young one from last night, the foreign bird in the hotel, she's just rung me and asked for a date. I told you she fancied me." John puffed his chest and surveyed the mere mortals around him.

"And I suppose you have made a date with her is that it?" Jones obviously disapproving but still examining the file on his desk.

"Why not? If you're attractive you just have to put up with these things. Know what I mean?" John leered and winked at Jones.

"No I am afraid I do not. As far as I am concerned all sexual intercourse outside the bounds of marriage is against Canon law and is therefore a sin against God." Jones delivered this withering assessment of his usual late night activities. Briggs was unsure whether Jones was serious or winding John up.

"Oh fuck you, you pompous prick." Barking stormed out of the office. Jones winked at Briggs.

The day proceeded as had many others with Jones and Briggs doing the things they did everyday and would no doubt be doing the following day as well. In the course of this grinding boredom, they completely forgot about John Barking and his imaginary assignation until the following morning when sitting in the canteen contemplating another day of chasing small villains about even smaller offences, Joyce joined them. "What happened?" She asked expectantly.

"Happened Joyce, about what?" responded Briggs, suddenly realising that Joyce's make up was applied crookedly. "Perhaps she does it that way to straighten her face up," thought Briggs.

"The wind-up with John Barking," Joyce amazed that her Sarah Bernhardt performance had been dismissed from his mind so quickly. "Did he turn up?"

Briggs was apologetic. "I have to tell you Joyce, I don't know, we've not been up there yet. Hold on he's coming in." They sat quietly whilst Barking got his tea and came across to join them.

"Alright Tel, Ron?" asked Barking; being sexist he could not possibly acknowledge Joyce.

Briggs thought there was something in her assertion that he was a poof, but why the performance. "Fine John, by the way how did it go last night."

Barking seemed puzzled. "You know the Dutch girl you pulled in the hotel," prompted Briggs.

"Oh yeah the Dutch girl, she didn't show," but before the trio could get in a cheer of success he said, "she left a message for me behind the bar, said she would ring again." Joyce and Ron looked at the floor suppressing laughter.

Briggs being of sterner stuff managed, "Oh I see she didn't stand you up then?" Barking seemed surprised.

"Me get stood up, Tel come on you must be joking, there are women out there who will pay good money just to be seen with me."

Joyce, unable to stand it any longer, got up and rushed out.

"I think she's got a dose of the trots, unsound tummy and all that." Briggs smiled pleasantly.

"Tel, please, not first thing in the morning." Barking made a distasteful face.

"Yeah sorry, but back to the Dutch bird, silly mistake, obvious really." Jones and Briggs finished their tea and left.

They both rushed upstairs and knocked on Jack the Hat's door "Come." Briggs pushed open the door. Jack the Hat looked up "What are you two bandits up to?" Jack the Hat was not at his best in the morning. Briggs thought this had something to do with his preferred drink of neat gin and water in large quantities every night, and sometimes lunchtimes too.

"It's about the office meeting guv, the thing with Barking well we think we may have something." An early morning grin spread across Jack the Hat's face.

Briggs then explained what had transpired so far, including Joyce's involvement and the fact that Barking had not sussed it as a wind-up. "Would Joyce be game to go again do you think?" Jack the Hat asked hopefully.

"She might want taking to dinner and wining and dining after the event guv." Briggs treated Jack the Hat to one of his knowing looks.

"At the end of which a large session of horizontal PT right?"

"Absolutely guv."

Jack the Hat pondered. "Right then ask Joyce on my authority to do you this favour." Jack the Hat emphasized 'you'. "If she is agreeable set it up. I want all of them here early lates and nights, get them assembled in my office. Make parade time 6.30pm which will be about the time he's off to get his dick seen to." Jack the Hat was gleeful at John Barking's expected downfall.

Jones and Briggs re-entered the switchboard room. Joyce was answering the dings and rings of the antiquated system. "Wotcha, that was hilarious, imagine not sussing it as a wind-up, what a prick." Joyce giggled as she plunged a cable connector into the requisite socket.

"Joyce, how about having another go at him?" Briggs pleaded as he leaned across the board at Joyce.

"What another set up you mean?" Joyce seemed doubtful, "It's a bit risky, if any of the guvnors found out I would be for the high jump."

Briggs touched her hand. "Joyce I don't think you have a problem. Our guvnor, Jack the Hat is behind all this, he wants Barking so much it hurts." Briggs pleaded the guvnor's case. "And Jack the Hat has said if we are successful I am to take you out to dinner and make a fuss of you – after. How about it then?"

Joyce looked thoughtful, after a pause, "Yes to all parts, the wind-up, the dinner and afters." She smiled almost winsomely. "But one thing more – I would like to be in at the kill, when the prick discovers that that is what he is, just that," Joyce exposing more than a malicious streak.

"Right then we are in agreement. Here's what we do." All three huddled together and discussed the forthcoming conversation with Barking. Joyce giggled throughout like a series of commas. "I hope you can control yourself whilst its going on, he susses us and he'll go ballistic." Briggs was thinking that really he wouldn't mind having what is known as a 'straightener' with Barking and, in a strange way would quite enjoy hurting him. This strange thought troubled him but continued, "Right let's ring him. Now don't forget it's all down to her sister and same place tonight right?!" Briggs briefing Joyce and thinking that he had often made more serious preparations, where much more had hung in the balance.

Joyce picked up her handset, indulged in some deep breathing exercises, then dialled the extension. The switchboard room went quiet with tension. Barking answered, "Yes CID Rodney Road," pausing expectantly.

"John iz zat you?!" came the continental voice, quiet and intense.

"Yes, and I don't want to talk to you, you stood me up. You made me look a right twit." Barking sounded sulky, like some big old tart.

"Jan believe me I could not help it, my sister, she found out and I could not get out." Joyce in make believe tears. "Jan, Jan pleaze believe me, anyzay Helga has now gone home for a few days, there is trouble wiz ze family biznezz in Amsterdam she has to attend to. So vee will be on our own. Jan we meet ja."

"Er ja, or rather yes I suppose so." Barking sounded somehow defeated. Perhaps he had decided no way, and was now dissatisfied with himself for giving in. Briggs wrote quickly on a piece of paper. 'Build him up with bullshit! Make him feel sexy.' Joyce nodded.

"You know John I was sinking of you in ze bath, tell me have you ze hairy chest" she paused "and ze ozzer zings?"

There was pause eventually Barking gulped and said, "Well er yes."

Joyce or rather Tulip continued, "Wiz ze hairy chest and ze broad shoulders wizout your clothes you look magnificent ja?" Joyce finished up with a series of short panting breaths which sounded like the dying gasps of an asthmatic dog.

"I don't know, I suppose so, I hope so." Barking was unsure of himself. Briggs waved his hand in a circular motion, meaning give him some more.

"John, I love ze clothes you wear, the colourful clothes, zat shirt ze other night, wiz ze yellow fluffy front and ze purple suit. I love men who wear these things, but you do know that only really handsome men can carry zis off. Also I love ze strong perfume some men wear, ow you say after shave? zis gets a woman's senses and makes her, how you say? do zings." John coughed, almost Briggs felt to hide shyness or embarrassment. "We've overdone it," thought Briggs.

But Barking was still firmly on the hook. "Tulip where shall we meet and when?" Barking truncated his sentences with smouldering passion."

"Oh yes Jan at ze otel as before, seven o'clock tonight, oh and Jan."

"Yes Tulip." Barking waited expectantly.

"Jan I ask you to bring flowers, I love men who bring flowers, it is how you say romance."

"Romantic," corrected Barking and responded, "Yes I will bring you flowers at seven tonight, till then my love." They heard Barking kiss the handset and the line went dead. Briggs and Jones both kissed Joyce, which she seemed to enjoy.

Jones and Briggs sauntered into the CID office with the hope that their casual attitude would conceal their secret knowledge. They sat down opposite each other. Briggs winked at Jones and nodded towards the latest case file. Ron picked it up and started to riffle through it. Barking was sitting at his desk day-dreaming out of the window. "You alright John?" Briggs engaged Barking in conversation.

"You know the Dutch bird, is it on for tonight?" asked Briggs looking down at his papers.

"Of course it is mate, she can't resist me can she?" Barking answered as he came down from his erotic day-dreams.

"I reckon your being had my old son, it's got to be a wind-up." Briggs sensed that all the officers around him stiffened with stress.

"A wind-up, me? You sure?" Barking offended at such a suggestion.

"Not from your mates here, John, but what about the villains from down the lane, could they be trying to get you at it?"

"Nice thought Tel and thanks, but really she's Dutch for Christ's sake, not from Walworth Road. Where are they going to get a Dutch bird from?" John open mouthed in amazement.

"Yes I suppose so, just thought I'd mention it, you know, it seems an awful lucky stroke." Briggs looked down at his files, but was aware that everyone else in the room was on the edge of their chairs after his impudent manoeuvre of getting Barking to confirm the wind-up against himself.

"Your trouble is Tel that, being well sort of plain." Barking studied Briggs' battered face as if for the first time. "Ugly almost, well just not handsome, you never get into the position where someone is overcome by your sexual attraction – know what I mean." Briggs feigned puzzlement. Barking continued. "Look, you're a nice good person, but being well, plain, no bird is going to fall head over heels for you as Tulip has for me. Anyway thanks for the thought." Briggs tried to look sad at this welcome assessment of his maschimo. Barking began going through his preparations for the sexual fray, sorting out toiletries.

Briggs eventually recovered what he thought was complete control. "Yeah fine John, no problem, just thought I would mention it you never know, but you're right, I can see that now." The line was played deadpan. Briggs looked around the room where everyone else was studying their diaries, files or newspapers, all grim faced, which to Briggs was a sure sign they were holding back howls of laughter.

Throughout the day Barking fussed around, collecting his spare suit, colour bottle green, from the dry cleaners, together with his fluffy fronted yellow shirt which Tulip had mentioned specifically. He borrowed Briggs' extra strong after shave. This had been given to him by his Auntie. Briggs had worn it once and thought it might be excellent for repelling mosquitoes and the like, but probably no good at attracting women. About 4.30pm Barking arrived in the office with an enormous bunch of flowers. "If she performs like she said for a bunch of flowers they will be at it for a month of Sundays," thought Briggs. Barking was at it again. "You lot don't know what it is like, birds are chasing me all the time," preening himself in the window.

"Why do you owe them money or what?" Sid hissed, having had enough of John's daylong performance.

"Sid, the 'or what', is pure animal magnetism, they can't resist it," Barking shimmying in the reflection on the filing cabinet. Sid shook his head in disbelief.

About 6.15pm Barking began his preparations in earnest, having showered and rubbed himself down with talc etc, on with fluffy yellow shirt, bottle green trousers and highly polished wedge heel boots. "Tel, honestly mate what do you think?" Which is best, the kipper tie or the gold medallion and open neck with the shirt?" Barking turned to Tel with both bits in his hands and changing from one to the other in order that Briggs could have the benefit of the likely effect of each.

"John I really don't know, you know the girl and what pleases her. I mean would she be offended by the presence of a hairy chest and gold medallion, only you would know mate." Briggs pointing Barking to the gold medallion and further ridicule.

"That's it you're right. She said she likes geezers with hairy chests and the medallion is only the icing on the cake. Know what I mean?" John put the chain over his head and adjusted the medallion in front; he opened his shirt to the waist to accommodate it. Equal portions of flab and hairy chest were now on display. "What do you think?" John asked posing in front of Briggs. Those behind John were grinning at his expected downfall.

Briggs stared at Barking intently feigning interest, "I tell you what John, that really completes the picture, makes you look like sex on wheels." Briggs had his fingers crossed behind his back "and those flowers John they're terrific, what you really need is some music to march in to, like Gary Glitter or something. But they haven't got music at the hotel. Shame, but there we are – just a thought."

John got himself together, finally he combed his hair into what he thought was a Tom Jones style, picked up his flowers and with a flourish, "Right lads, see you tomorrow, if she will let me go that soon." Barking winked. Briggs felt the resultant laughter a bit over the top, but Barking didn't sus it so it was probably Briggs being anxious. Barking left the office and could be heard clumping down the stairs in his wedge heeled monstrosities.

As soon as Barking's car started up, Sid ran into Jack the Hat's office, where all the Aids, some of the Detective Constable and a couple of sergeants were perched. They all entered the main office. Once they had settled down Jack the Hat addressed them. "Right then settle down you lot, I want this to run like clockwork, no fuck ups, no nothing. I've arranged for us to assemble in the basement of the hotel and I want our entrance to be precise. As you enter the bar it is essential that you do not speak to Barking until I give the word, got it?" Mutters of agreement floated across to Jack the Hat. "Briggsy you pick up Joyce on the way round, okay?" Jack the Hat waited for Briggs' nod. "Right then, just make sure it runs right. Now off you go and assemble in the basement. I'll sort you out from there."

Briggs, entering the basement with Joyce, saw Jack the Hat approaching him. "It's on guv, he's in the bar, in the corner opposite the door and the bar. Couldn't be better," Briggs drawing a picture with his hands.

"Right then here we go, all you lot upstairs, in the hallway leading to the bar, and quietly." Jack the Hat ushered them along the passageway and up the stairs. Sid Mills was standing in the hallway and got them organized into sections with reference to rank. When everyone was arranged according to rank and seniority and to Jack the Hat's and Sid Mills' satisfaction, Jack the Hat said quietly, "Right then, Aids form up." and once they had got into position, "Quick march, halt when you get to the end of the bar." The Aids marched into the bar in step and halted at the end of the bar. Briggs, who was looking through a crack in the door saw Barking sit up straight and his jaw drop.

"Right, DC's quick march." and a further ten bodies, marching in unison, entered the bar which, luckily, was a long one. They halted as one by the Aids and turned left to face the bar as the Aids had done. Jones and Briggs were in this contingent. They were followed by six second class sergeants and two first class sergeants and then by Jack the Hat, who, once he had a glass of beer in his hand, called down the line, "Ready lads?" and, receiving the confirmatory nod, "About turn," which they all did, heels crashing into the floor together. Jack the Hat spoke up. "Detective Constable Barking we are here to sing you a song, all together lads one two three, WHEN IT'S SPRING AGAIN I'LL BRING AGAIN TULIPS FROM AMSTERDAM " As they were singing Joyce came in waving a bunch of tulips in time to the music. They carried on singing until all verses had been rendered and Barking was crimson.

Jack the Hat walked forward and pulled a large plastic penis from his pocket, he place it in the top pocket of the bottle green suit, Jack the Hat smiled, "There you are my son regard it as a badge of office." They all cheered.

The Snout

One of the very necessary weapons a good detective needs in his pocket is a snout, grass, or formally an informant. Call them, him or her, what you will but without them the system tends to run dry. In the memoirs of a number of very senior CID officers, their informants are numbered in twenties or thirties, and in one learned tome, hundreds. The most that Briggs and Jones ever managed was three, and even then they found it difficult to keep up. But then again Tel and Ron were only Detective Constables and not issued with the super powers with which Senior Detectives would have you believe they are blessed.

There are a number of reasons and circumstances which makes the apparently 'sound' person turn informant, be it the result of revenge, greed, jealousy or ambition. In fact any emotion which, if powerful enough, will turn the apparent 'staunch' into a grass. It is remembered with amusement the headlines of an East End newspaper which read "In the East End We Never Grass" referring to the mythical East End code which dictates just that. There should have been one or two provisos added. One, except when money is involved or offered, the larger the amount the deeper the treachery and, two, except when in a Police Station and it is on you, meaning that you have been caught bang to rights and, three, when it suits you to blow the gaff on a friend or accomplice.

For certain what you did not do is to publish his or her name to your superiors, even in reports for a reward from the informants fund or to insurance companies, you always used a pseudonym. The reason for all this cageyness was that it was not unknown for superiors to 'sell' your informant, or else convert him to their own use. So to be an informant was a very dangerous game, and they needed special handling, and always had their own agenda – something else they wanted out of the deal. This was sometimes known as the 'x' factor.

One such grass was Christine Moffat the daughter of the donor of the famous 'Moffat' pens. Her arrest was requested by officers of the Surrey Constabulary for offences of 'kiting', – writing worthless cheques to obtain goods. The way this worked was the burglar would take any cheque books found to his local fence (receiver of stolen property) The fence would farm them out to one of his agents and a deal would be struck on the resultant income. Alternatively he might sell the cheque book and card to Christine or some other agent. Christine was obviously 'at it' for a local fence and had been tracked down by the Surrey officers.

Having been given the task of arresting Christine, Briggs and Jones and immediately contacted Charlie Moffat who was as helpful as could be but didn't know where Christine lived, she was cohabiting (married sort of) to a Bobby Collins who was very cagey about where he lived. Further, that Collins was the author of numerous burglaries and the like, and who was the top of every detective's list who knew him. Charlie however promised to pass the message on to Christine when he saw her – 'and would it be alright for her to attend Rodney Road with Mr. Beamish of Beamish and Beamish?' Which, as it was for the Surrey Constabulary, was perfectly in order.

After leaving the message with Charlie, Briggs and Jones went about their business waiting for the bird to land with Beamish in tow. The newly disclosed liaison between Christine and Collins was plotted in the collator's office. Jack the Hat expressed an interest in Collins, as it was his belief that he was a one man crime wave, and his apprehension could well affect his long awaited promotion to Superintendent. The arrest of Collins would not immediately cause Jack the Hat to rise the slippery pole, but it would cause the crime figures to drop and therefore a more healthy crime detected figure might well improve Jack the Hat's chances of rising to the top of the pile.

About a week after dropping the message to Charlie, Briggs was called to the front office by the duty station officer,. When he entered the office he was greeted at the counter by Mr. Beamish. Briggs guessed it was to do with Christine and knew that Beamish would want to talk in the interview room. "Ah yes good morning Mr. Beamish, about the Divisional Ball, please step this way and we'll sort out your seating requirements." Briggs ushered the puzzled Beamish into the side room.

"Tel it's not about the ball, it's about Christine," hissed Beamish.

"I know that, but I would have thought you would want to talk in here rather than out there, am I right?" Beamish settled himself down behind the table and lit a cigarette.

"Ah good, so anyway Christine." Beamish studied his lit cigarette. "She is happy to surrender, however they insist there are no verbals, and are willing to pay for the service." Briggs listened intently, amused by the request –'verbals' are allegedly oral admissions made by the accused. One of Briggs' friends, when questioned in court, about 'verbals' defined them as "statements made in surprise on arrest and later retracted on legal advice." Beamish continued. "Old man Moffat was well pleased with the way it went in court about the other thing, his lot you know, and has said that you are to be trusted, well sort of." Briggs nodded at the implied compliment.

"I'll play it straight, well as you say almost, Christine is wanted by the Surrey Constab, we won't verbal her but they might, so no deal OK?" Beamish nodded and made a note in his file.

"Well then when and where?" Beamish looked up into Briggs' face.

"As soon as you like Frank, it makes no odds to us, we are only passing her on." Beamish got up put his files into his briefcase, straightened his coat, shook Briggs' hand, said, "We will be in touch" and left.

Briggs returned to the office. Ron was at his desk intent on a section of General Orders, which were at that time the subject on which promotion examinations were based. In the provinces the examination was on pure law as this was what you were supposed to be enforcing. In the Met it was purely on General Orders or G.O's as they were usually known. So to get on, one had to learn great reams of G.O's which were really compiled of other people's mistakes. Briggs eventually rose to having almost his own section of G.O's. "Still trying to become Commissioner then Ron?" Ron folded the book almost as though he did not want Briggs to see what it was. "What have you got some porno in there or what?" Ron looked sheepish not thinking that his act had been interpreted so quickly.

"Well no actually it's the latest tip for the Inspector's examination." Ron was already qualified for Sergeant, but if the officer wanted he could become qualified for the next rank whilst still a Constable. For the rank after – Chief Inspector – it was rumoured that they sent you St Thomas's Hospital and removed your brain.

"That was Beamish, he's going to bring Christine in by appointment, but they are willing to pay for no verbals." Ron smiled, "What an opportunity, Winkle would be there like a rat up a drainpipe." Briggs finished the sentence "And just hope that Surrey don't verbal her up to the hilt, it's a sweat I don't want."

Some officers however actually courted the grief that this sort of endeavour brings home. Briggs well remembered being in the corridor of Tower Bridge Magistrates' Court standing next to his prisoner who was on a charge of dishonest handling a packing case of cigarettes from the nearby docks. The prisoner turned to him and said, "You know the script don't you?" Briggs was taken aback as he had nicked the prisoner on the usual "bought them off a man in a pub evidence."

Briggs nodded the conversation on "Go on tell me," half expecting something of the sort that followed.

"Well Winkle said it would be OK for you to say that I took them in payment of a debt, know what I mean."

Briggs thought for a moment. "And how much has gone in on the strength of this little fiction?"

"Always the same, a double ton for 'elp, innit." Briggs heaved a sigh.

"Yes I suppose so," for to oppose this insertion of a tall story would be to drop Winkle in the veritable. Needless to say Briggs called Winkle to order when he returned to the office, but it made no difference. Winkle shrugged and never shared the double ton.

"Tel it's for you." Richards held the phone for him.

"Yes Briggs." There was a pause and Frank Beamish said, "Hi ya Tel, Christine tonight 7.30pm OK?" Briggs nodded "Fine, that'll do." Briggs replaced the phone.

In reply to Richards' questioning look, "It was Sophia Loren begging me to shag her." He went back to his desk and sat down. Ron was lost in some file or other, Briggs could see that with his predilection for files and paper dust etc that Ron might be a good candidate for C6-Company Fraud Office. "Oi Ron, Christine tonight at 7.30pm Beamish will be with her."

Ron placed his finger on the point at which he had read up to and looked up. "Right I'll look forward to seeing her again," and immediately immersed himself in the file.

At 7.30pm Ron and Briggs were in the front office waiting. The street door opened. Frank Beamish entered accompanied by Christine. Frank was always well dressed and presented himself well. Christine complemented this appearance, very expensively dressed in brown leather jacket with matching shoes. If it was fake crocodile they were a good copy, even the scarf around her head screamed money.

"Mr. Briggs." Frank spoke to Briggs as he rarely afforded Ron the compliment. "This is Christine Moffat," indicating Christine. "I understand she is wanted by the Surrey Constabulary for an offence of obtaining property by deception." Christine flicked her headscarf off her shoulders and was plainly irritated by this whole event.

Briggs would later describe Christine as being a 'bit tubby'. Ron described her as 'voluptuous' which to Briggs meant fat with sexual overtones – same thing really 'tubby'. Briggs said, "Thank you Mr. Beamish."

He then addressed Christine, "Miss Moffat." Briggs paused for effect, needless really for all participants in this little drama had travelled this path before and none were particularly nervous about any of it. "I am arresting you for obtaining property by deception in the County of Surrey; you are not obliged to say anything unless you wish to do so but what you say may be put into writing and given in evidence."

Christine stared at Briggs deadpan. "Am I supposed to be impressed officer?" She spoke in an assumed high class drawl, which Briggs judged to be reasonable, so reasonable it almost made him feel servile.

"Come this way Miss Moffat." Briggs ushered her and Frank Beamish towards the charge room. Briggs was holding himself in check, because he was really dying to enquire as to the fate of the spider and the spilt curds and whey, but didn't.

In the charge room the duty sergeant took Christine's details and recorded them in the book 12a. She gave her address as her father's where Charlie's hoard had been discovered. Briggs made no comment, as it might be that he could obtain Collins' address in exchange for some future favour with Beamish. In any case he didn't want Christine to know that he was aware of her domicile and who was keeping her happy nights.

As Christine was unlikely to kick over the traces she was placed in the detention room and given a cup of tea by the matron. The tea had slopped into the saucer. She stared at the cup with assumed horror. "Oh God no. Take it away, have you got any Malvern Water?"

Matron, who had seen it all and been involved in much of it said, "Of course my dear, hang on and I'll pass some through my kidneys into a glass for you. In the meantime drop that stupid voice you fat slag." Christine's face was a picture.

"Well fuck you an all, if you had any arsehole you would be doing a proper job not cleaning up for the filf."

Matron laughed, "That's better dear we all recognise you now." Matron left and locked the door behind her.

Briggs rang the Guildford CID office and informed them that their prize prisoner was in custody. He didn't mention the offered deal about buying the verbals, as to Provincial officers, this would have been alien territory, and being straightlaced they would not have understood. On reflection, Briggs was not sure he understood, preferring to think that such things were labelled as 'Copper's logic' and filed in his conscience as excused liability. Briggs and Jones then awaited the arrival of the escort from Surrey, content that their prisoner was going to receive her just desserts in the County of Surrey.

The next day Briggs and Jones were about to go out and investigate the accumulated burglaries on the manor when they received a call from the Guildford CID. Briggs heard one side of the conversation which consisted of Ron saying "OK, but why?" with a pause and "She is going to be surprised." Ron put the phone down and turned to Briggs. "It was Guildford they want us to release Christine." Ron was plainly bemused.

Briggs thought for a moment. "Ron get back on to them, tell them to send a telex, else it could be the station cleaner calling, also it would be nice to cover ourselves just in case."

Ron brightened, "Good thinking Tel." He picked up the telephone again and immersed himself in making contact again.

Some time later, after receipt of the telex, Ron and Tel entered the Detention Room. Christine was sitting on the bench surrounded by the remains of a cell breakfast which looked even more unappetizing than when it was prepared. "Morning Christine did you sleep well?"

Christine nodded, "Not bad actually, 'cept for the drunks who came in later." Briggs did not enquire if they were prisoners or CID officers on the razzle – not a lot of difference really.

"Good, Ron and I have got some good news for you, which maybe will make your overnight stay a bit more bearable." Christine brightened, but yesterday's immaculately applied make up had turned into today's nightmarish appearance.

"Yes Tel, I could do with some good news."

Briggs breathed deeply, "Well love it's like this, we've had a word with our mates at Guildford, and they have decided not to charge you and left you with us so to speak."

Christine looked puzzled. "What no charge at all?" Briggs immediately noted that she had obviously been tearing their ground apart and was obviously surprised no-one had cottoned on to her.

"No dear you are free to go."

Christine hardened a little. "I don't believe all this bullshit – How much? We'll do it through Beamish as a middle."

Briggs laughed, "No you misunderstand dear no charge, we have done you a favour nothing more, no charge."

Christine's head went down. She pondered. "Alright," she said it slowly as though her brain was catching up with this new development. "What do you want for this favour of yours." Briggs knew she had been well briefed by someone as to the machinations of the old bill.

"A favour in return if you like dear, just a favour."

Briggs could see that Christine was suspicious, "What sort of favour?"

Briggs drew another deep breath. "Well any information that comes your way we would obviously appreciate."

Christine flinched, "I'm no grass, no way, I'll stay, we don't grass."

Briggs thought, "The same as you don't plead," but said, "Not grassing Christine, just returning a favour, you can put in anything you like, it doesn't have to be close to home. or anything like that.

Christine smiled, "Oh like child molesters and rapists." Briggs nodded. "Oh yes I could put them away like there's no tomorrow."

Briggs was relieved. "When you have something just ring me love. In the meantime, come this way and I'll get you released." Christine gathered yesterday's expensive accessories which had become today's bits of tat.

They filed into the charge room and the station sergeant released her formally. Ron and Tel stood in the foyer of the station as Christine took her leave. She shook their hands and gave Briggs a look, a leer more like, which made his blood run cold. "I'll be in touch Briggsy." She assumed that she had the look of Lauren Bacall, to say the least it didn't come across that way, She turned at the door and smiled at them both, gave a little wave and kicked her heel up slightly.

Briggs could see that Ron was smitten. "I wouldn't' not even with yours."

Ron bristled out of his reverie "Nor I Tel, nor I, Audrey," He didn't get any further as Tel was already making his way to the stairs.

Some weeks later Briggs was at his desk sorting his property register stuff, Ron was compiling a legal aid report, correlating statements and exhibit lists. The telephone rang. Briggs answered it "Er hello Tel isn't it, I recognise the voice."

Briggs was puzzled "Yes Briggs, who's this?"

"Tel it's Christine, about your favour you were looking for." Briggs paused, he was off balance, this was not expected at all.

"Right Christine, what have you got for us?" Briggs felt uncomfortable with this approach and now twenty odd years later he could not say why.

"Not so fast, Dick Tracy, let's have a meet and I'll explain everything."

Briggs was still thinking on two plains. "Alright Christine when and where?"

She paused then said, "The Crown and Greyhound tonight at 8 don't be late big boy, oh and bring Ron with you." Briggs put the phone down Ron looked up from his papers.

"Ron we have ourselves a snout."

Doing the Business

"She said the Crown and Greyhound, East Dulwich, do you know it?" enquired Briggs intently over tea in the canteen.

Ron shook his head. "It's the haunt of stockbrokers and the like, the area is becoming gentrified."

The word sunk in with Briggs. "Gentrified, what a peculiar word. I bet it's American somewhere along the line." Ron seemed edgy, frightened supposed Briggs. "I am against going on the meet. It's bound to be a set up, she doesn't love us, why should she grass?" There followed a lengthy discussion about should they go or stay, was it a fit up. Eventually it was decided to go and chance it, a policy which Briggs regretted in later life and service.

Briggs knocked on the office door. "Yes?" Jack the Hat bellowed. Briggs eventually followed by Jones entered. Jack the Hat looked expectant "Well?" he said.

"Jones and I have a snout." Jack the Hat leaned back in is chair, and appraised the two scaleys in front of him.

"Have you now, tell me more." Jack the Hat waited.

"Well guv he's" Briggs lied, "connected to a very well known local firm and wants to go to work."

Jack the Hat's eyebrows arched in surprise, "For you two? God he must be desperate."

Briggs ignored the insult "Well he does guv, and we feel he can do a bit of good. and we are going to meet him tonight, with your permission of course." Jack the Hat fell silent, for a moment, considering the dangerous information laid before him.

Eventually he said, "He's not a participating informant I hope."

Briggs "No guv, he's not." Well anyway Briggs had his fingers crossed so it didn't count anyway.

"Well why is he going to snout?"

Briggs thought it through and said, "Well as near as I can make it out it's revenge, he caught one of the others shagging his wife and is upset by it all."

Jack the Hat was surprised, "Is that all? Seems a bit moody to me, so be careful, and I mean very careful." Briggs nodded with Jones in unison. "Remember either you have your boot on the informant's neck or he has his on yours, got it?"

"Yes guv." Jack the Hat made a note in his diary, Briggs supposed this to be a note of their conversation, but it might not be.

"Go on then, go on your meet, if it all goes boss-eyed I will try and help as you have told me." They both left the office.

They arrived outside the pub and were ten minutes early. They toured the area examining the parked cars closely. Christine's Lotus was very prominent on the opposite side of the road. "Trouble is," grunted Briggs, "You never know what motors they will be using, they can hire whatever they like."

"Yes." replied Jones "but if they are off a decent team they might show out on the motor, leave something on display like, be a shame to be set up for the want of looking like." Jones parked his old Wolsely near the pub and they got out. Jones looked up and down the road. He went up to the car behind his and examined the tax disc closely.

"Ron for fucks sake pack it in, we aren't doing anything wrong. We are entitled to meet informants, she is an informant and she is going to set someone up for us." Briggs voice had the hard edge of irritation on it produced by Ron's caution.

"What worries me Tel is that it might be us she is setting up." Jones was morose and nervous.

"Well either way we won't find out unless we go in will we?" Briggs said, looking hopefully at Jones but he didn't reply, just shrugged his shoulders as they made for the pub entrance.

At the stroke of eight they entered the bar. There was no saloon or public bars, just one bar that went round the pub. They looked around for Christine and would have missed her but for her waving from the corner. She was dressed to kill. She had an expensive chiffon dress on, with gloves, handbag and shoes to match. Her hair had been done for the occasion, although the hair spray bit had been overdone. She glittered with gold, necklace, earrings and the obligatory sovereign ring sparkled dully in the low light. "Hello Christine, what'll you have?" Briggs asked because Ron rarely did.

"Southern Comfort and Babycham my dear." She smiled sweetly as though ordering a lemonade. Ron winced, it was his round next. Briggs got the drinks. He nodded to a corner which was fairly isolated with little danger of being overheard. Christine sat in the corner. She arranged her expensive dress around her and struck a pose straight out of Vogue. Briggs put the drinks down on the table and sat opposite. Ron perched on the edge of the corner settee near to Christine but careful that he did not touch the misty dress. "Cheers love." Christine downed a good half of her volatile mixture.

"Cheers Christine, you look nice tonight," Briggs committing his usual mistake. Women when dressed to kill never want to be described as nice and, by inference, 'mumsy'. The required description is sexy, stunning, voluptuous maybe, but certainly never nice.

"Thank you my dear." Christine smiled a secret smile well knowing Briggs' mistake.

"Now what do you want us for Christine?" Briggs diving in at the deep end.

"Well my loves, as you are both men of the world I'll speak plainly." Briggs had come to be very wary of being described as being worldly wise and such, as if you disagreed you became a wally by default.

"Please do." Briggs ushered Christine along her path as a snout. Briggs looked to Jones for support, but he was studying the weave of the cloth on the settee in great detail.

"Well I know you want my old man." Christine dropped the bombshell on them both. Ron shaken from his attention and study of material used in the construction of settees looked to Briggs, apprehension was the only discernible emotion.

"Yes your old man is overdue, but anyone will do. Does it have to be him?" leaving the ball firmly in her court.

Christine seemed to re-appraise the situation, then she said "Well, I know I owe you and he's" she paused and Briggs thought she might say "My lover," "The light of my life," or perhaps "My husband," but she continued "at it in a big way."

Briggs was stunned, not expecting treachery of this magnitude. He mulled over what she had said and was thinking as fast as possible. After a while Briggs came back "And you want something in return is that it?"

"You've caught on at last. I think they heard the penny drop in the next street." Briggs glanced at Ron hoping to elicit some sort of opinion from him but nothing was forthcoming.

"Okay my love, what is it that you want from us?" Briggs asked quietly but included Ron in the 'us.'

Her eyes flashed, she leaned forward. "You're interested then?" Briggs caught a waft of her perfume, quite overpowering, causing Briggs to sneeze.

When he recovered he said, "Yes of course we're interested, but first I need to know why you're putting him away, completes the picture like." But in the back of Briggs' mind the real reason was to discover the 'x' factor and if this did not sound convincing then they would take the appropriate steps – big ones in the direction of home.

Christine studied her lap in a manner which she thought was demure, but unfortunately was only from memory. "I don't think I can tell you that, it's sort of personal." She then lapsed into an awkward silence.

"Well anyway we'll have another drink whilst you think on it. Won't we Ron?" Briggs trying to lessen the tension and nudging Ron into life.

"Oh yes, I'll miss this one out, don't want to end up drunk do we?" Ron was thinking with his wallet.

"Well I want one and so does Christine, and as it's your round you can decide if you want one or not, but don't leave us out as well," Briggs, sniping at Ron's legendary meanness. Ron got up and sullenly made his way towards the bar.

Whilst Ron was away, Briggs thought a little small talk and judicious compliments were in order. It might make their future task easier. "I do like your dress Christine – very nice." There he'd done it again, committed the nice offence. But Christine didn't seem to mind.

"I got the whole outfit on a shopping spree in Guildford some months ago, remember? I can get your missus one if you like."

Christine offered being very helpful.

"Oh it was on that shopping spree was it?" Briggs remembering how they had first come into contact with Christine. "No thanks love, you know how it is ladies usually like to choose their own don't they?" Briggs paused and surveyed Christine "But a dress does suit you ever so well. We usually have to imagine your legs as they are encased in jeans." Christine leaned forward, giving Briggs an excellent view of her melon size breasts.

"Well Tel under certain circumstances a dress is certainly more – well practical " She leaned back in her chair and gave Briggs a leer that chilled his soul. He was beginning to catch on.

Ron rejoined them and sat down with a wheeze. "There you are, but it's the start of the greasy road to alcoholism." Briggs could feel the onset of a sermon, brought on not by erring principles but by expense from Ron's pocket.

"Don't tell me Ron, for Christ's sake live clean, or something like that, yes?" Briggs, stopping Ron dead in his intended speech.

Ron seemed crestfallen "Well something like that yes," replied Ron.

"Ron I've heard it several times before. Book it down that you've run the alcohol programme past us yes?" Ron nodded sullenly. Briggs was irritated as he always was when Jones got out his white horse and cantered around on it.

"Now Christine, why are you setting up the old man?" Briggs punched the question at Christine. It was obvious that he was not in the mood for fairy stories.

"Well love," she started quietly, looking left and right in case they were being overheard "You know Sylvia Peters?"

Briggs did indeed know Sylvia. It was rumoured that she did it for friends and didn't have an enemy in the world, but confined himself to "Yes I know her she lives down Kennington way."

"That's right." Christine nodded "That's her. Well I caught Bobby up Dog Kennel Hill with her in the back of his motor, they were at it." Christine looked at the floor, apparently ashamed that she could not control her man.

"And?" Briggs knowing that this sort of behaviour was nothing more than the norm, and that girlfriends and wives got passed round like ganja cigarettes.

"Well, he's changed," said Christine, "he's sort of different, a bit cold maybe." Briggs was relieved that the 'x' factor was so simple – hell hath no fury etc.

"I see Chris and what's the catch?" Briggs asked quietly approaching that subject on which would hang Bobby's liberty. "What do you want from us – money?"

"No Tel not money, I can always get my hands on some dosh. It's more like returning a favour if you like sort of personal, know what I mean?" she grinned from beneath her lacquered fringe.

Briggs was exasperated. "Chris you'll have to speak plainly, I am afraid I don't follow." Briggs was wondering where all this was leading and Jones was still studying the sofa.

Christine paused, glanced at both of them. "Well," she said slowly, "with Bobby away I would need to be looked after and I don't want to catch anything do I now." Christine placidly describing her contract of employment as a snout, which appeared to be "I get laid, you get the old man." Ron fell in. "Us?" he cried mortified, "Us?" Chapel, wife, kids and dog looming large in his mind.

"Yes." said Christine firmly, "either of you, I quite fancy either of you, but not both together as I'm no whore." She beamed at Briggs and Jones as she spoke as though bestowing some great gift. Both Briggs and Jones were stunned by this bombshell, both were silent, a couple of times Jones went to say something but thought better of it. Christine waited content that her 'deal' was being considered in the highest available court.

Eventually Briggs said, "You'll have to excuse us for a moment, but we have to go to the toilet." He got up and waited for movement from Ron.

"No I'm alright thanks Tel," Ron smiling content and secure.

"Not on this one your not mate. Come on." Briggs grabbed Ron by the coat lapel and pulled him to his feet. Jones followed compliantly and morosely.

They stood at the urinals, contemplating the glazed tiles and the notice that informed you that 'Venereal disease is a dangerous disease' and giving details of the available clinics that sort out this problem in confidence. Briggs smiled at the thought and decided not to mention the notice to Ron. "Well Ron what do you think?" Briggs knowing the answer before posing the question.

"Down to you Tel," Ron muttered shaking his weaponry at the porcelain. "Your idea to come, you can do the rest."

"And you're just a passenger who becomes important when the bodies get nicked is that it?" Briggs could feel his temper rising and decided that this would not help Ron into the chair as a sex object. "Look Ron are you game to get Bobby at the end of it?"

Ron brightened up. "Oh yes, he's well wanted, make a nice entry in the back of my book he will."

Briggs noted that Ron mentioned 'my book', not 'our books', also that Ron was almost preening himself at the expected glory to come "So you want to be on board when the glory is flying about, but not when the dirty work has to be done, yes," Briggs snapped the question at Jones. Ron made a face as though sucking a lemon.

"Not really my scene you know, cold bums and flapping sheets and all that." Jones' face showed distaste. "And anyway Audrey…" Jones never finished the sentence. Briggs erupted, "Bollocks to Audrey and to the bloody chapel, you're a bunch of hypocrites anyway." Jones seemed crestfallen showing no opposition. "Listen you prick, you don't mind having a lump of the cake if I go and get it for you is that it?" Jones looked into Briggs' angry face and looked away.

"Well I wouldn't put it like that you know, anyway it's different for you." Ron looked like a little boy pleading to be let off PT, which is probably what he was.

"Ron tell me how is it different for me?" Ron drew a pattern in the wet floor with his shoe.

"Well you know, you're atheist, no enforced principles, know what I mean."

Briggs could feel his temper rising and was getting fed up with this discussion, "You mean no conscience Ron. Well I have and mine doesn't disappear when I have had a beer." Briggs grabbed hold of Ron's coat and shook him. Jones flinched, he thought that Briggs was going to hit him. "Ron we have been in everything else as partners why not this?"

Ron was very aware that anger and violence could break out at any moment "How do you mean – exactly?"

"Well we toss a coin and the loser has to do the superstud bit for Christine," said Briggs hopefully and in desperation. Briggs let go of Ron's coat, Ron smoothed down where his hand had been. Ron looked hurt, but was silently contemplating the odds.

Eventually he said, "Right it's a deal." Almost as soon as he had said it he regretted it.

Briggs fumbled in his pocket and found a florin (10p) and balanced it on his thumb. "What do you want heads or tails?" asked Briggs, standing under the only light in the toilet. Jones considered his two options momentarily.

"Tails," he cried. Briggs flicked the coin into the air where it sparkled and then flopped down on his open palm. Ron leaned forward for the result and lost.

Crestfallen and desperate Ron pleaded. "Tel you've got to help me."

Briggs laughed at Jones' discomfort (and his own relief) "How the bloody hell can I help you, what do you want me to hold it for you? Would I be able to charge a stud fee?"

Ron seemed helpless "Tel you're not helping, I don't think I can manage." Ron winced, forlorn at Briggs' amusement."

"Ron don't worry I expect she'll do it all for you, just lay back and think of the Commissioner," Briggs offered, being well, almost helpful. They left the toilet, Briggs with a lighter step and Ron dragging his feet.

Christine straightened herself on the couch and fluffed up her chiffon dress. "Well who is it to be?" she asked brisk and business like.

"Ron," Briggs blurted the word before Jones had time say to otherwise. Christine seemed relieved.

"Well that's nice," she said. "I have a really soft spot for our Ron." Briggs could just imagine what that might be. Christine gathered her handbag and gloves together. "We'd better go before it's too late" and made for the door with her hand firmly on Ron's, almost dragging him with her.

Briggs stood outside the pub and watched Ron and Christine get into the old Wolsely. Well the Lotus would hardly be suitable for such an endeavour would it? Briggs waved to Ron as he drove off to his carnal fate, almost in the vein of a French nobleman going to the guillotine. Briggs was firmly of the opinion that she would eat him and come up for more and consoled himself on the fact that it may well kill Ron's drunken romantic endeavours, or maybe not.

Getting it Done

The next morning Briggs drove into the back yard of the Police Station. Ron had made it before him. Maybe she had not been as demanding as expected. Ron's old Wolsely sagged in its bay like an old hen squatting on eggs. Briggs entered the canteen and Jones was at their usual table, studying the inside of a tea cup, reading the leaves no doubt. Briggs got a cup of tea and sat down opposite him. Ron was pale and sullen, almost like a blood donor who had attended too many times. "How did you get on mate?" Briggs enquired quietly.

Ron looked up from his studies, heaved a sigh. "Oh alright you know." Ron looked away almost evasive.

Briggs was impatient."Come on tell me, when is she going to feed him to us." Ron looked to either side and spoke quietly. "That's it you see, she wants another payment in the bank." Ron looked pained but not pleading. Briggs became cautious. Was he to be called upon to give his all in the cause of capturing Bobby? More importantly, would his all be enough?

"So I've got to do the business as well is that it?" Briggs spoke as quietly as Ron. Ron gave an enigmatic half smile.

"Well that's it you see, I tried to put you in, but she wants more of the same." Ron looked apologetic.

"Then you must old son. If you don't enjoy it, think of it as duty for Queen and country and all that garbage." Briggs' voice showed his relief that he would not after all have to engage in carnal combat with the mighty Christine. "Anyway she can't be all that bad, a bit rough maybe."

Ron shook his head, "Not the problem boyo. She's pleasant

enough, but big and energetic. That's what worries me, she swamps me. I can hardly breathe, and as for that fucking perfume, I got on the vinegar strokes and it made me sneeze." Briggs grinned at his friend's predicament.

"Anyway a cautionary word." Briggs leaned across the table. "Not a word to the others about Christine being our snout okay?"

Ron looked up, "Why's that then?" Cautious and quiet.

"Well we don't want them selling her name to Bobby and the others, do we?" said Briggs exhibiting his inbuilt distrust of others.

"Oh, I don't think they would do that." Jones was surprised and hurt on behalf of his brother officers.

"Well, just in case, we won't give them the opportunity to will we?" Jones nodded to Briggs' forcible stance as usual.

As they talked generalities, Briggs could sense that Jones was becoming comfortable in his role of sex machine, stroking the sauce bottle in a peculiarly phallic manner, and punctuating his comments with finger stabs in the air in a Freudian manner. "Anyway Tel, you don't know what it is like. After all, women don't find you attractive do they?" The imagined spectacle of Christine and Ron sprang before Briggs' mind and he was grateful that he was plain or ugly or both.

Ron's next deposit in the sperm bank was to be paid that evening, and all day Ron was ultra quiet, no doubt pondering his carnal fate and wondering maybe would he die in the breach. As Ron was preparing for his assignation, there was an in-depth conversation about the relative value of condoms in the war against venereal disease. "Are you sure it stops you getting VD?" Ron asked, plaintive and little boy like.

"I wouldn't know old son. After all, as you say, I am plain and dull and therefore never get a chance to find out," said Briggs leaving for home. A book crashed against the door behind him.

Briggs retired to his home, wife, kids and lunatic dog. About 11pm he received a phone call. It was Ron. "You alright mate?" Briggs, concerned.

"Bit tired maybe." Ron giggled, Briggs guessed he had enjoyed himself, "I'll be round in about ten minutes."

A short time later Ron appeared. He wore the satisfied grin of an old tom cat that Briggs once knew. "That's it boyo, she's given me loads of names and addresses. Bobby and his mates did a record shop a few nights ago, the gear's at these gaffs." He flourished a list of names and addresses,"and he's got a music centre at his and Christine's place." Ron was enjoying his moment of supreme manhood.

"Any more deposits required?" Briggs enquired with fingers crossed behind his back hopefully.

"No, no, Tel, put that end of things down to me." A vision of the old Wolsely bumping up and down in some secluded car park swam before Briggs' eyes. Jones was grinning, perhaps he had got used to being swamped, liked it even. "No point in sending a boy to do a man's job is there?" Ron looked searchingly at his buck, but Briggs was not biting today, content to be a boy in a real man's world.

Briggs could see no reason for Ron to hustle round and inform him of his success in the sexual gymnastics competition, unless imminent action was involved. Briggs looked to Jones who, by now, had noticed the scotch bottle on the sideboard. "When's it to be then Ron?" asked Briggs hoping to break Jones' concentration on the scotch.

"What?" Jones asked in monotone to the scotch bottle "The raids, when do we do them?" persevered the exasperated Briggs.

"She says we have to do Bobby and the girls early tomorrow, as Bobby is off to Wales to do something else." Jones spoke evenly to the scotch bottle.

"Would you like a drink Ron?" asked Maggie Briggs embarrassed at Jones' concentration on the scotch bottle, not understanding her husband's reluctance to offer a colleague a drink when he obviously desperately needed one.

"Yes love, a tea or coffee would be fine, fortify us all if we are going to work, won't it?" Briggs defending his scotch to the last drop.

"No dear, Ron deserves a real drink, after all he's been working hard, while you have been at home enjoying yourself." She smiled and got the glasses.

"Does she know, or is she just being pleasant," thought Briggs, and concluded that one rarely knew with women, they being a perplexing breed and what they say is very often what they don't mean. This probably explains Briggs' lifelong policy of being plain and ugly.

Briggs poured a measure into each glass and handed one to Ron, who accepted his after examining the contents. "What! Are we on an austerity drive Tel?" Jones holding his glass up for ridicule. "Well we don't want get drunk do we?" Briggs responded mimicking Jones' Rhondda accent. Ron snatched the bottle and poured a giant measure into his glass. Briggs winced. Maggie Briggs giggled.

Over several trips to the scotch bottle, Briggs and Jones decided the plan of battle for the following morning. Meet at the nick at 5am, borrow some woollies, brief them and the van driver, then cause mayhem and panic on the ground. Jones staggered off up the drive towards his trusty rusty Wolsely, a sheaf of papers under his arm. Briggs looked at his retreating back and thought he looked quite the mad professor. Well a stumbling drunken mad professor. Briggs wondered what the Justice of Peace would make of his buck when he swore out warrants later that night.

5am, parade room Rodney Road Police Station. The woollies were near the end of their night duty shift and attention span was diminishing. Jones looked awful, sex, no sleep and the ravages of the scotch taking their toll. "Right then listen up. Before we start the briefing proper, let me state that overtime has been authorised for this operation and it is under my hand as to exactly what time you book off." Jones paused to allow those almost asleep to focus their attention on their bank balances. "Should it be that you perform your duties without giving me a moment's problem, I feel fairly sure that by the time you are actually booked off you will be home in bed for a good two hours, or in someone's bed anyway," Ron paused and was pleased to see most of the heads come up and pay attention. He continued. "If on the other hand you give me shit service, I will make a mistake and book you off at 6.00am. Anyone not understand me?" Jones looked around the room. They were all sitting up straight and paying attention. Jones paused for anyone to say anything – silence. Briggs thought this was probably down to Jones' wild attitude. "Good we understand each other then." Jones shuffled his papers continuing without a pause "Now the situation is this. We have four search warrants to execute, the first being Bobby Collins, the second and third, mates of his, and the fourth being Dolly Bryant, that well known purveyor of gonorrhoea and syphilis."

"Do you mean she is a prostitute Sergeant?" asked Sims, a callow young probationer, who Briggs thought looked about fourteen.

"It's Constable actually, but call me Ron, and yes she is a tom. She runs a brothel – be a new experience for you. Stay by your senior Constable and you will be alright." Ron ended by smiling at the young copper to give him some confidence. "Right then, usual arrangement. Charlie you take the van to the front door with two (make it Sims and his guvnor), the remainder around the back. Briggsy and I will enter at the front. If we get into trouble the two at the front can bail us out. Likewise, if anyone tries to exit stage left from the back, just nick 'em and bring 'em round the front – right?" All nodded. "Then if DC Briggs and myself find any property, it's loaded into the van together with the prisoners, if any, and taken back to the nick. Do not list prisoners and property at this stage but straight out again and onto the next address where we will be waiting for you. Now do we have anyone who doesn't know what he is supposed to be doing?" Ron paused to give a response time to rise, but none did. "Right then mount up. We'll meet at Clapham High Street at its junction with Clapham Park Road, Bobby's place is just around the corner."

They all met up as planned. Briggs posted the back stop woollies where he thought Collins might appear. They, Jones, Briggs and the three in the van drove around to the front of the premises in time to see Collins disappear over a side wall, he being warned by some inbuilt sixth sense of the arrival of police. Jones leapt out of the car and pursued Collins. Briggs retraced their previous route as fast as the clapped out CID car would go and was in time to see Jones rugby tackle Collins in the middle of Clapham High Street. Briggs parked the car and wandered across the to the struggling scrabbling pair on the ground. Buses and cars whizzed by within inches. Briggs took hold of a clump of Collins' hair and hauled him to his feet and clamped an arm lock on Collins' arm. It was then that Briggs realised that Collins had no shoes on and was the cause of Collins screaming in pain. Also, by flinching he had increased the leverage of the arm lock.

"Leave off for fucks sake you're breaking my arm," screamed Collins, on tiptoe and in obvious pain. Briggs smiled pleasantly. Jones got up and dusted himself down. He was irritated. "What kept you?" he snapped.

"I was just admiring you in action. I am not surprised you are a success." Jones scowled at Briggs' jibe. Briggs hoisted Collins onto the arm lock, which was met with a scream of pain, and marched him across the road. "Come on Bobby, we have a warrant to search your gaff." Briggs noticed that he was walking as though on a bed of nails. He hadn't been so bothered when Jones was in pursuit.

Christine greeted them at the front door. "Get your fuckin hands orf him you slags!" She looked bedraggled – not quite the flash lady of the Crown and Greyhound a few nights earlier. Sleep lay in her eyes, her hair was tangled and uncombed, the nightdress was soiled and falling forward exposing her melonous breasts. "Either of you, I quite fancy either of you, but not both together as I'm no whore" Briggs thought wistfully.

"Don't worry Bobby, I'll get you a good brief. I'll get Mr. Spinks. He'll sort this lot out for you, don't worry." Christine was stroking Collins' shoulder as though trying to placate him. She had mentioned Spinks, a well known local solicitor whose main armoury in defence was one of verbals and fitting up. For this vast array of legal weapons he had been known to accept bent money on top of a legal aid brief. Briggs smiled to himself. Christine was really intent on doing her man down. Spinks was bad enough to get Bobby a good seven or eight years worth, taking his previous convictions into account.

They entered the small tumbledown building, Jones wandering around doing the searching and Briggs keeping the arm lock very firmly on Collins. Christine came up to Briggs. "You're just the type who enjoys all that, you arsehole." She nodded at the painful arm lock. Briggs looked deadpan and said nothing.

Jones made the search look good. He rummaged around under the stairs, in the kitchen drawers and, in the broom cupboard, he found a sawn off shotgun which, when examined, was found to be loaded. This was a bonus, Christine had not mentioned this as, probably, she knew nothing of it. Jones unloaded it and showed it to Collins. "Anything to say about this then Bobby?" asked Jones, holding the broken gun under his nose.

"Never seen it before – you pricks planted it," Collins snarled.

Then he screamed "Leave off for fucks sake!" as Briggs increased the force of the arm lock.

"That's unusual even for us, we always run around with sawn offs in the motor, don't we Tel?" Jones asked, looking to Briggs for reply.

"All the time." Briggs laughed. "Well that's you nicked anyway Bobby, I must caution you…" Jones stopped short as Bobby said. "Alright I know that bit don't I."

Briggs, with Collins attached, lumbered into the front room. The music centre was duly found behind the settee, exactly where Christine said it would be. It was still in its cardboard box. "What about this then Bobby? Where did it come from?" Jones pulling the case into the middle of the room.

"Bought it didn't I," Collins muttered.

"Did you now, who from?" asked Jones, patiently playing the game that always had to be played.

"Off an ice cream in a pub." (ice cream = freezer = geezer) Collins said it quietly and knowing, as he said it, that it was not going to help his cause at all. Briggs had often pondered the extreme lack of imagination which made them come up with this mythical man in pub routine – perhaps there was a man somewhere who had loads of gear and who knocked it out round the pubs of South London, but on the other hand….

"That's another charge Bobby, added to the sawn off, should be good for a sound seven or eight stretch." Collins' head went down, beaten. As he was being questioned, Christine stood behind him facing Ron. She winked at Ron, pulled her nightdress to one side and exposed a large breast. Briggs was immediately put in mind of St Paul's Cathedral. Jones coughed, smiled secretly and lost his concentration completely.

After the usual protestations from Bobby and the obligatory abuse from Christine in an effort to gain or preserve credibility, Bobby was cuffed, placed in the police van and whisked off to the factory in the manner to which he had become accustomed.

Three houses remained to be searched. The first two were occupied by henchmen of Collins. In each case the search went off as sweet as a nut and large amounts of electrical gear were recovered, which both occupants assured the officers were bought "off a man in a pub." They were all carted off to Rodney Road and lodged in cells.

This left Dolly Bryant's place. The team arrived outside her home, which was also her place of business. A dingy hovel, peeling paint and stucco, dirty cracked window panes and a backdrop of grey net curtains. The other houses in the street stood out in their comparative smartness. Briggs noticed that next door's front step was whitened. This sparked a memory of his mum blancoeing their front step and washing out the milk bottles until they sparkled so that "The neighbours would not look down on us." He suspected that, in this present case, being next door to a brothel was liable to bring out an excess of cleanliness in one.

After checking that the woollies were in their respective stations at the rear, Jones knocked on the front door. They waited. There was no response. Briggs looked at Ron – he was visibly wilting. He leaned up against the door jamb. "I don't think that was quite loud enough Ron, after all they have been at it all night." Briggs kicked the door several times until it rattled in its frame.

A voice came from inside "Alright, alright, I'm coming don't take the door down." Dolly screamed from the inside. She opened the door slightly, a foul stench escaped with the door opening. This made Briggs gag. She looked horrible. The remains of last night's make up was smeared across her face, her age was showing to her commercial detriment, as were most of the tools of her trade.

"What do you want Briggsy?" she sneered, coughing and blinking in the early morning light. Judging from the smells that wafted out of the place fresh air might be classed as a health hazard to an inhabitant.

"Business call Dolly but not yours dear." Briggs smiled his insincere "Please don't give me hard time" smile.

"You're not coming in here," she snarled, showing her broken stained teeth, which caused Briggs to reflect that her rumoured speciality was oral sex, and shuddered.

"I've got a warrant love," Briggs said evenly. Dolly pondered, she knew the score. If she didn't let them in she would be nicked anyway.

Eventually she said, "I'll let Mr. Jones in, he's a religious gentleman, but not you Briggsy cos you're a slag and one no-good bastard." Briggs could see that the easiest course was to let Jones go in on his own, thereby saving an out and out fight with Dolly.

Briggs turned to Jones, "Go on my son, your fame has spread."

Dolly stood at the foot of the stairs confronting Briggs who waited on the front step. Briggs studied Dolly, her arms crossed, just, over her flacid breasts, bare feet, body odour and the smell of stale urine. "How could anyone pay for this" Briggs wondered, "Perhaps she pays them." With such idle thoughts Briggs spent the few moments while Jones was out of his sight. Dolly and Briggs eyed each other like two wary tom cats. She was muttering threats and swear-words under her breath. The cause of all this enmity was that some weeks earlier Briggs had occasion to arrest one of her customers before he had received or paid for her services, so Briggs was a sort of business threat, not quite in the league of the VAT or Inland Revenue Service, but still a business threat for all that.

"Sorry about that the other week Dolly, but he was well wanted you know." Briggs, trying to convince her that he was a nice person really and that she had got him all wrong. Her erratic pencilled eyebrows arched. She flushed bright red, broke wind loudly and involuntarily. She shrugged her breasts into another position.

"You bastard," she screeched, "You don't want a working girl to earn a living." It was getting worse not better.

"You can't call this a living Dolly," Briggs said mildly, waving his hand around.

Dolly got redder. Briggs thought she might explode, or at the very least fart again, but she didn't. "I suppose you're going to ask me what a nice girl like me is doing on the game." Dolly was in full flood as Briggs was about to try a little humour to ameliorate the situation. She added "I bet you're a turd burglar." Briggs had never heard this term before and looked puzzled. "A poof you dumbo, I bet you're a poof."

"Not me Dolly, I've got piles," Briggs trying to calm her with his quick wit.

Dolly looked scornful, "Got piles have you? I hope they itch and you scratch your arse to pieces, you shit." Dolly was screaming at the top of her voice. Briggs gained the impression that she didn't like him very much, and that maybe silence might be the best course.

Suddenly Jones called, "Tel up here quickly." He sounded agitated and in fear. A vision of Ron grappling with some violent sex pervert swam before Briggs' mind, and thinking that maybe, just maybe, this was his moment when he would win the BEM for gallantry, Briggs rushed forward along the corridor intending to ascend the stairs at speed. Dolly grabbed a child's pushchair and threw it into Briggs' path causing him to crash to the floor. As Briggs was getting up, Dolly was at him, kicking and scratching. Briggs pushed her off and made for the stairs – marks on the face are difficult to explain and may give rise to such wifely comment as "She finally said no did she?" or perhaps, "You really ought to get a non-violent girlfriend."

In that moment, with his friend upstairs facing death or, at the very least, extreme danger, and him desiring to be decorated for gallantry, Briggs caught Dolly a full blow on the jaw which sent her spinning into the back bedroom with a crash. Briggs went up the stairs two at a time. Jones stood on the landing alone and composed. "Ron why the shout?" gasped Briggs slightly out of breath from his bout with Dolly. Jones laughed.

"Oh that, I thought you might need the exercise, or do we toss the coin for that as well?"

Briggs glared at Jones, too annoyed to respond. Dolly had recovered and was arguing the toss with young Sims, the probationer. Briggs called down to him "Nick her, put her in the van" which brought on the usual and expected wail, "Fuckin' hell, what for, I ain't done nuffink?" Dolly was plaintive and pleading, with a fast appearing bruised jaw.

"Sergeant, she says she hasn't done anything wrong," Sims called up the stairs.

Dolly, feeling there might be a chink in the armour of police solidarity, wailed, "Not only didn't I do nuffink, I've got a good hiding into the bargain. It's all down to that Briggsy, fucking animal he is." Briggs was exasperated, partly by the young copper, but mainly by Jones having him over.

"Listen mate do me a favour and exercise my power of arrest, got it, mine, and put that old tart in the van." Briggs shouted at the young officer, and was immediately sorry he had done so as Sims looked as though he was about to burst into tears. In a softer tone Briggs added "Go on then now, put her in the van, and you Dolly, don't give the young officer any trouble now." Briggs was satisfied as they disappeared from view.

Jones was standing by the door to the front bedroom. He raised his eyebrows at Briggs who nodded. Jones opened the door and they both walked into the room. The bed was behind the door facing towards the window. It had two occupants, one male who was endeavouring to be invisible under the bedclothes, and the obligatory tart, who was sitting upright holding the sheet to her chin as they do in all the best movies.

"Whatever do you want?" she cried, her eyes open in wonder, or surprise perhaps, a younger version of Dolly.

"Not you that's for sure darling, we have a warrant to search – now out the pair of you," Briggs shouted. He noticed that the sheet clinging girl flinched, the hiding Romeo shuddered. They both climbed out naked – well, almost – he still had his vest on in true English style. Briggs smiled. He had heard it said that if you watch a blue movie and the stud is wearing a vest he is English, and if he wears socks and a vest he is from the Walworth Road area. She had a poor figure and sagging breasts, hardly the stuff of masturbatory dreams. Briggs noted that Romeo's vest was soiled from his night's adventure and, together with his bald head and out-of-condition body, was hardly an Adonis. "Now get dressed both of you, unless you want to be down the nick naked." They shuffled around picking up pieces of clothing here and there. Briggs considered that the performance of undressing last night must fall into the frenetic activity class. Jones was rummaging under the bed. Briggs noticed the floor was wet, also that the dressing pair were paddling about in it, as well as having it on their clothes as they dressed. "What's that on the floor Ron, smells like piss." Briggs studying his shoes and also "Loves Young Dream" paddling about in it.

"It's piss Tel, I knocked the jerry over whilst getting this lot out," indicating a small pile of record players and records. Jones laughed at the predicament of them all. Whilst Jones and Briggs examined the stolen gear, Briggs could feel that Dolly Junior's customer was weighing them up.

Eventually he tapped Briggs on the elbow. "Will my wife have to find out, I'm supposed to be in Birmingham?" His eyes showed the terror of imminent discovery. Cruelly Briggs laughed at this discomfort.

"One thing's for sure old son, you would be less likely to catch clap in Birmingham, and now you're nicked as well." Briggs waved his arm at the growing pile of stolen property.

'Loves young dream' pulled himself up to his full height, which wasn't much over five foot eight inches.

"Now look here officer" he said pompously, "I know the Commissioner personally." Dressed, clean and smart, Briggs imagined he could be quite impressive, imposing even, but now with his trousers half on, the vest bearing the dishonourable badge of his night's adventure, the early morning sun reflecting on his bald pate and underlining his insipid features, he was anything but impressive.

"I didn't know the Commissioner came here as well, probably all he could afford on the money," Briggs joked and, in the worst taste, laughed at his own joke. Briggs did not see it in this light but just the fall to earth of this stuck up prick. Briggs enjoyed the situation immensely.

"Can't we sort this out officer? The Commissioner and I are members of the same charitable organisation, so things can be accommodated very discreetly and with no risk." Briggs had illusions as to the meaning of all this, he was being offered a bribe, with the Commissioner as a middle man. It would be nice if it could be arranged, as Briggs was sure this middle aged Romeo would never re-offend and would probably never again indulge in masturbation, never mind illicit sex, but the thought of Dolly's fast appearing bruise decided him.

"Certainly sir, for a friend of the Commissioner's, anything at all, including free transport to the nick." Briggs pushed the man towards the door. "Come on Romeo you're nicked." They finished dressing and went downstairs to the van like a couple off to the gallows.

The situation at Rodney Road was chaotic – property and prisoners everywhere. Briggs and Jones would be hours, if not days, sorting this lot out. "Well done you two, I booked you down as a pair of Ghurkas, just shows how wrong you can be." Jack the Hat delivered the closest thing to fulsome praise that ever came from him.

"Ghurka guv?" Jones puzzled at the description.

"We take no prisoners – Ghurka creed got it?" Jack the Hat enjoying spelling out the insult.

"Oh I see guv, immensely funny," Jones not amused at all and, to some extent showing it, his irritation going completely unnoticed by Jack the Hat.

"I wonder if I might have a word with you on a delicate matter?"

Briggs speaking quietly into Jack the Hat's ear. Jack the Hat did not reply but nodded towards the detention room which was empty. They walked across the charge room. Jack the Hat entered and pulled the door to. "Right then young Tel, what's the problem?" asked Jack the Hat, leaning up against the door jamb.

"No trouble guv, only the brothel customer who we captured in bed with a tom, reckons he's an old friend of the Commissioner, and how he's sure the Commissioner would dollop out some help if he was made aware of his friend's predicament," Briggs whispered to Jack the Hat. Briggs noticed that Jack the Hat's eyebrows arched at the mention of the Commissioner.

"And apart from dirty nastiness with a tom, what have we got against the Commissioner's pal – if that's what he is?" Jack the Hat asked expectantly of Briggs.

"Well guv, only that he was having his end away on a bed under which was stored bent gear, of which probably he had no knowledge" Briggs replied, awaiting the decision from Jack the Hat.

Jack the Hat made some notes on the back of an envelope. After he had noted the name and address he said, "Any form as such?"

Briggs hesitated. "No guv no actual convictions recorded. The problem with all this is that I had to give Dolly a slap and it has caused a rather heavy bruise to her face." Briggs was ashamed at having hit a woman.

"I bet she loves you then. Didn't you have a run in with her before, something about nicking one of her customers?" Jack the Hat laughing at Briggs' embarrassment "And why did we kick the shit out of this poor woman?"

Briggs paused. "Well guv, she threw a kid's pushchair at me and when I fell over she came at me tooth and nail." Briggs hoped against hope that Jack the Hat's questioning would not go any further and that he could conceal the fact that the whole violent episode was the result of a humorous wind-up by his buck.

"She no doubt being angry that you and Jones were going to search her pristine palace of love, the two of you having previously upset her by nicking one of her paramours, so to speak?" Jack the Hat arched his eyebrows waiting for a reply.

"That's about the size of it guv," Briggs relieved at having been able to conceal Jones' prank.

"So, if necessary we could say that the evidence against Dolly, the tart in bed and the Commissioner's friend (if that's what he is) is very slim, except of course, Dolly has assaulted a Police Officer in the execution of his duty – yes?"

"That's one way of putting it." Briggs was cautious.

"Right then, what we'll do to preserve the situation is, bail all three under Section 38(2) of the Magistrates' Courts Act to return to this nick after the conclusion of enquiries, those enquiries really being about whether the Commissioner knows him or not – agreed?" Jack the Hat looked to Briggs for affirmation.

"Agreed guv. I'll get on with getting rid of these three. I'll prepare the ground with Dolly for no action on the assault. That way at least we'll know if she's amenable. Just one problem guv, there is obviously an informant on this one, and I think it would be encouragement for the snout to receive a reward. I understand the insurance company on the shop in Clapham is up for ten per cent reward, but obviously we need your sanction guv." Briggs waited for Jack the Hat's decision, knowing what was likely before it came.

"Can't see a problem young Briggsy, providing of course the correct amount of respect is shown." Jack the Hat gave Briggs a meaningful look. Briggs nodded assent for himself and Jones. They left the detention room.

Briggs noted that Dolly was sitting on the bench in the charge room. He nodded Jones to leave and sat down beside her. "Right then Dolly my love, let's have a little chat," Briggs nudging up to the Queen of Body Odour.

"Don't you 'my love' me you shit, look at my boat." (Boat = boat race = face)

"Now come on Dolly, just for once try and be a bit sensible and listen to me as I am trying to do you a favour," Briggs said, giving his version of sympathetic and hopeful. He had wanted to add 'you dirty, filthy, disease ridden old tom' but decided against it as being counter-productive.

Dolly paused for a moment in thought. "A favour you say, what sort of favour?"

"Well" Briggs responded, elongating the word and pursing his lips. "How about you eventually walk away from the assault charge?" Dolly straightened up and was immediately very attentive.

"What about the dishonest handling charge?"

Briggs hesitated, he didn't want to be seen to be lenient or, by inference, soft. "Well, that as well. I can't promise obviously as it's not my decision, but the guvnor has mentioned the possibility, but obviously you must say that the assault is the result of a mistake between friends, otherwise no deal." Briggs could see that Dolly was very keen on the prospect.

"And say I go for all this, what's in it for you Briggsy?" She gave Briggs a sly look.

"Whatever Dolly, whatever. If in the future you fancy doing a bit of snouting I'll always listen to what you have to say," Briggs whispered the deal to her.

"Well." she said slowly, "I do not normally snout, but on this one occasion, provided of course we all walk, I will go to work for you and see where we go."

Briggs was relieved. He had hoped that Dolly would see things his way, but had doubted that that was possible due to the enmity between them, but here she was eating out of his hand. "Right then Dolly, what we'll do is to bail you to three weeks' time, during which the guvnor will make a decision."

The next day, Briggs and Jones were in the property store sorting and recording the property they had recovered when Jack the Hat came in. "Briggsy, about the geezer in bed with the tom, he is in the same outfit as the Commissioner and all concerned would be very pleased if he was released without charge so to speak." Jack the Hat waited for a reply.

"Of course guv, I have already sorted Dolly. She will say that it was all a big mistake between friends." Briggs laughed at the 'between friends' bit.

Jack the Hat laughed, almost giggled, with Briggs "And will she make a statement to that effect?"

"Yes, providing all three walk on the dishonest handling charge which of course they all will." Briggs waited and almost expected Jack the Hat to disagree.

Eventually he said, "You will not lose by this my son." He sounded almost priestly.

Briggs thought, "Neither will I gain very much either" but said, "Oh that's nice to know guv."

Some three weeks later, after Dolly, her lady of the night and the Commissioner's friend had surrendered to their bail, and whilst the sheets were being written down as "No crime – insufficient evidence" (Dolly having, of course, made her statement which exonerated Briggs' right fist from any evil intent) Jack the Hat suddenly called for the presence of Briggs and Jones in his office. On entering, they found Jack the Hat sitting behind his desk grinning. "The big house has shown it's appreciation." Jack the Hat then pulled an envelope from his inside pocket and handed it to Briggs. Briggs opened the envelope, it contained twenty pound notes. Briggs counted the notes. In all there was three hundred pounds present.

"That's handy," said Jack the Hat "It saves all that division and mental arithmetic. There are three of us and there is three hundred pounds, that doesn't take a lot of working out does it. Briggs divided the money out into one hundred pound lumps and gave one to Jack the Hat and Jones.

Jones said, "I am not sure about all this" looking at the hundred pounds nestling in his palm. "It does seem a bit on the warm side, know what I mean." Jones appeared like a little boy pleading with his head teacher.

"Listen Jones, you can regard this as a present from the Commissioner, it's actually from a mate of his, but it is absolutely Kosher as far as I can see. If you don't like it go out and give it to the poor or to that sanctimonious church you're always bleating on about." Jack the Hat was angry and Jones flinched at his harsh words,

"Well that is what I will do. I will make evil money do good works." Briggs suddenly realised the almighty struggles that went on in the mind of his partner.

"Good luck with your conscience" Briggs muttered.

Later in court Bobbie, because of the sawn off shot gun and his previous, received a ten stretch and his henchmen received three years. This cleared the way for Jones to continue his frequent 'questioning' of the snout with further successful results.

Murder – The Arrest

With her common law husband safely inside and without any hope of bail or remission, thanks to the legal ineptitude of Mr. Spinks, Christine really blossomed as an informant and, although the deal was still "I get laid, you get the information," there developed a strong bond between Christine and Jones. They took to having assignations in friends' flats and late night meals in out-of-the-way restaurants, all of which Briggs covered in case Jones' absence was noticed. Jones had got himself so deeply involved that Briggs rarely mentioned Christine, other than to comment on the high quality of her information and certainly never took the opportunity of winding Jones up on the subject, as Briggs was uncertain how this would be taken.

It was during this period of almost domestic bliss between Christine and Jones that a murder was committed. The offender was known, he having kicked an old drunk to death in the toilet of a local pub whilst engaged in the business of selling cannabis. Cocaine, heroin, crack, were at the time things of the future. The offender, Johnny Harris, an ex Para, fancied himself as the local hard man, although Briggs had, for a long time, suspected him of being just a bully, his exploits all being against the old, the young and the inexperienced. The main problem with Harris wasn't the supply of evidence linking him to the death of the drunk Gaffa Haynes, for there was ample coming forward from the licensee, his wife and the occupants of the pub at the materiel time, but that Harris' whereabouts were unknown, he having gone to ground. Thus it was not a difficult case. It just remained to find Harris, who given time, would surface somewhere and be nicked. However, in accordance with Metropolitan Police policy at the time, a murder squad would have to be formed under the stewardship of at least a Detective Chief Inspector, possibly higher, and the usual form gone through. It was accepted practice on these squads that, as and when the offender was nicked, the Officer-in-Charge would always be shown on the charge sheet as the officer arresting, irrespective of who actually 'felt his collar', that person only being accredited with bringing him to the station for the attention of the guvnor. In this case, the murder squad had moved into offices in Rodney Road, on the floor below the CID office, and had begun their enquiry under the leadership of Detective Chief Superintendent Bolton, the Divisional Detective Chief, who both Briggs and Jones accepted had merely moved onto this squad to gain another feather in his headdress for nicking a violent murderer. The Officer in Charge of the day-to-day running of the squad was Detective Inspector Wiseman, who really could not work up a sweat over Harris, knowing full well that Harris would put a foot wrong shortly and be nicked. In addition, even when nicked, no credit would be showered on Wiseman for any hard investigation work he had put into the case.

The information at the moment was that Harris had fled immediately after the offence to Chester, where he came from, and where his parents still lived. Consequently, two officers were dispatched to cover this aspect of the enquiry. Harris had not been near his room in the local doss house since the night of the offence and most of his personal gear was missing from the room. It was at this point, when the murder squad were not trying particularly hard and when the Officer in Charge of the enquiry was lying back and awaiting his undeserved moment of glory, that Christine, via Jones, came up with the address at which Harris could be arrested, he having moved in with a friend of Christine's, June Sheehan. Miss Sheehan had become thoroughly pissed off with Harris as a long term guest, even though, previously, he had been quite entertaining as an overnight bed partner. She had spoken to Christine as to whether she knew of anyone who could extricate her from this embarrassing position of harbouring a murderer, obviously without getting herself nicked for so doing.

Jones and Briggs had an in-depth conference about Harris and his location at the present time. One aspect which particularly worried

Briggs was had Christine's cover been blown? Jones was sure it had not but, in any case, after the event they would all assume that June Sheehan had blown the gaff. They agreed between them that they should inform Detective Inspector Wiseman and let him carry out the arrest, at the same time acquainting him with the situation regarding the informant, who obviously needed payment for this kind service. Thus the guvnor would get his body; they would not have to face Harris, just in case he was a real hard man, and Jones would get his paramour's expenses, or stud fee, as Briggs took to referring to it as – a happy solution for all concerned.

Briggs and Jones entered the Murder Squad offices. A number of officers were in the room, including Detective Inspector Wiseman who was sitting at the corner desk facing towards the office centre. Briggs and Jones went up to his desk. "Excuse me guv, DC's Briggs and Jones from upstairs." Briggs announced themselves deferentially, "Could we have a word?" Wiseman looked up, put his pen down on his blotter, (Briggs noticed it was a "Moffatt" pen – nice to know he hadn't missed the boat).

"Yes, what do you want?" He was both surly and superior which, Briggs thought, being a Detective Inspector he supposed he was. Briggs noticed that he also had a silk handkerchief in his top pocket, a la Bolton. He also had a framed photograph of his wife and kids on the desk. It was rumoured that he was a protégé of Bolton's but Briggs didn't expect it to be so obvious. He felt like asking if one of the squad had nicked his specimen glass that should contain a single rose, but of course he didn't.

Instead he said, "It's about Harris guv. We know where he is, location on the ground."

"And how do you pair come to know that?" Wiseman's question was almost a sneer.

"Well guv we have an informant who says…" Briggs got no further.

"I have heard about you and your informants. Mr. Bolton mentioned it the other day." Wiseman almost bowed as he mentioned the golden name which he hoped was going to enable him ride to higher things. "You're both full of bullshit. I know Harris is in Chester and I have my best men on the job – Detective Constables Barking and Hobbs. They'll bring him back." Briggs was stunned by Wiseman's arrogance but, thinking on it afterwards, was not unduly surprised.

"Look guv, Harris is not in Chester. He's here, on the ground, gone to earth so to speak and we know where," Briggs anxious to give away a body for murder. Wiseman was right on one thing, Briggs did not relish taking on Harris just in case he was a real handful – always better to let someone else do the fighting if you can.

Wiseman studied both Briggs and Jones and chuckled, "If you know where he is you go and nick him. I'm not getting involved in any of your wild goose chases, got it?" Wiseman resumed his examination of a piece of paper on his desk. Briggs breathed deeply trying to control his temper.

"Right guv, that's what we'll have to do and, as he's wanted official, shall we take the details for the charge off the crime report?"

Wiseman looked up again, "Not a lot of point in discussing it really, but yes okay, take the details from the crime sheet," Wiseman showing his exasperation with this conversation. "But you two haven't the bottle to take on Harris, even if he is here – which he isn't." Briggs leaned over the desk and spoke very quietly.

"We'll find out about bottle later on guv, both yours and mine."

"Leave it Tel." said Jones nervously, feeling his partner's anger beginning to climb out of his collar.

"What was that you said Briggs?" asked Wiseman, aware that Briggs had said something and that it was threatening, but couldn't quite catch it. "What was that you said to me Constable?" Wiseman beginning to get on his high horse of rank and maybe ride it around for a while.

"Nothing of importance sir," Jones ushering the angry Briggs out of the office. "Just that we will leave Harris in the cells for your attention." Jones almost pushed the red faced Briggs out of the Murder Squad office.

Once in the privacy of the CID office, Briggs exploded. "The bare faced cheek of that Wiseman, he's so far up Bolton's arse he's looking out of his belly button." Briggs slammed his chair against the desk and stood fuming.

"Never mind, whatever, it doesn't matter" said Jones, placating Briggs. "He's given us permission to nick and charge Harris, let's leave it at that." Jones returned to his desk and picked up the phone.

"I'll ring Christine and tell her that we'll be round tonight, okay?"

Briggs nodded, "Tell her to tell that Sheehan bird to be out all night. We will call about 11.30." Briggs looked to his partner for confirmation.

Jones nodded and dialled the number which would always give him erotic thoughts. "Hello love, er no I'm not on my way round, can you give that Sheehan bird a ring and get her to be out all evening." Jones paused and smiled whilst listening to the reply. "Yes, of course we will be careful and, anyway, I think Briggsy likes to go in first" Jones added, nodding hopefully at Briggs. "You know I do, of course I do love." Jones kissed into the handset in farewell. Briggs erupted into laughter once the handset had been replaced, his anger finally dispelled by this drivel.

"Will you include all this in your next sermon on the sins of the flesh Ron?" enquired Briggs getting his truncheon and handcuffs from his locker. "Nothing wrong in bringing a little light and pleasure to someone's life is there? replied Jones, grinning in remembrance of sexual gymnastics.

"I don't think the church elders think you should blow it out of the eye of your whelk and enjoy it all quite so much mate," Briggs continued, stowing his aggressive tools about his person. "You'd better get tooled up as well Ron, you never know, he might just be a handful, can't see it though."

Jones busied himself at the back of his locker trying to find truncheon and handcuffs. Eventually Jones located and presented a pair of ancient handbolts, but without a key. This effectively means that once the prisoner is manacled, they can't be undone without a blacksmith's assistance. "I can't find my truncheon and someone's swiped my ratchet cuffs and left these," Jones dismally holding up the relics.

"Okay, leave it, we'll go with mine. If he comes through me then you hit him with your handbag," Briggs added grimly.

Ron left Briggs making up case files of those who had already been fed through the sausage machine of justice. Whilst Ron made a fleeting call on Christine to keep her happy, Briggs' warning hung in his ear, "Don't expend too much energy my old son, we might need you to be energetic in upholding the law for a change." Briggs spoke without looking up. Jones scowled and left.

Briggs and Jones spent a quiet half hour in their personal pub before closing, having a beer or two. In the public bar, the darts crowd were getting noisy and singing. One of their number, 'Soapy Cussons', shouted across to them, "Oi Briggsy, fitted anyone up today?" The assembled darts team roared at his expression of foolhardiness.

"Don't take offence Tel, he's just had too much to drink, just a wind-up, nothing in it like" Bill Drewery, the licensee trying to pour oil on troubled waters. Briggs smiled, but in heart seethed.

"That's alright Bill, I quite understand. I have kids of my own at home." Briggs looked at his watch." About time we made our way Ron." He then put his hand in his pocket and pulled out a note. Briggs then beckoned the flousy barmaid to him. She waltzed over. "Yes." She spoke more with her eyebrows. "Get me large scotch will you love?" She nodded, got the drink, Briggs paid over his money, got the change. He said quietly to the girl, "Do us a favour love, give this to Soapy over there." The barmaid looked puzzled but took the drink anyway. Briggs and Jones made their way towards the door and, holding it open, Briggs looked across the bar at Soapy and friends. Soapy stood there puzzled and mesmerized holding the glass as though it was a used condom. "Thanks a lot for that favour Soapy, worked a treat." Briggs grinned and waved, then they both left quickly, got into Jones' car and clattered off into the night.

"That was a shitty trick Tel," Jones' conscience getting to him. "He'll probably get a good kicking out of that scotch."

"He laughed at us and now I am laughing at him – seems eminently fair to me," Briggs studying the street names as they went along.

They arrived outside the address which Christine had given them. A big four-storey Victorian building, all now bed-sits. Briggs studied the name boards next to the bell pushes and pressed one marked 'caretaker'. Eventually it was answered by an elderly man who wheezed and had the open-mouthed attitude of an emphysema sufferer. "Whad'ya want?" he panted, releasing a hacking cough full of bad breath in their direction.

"Department of Health and Social Security come to check on Miss Sheehan's residence." Briggs flashed his warrant card, but not long enough for the man to read it. "She does live here doesn't she?"

The man hesitated. "Er yes, that's right, third floor front, flat C." The caretaker seemed at ease with Briggs' questions "Why, is she in trouble then?"

"No just checking on address records. She's made an application for an additional benefit." Briggs indicated the sheaf of papers held by Jones. "We'll just pop up and have a word."

The old man moved aside and allowed them to enter. They walked slowly up the stairs as befits men from the Ministry and arrived outside the door marked 'C'. Jones gently put his ear to the door. He shook his head at Briggs and whispered, "The telly's on. I can't hear anything else." Briggs nodded. He reached into his inside pocket and extracted a small leather wallet and indicated to Jones to hold his hands out. Jones put his file of papers on the floor and held his hands open in the form of a table. Briggs laid the wallet on Jones' hand and opened it up. There was displayed an extensive selection of picklocks. Briggs selected two, pre-loaded the cylinder lock and jiggled the tumblers with the other picklock. There was a slight click and the lock opened. Jones closed the picklock wallet and placed it in Briggs' side coat pocket. Briggs nodded an enquiry at Jones. Jones nodded. Briggs flung open the door and they both entered quickly.

Harris was sitting down, watching television. He jumped up and grabbed a small baseball bat and, without a word, came towards them, bat raised. Harris swung the bat at Briggs who stepped under the blow and hit Harris a heavy blow to his left eye, making sure that his thumb came in contact with the eyeball. Harris dropped the bat, screamed and placed both hands over his injured eye. "You bastard you've blinded me," Harris screamed. Whilst his hands were engaged, Briggs kneed him in the testicles and Harris immediately transferred his hands to his nuts, screamed again, and fell to his knees. Briggs pulled his truncheon out and hit Harris across the back of his head with it. There was a resounding 'thunk' as wood came in contact with cranium and Harris fell forward unconscious. Jones rushed forward and examined Harris.

"Is he dead?" asked the worried Jones.

"Too bad if he is, shouldn't piss about with baseball bats should he?" Briggs knelt and felt Harris's jugular. His heart was pounding along quite healthily.

"Give us a hand Jonesy." Briggs pulled Harris's arms behind his back. Jones held them and Briggs put the cuffs on. Briggs rolled him over and tapped his face. "Come on Harris, wake up, we've all got to go down the nick, now do come along." Harris was now groaning and swearing. Together Jones and Briggs hauled him to his feet. Harris stood with head hung. "You alright mate?" Briggs enquired. "You with us yet?"

"Wait till you let me out of these cuffs, I'll show you if I'm alright you arsewipe," Harris spitting anger and venom. Briggs took hold of Harris's testicles and yanked them up and held them.

Harris screamed as Briggs whispered menacingly, "Now listen to me very carefully, keep a civil tongue in your head or life is going to become very painful for you my old son. You're probably the business with old men in dark toilets but this is a different game see?" Briggs gave Harris's testicles a tug upwards and let go just to emphasize the point. Briggs could see the sweat standing out on Harris's forehead as he fell to his knees. "Come on up. I think you like it on your knees, must be a Catholic." Together Jones and Briggs pulled him to his feet again.

"Right then, are we going to be friends or enemies, shithead?" Briggs said, as he was holding Harris by the elbow, the other hand poised to take possession of sore bruised testicles.

"Friends," muttered Harris.

"If we are going to be true friends, let me enlighten you on one of my philosophies of life," Briggs chatted amiably. "I don't give any shit and I don't take any either, especially not from a prick like you. When we get to the nick we can make special arrangements if you fancy your chances, but you let me know yes?" Harris nodded, subdued and in pain.

They led Harris down the stairs. The caretaker stood at the bottom, still wheezing. "I told her she shouldn't have someone staying with her permanent like."

Briggs smiled, "Quite right, we'll just whiz him down the local office and stop his benefit, shan't we Mr. Jones?" Jones smiled and nodded. The caretaker shuffled to his flat.

On arrival at the Police Station, Harris was placed in the charge room. Jones kept him company whilst Briggs called the custody sergeant. On entry into the charge room the custody sergeant sat down behind his desk. Briggs said, "Sergeant this is John William

Harris of no fixed abode. We have arrested him this evening for the murder of Henry Haynes in the toilets of the Rising Sun Public House on the evening of Thursday, 17th July 1971. When arrested he made a determined attempt to resist arrest and assaulted both DC Jones and myself. I therefore request he be charged with murder, resisting lawful arrest, and assault on police."

Almost before Briggs had finished his monotone, the custody sergeant said, "Granted. Harris come here and stand before me." Harris hobbled over and demonstrated that he was still feeling very sore. The custody sergeant rumbled out the charges in time honoured fashion and cautioned Harris, who made no comment. The sergeant explained that he, Harris, was entitled to a solicitor. Again Harris made no comment.

"Right then who is arresting officer?" the custody sergeant asked with pen poised. Briggs felt that Jones was about to announce his intention of claiming the fame and glared at him. Jones coughed apologetically for his mutinous thoughts.

"I am, sergeant, ably assisted by Detective Constable Jones." The custody sergeant made a note on the charge sheet.

"Right then uncuff him and put him in the cell." Briggs and Jones looked at each other.

Briggs spoke to Harris. "Right my old son, we are going to uncuff you, if you fancy your chances just go for it, but if you do I promise you a hospital breakfast. Do you understand?" Harris's head went down and he nodded.

Briggs unlocked the handcuffs and took them off. He took Harris by the arm and led him to the cell. As he was being put into the cell Harris said, "What will I get for this lot then?"

Briggs leaned against the open door. "You must know that if you go down for murder there is only one punishment – life imprisonment and, as far as I can see, you will cop just that." Harris sat down; he winced as his sore testicles came in contact with the bench.

"How did you know where I was?" he muttered. "Was I grassed?"

"Well let's put it this way, we didn't call by chance, did we?" Briggs slammed the cell door and checked that it had locked.

He joined Jones in the canteen. "Not a bad day's work Jonesy. Do your pocket book now and I'll sign it." As an afterthought, Briggs said, "Make sure you put his CRO number (Criminal Record Office) underlined in red." This ploy was an insurance against any smart brief calling their notebook into question for, to do so, they would have to admit that their client had a criminal past. The usual form was that the brief would ask for the pocket book, examine it, see the red underlined CRO number and give the book back without comment. Together, over the canteen table, they compiled the notes of evidence to the night's events. When finished, Briggs read them over and initialled them. "Right then before we go off duty, we'll leave a little note for Detective Inspector Wiseman." They both smiled an evil smile.

Briggs left the note on Wiseman's blotter. It read, "As ordered, Harris is in custody downstairs, charged with murder and other offences – signed Terry Briggs, Detective Constable."

No comment was ever made by Wiseman or Bolton, directly to Briggs or Jones but, through gossip, it was learnt that neither of them was happy with the situation especially when Jones' informant's report hit their desks.

Up the Bailey

Briggs looked up at the vaulted roof. It was lofty, dusty and definitely in need of a coat of paint. He paced the corridor waiting to give his version of the evidence. Sounds echoed eerily around him, barristers and instructing solicitors scuttled about the place, as such, lost in their own thoughts, as he was. Jones was in the box giving evidence. Briggs sincerely hoped that this wasn't the occasion when he truly found God and told the truth, the real truth, or they would both end up gripping the bars instead of that animal Harris. Harris's relatives and friends were in the corner opposite, eyeing him and talking quietly amongst themselves. One big man kept looking at him and motioning towards the gents' toilet. Obviously he wanted to talk, or perhaps structure some sort of deal, but it was too late for all that nonsense and Briggs kept blanking the invitation.

A shambling drunk, one Harry Lambert, had given his evidence of stumbling over the broken, barely alive, bleeding body in the gents' toilet of the Rising Sun Public House. Surprisingly, he had been quite good as, for once, he wasn't only sober but completely dried out. The barmaid and the licensee's wife could both remember Harris and Haynes being in the bar at some time during the evening, also that Haynes had slagged Harris off for being a drug dealer and user. The licensee's wife had hotly denied that her pub had ever been used for exchanging drugs for money and further described both the victim and alleged assailant as being 'jolly' but not drunk, as there is a separate offence of 'allowing drunken persons to frequent the premises' under the Licensing Act – so, not 'pissed' but 'jolly'. When he heard this, Briggs smiled. He could never quite understand this offence as there can be no other result of drinking beer and spirits than ending up pissed to one degree or another.

The forensic scientist had found an imprint of Harris's boot on Haynes' head, where Harris had stamped on him. Blood from Haynes had been found on the bottoms of Harris's trousers. Briggs personally thought this might have been planted by some over-enthusiastic Murder Squad Detective but didn't see that it mattered, Harris had it coming anyway. Then Jones had been called and was still in court. Briggs looked through the porthole in the doors and saw Jones bobbing and weaving under heavy fire from the defence barristers. He definitely did not look comfortable. Briggs crossed his fingers.

Briggs fidgeted. He checked his dress for the umpteenth time, also his flies – wouldn't do for jury to get an eyeful of his old chap. His father had always advised, "Got something to do which tests your bottle, tighten your boot laces and your belt and you'll be okay." Well here he was, bottle under extreme test and his shoes laces were singing with strain, as was his belt. He certainly felt no more courageous, less in fact, now he was uncomfortable as well as being about to give evidence before His Honour Judge Hiscock, a fearsome red coat Judge who had a reputation for chewing off PCs a dozen at a time. "Did he really make that PC leave the job?" Briggs wondered.

"Call Detective Constable Briggs" – the usher's deep brown voice rang round the corridor. Briggs straightened himself, breathed deeply, "I'm on," he thought and entered through the glass panelled doors. Jones passed him on his way out. "As per pocket book – no changes," Jones whispered. Briggs walked along the gallery behind the jury box. Heads craned around to look at him. The carpeted gallery felt like cotton wool beneath his feet. The elderly lady with the twenties hat at the end of the jury box turned and smiled at him but it seemed that everyone else in the court glared at him. Briggs pressed on, turned left at the end of the jury box and started to descend the steps to the well of the court. The Judge was up high on his perch. He glared over his half moon glasses.

"Come along officer don't keep the court waiting." Briggs was looking around as he descended and was so intent on being impressed and terrified that he missed the last step completely and cannoned into counsel's table, knocking his carafe of water over and onto himself as fell down with a crash. There followed what can only be described as a stunned silence about the court. Briggs got up, brushing the water from his newly cleaned Marks and Sparks suit. Defence counsel, the dreaded Roger Ashburn, broke the spell.

"Oh dear my lord, the officer seems to have taken a fall from grace." The court erupted in laughter which heightened Briggs' embarrassment.

"Are you alright officer?" His Honour asked, peering from his lofty lair.

"Yes my lord," Briggs managed to mutter. A stray giggle could be heard rattling around the back of the court.

"You are giving evidence before me for the first time young man?" his lordship giving his version of a pleasant smile, but it was lop-sided, probably due to lack of use.

"Yes my lord," Briggs pleading for understanding and kindness maybe.

"Well I doubt you will ever forget it." His lordship's head went back and he cackled at his version of wit, and the assembled court duly roared in unison as if on cue. Briggs stood disconsolate. "Well, as with most things of this nature, try and put it behind you and come and give me some evidence to take your mind off it." His lordship waved a withered hand at the witness box which towered above Briggs, almost on a level with his lordship.

Briggs made his way up towards the witness box. The court usher was tucked away in her little alcove at the back of the box, smiling a sympathetic smile as he passed. He arrived before the lectern. Jones' notebook was on the top of the ledge. The usher handed him the testament and the card on which was printed the oath. Briggs recited the oath, gave his name and rank and station and looked around the court. They were all laughing or grinning at him, or he thought they were.

His lordship broke the spell. "Well now officer, after your adventures, you're here, so perhaps we could have some evidence from you." His voice had the crackling quality of ice. His lordship coughed. "Was he covering a laugh; were they all about to cascade again into laughter?" but they didn't.

Prosecuting counsel, whose name Briggs never knew, led him

through his evidence, prompting him this and that to elicit all the salient facts. He glossed over the actual arrest, "suffice it say officer, it is true, is it not, that there was a violent struggle when Harris was arrested?"

Briggs replied, "Yes my lord" as firmly as he could.

"Just wait there will you officer." The prosecuting counsel sat down. Briggs, shorn of his protection, stood and quivered with fear but desperately tried not to show it. That stilton ploughman's lunch and its accompanying pint of best bitter was having disastrous effects on his stomach and lower bowel. This was all accentuated by the thought of being cross-examined by the fearsome Roger Ashburn QC. Briggs felt an urgent need to break wind and clenched his buttocks together to prevent the worst excesses of noise. There was little he could do about the lavatorial aroma accompanying the fact. There was a discernible squeak of wind which was prolonged by the clenched buttocks. The usher sitting behind him suddenly found some urgent task which called her attention to another part of the court. Briggs didn't think anyone heard his strangulated fart – or did they?

The dreaded Roger Ashburn QC rose slowly from his bench. In standard custom he shrugged his gown around his shoulders and adjusted his old grey wig. He paused and fixed Briggs with the cold stare of an arch enemy.

"Officer, you have told us that you used force on my client." He waved without looking at the dock.

"Yes my lord." Briggs directed his reply to the Judge as was the proper course. His Honour nodded and smiled almost as if he agreed with the course of action.

"You firstly hit him in the left eye – is that right?" Ashburn held his head on one side as though deaf in one ear.

"Yes my lord." Briggs was trembling, but not showing out.

"How hard did you hit him officer?" Ashburn again tilted his head, this time accompanied by a cobra smile.

Briggs spoke slowly and firmly. "As hard as I possibly could my lord."

Ashburn paused and screwed his face into his concentrated searching look. "Was it absolutely necessary to hit him quite so hard? After all, you are a big man, could you not have overpowered him in some other way?" Ashburn stared coldly into Briggs' eyes.

Briggs smiled and said. "Well I don't see how sir. It was all so quick. He had a baseball bat." Briggs got no further.

"I didn't ask you that officer" roared Ashburn.

"But if it's true we should hear it shouldn't we?" Not waiting for an answer from Ashburn his lordship continued to bat for the good guys. "He had a baseball bat you say officer? What was he doing with this bat thing?"

"He was coming towards me with it raised as though to strike me my lord." Briggs said it slowly and firmly

"And you, realising that you were about to be struck, hit him first is that it?" asked his lordship giving a knowing smile.

"Yes my lord," Briggs replied, happy to be under the protection of the most powerful person present.

"I see," His lordship made a note. "Please carry on Mr. Ashburn." He waved at the dreaded Ashburn and unleashed him.

"You hit my client on the left eye. Do you realise that my client had to have surgery to save that eye after it had been damaged by you?" Ashburn waited with a look of blunt belligerence.

Briggs yearned to say, "I wish I had taken the prick's head off" but instead said, "No sir, I wasn't aware of that."

"Well that is a fact. The point I am making is that this assault by you was surely enough to overpower him, but you did not leave it there did you officer?" Ashburn added darkly.

Briggs felt another blast of bitter and stilton coming on and stood on one leg in an effort to control it. "No sir I did not" he replied, half his attention on his suppressed flatulence.

"Perhaps you would enlighten us as to what you did next" asked Ashburn coldly.

"I kneed him sir." Briggs said it ever so quickly so perhaps no-one would notice.

"I see, you kneed him. Where exactly did you knee him?" Ashburn asked the question in the pleasant tone of one about to deliver a crippling blow.

"In the testicles sir." There were gasps from the public gallery. Someone, obviously one of Harris's cohorts or relatives, shouted "You arsehole Briggs, you've got it coming" – a strangely prophetic announcement. The shouter found himself being ushered out by the city copper on duty in the public gallery. Briggs looked across at the jury. The middle-aged guy sitting back left had his arm across the back of his neighbour resting on the top of the jury box. He slowly lifted his hand to the thumbs up position and smiled at Briggs.

"In the testicles!" roared Ashburn, "in the testicles!" feigning incredulity. He threw his brief down in the usual theatrical manner and looked meaningfully at the jury.

"Yes sir, I kneed him in the testicles" Briggs affirmed in a matter-of-fact tone.

"And what did he do then?" asked Ashburn, quietly and expectantly.

"Well my lord, he transferred his hands from his eyes to his testicles," Briggs answered looking directly at the jury.

"And what did you do then?" Ashburn questioned with bated breath. Briggs answered slowly and with definition.

"I took my truncheon out and knocked him unconscious my lord." This bald statement was followed by a stunned silence. Ashburn acted it as being a reasonable barrister. He knew the answer to the question before he asked it but the court, jury and onlookers if you like, were stunned. The young lady sitting behind the prosecution counsel, who Briggs thought might be a bit of spare for the benefit of prosecuting counsel, was open-mouthed.

Eventually, after a suitably theatrical pause, Ashburn said, "My lord, surely this officer has overstepped the mark? He has abused my client and has damaged his health in so doing." The Judge looked up as though awakened from a short nap. He ignored Ashburn and turned his attention to Briggs. "Officer, tell me again, when you entered that room Harris lunged at you?" His lordship waited expectantly.

"Yes my lord," answered Briggs, compliant and realising that this wizened old man was firmly on his team.

The Judge smiled pleasantly – sort of. "What do you think his intentions were when he did that?"

"That he intended me some personal injury my lord," Briggs with all the certainty of truth.

"So you were defending yourself initially and then overpowering him so that an arrest could be effected?" His lordship made a note.

"That is correct my lord" Briggs said firmly.

The Judge continued. "From your enquiries, had you formed an impression of this man's attitude to police?" scribbling in his book without looking at Briggs.

Briggs was getting more confident by the second.

"And what did you ascertain that attitude to be? Be careful how you answer," his lordship advising caution not to disclose any of Harris's many convictions.

Briggs thought deeply as to how to construct his answer. He was aware of Harris's convictions for violence and possessing offensive weapons etc, but confined himself to, "I ascertained him to be an extremely violent person who hates police."

Ashburn leaned forward anticipating the disclosure of Harris's convictions, but it was not to be.

"So then officer, you formed the opinion that if you did not overcome this man physically he could injure you?" queried his lordship inclining his head towards Briggs.

"Yes my lord."

The Judge continued, "And therefore leave himself open to a further charge or charges?"

Briggs nodded. "Yes my lord." Briggs looked across at the jury box; the middle aged chap who had earlier given Briggs the thumbs up, winked at him. The elderly lady who had the strange hat gave him a look that she hadn't used since she was a young girl.

"Mr. Ashburn, I think I may be of some service in the saving of time in this matter. It is my view that this officer acted in the best interests, firstly and most importantly, of his own well being, and secondly, of the hallowed traditions of the force."

The Judge looked icily at Ashburn who replied, "I am obliged to my lord for his valuable assistance in this matter." Ashburn seemed to be speaking through gritted teeth. "I may of course raise this matter before another court and I will be referring to this incident again when dealing with this officer's brutal treatment of my client."

"Yes of course Mr. Ashburn, please carry on." All this ruthless politeness was quite beyond Briggs.

Ashburn again adjusted his robe, proving that the action was the exercise of long practised habit. "Now officer, perhaps you will be good enough to tell me how you gained entrance to this house in the first place." Ashburn was now smiling like the proverbial

Cheshire cat.

Briggs braced himself for further onslaught. "Yes sir, I told the caretaker that we were officers from the Department of Health and Social Security and wanted to see Miss Sheehan," Briggs with the open face of one telling the truth.

"So you went in by subterfuge?" Ashburn hissed the word and glared malevolently at Briggs.

"Yes sir" replied Briggs, with the open aimlessness of innocence.

"Don't you regard that as cheating?" Ashburn lowered his voice and studied his brief as though some fact had been missed. Briggs considered the possibility for a second or two.

"No sir, I do not regard that as cheating," said Briggs, with as much certainty as he could muster.

"Allow me to summarise. You tell lies to get into a house to arrest my client and you don't think there's anything wrong in that?" Ashburn waited expectantly.

Briggs thought, "Was there something wrong in it, has this arsewipe got me?" However he cleared his mind and replied, "No sir, I do not think there is anything wrong in that." Briggs spoke with more certainty than he felt.

"Officer, do you go about your duty telling lies willy nilly to the public?" Ashburn smiled his horrible smile.

"Well no sir, it has to be for a special reason," Briggs becoming unravelled by the second.

"I see, a special reason eh officer? I suppose coming to court could be viewed as a special reason. Are you lying now as you were lying then?" Ashburn delivered the sucker punch with aplomb.

"No sir, most definitely not sir," said Briggs hotly. "I am not lying sir."

Ashburn adjusted his wig and looked confidently at the jury, "And how do we ascertain the difference? You are the sole guardian of the truth, is that it? When you say it's the truth it is and when it's not it's not, is that it?" roared Ashburn.

"No sir, no sir that's not the case at all," Briggs almost pleading.

"Mr. Ashburn." His lordship spoke and took the sting out of what Ashburn was about to say. "Perhaps I might assist you once again in this matter." His lordship now sounded a bit testy, but smiled the sweetest smile at Ashburn, who didn't seem unduly affected by it.

"Officer you have already told us that you ascertained that Harris was a violent man; extremely so I believe you said?"

"Yes my lord." Briggs was relieved once again to be under the protection of the most powerful man in the place. His lordship almost grinned at Briggs.

"Is there some connection between that realisation and your subterfuge which operated against the caretaker?" Briggs suddenly realised that this bewigged old man was throwing him a lifeline.

"Oh yes my lord, I wanted to catch him unawares."

His lordship nodded, "So you would have the advantage in any forthcoming confrontation no doubt?"

"Absolutely my lord," Briggs relieved that he had been assisted out of this tight corner.

"So you thought it through and decided that you must keep the advantage throughout or maybe you wouldn't be able to effect an arrest and this man would escape justice?" The Judge inclined his head to enforce the question.

Briggs answered in a relieved voice, "Yes My lord."

His lordship turned to Ashburn. "Mr. Ashburn it is my view that had this officer announced his identity, ab initio, he may have been putting himself and his colleague into danger, and therefore I support his action." Briggs felt that had the Judge had a gavel he would have banged it at this point.

Mr. Ashburn stared stonily at the Judge. "I am obliged to his lordship for again assisting me in this matter." His lordship inclined his head and smiled in acknowledgement. Briggs had the definite impression that the Judge would have none of it as regards impugning his officers.

"Now officer" Ashburn said, on returning to his feet, after referring to his notes. "After you had arrested my client, I understand you communicated with him by causing pain in his testicles by holding them very tightly?" Briggs felt that Ashburn got some sexual emotion from asking this question and he laughed to himself, partly at the thought of Ashburn getting off on the prospect of squeezed testicles, and partly at the question.

"No my lord, I did not squeeze his testicles," said Briggs grinning.

"Officer you may laugh but these are my instructions. You squeezed his testicles and said," Ashburn looking down at this brief and reading from it, "Keep a civil tongue in your head, or life is going to get painful – got it prick?" Ashburn looked unexpectantly at Briggs.

"I certainly never said that my lord," replied Briggs straight-faced and excused himself as it was not an exact quote of what he did say – not that that would have effected anything other than complete uproar.

"My client will say that, when you released his testicles he fell to the floor and had to be helped to his feet by you and officer Jones. That is the situation isn't it?" Ashburn again quoting from his brief.

"That did not happen my lord" denied Briggs, brassing it out.

"I see, my client is in error according to you," Ashburn waiting.

"Yes my lord he is" Briggs replied with certainty.

"How is it that you came to call on my client at such an unusual hour?" Ashburn tilted his head to one side, adjusted his wig and shrugged his gown in the manner of one practicing an ingrained habit.

"Our actions were the result of information received my lord," replied Briggs knowing the next step.

"From whom did you receive this information?" Ashburn looked at a point above his lordship's head, staring as though reading something.

"I understand I do not have to answer that question, unless directed to do so by His Honour." Briggs looked to his, by now old friend, the Judge.

"He's quite right you know Mr. Ashburn, unless you can show that details of the information are essential in some material respect to your client's case, I shall not order disclosure." Mr. Ashburn nodded his understanding, if not assent.

"Now officer Briggs. When you got to the flat you opened the door by artifice, not by a key as such but you, in fact, picked the lock?" Ashburn looked towards Harris in the dock.

"Yes my lord that is so."

"I would have thought that the necessary skill which enabled one to pick locks would not have been taught in a Police Training School, am I right?" Ashburn made a note on his brief.

"Yes my lord counsel is right," Briggs acting as though on the defensive.

"You were born, were you not, in Central London?" Ashburn reading from the preamble on Briggs' statement.

"Yes my lord."

"And brought up in which area?" Ashburn was still looking down.

"Notting Hill Gate, West London, that sort of area." Briggs momentarily considered his beginnings in the council flat on the seventh floor and how pleased he was to be away from it.

"And you must know many friends in that area who could teach you such skills?"

Briggs smiled, "I don't know my lord."

Ashburn roared the theatrical roar which seems to be issued to all counsel for just such a moment. "What do you mean you don't know? You were brought up in the back streets of London and must have picked up your criminal habits there, that's it, isn't it?" Ashburn was glaring eye-to-eye with Briggs.

Briggs again smiled, not because he was feeling pleasant but because it did seem to upset this Queen's Counsel so much. "No sir, you are completely wrong, I learnt about locks whilst in Her Majesty's Forces," Briggs leaving the question to be asked.

"Which branch deals with locks?" snorted Ashburn. "I put it to you that your ability to pick locks is an indication that you have criminal associates who pass on instructions about such matters, as well as criminal information." Ashburn looked expectantly at Briggs.

Briggs sighed as though he was tired or exasperated, which he was. "I cannot tell you any more about lock picking as it is covered by the Official Secrets Act. As for criminal associates, I of course know some criminals. It is, after all, my job to arrest them and bring them to book as I have in this case."

Briggs looked to His Honour for guidance and support.

"Mr. Briggs, I wonder if you would be so kind as to write down which arm of Her Majesty's Forces has the ability to instruct one on lock-picking, and pass the note to me for my eyes only," His Honour smiling at his reference to James Bond's escapades.

The usher handed Briggs a piece of paper. Briggs took out his Moffat pen and wrote 'Special Air Service Hereford' on it, folded it and passed it to the usher who carried it to the Judge. The Judge opened the paper, read it and with a half smile said, "Much as I thought. Mr. Ashburn, this officer learnt to pick locks in the defence of the realm, you will ask no further questions about it at all."

Ashburn looked puzzled. "As your lordship pleases. In which case, I have no further questions for this officer." Ashburn sat down, dissatisfied with the results he had obtained.

Prosecuting counsel rose. "May this officer be excused now my lord?"

His Honour was busy writing up his journal and looked up. "No, I think not, I may have something further to say about him and his colleague later."

The defence, via Ashburn QC, ran its course of verbals and fit ups. They were hard put to to challenge the evidence of the witness who put Harris and Haynes in an argument in the pub on the fateful night. Ashburn did not mention or challenge the forensic evidence of the blood on the trouser leg, almost as though it didn't count.

After both sides had summed up, the jury retired and almost immediately returned with a verdict of 'Guilty'. Harris shouted "Bleedin' fit up." His friends and family in the public gallery erupted into curses and oaths. When order had been restored by enforced ejection of the Harris firm, His Honour curtly sentenced Harris to life imprisonment and regretted he no longer had the power to sentence him to death. Harris was taken down to the cells.

His lordship smiled, obviously he had enjoyed treating Harris to his come-uppance. Briggs recognised the feeling as he had experienced it earlier. "I would now like Detective Constables Briggs and Jones to appear before me in the well of the court."

Jones and Briggs walked out from behind the prosecuting counsel's bench and stood to attention before the Judge.

The Judge coughed and cleared his throat. "I would like to commend both these officers for bravery, tenacity and devotion to duty and to Mr. Briggs for remembering the instruction on how to pick locks. Thank you both." Briggs thought it might have been nice if Jones had got a mention for shagging the information out of the informant, but he didn't. They bowed and left the court.

They were both standing outside the court when Ashburn came out. "Good show officers." He shook Ron's hand and turned to Briggs, who made no effort to put his hand forward. "No hard feelings surely officer?" Ashburn spoke, secure in the superiority of Queen's Counsel.

"Sir there is a lot more to life than coming along here in seventeenth century dress with a soppy wig on your head and talking about things in a plummy public school accent. Things which you have never been near nor by when they have gone down, nor ever had the bottle to be there in the first place. Just fuck off."

Jones and Ashburn looked shocked. Ashburn walked away shaking his head.

The Pringles Attempt Robbery

"Tel, message for you – contact Doll, phone number 705 3586. Says she's repaying a debt or something." Ron passed over the details on a piece of scrap. Such things were rarely put into the official message book. Briggs took the scrap of paper and rang the number. It was answered almost immediately by a woman's voice, "Ello, who's that?"

"Returning your call Dolly, it's Tel." Briggs waited.

"Er yeah, can you call round, it's sort of secret, know what I mean, and I fink it might be urgent." Dolly sounded hunted or haunted maybe. Dolly's worried voice triggered something within Briggs' apprehension but said, "We'll be round in a minute."

Briggs put the phone down and called to Jones. "Come on Ron we've got a meet with a snout." Jones put his files away and they both went to the table at the end of the room and wrote in the duty book. "Enquiries Penrose Place back 6.30pm," which wasn't where they were going at all, but the estimated time of return might be right.

Together they turned out of the Police Station and walked south along Rodney Road, Dolly's little emporium of love being in the back streets. They arrived outside Dolly's place. Both of them looked up and down the road as they arrived at the porchway of her house-cum-brothel.

Briggs knocked on the door and, some moments later, Dolly arrived. She also looked up and down the road, as far as was possible, before indicating for them to come in. They followed her down to the back kitchen where Dolly made herself comfortable behind the kitchen table and pointed to two seats opposite. "Drink?" she enquired indicating a bottle of scotch and three glasses on the table.

"Don't mind if I do" said Ron, helping himself to a liberal measure of Scotch.

Briggs said, "How about you Dolly?" After she had nodded, Briggs poured out two glasses of scotch and settled down next to Jones. "Well Dolly what's this all about then?" Briggs asked, holding his glass up to the light and deciding that the scotch was clear but the glass grimy.

"Look, can I tell yer about it and then if there's nuffink you can do for us can you just forget it?" Dolly looked hopefully at Briggs.

Briggs paused, he could sense that this was fraught with danger and if he had any sense he should exit stage left now before he got involved. However he said, "Well Dolly tell us and we'll see. We'll obviously do the best we can but if you've been at it, be careful as we may have to feel your collar."

"No. no, it's not me, it's someone else taking the piss out of me." Dolly seemed very anxious.

"Come on Dolly spill the beans, if we can't help we'll forget all about it, won't we Ron?" Briggs looked expectantly at Jones who shuddered his response. Dolly took a deep breath.

"Well it's down to the Pringles, they're keeping their guns here, no by your leave or kiss your arse." Dolly was undoubtedly upset. "I can show them to you, but if you take them the Pringles will know I've grassed."

"And we end up only nicking you, which doesn't seem very fair does it?" Briggs trying ever so hard to be nice to Dolly. The main obstruction to this affection was her almost corrosive body odour.

"Not if you want to keep me as a snout" Dolly added forcefully.

"Right then my love, show us the guns and we'll try and come to a decision, won't we Ron?" Briggs spoke with all the forced sincerity usually heard on the hustings. Ron nodded but didn't seem too happy.

Dolly nodded and got up. she went to an old kitchen cabinet and opened it. She said, "Here you are then." Briggs and Jones moved forward and looked in. There were two sawn off shotguns and two 9mm Browning handguns, together with a load of ammunition for all guns.

Briggs picked up the sawn off shotguns, examined them and said to Jones, "They're class guns and have been shortened recently," cleaning his fingerprints off as he spoke.

The Brownings were both loaded, but without one up the spout. Briggs emptied the magazines and reloaded them, noting as he did that they had been loaded by someone used to handling the Browning. The guns were scrupulously clean with just a trace of oil. The rounds had been highly polished and were coated with a thin film of Brylcreem, a dodge to make sure the weapon does not jam under operational conditions. Briggs wiped them down and put them back where they had been. "Right then Dolly, tell me how you came to be gun minder for the Pringles – the whole truth now love."

"Well, as you know, I don't mind holding bent gear from time to time and Mickey Pringle came up with the business about holding guns for 'em. Again, I wouldn't have minded but the bird for this is a lot more than bent gear that's for sure. I just don't want to be involved, who needs it?" Dolly looked genuinely afraid.

"Why didn't you just tell them no?" Jones interposing his character and naïvety on the proceedings. Dolly looked at Jones in amazement.

"Are you fucking mad or what?" she exploded. "You don't say no to the Pringles, you are liable to end up floating in the canal. Mickey's not so bad but that Dessie, his brother, he's not all there you know. Have you noticed his eyes, a right nutter?" Dolly was getting more agitated by the second. Her voice was rising and she was becoming red faced. The last time this happened it brought on a near fatal dose of flatulence, and in this small kitchen Briggs didn't think he could bear it.

"Alright, alright, calm down Dolly, let me think for a bit. What about another scotch love?" Briggs said, resting his eyes on the guns whilst he thought. He turned to Jones. "Any ideas Ron?" As usual, in time of decision Ron's face was blank. "Might have known it" grunted Briggs, "About as much use as a concrete parachute."

Dolly put the glasses down on the table, all with the same amount of scotch. Which glass was which was anybody's guess and Briggs didn't relish the prospect of drinking out of Dolly's old glass but, almost as if she had read his mind, she said, "It's alright love, I've washed them." With relief, Briggs picked up a glass and Jones followed suit. "Well?" Dolly asked.

"Yes, well the best thing I can see is that, for the moment, we let sleeping dogs lie. Leave them where they are and I'll take advice from our guvnor. I won't give your name Dolly, just that we know who the armourer for the Pringles is, and that HE is willing to go to work for us – right? We'll get back to you as soon as we can." Briggs sank his glass. "In the meantime, you get on to Mickey Pringle and say because of the turnovers you've had, you don't feel this is very safe and would he mind you putting the things with one of your mates. Hopefully he'll go along with it, then they'll have to give notice to get the guns for a job."

Dolly sat and thought for a moment, her dressing gown hanging open showing her wrinkled breasts, the veins on her legs standing out like blue ivy stems. "I can ask and see what he says, but it makes sense, 'cos then even they don't know where the guns are. If they agree, who is going to hold the guns?"

"Leave that to me but, for the time being, leave them where they are and we'll get back to you. Don't worry about our side, we'll both remember that we spoke to you on this matter won't we Ron?" Briggs turned to Jones.

"Of course Tel absolutely," Jones lying in his teeth. They both got up to leave and as they went along the hall, they could hear laughter and frivolity going on upstairs.

"I hope it's not the Commissioner's mate again," they both laughed in memory.

As they strolled along on their way back to Rodney Road, they discussed the information Dolly had given them and how they were going to utilise this new found avenue of crime intelligence. Eventually Ron suggested that it should be left to Briggs to decide what to do about Dolly and her armoury.

"Morning guv," Briggs said at the entrance to Jack the Hat's office, "Have you got a minute, Jonesy and me have got a problem."

Jack the Hat was looking down at the morning state on his desk, unwilling to acknowledge Briggs in the knowledge that a 'Briggs' problem could be disastrous, but also knowing that he has to deal with it, come what may. "Come on then," Jack the Hat answered wearily, waving them in and indicating two chairs opposite his desk. Sit down."

Jones and Briggs settled themselves in the chairs but Jack the Hat continued, "Jonesy, I wonder if you would do me a favour?" Jack the Hat was obviously about to ask for something he could not strictly order.

"Of course guv, no problem whatever" said Jones, squinting in the early morning sunlight.

"Get me a cup of tea from the canteen would you, I haven't had one yet, and if you two live up to record I won't get one at all." Jack the Hat leaned back in his chair and adjusted his famous hat.

"Yes of course guv, no problem, I'll bring one up for Briggsy and myself." Jones got up and left the office.

Once Jones was out of earshot, Jack the Hat said. "Right, what's up, no need for the preacher to be here is there?" Briggs quickly related the events of the previous evening, what they had seen and what Dolly had said. He did not, however, as was the norm at the time, disclose who Dolly was or where she lived. "And what do you propose to do about all this then Briggs?" asked Jack the Hat, placing the ball firmly in Briggs' court.

"Well as I see it, if we take the guns and leave my snout in place as being genuine, as I explained, we'll probably get twenty four hours' notice of a job the Pringles are going to do. We then get the guns back to my snout, he gives them to the Pringles and off we go," Briggs stated with the alarming logic of the absolute fanatic.

"And where are the guns whilst they're out of your snout's possession?" asked Jack the Hat, half knowing the answer before it was stated.

"Well we have them of course guv, but not officially," Briggs now reaching the most difficult part and waiting for the dam to burst.

"*We* have them, *we* have them? Are you barking mad Briggsy? What happens if it all goes boss-eyed?" Always the first reaction of a senior officer to any unorthodox plan, except of course, in this case, it was not just unorthodox but probably highly illegal as well. Jack the Hat was shaking his head, "What then?"

"Well guv, only Jones and I know the ID of the snout and only he, you and I will know the guns are in the nick, so if it goes boss eyed, as ever, it will be down to Jones and me. We'll never admit to taking the guns into police possession."

"Right then, let's have an in-depth session of 'what happens if'. Like, what happens if the Pringles pull the job, we lose or don't know where to go because, let's face it, we might know the day, but as yet we don't know the place, and they might just calmly shoot some poor bastard. What are we going to do then?" Jack the Hat spoke and looked expectantly at Briggs who, in turn, was deep in thought. "Well come on Briggsy what do we do?"

Briggs spoke after a few moments had elapsed, slowly and with precision. "We do nothing. If it happens, it establishes our snout's credentials and we are ahead for the next one, plus we know some of the team who did it. What we basically have is an 'in' into the Pringles' armoury, or are you suggesting we blank it guv?"

"No, I'm not, but it's not a simple situation. We have to think and plan this one, else we can make ourselves look right pricks and probably do some bird if we aren't careful. What's the situation with the guns; are they real, would you expect a professional team to have them?"

Briggs nodded, "Very much so guv, they're class equipment and well maintained."

"So, no chance in tampering with them before they go back if that's the way we go," Jack the Hat mused, hopeful that he didn't have to risk his pension.

"Not really guv. If the same guy who prepared them for being put away gets 'em out, he's almost sure to check them before service. All we'll achieve is getting the snout a good hiding – you know the Pringles guv."

"What about Jones? Is he alright – tends to give me the horrors?" asked Jack the Hat maligning Briggs' partner.

"Sound as a pound guv. I know he doesn't look it but when we come under fire he'll make one, but don't ask him about religion, tends to get a bit silly about all that." Briggs spoke confidently, defending his partner and not really knowing why he was doing such a thing.

"What happens if they sus your snout, what then?" Jack the Hat started to make notes.

"Guv, I would feel a lot safer if we didn't have any notes on anything, nothing written down at this stage," Briggs pleading and tentative.

Jack the Hat nodded. "Good thinking Batman" and put his pen down. He looked expectantly at Briggs "And?"

"Well if they sus our snout, he takes his chances in the normal way."

"You do realise that the Pringles might waste him under such circumstances?" Jack the Hat was painting the grimmest scenario.

"I don't think so guv, if they know he's a grass, he must be working for old bill and with such connections it would be risky to waste him, probably give him a good kicking, or break his legs, but not blow him away." Briggs didn't think he over emphasised 'he' and thereby gave Jack the Hat some indication of what was going on.

"Okay," Jack the Hat continued, "What happens if your snout is a double, designed to fit us up with the guns, what then?" Jack the Hat explored as many possibilities as occurred to him.

"Can't see it guv, but if it is we just deny it completely. Jones and I are the only ones who know where the guns come from. I will be the only who knows where they are stashed, – not the safest arrangement I know, but it's the best I can do for the minute." In desperation, Briggs added, "Anything else I will have to react to as it happens?"

Jack the Hat grimaced. "I was afraid you were going to say something like that."

Jones entered with the teas on a tray, together with biscuits which he served up without question or knowing looks. Jack the Hat continued without pause except to slurp a mouthful of his tea. "Cheers Jonesy. Now you two, the situation is this as I see it. We have the guns, maybe, if the Pringles go for it, yes?" Jones and Briggs nodded. "Then with us holding the guns we wait for the Pringles to call for them for a job, again yes." Briggs and Jones nodded in silence. "And hopefully, if we've managed to work out where the plot is, we go for it and nick the Pringles, yes?" Briggs and Jones again did the nodding dog impersonation. "Now the downside. If we get captured with the guns it's down to you two. I know nothing. If the Pringles sus the snout we all blank it, right? However, in case it's a deep down set up, I'll inform Bolton but will omit to tell him that we have the guns but just that you two are sailing in dangerous waters again, okay?" I think it's best to have a little bit of insurance." Jack the Hat looked at his watch. "Anything else?"

"No guv," came the chorus from Briggs and Jones.

"Right then you two listen up. Briggsy, I don't want to know where the guns are, just that they're safe. New developments I want to know about as soon as they happen, even if I'm at home off duty. I want no action on new developments until I have been advised – got it?"

"Right guv – I'll contact the snout and then give the okay for the guns and see where we go," said Briggs tidying the cups on the tray. "Any chance you could contact someone in C11 guv and find out if the Pringles are serious crime targets, or whether any of them are hooked up?" Briggs motioned a imaginary telephone handset to his ear. "I'd do it but I don't know anyone high enough."

"Right I'll ring in the morning. I do as it happens know someone who would be extremely helpful. I'll let you know." Jack the Hat dismissed the dynamic duo with a wave. They returned to the CID office to continue to plot the downfall of the Clan Pringle.

"Tel, bird for you on four." The voice of Richards rang across the office. Briggs picked up the telephone and dialled on to extension four. "Hello, Briggs." Briggs answered with pen poised.

"Hello Briggsy recognise the voice?" Dolly was very quiet and controlled.

Briggs hesitated, "Er yes, yes I do, can you help me?" Briggs continued doodling on the blotter.

"Yes my friends want you to hold their tools for them" – Dolly giggled at the inference to her trade – "Until they need them."

"Okay I'll be around to pick them up." Briggs replaced the handset and nodded to Jones.

They collected the guns late at night after late turn and certainly did not mention it in the duty book. Dolly was careful and, even though no-one was in, spoke in whispers. Briggs put the guns into an old holdall and placed an oily rag over them. "Dolly, listen, we need to know where the blag is going down. Any ideas?"

"Not really Tel, you know the Pringles, tight-lipped lot, never say anything to anyone outside their firm." Dolly leaned up against the door jamb with her arm extended up the door frame as she had seen Rita Hayworth do in a film she once saw, unaware that the effect wasn't quite the same.

"Have you ever heard them talking together, even snatches?" Briggs asked hopefully.

"When Dessie was round here the other night he was saying

something about sissy giving them 'the off', and how much, but who sissy is and where?" Dolly shrugged her shoulders to complete the sentence.

Jones and Briggs left. They walked along the mean street with Briggs holding the armoury. Jones was almost on tip-toe and periodically holding his breath. "Ron for fucks sake relax, you're walking as though you've got something stuck up your jacksy, relax," Briggs exhorting Jones to achieve the impossible.

They entered the CID office and sat down at their respective desks. Briggs got out his personal keys and opened his locker, placed the holdall in it and locked it again. "Tel you cannot be serious, what if A10 come to call and give us a spin?" Jones sounding a touch unravelled.

"I'll find somewhere else tomorrow. Now stop worrying, you're like an old tart at the wrong time of the month." Briggs thus dismissed Jones' worries.

They both booked off duty and made their way downstairs. As they passed the collator's office Briggs said, "Hold up Ron, let's have a little look in here." Not waiting for Jones to answer, he opened the door and entered. Briggs went over to the card index drawer and opened the drawer covering the 'P's." He extracted all the cards covering the Pringle family. Briggs divided them and gave Jones half. "Look through them and see if there's a mention of a 'Sissy.' Could be a name like Cecilia or it's more likely a sister." Jones and Briggs settled down at the collator's desk and got busy reading the cards.

"Tel, there's a mention of a wedding on this one; doesn't say exactly who, what where or how, but they were all there," said Jones, holding the card up.

"Has it got a church and a date on it?" Briggs asked looking down at his cards, still reading.

Jones read on, "Yes there is."

"Then note the details and we'll follow it up tomorrow." Ten minutes later they left the office and went home.

The next morning Briggs found Jones slumped over his desk. "You alright Ron?" Briggs shaking the slumbering Jones.

"Yes boyo, just a bit tired see." Jones rubbed his eyes.

"I thought you were going straight home last night." Briggs emphasized the 'straight'. Briggs stared searchingly into Jones' eyes.

"I decided to go and see a snout to see if any light could be put on our people, know what I mean?" said Jones with just the hint of smile.

"I can imagine. What have you got on today?" asked Briggs looking at the duty book. Jones thought for a moment.

"Well Sid has put me down for a couple of break-ins apart from that, nothing, why?" Briggs indicated the door.

"Well come on, book out on the break-ins and we'll do the wedding enquiry at the same time. Briggs began writing in the duty book. "Wedding enquiry, what wedding enquiry?" asked the puzzled Jones.

"Come on copy my entry. You know what Ron, your memory is leaking out of the eye of your whelk" Briggs spoke, as he continued writing.

"Oh that enquiry. Quite, old son." Jones peered across, copying Briggs' entry and adding the two burglaries to the entry. "What about the 'you know what'?" Jones made a movement with his hand as though firing a gun. "I'll sort it out later," Briggs making for the door.

They visited the scene of the two burglaries and spoke sympathetically with the losers, preserving the scene for examination by the Scenes of Crime Officer. Having paid lip service to the investigation of the burglaries, they went to St Barnabus Church, John Ruskin Street. After wandering around for a few minutes trying to find someone connected to the church, a large man in a cassock came out of a nearby house. "Can I help you gentlemen?" He had the manner and look of someone who is used to being obeyed.

"Yes sir, we are looking for the Vicar of St Barnabus, would you be him?" which seemed a fair bet, cassock, plus cross on chain round neck.

"Yes, well I am the curate." The big man looked closely at Briggs. "I know you from somewhere." Briggs looked up.

"Do you sir, I must admit your face is familiar, what is your name?" The curate sat down on the garden wall. "Tim Crawford."

Briggs smiled. "At one time your holiness, were you called Tanky by your fellows?" Crawford leapt up.

"Briggsy it is you, I couldn't be sure" and began to pump Briggs' hand as though trying to draw water. "It's great to see you, great,

Who Dares Wins eh?"

Briggs laughed, "Who cares who fucking wins, let's survive." They roared together and hugged each other.

"I take it you two know each other?" Jones spoke tetchily, a little peeved at being left out of things.

"Yes, we were in the forces together. A few years ago now eh Tanky? This is my partner Ron Jones. For our sins we are both detectives at the local nick." Briggs spoke with his arm around Crawford's shoulder. "Whatever possessed you to become a sky pilot?" indicating the cassock.

"I don't really know, after everything it came to me that there had to be something more. The more I searched, the more this seemed right and is now right. Doesn't that ever concern you Briggsy?" Crawford asked, being ultra serious.

"You mean the meaning of life and all that, it's a boat that never docked with me. Ron's a bit of a sky pilot, lay preacher or something with the Methodist lot, that's it isn't it Ron?" Briggs waited for Jones to join the conversation.

"I do my bit to spread God's word," said Ron stiffly and pompously, instinctively not liking Crawford for his previous association with Briggs. Briggs thought it would have been truthful to add, "I also do my bit for spreading semen about the place, any port in a storm that sort of thing."

"Anyway what do you want with a poor sinner who is now of the cloth?" Crawford asked with that sing-song voice that the clergy use when leading others in prayer. All three laughed.

"Well we have to enquire into a wedding that took place here last year, just a matter of record really Tanky." Briggs dug a scrap of paper from his pocket and showed it to Crawford, who took it and read it.

"I remember this one. Come on, I'll look it up for you. By the way Briggsy, don't call me Tanky if you don't mind, I don't want to remember how I got the name." The picture of a tank blazing from a rocket launcher hit, bodies running alight and screaming, small arms fire-fight swam before Briggs' eyes. "I can go with that Tim," said Briggs quietly.

They all three entered the church and went to the vestry. Crawford got out the register of marriages and flicked through the pages until he came to the one mentioned on the paper.

"There you are help yourself. I'll be next door in the vicarage getting a brew on – see you in a minute."

Briggs and Jones examined the entry carefully. The marriage was between Tracy Pringle and Steven Coker. The witnesses to the marriage were given as Desmond Pringle (brother) and Cecilia Coker (mother) "This looks like a sister of the Pringle clan, question is, are there any more?" Briggs made a note of both addresses given for the bride and groom.

Briggs and Jones entered the vicarage as the door was ajar. Briggs could see the room at the back was a kitchen and entered. Crawford was sitting at a table. "Help yourself to sugar. I don't use it myself."

"I don't believe this Tim, you've become an opposite. Can we play 'do you remember when' sometime?" Briggs settled himself behind the kitchen table and helped himself to a mug of tea.

"I would rather not Tel, there's so much that's painful to remember you know." Silently Briggs agreed with him.

"Got it. How do you find being a priest? Is it all hatches, matches and dispatches?"

"What?" asked Jones, puzzled.

"Births, marriages and deaths" explained Briggs.

Crawford laughed, more at Jones' inexperience than the joke. "It's not too bad, dealing with people's weaknesses and counselling when it's asked for, very rewarding really and it's where I want to be."

"Oh I see, well good luck mate, I hope it stays happy for you." Briggs finished his tea, nodded to Jones and got up. "Must get back Tim, the guvnor will be asking where we are," said Briggs extending his hand.

"Drop in when you're passing Tel. It's been good to see you, but a little painful. You know what I mean?" Briggs nodded but did not speak. They left with Briggs in pensive mood.

They got into the CID car. Jones put the ignition key into the slot but did not start the car. He turned to Briggs. "What was all that about then?" Briggs was shaken out of his mood and away from his thoughts that Tim Crawford had engendered.

"What's up Ron, just an old mate from the mob."

Jones seemed annoyed. "Yes but what mob, you and him are ex SAS aren't you?" Ron stated belligerently rather than asked. Briggs snorted a laugh.

"It's no good officer you have got me this time. Yes that's right we were both in the same troop together. What difference does it make?" Briggs smiled, poking fun at his serious partner.

"None really I suppose, it's just that I would have thought I could have been told that's all," said a petulant Ron.

"I never told you or any of the others because it just doesn't matter and, like Tim, there are some things I would prefer to forget. Okay?" Jones started the car and they drove back to Rodney Road shrouded in an awkward silence.

After the obligatory or usual cup of tea, Briggs adjourned to the collator's office where he again looked up the Pringles' and the Cokers' addresses, making a note of the details and the subjects supposed to be living there. "Looking for something in particular Tel?" asked Tom Stephens the Local Collator, returning to his office.

"Not really – someone came up with name of Tracy Coker for something and I was just trying to work out her home address," said Briggs, lying, and careful not to mention the Pringle connection.

"Oh yes, she was a Pringle, got married last year, her father-in-law is the local builder 'Uni Build', Tom rattling off the details better than any computer print out.

"Any idea where she was living – better still, where she works?" asked the ever hopeful Briggs. Tom went into pensive mode.

"Ah yes" he said brightly. "She used to live in a house which was part of a development by pa-in-law. At the time of her marriage she lived in one of her pa-in-law's houses and worked at St Olaves Hospital over Rotherhithe, both bits of history I'm afraid." Tom was apologetic.

"What was the address, can you remember?" Briggs was ever hopeful.

"Yes, I think so 14 Evergreen Crescent, just the other side of Crystal Palace Park Road" Tom announced, whilst pointing out the venue on a road map as he spoke.

"Tom, a complete shot in the dark, do you know what sort of job she does?" Briggs asked writing furiously in his notebook.

"Well old man Pringle was always on about her having brains and her working in an accounts office somewhere," Tom answered off handedly, sorting out the makings for his mid morning cuppa.

"Well done again Tom. Is this recorded anywhere apart from your brain cells?"

"No I don't think so Tel, why do you ask?" Tom speaking over his shoulder while he attended to cups and kettle.

Briggs hesitated, he didn't want to explain the whole job to anyone at the moment so he said, "It's all a bit tentative at the moment, but I'll keep it under wraps for the moment. If it comes off I'll see you alright. Okay?"

"It's already cancelled Tel, but you will let me know how you get on won't you?" Tom settled himself down with his cuppa to do some serious cross-referencing and filing.

Briggs returned to the CID office where Jones was studying the accumulated intelligence file on the Pringles which, for security reasons, was labelled 'Fraud Anglo-Indian Trading Corporation.' Briggs sat next to him and very close. "Ron," whispered Briggs. "How about some late night secret squirrel tonight after close down?"

Ron whispered his reply. "Always game for a bit of extra overtime Tel, you know that." Ron was still concentrating on the bogus file.

"Well this won't be recorded as overtime immediately. In fact, it won't be recorded at all. Let us say that in the fullness of time your investment will be repaid yes?" Briggs wrote "Robbery suspect" on a scrap of paper and placed it in front of Jones.

Jones read the message. "Ah yes of course, always a pleasure to do some for the Queen," said Jones taking the scrap of paper and screwing it up into a ball. Briggs thought that Ron might, in an excess of security zeal, chew the paper and pass it through the Jones re-cycling unit. However, he threw it into a waste-bin.

That evening, after booking off in the duty book, Briggs and Jones drove their cars to Crystal Palace Park Road where Jones parked his in the side road. Briggs, with Jones as his passenger, then drove to Evergreen Crescent, a small development of tiny houses of the doll's house variety. Every last scrap of available space had been taken up with houses. In front of each was a postage stamp of a lawn, some had acquired the taste for plastic gnomes and some had retained sanity without. No 14 was typical, ruched curtains and brass front door furniture. A surreptitious look inside revealed an imitation leather suite and the obligatory sixties blue Chinese lady on the wall. The television was on and two people were sitting on the settee watching "Steptoe and Son." Briggs returned to the car. "Well what do you think?" Jones was not keen on secret squirrel missions which is why he always got Briggs to do them.

"The place is very well furnished, if it's them that lives there that is. But we can soon find out from the Local Collator." Briggs made a note in his personal pocket book. Whilst doing so, he was thinking that it might not be such a good idea to speak with the Local Collator; there might be a contact between local police and the Pringles. "Let's have a look round the back, there are probably garages, might be something for us."

They drove up the crescent and parked by the junction. Briggs got out and locked the car. "Well Ron, you coming?" Briggs to still-seated Jones.

"I'm alright mate, I'll keep cavey from here," Ron settling himself down so as not be immediately visible.

Briggs spoke with an edge to his voice. "I don't think so Ron, I may need some back up on the plot if it all goes boss-eyed, so you keep me company, yes? Just in case I get lonely like." It was obvious to Jones that this was not a good time to be dodging the column so he got out and joined Briggs on the pavement. They walked down the crescent together and turned into a service road behind the tiny houses. The garages stood like serried ranks of soldiers, again occupying as little space as possible. They walked up and down and eventually found No 14 which, as expected, was locked. Briggs got his lock-picking instruments out and, in seconds, had the cheap lock on the garage door open. As quietly as they could they lifted the up and over door. There was van inside the garage, a Ford Transit, the robber's favourite. They stopped and listened to see if the very small noises had made anyone aware of their presence, but all was quiet.

Briggs whispered to Jones, "You stay here and bang the door if someone comes." Briggs entered the garage and quietly dropped the door behind him. He turned on his small pocket torch and examined the Transit closely. It had recently been re-sprayed in dark blue. Briggs scraped the paint on the lower wing and saw that beneath the blue the original colour was white. He opened the driver's door and took note of the chassis number from the plate on the door pillar and also recorded the registration number as KKP 466J. Briggs searched the inside of the vehicle and noted that the ignition barrel had been removed, but found nothing else of note.

He left the garage, and with Jones they closed the door as quietly as they could. Briggs relocked it. As they were walking across the area towards the exit a stray dog, startled by their presence, began to bark furiously. Briggs called to it softly and made out by pursing his lips and holding his fingers to them that he had some treat for the dog, thus gaining the dog's attention and interest. Briggs made the dog follow them in silence until they had gained the pavement of the Crescent, then dropped all pretence and walked away quickly. They drove around the area taking note of all vehicles parked in the Crescent and any likely ones parked elsewhere. Briggs then drove Jones back to his car and they went their separate ways home.

"Guv, could Jones and me have another of those conferences?" Briggs spoke quietly and emphasised the 'conference'. Jack the Hat was examining the crime book. "My office in ten minutes," grunted Jack the Hat.

At the appointed time, Briggs and Jones entered Jack the Hat's office where he nodded them to the two empty chairs while he finished a telephone call. They sat quietly whilst Jack the Hat spoke with someone of exalted rank, judging from the number of times he called the caller 'Guv'.

"Right then, what have you got? Be quick 'cos I've got to be at Southwark on a Senior Officers' Conference," Jack the Hat ever impatient.

Briggs took a deep breath. "Right guv, we have a suspect vehicle. It's actually a Ford Transit but is showing the number of a motor cycle from somewhere in Kent although we haven't tracked that down yet. The vehicle is in the possession of a Pringle but stowed away in a lock-up. The chassis number matches a stolen Transit nicked from Peckham two months ago but has had a change of colour. That's the vehicle taken care of. Further we have a Pringle connection within the cash office of St Olaves Hospital,

Rotherhithe and also a connection from that person, not only to the Pringles but also to the bent Transit. My view is that if we get a request for guns from the Pringles via our snout, we now know the robbery vehicle and where the robbery is going to take place. Or, to be more honest, where we think it most likely to take place." Jack the Hat leaned back in his chair, assessing this new development.

"Do we know how long this plant has worked in the cash office?" asked Jack the Hat.

"As far as I can make out guv at least nine months." Briggs looked to Jones who nodded.

"And how old is the plant?"

"About twenty two guv." Jones nodded again.

"Right then I've been in touch with my contact in C11. The Pringles are all hooked up on the tinkerbell but, as usual, don't say anything on the phone. The robbery squad are of the opinion that this is too big for us to handle – what do you think?"

"And they would like to take it over guv is that it?" Briggs studying Jack the Hat to try and assess his view, if any, of the subject.

"That would appear to be the size of it. They say that this is a serious robbery of which there is intelligence and they should be running it."

"And our view is no way, definitely no way! Ron and I have worked this up from fuck all. Now it looks as though we 're going to get there, the robbery squad want to take over. They're supposed to be the super tecs so they should be there miles before us." Briggs showed he was annoyed by this approach. Jones kept quiet and awaited the result of this discussion.

"Something else, they want to run your snout," Jack the Hat dropping a bombshell on the Dynamic duo

"Guv they have to be joking. I won't say why, but there is no way they can run our snout, can't be done. If they carry on like this, we'll forget about this job and get on with something else."

Jack the Hat laughed at Briggs' intensity. "Come down Tel, it's only politics and ruffled feathers; they'll either come round or they won't but we carry on as before – agreed?" Jack the Hat looked to Briggs and Jones for response.

"Absolutely guv." Briggs spoke with Jones in assent.

"Right then, we have it all set. What do you think about approaching the security officer at St Olaves?"

"Good idea guv, I'll do that, but I'll only tell him the bones of the thing. Perhaps he can help with possible sniper posts and obbo sites." Briggs made a note in his pocket book. "Guv it might be an idea if you put the firearms branch on notice about this one. We're going to need some people with operational skill with firearms. Ron and I are authorised shots but I think we might need snipers and Brownings."

"I'll get on to them as soon as you two are out of the way," Jack the Hat said, picking up the internal telephone directory. "Right then you two, the might of the Metropolitan Police awaits your instructions with bated breath – God help us." Jack the Hat closed the conference by saying "Keep me informed as before, and, if you're contacted by C11 refer them to me."

Pringle Politics

"Are you Detective Constable Briggs?" The speaker was tall, well dressed and obviously a member of the officer class.

"Yes, that's me and you are?" Briggs was immediately on the defensive thinking about the mini-arsenal he had stored in his private locker, which he should have moved but had not.

"Chief Inspector Hollis, Crime Intelligence. That's C11 to you. I want to talk to you about this business of the Pringles and the subject of co-operation." Hollis placed his expensive briefcase on Briggs' blotter. Briggs considered the case for a moment, and in that moment decided that he would never be able to afford such a thing, and therefore doubted that the Chief Inspector had ever purchased it, but probably got it on a blag. Briggs took the briefcase off his desk and placed it on the floor.

"Yes guv?" Briggs queried and sat down at his desk. "You should be talking to Mr. Parris, he's the guvnor here."

Hollis pursed his lips. "So he is, but you're the one with the inside on this little job aren't you? So my life, cut out the middle man and go direct I always say." Hollis paused and launch himself into his sales pitch. "Now what I want to know is, firstly, who your snout is. Is he a participating informant, can we use him – please? Hollis reached across and idly started to riffle through Briggs' correspondence. Briggs stood up and treated Hollis to his cold hard stare.

"Guvnor, do yourself a favour, leave my corres alone and don't ask silly questions. Or if you do, go and speak to Mr. Parris. In the meantime go away." Briggs ached to say 'fuck off' but managed to hang on to civility – just.

Hollis grinned. "But my dear chap, I am Chief Inspector from the big house. I can do you lots of damage and lots of favours, best thing for you is to stop being bolshy and work with me. I'll see you right, just you see." Hollis spoke with the confidence of one who is used to getting his own way.

"Look guv, I'm not interested in big house favours or ticket punching if that's what you mean, just speak to my guvnor will you." Briggs looked down at his blotter, but his left hand rested on his pile of correspondence and files. "I don't know what you are on about, but you are certainly giving me the shits now piss off."

Heads lifted in the office. There was a pregnant silence. Hollis began to redden. "You cannot speak to me like that, I am a Chief Inspector." Briggs stepped forward and adopted a threatening pose.

"Listen you soapy bastard, I've tried to be polite and you won't have it. I've requested you speak with my guvnor and you won't and you keep interfering with my corres and won't stop. Now fuck off or you're going to be looking at the ceiling." Briggs stepped forward, again causing Hollis to step back.

"Alright Briggs that's enough," Jack the Hat, speaking forcefully and loudly from the far end of the office, "stand fast."

"Jack Parris, DCI at this nick and you're Chief Inspector 4 Area C11, yes?" Jack the Hat spoke directly to Hollis and motioned Briggs to sit down.

"Yes I am and your DC has just threatened me with personal violence and told me to fuck off." Hollis appeared flustered and a bit confused, no doubt because the confrontation had not gone the way he had hoped.

"Did he now?" said Jack the Hat. "Well he's a bit like that, does that to me all the time, so why should you be any different?" Jack the Hat smiled pleasantly. "My advice is that if Briggsy here told you to 'fuck off' I would make travelling arrangements right away."

"I am here to get information on the Pringles and I understand this officer has an informant who might be able to assist." Hollis looked longingly at Briggs' corres bin. "It's co-operation I'm after," Hollis finished rather lamely.

"Come into my office and we'll discuss the matter but, for the record, do not come to my nick and interfere with my officers' operations without consulting me first." Hollis's head went down and he meekly followed Jack the Hat.

Hollis and Jack the Hat were involved in a heated argument in the guvnor's office for about ten minutes. This was known because Briggs and two others were listening at the door. Briggs stood back as the door rattled. Hollis came out, looking even more flustered than when he went in, and left the station in a huff.

"Right Briggsy, handy that you were standing outside, come in and cop a bollocking, bring your pocket book with you."

Briggs' face fell, "But guv, what chance did I have?"

Jack the Hat laughed, "Not the point I am trying to make. If I give you words of advice on the subject of modes of address to senior officers and record it as such in your pocket book, there's no way that that slimy shit can then discipline you officially, cos it's already been done. Now are you with me?" Jack the Hat beamed his version of Cheshire cat. Jack the Hat took the pocket book and opened it at the last used page. "Is it up to date, have you got all your evidence in?"

"Yes guv." Jack the Hat wrote the discipline entry in the pocket book and handed it back to Briggs. "Thanks a lot guv." Jack the Hat looked up, surprised at Briggs' comment. "No guv, I am not taking the piss, I mean it, thanks."

"That's OK, but don't leave anything lying around the office. They have been known to slink in, in the middle of the night, so be careful." Briggs nodded and left.

Briggs sat and pondered at his desk, then, after about half an hour, went to another desk and collected a typewriter, put it on his desk and began to type intelligence forms and various file covers which read 'Pringle job – Maybe Robbery'. In one of these files he recorded fictitious meets with an informant whom he named 'Cicero', betting that the robbery squad or whoever had not the wit to know who Cicero was. He stapled a sealed envelope, which he signed across the flap, on the inside of the file cover. Inside the envelope he placed a plain card on which were written the name and address George Harris, 42 Manor Place, Walworth, his date of birth and Criminal Record Office reference number and the comment 'Kings College Hospital Friday sometime soon'. On the intelligence sheets he recorded details of Christine's information, the jobs she had put up, also copies of the informant's reports which Ron had successfully submitted, together with a grand total already paid to this very important informant.

Briggs took the file with the informant's report and put it on Jones's desk. On the front of the file he pinned a note, which read, "Ron put this back in the drawer when you have finished with it. Tel" Jones seemed be amused by it all, mainly because he could not countenance C11 pulling a secret squirrel operation on them. "Ron don't worry about it, just leave the file there and see what happens, if nothing I'm wrong." The weary Briggs pulled a hair from his head and marked the locked drawer with it. "I'm sure I'm not the only one who can pick locks." Briggs leaned back and gauged whether he could see the marker and was satisfied he could not, unless very close.

"Anyway these locks are rubbish, a child could pick them with a bent hair pin. The robbery squad could be in difficulty then." They both winced at Jones's sarcasm.

The next morning Briggs sat at his desk and contemplated his partner opposite and came to the conclusion that morality was not the only bar to extra-marital sex, stamina must enter into the equation somewhere. Jones looked awful. "Which one Jonesy the wife or...?"

"Both" grunted Jones, not looking up from his report.

"Ron you're my hero, to rise to such heights, both, jeez." As he spoke, Briggs moved a file on his desk. Underneath it was an envelope addressed to 'Briggsy' in child like handwriting. Briggs studied it for a moment and opened it. It read 'Briggsy they're watching me, that Des is here on and off all day. They want the gear for Friday but I don't know where. Ring my number and say you want a blow job from the one in the French waitress gear and you would like the strawberry treatment as well. I'll meet you in the side road alongside Manor Place Baths, where the boxing is, ten to fifteen minutes after the phone call. Love Doll."

Briggs studied the sheet for a few moments and then handed it over to Ron saying, "I'll do this one solo."

Jones read the letter, and nodded. "I'll be in the motor at the corner of Penrose Place. If it goes boss-eyed, at least I'll be about." Jones laughed, "The bit at the end 'Love Doll', you're in there Tel, I bet she would do it for nothing for you."

Briggs took the envelope and placed it in his inside pocket. To do it for nothing would not be good enough, she would have to pay, and some. Briggs opened his personal locker and checked that the guns were still in place. "Ron, I'll go and tell Jack the Hat what's happening. Friday is only two days away."

Briggs strode off down the office and knocked on Jack the Hat's office door. "Come in," bawled Jack the Hat. "Oh it's you Briggsy any news?"

"Yes guv," Briggs reminding himself that he musn't show the letter to Jack the Hat as this would 'show out' his informant. "Snout's been in touch, it's on for Friday. I have got to meet to hand over the 'you know what'."

"Right then, I don't want to know anything about that meet while you're out I'll get on to D11 and get some shootists down here for early Friday morning, say 6am?" Jack the Hat arched his eyebrows to emphasise the question. Briggs nodded.

"About the meet guv, it would be nice if I had some protection or rather insurance," said Briggs hopefully.

"Why do you want insurance, don't you trust your informant?" Briggs had always considered this a strange question which was always being asked by senior officers, usually those who had never had an informant, although this did not apply to Jack the Hat. The essence of a snout is usually that he or she will sell out close colleagues for cash, or some other valuable security. Being the ground rule for snouts, it is unlikely that anyone will ever knowingly trust them again. But instead Briggs said, "Not really guv, he's being leaned on by the Pringles, they've got wind of something and I don't want to be in the situation that they can set me up and get away with it." Jack the Hat leaned back in his chair and studied the scaley in front of him.

"Well guv, how about I write something out that I think will save me in the event of it being all horrible, seal it in an envelope and you can sign across the flap as well and we leave it in the station officer's safe addressed to me," Briggs explaining his life saving ploy.

"Yeah fine, so long as I note that I don't know the contents okay?" Briggs nodded enthusiastically.

"Well that way, at least if I get fitted, I only get dismissed from the force, not any bird," Briggs stating his damage limitation procedure in the event of failure.

Which is what happened. Before making the all-important telephone call to Dolly, he sat down behind a typewriter and wrote himself a letter, which basically stated what had transpired and that no-one else was involved. Further, that Jones was only there because he had told him to be. Briggs sealed the envelope and signed across the flap. He then went to Jack the Hat's office who also signed across the flap and timed and dated the act. Jack the Hat looked soulfully at Briggs and said "Be lucky old son." Briggs nodded, "I'll try guv." Briggs took the envelope and went to the front office and spoke with the station duty officer who, although puzzled, put the envelope in the safe, logging the event in the occurrence book which is what Briggs had requested.

Having accomplished his own safety as best he could, Briggs sat behind his desk and contemplated his next move. Obviously it had to be the phone call to Dolly. He rang the number and waited a few seconds. A woman's voice responded, "Hello, Paradise Lost." She spoke with her version of a plummy accent, but Briggs could discern the Walworth Road accent beneath the bullshit.

"Er hello is Dolly there?" Briggs was cautious just in case it was not her.

There was a pause. "Er yeah, speakin, what can I do for yer?" asked Dolly, dropping her fake upper class accent.

"Well how about a blow job, French waitress gear, plus the strawberry treatment?"

"I shall be able to see you in about ten or fifteen minutes sir. Do you need bondage this time or not?" Briggs sensed that Dolly was enjoying this conversation.

"No thanks no bondage. I'll be there in ten or fifteen minutes." Briggs grimaced at the awful prospect as he spoke.

"Well sir" said Dolly brightly, "As an alternative we could offer you an exotic enema with bondage overtones." Dolly giggled at Briggs' gagging reply, "As I said, I'll be there in fifteen minutes."

Briggs removed the holdall from his personal locker, sat at his desk with it between his feet and surreptitiously checked on the contents. Once he was sure that all was in order he zipped up the bag and stood up. "You ready Ron?" Briggs nodding to the holdall on the desk.

"Yeah right just finish this." Jones finished his all important line of lies in his diary and got up. They booked out "enquiries Kennington Park Road area re robbery. Back conc." Which anyone conversant with the CID at the time would have translated as "We are going out and do not know when we will be coming back, if ever."

Jones parked his car in Penrose Place. Briggs got out, taking the clanking holdall with him. He looked around but could see no-one taking an obvious interest in him. He sauntered around the block twice, checking the reflection in corner shop windows to see if he was being followed. Once satisfied, he made his way to the designated meet, the side road alongside Manor Place Baths. Briggs stood at the end of the road and surveyed the short road about one hundred yards long, tenements to the right and overgrown gardens to the left adjacent to the baths. Briggs strolled along with his lethal holdall and tried to look unconcerned. He stopped by the gap which was overgrown with that favourite bomb site shrub buddleia. He could vaguely discern a pair of legs in the corner by the doors, below the shrubbery. Briggs entered this inner city arboretum where Dolly was standing in the corner. "Wotcha Briggsy" she said, flashing him a grin with gaps.

"Hello Dolly." Briggs noticed that Dolly was carrying a similar holdall to Briggs.

Noticing Briggs' stare she said, "Well, makes it look kosher don't it?" Briggs nodded.

"Any news on the plot, where it is etc?" Briggs opened his holdall to show all the gear was there.

"Fine" Dolly nodded. "No news on the plot though, except sis had given it thumbs up for this Friday, whoever she is." They exchanged holdalls. Briggs thought his a little heavy and opened it. Inside there were five housebricks nestling in the bottom. Briggs laughed. "Nothing like dropping a brick is there?"

"Eh?" said Dolly.

"Nothing" said Briggs. "Don't worry about it, silly copper's joke. Now listen carefully Dolly, just go back and hand the guns to Pringle, don't try to find out anything, no pumping or anything like that, just hand the guns over and forget the rest, we may have that covered." Dolly nodded and Briggs continued, "If this comes off there will be an informant's reward. I'll see you get most of it, but you realise other palms have to be greased don't you?" Again, Dolly nodded. "Right then Doll you leave first." Dolly waddled away, humping the holdall, thankfully she didn't have far to go.

After a few minutes, Briggs emerged from behind the shrubbery and walked off quickly up the road and joined Jones in his car. "Go alright did it Tel?" Briggs nodded. "What did you get?" Jones leaned forward as Briggs opened the holdall. "Housebricks, that doesn't seem much of a swop for our pristine guns." Briggs laughed.

"Let's put is this way, I feel a lot happier with housebricks than that arsenal we had there," Briggs throwing the now useless holdall onto the back seat. "Right then back to the ranch before the Indians get us."

As Briggs sat down behind the desk he checked the hair he had placed across the drawer of his desk. It had gone. He couldn't be sure that it had not been there first thing in the morning as he had forgotten to check it, but it was definitely missing now. Briggs unlocked the drawer. It may have been his imagination but he felt the lock to be gritty and stiff. "You got the file I gave you on the snout Ron?" asked Briggs forcing his voice to be even and controlled. "Yes here it is." Ron paused, "Or here is where it should be." Jones checked the other filing trays on his desk." Here it is, it's in the wrong tray. I am sure I didn't put it in there" said Jones, showing that he was not on the same wave length as Briggs. "Well I am sure nothing hangs on it, so long as we got the file." Briggs spoke fairly loudly so that he could be heard by anyone in the office. Briggs checked the drawer contents; they were in a different order than when he had left them, plus the file with the sealed envelope had been tampered with. "You must be mistaken Ron, no-one would muck about with our corres, would they?" Briggs locking the drawer and pleased that his bait had been taken by whoever, but had he been forced to wager, he would have put his money on the robbery squad. Jones thought for a moment and maybe realised his partner was up to something and said, "No I suppose not Tel."

Jack the Hat sat behind his desk brooding on the outcome of the operation with the Pringles. He'd taken care to cover his backside, which would save him from the ravages of A10 and the Criminal Law, but as far as his career was concerned it would be the end. He would remain a Chief Inspector for the rest of eternity, even granted that he had the legs on every other senior officer on the division, including Bolton. If the wheel came off this particular cart he would never have the chance to prove it and, whether it did fall to pieces, wasn't something over which he had any control. Having turned it this way and that in his mind, he decided his future career was linked to the actions of Detective Constable Briggs and, to a lesser extent, his partner Jones. Briggs entered the office.

"Ah wotcha Briggsy just thinking about you and the Pringles. How are we set – OK?"

"Yes fine guv, did you get the shootists from D11?" Jack the Hat nodded.

"Yes they are parading here at 6am, two authorised shots and two snipers. What time do they need to be in position by?"

Briggs pondered, "At least 8am, possibly ten minutes earlier, any later and we stand a chance of being sussed." Briggs sat down in the armchair opposite Jack the Hat's desk.

"Sit down Briggsy, why don't you," Jack the Hat displaying his sarcasm.

"Thanks a lot guv." said Briggs, ignoring it. "What we do need is more bodies and without any suggestion of a leak back to the Pringles."

"Have you got anyone in mind?"

"Yes guv. What about giving the uniform crime squad a run, together with the Divisional Aids Squad? That would give us a total of sixteen plus two sergeants – should be ample." Jack the Hat made a note on his scribble pad.

"You don't reckon giving the sub Div CID here a chance at this then?"

"Good idea guv, but that would denude the office for all of the day and, let's face it, with twelve to fourteen burglaries a day we need staff here"reasoned Briggs, not even touching on the real reason for his unwillingness to employ his colleagues.

"Fine OK." Jack the Hat completed his note. "Now you'll be briefing Friday morning how do you see it?" Jack the Hat waiting for a re-run in order that he could check the chances of a foul up which might affect his career. "Although of course I will be present."

"Well guv, what I have arranged is all based on supposition, but a fairly strong one. I reckon they're going to use the Transit to drive from Crystal Palace Park Road to Rotherhithe – St Olaves Hospital, we know the security van arrives about 8.45am. Therefore it's most likely that the Pringles will be on the road from 8.30am accounting for the rush hour. Every school crossing patrol, civilian and old bill along the way will have the number and colour of the van. Should it be sighted it will be called into MT control and passed on to us on the plot – that is, direction of travel and number of occupants etc."

On the Plot

5.30am the next morning, Briggs entered the back door of Rodney Road. He went into the canteen and sat down. The night duty were still about, having about half an hour to go. Briggs took a spoonful of coffee from the night duty tea club and went to the ever boiling urn and made himself a drink. The canteen was quiet and the background noise from the front office was all about getting cleared away at the end of the shift, ready for the le Mans start to go home.

Albert Hendry, a middle aged affable Police Constable entered the canteen. "Oi, Tel, what's the matter, shit the bed then?" He struck Briggs as being over noisy for first thing in the morning, of course, the difference being this was last thing at night for Albert.

"No, got an early one starting this morning" Briggs grunted.

"Oh good you found our tea club then, I would hate to think of CID going without." Briggs nodded and flicked a silver coin into the margarine container that served as a kitty.

"Hear you're popular, had the robbery squad asking about you, what sort of bloke etc. whether you're approachable and all that. The skipper told him you are an arsewipe." Albert busied himself clearing away the tea club.

"Probably as near the truth as anything I suppose. Did you know any of them, any served here like?" asked Briggs, studying the scum on top of his coffee and deciding to leave the rest. "Yes one of them, he hadn't served here as far as I know, but I saw him last week with Barking. Well suited the pair of them – right flash bastards."

Briggs shrugged himself into action and went upstairs. Some of the Aids squad and the uniform boys had already arrived. On their own at the other end were the four D11 officers together with their Chief Inspector. On the floor were a number of aluminum cases. Briggs could guess what was in them.

Briggs nodded to the Aid and uniform lot, then approached the Chief Inspector who, unlike everyone else, was in full uniform and hatted to boot. "Hello guv, DC Briggs, it's my job you're on this morning," Briggs being as pleasant as an early start permits.

The Chief Inspector paused and studied Briggs who was not at his smartest for this one and said, "Sir, I prefer to be called Sir." Briggs looked past him to one of his soldiers who shook his head in disgust and shook his hand and forearm in a manner which says in universal language – "Wanker" Briggs was a little shaken, this 'Sir' was more Provincial than Metropolitan Police but said, "Oh fine, if that's the way you want it. But am I right that you are here from D11 – SIR." The Chief Inspector looked to his staff and said, "Yes that's me, I am here in charge of my men." He waved his hand at his four men.

"I'll introduce you to Detective Chief Inspector Parris when he arrives. No doubt you want to keep him company in the operational control room at MT sir," Briggs suggesting that which was operationally more desirable to him for there was no way he would want this toy soldier on the plot. The four shootists behind their senior officer all nodded their heads vigorously. Briggs returned to his desk as more officers filed into the room. Briggs counted the number present including Ron Jones who was asleep with his head on his desk. Briggs wondered if he had been gathering information again last night, but did not wake him to find out. With the exception of a couple of absentees they were all present.

Bang on 6.00am, Jack the Hat burst through the door. It was obvious that early starts did not agree with him. He was unshaven and had yesterday's shirt on. "Right, all here then?" as he bustled over to Briggs' desk. "Well Briggsy are they all here?"

"Yes guv as near as makes no odds. In addition, we have a Chief Inspector from D11." Briggs spoke and Jack the Hat nodded, not really taking on board what Briggs was saying. "Right then listen up you lot. I am Detective Chief Inspector Parris of this nick. I am in charge of today's operation. However you will be briefed by Detective Constable Briggs whose informant has come up with the likely offence on which this operation is based, so if it all goes boss-eyed – blame him." Jack the Hat paused and beamed at his humour. "And if it is a great success I will claim all the credit." They all dutifully roared at what they perceived to be the truth and the way things always ran.

Briggs took centre stage and ran them through what he thought might occur that day, including the number and description of the Transit which he hoped the robbers would be using. He then sectionalised them and dispatched them to various duties giving them all call signs for use on personal radios.

He briefed the D11 officers last and alone, apart from the now awake Jones and Jack the Hat, explaining that the two snipers would be secreted on second floor roof top situations about 100 yards from the operations site and would be warned by radio. The two authorised shots would be hidden with Jones and Briggs in a nearby boiler house, from where the entrance to the cash office could be seen through a ventilation shutter. They would also be warned by radio. Once the bandits had entered the cash office, the authorised shots would be on either side of the door to await their exit and challenge them accordingly. Briggs and Jones would be armed with Smith and Wesson Model 8's. At the end of this briefing Briggs said, "Any questions?"

Almost as if by magic the D11 Chief Inspector came to the surface. "Yes, have these operational sites been examined by someone from my department?" he asked, making a note on his clipboard.

"Yes sir, yesterday, your Sergeant Henderson" said Briggs, sure this was the start of something.

"I see. I am unhappy, I would wish to pass them myself." He looked earnestly at Jack the Hat.

"I am afraid that isn't possible sir, it's too late and too close to the operation, we stand a chance of showing out," Briggs putting the objection. He noticed that the D11 shootists were nodding in agreement with Briggs.

The D11 Chief Inspector shook his head "I'm afraid I must insist, as I do not like the sound of this cross fire routine with officers under the gun so to speak." The Chief Inspector looked down at his clip board as though reading from it.

"You've had plenty of notice of this operation and if you haven't taken it on board it isn't our fault. We will not allow another visit so all that you will achieve is that the snipers will not be used, is that what you want?" snapped Jack the Hat, who could be fairly described as a little testy.

"I just want to do my duty as I am supposed to under General Orders." The D11 Chief Inspector quoted that large collection of past misdemeanors which have been correlated into regulations for the guidance of Metropolitan Police, the truth being that if General Orders were obeyed implicitly nothing would ever be achieved.

"I will confer with the Chief Inspector in my office," said Jack the Hat curtly and, making for his office, beckoned the Chief Inspector to follow. There followed five to ten minutes of raised voices, one memorable part was Jack the Hat shouting, "Listen to me you fucking lame brain, this is about real policing, real coppers and real villains and someone could wind up dead, one of ours, or better still, one of theirs. If you want to talk about duty, get into it beside your men. If not shut up." Briggs could tell this went down well with the D11 shootists as they smiled and held their hand over their mouths to avoid making a noise.

Jack the Hat came out of his office followed by a crestfallen Chief Inspector. "The Chief Inspector will assist me in MT control. You will now all go to your assigned places and good luck."

They all went downstairs and waited in the yard whilst Jones and Briggs signed for their guns and ammunition in the front office. Briggs put both guns into a toolbox, together with the personal radios. They loaded all their gear into the boot of Briggs' battered Westminster and climbed aboard.

They drove in silence to St Olaves hospital where Briggs parked at the junction of the short service road which was a cul-de-sac and led to the cash office. It was very early and no-one was about. Briggs had a whispered conversation with the two snipers and they took their aluminum cases and followed Briggs. He sited them on a flat roof about 100 yards from the exit from the cash office, the entrance to which they had a clear view of. They could shelter in the meantime in an unused office on the floor below. Briggs promised faithfully to give them a firm warning of the 'off' so they could get into position. Briggs reminded them not to get into position until after the bandits had entered the cash office and they both nodded.

Briggs returned to his car and had another whispered conversation with the occupants. He pointed out the boiler house and instructed them to make their way singly to it to avoid arousing suspicion. Briggs waited until the two authorised shots and Jones had entered the boiler house, then he took his toolbox and holdall, and strolled across to join Jones and the others, with much more confidence than he really felt.

Once inside the boiler room and his eyes had accustomed to the gloom, Briggs found the ventilation shutter which he had noticed previously and enlarged the slits slightly. He then set up his coffee and sandwiches, gave a set of overalls from his holdall to Jones and took a set himself and got into them. He cleaned and checked both revolvers, loaded them and laid them on a shelf together with ammunition which he also cleaned. He then left the boiler house and strolled across to his Westminster. He looked up and down and noticed the Constable off the uniform squad walking towards him. Briggs made his way towards him. "Alright mate?" asked Briggs sorting his keys.

"Yeah fine, saw you coming out of the boiler house." Briggs noticed the Constable's hand shook as he accepted the key. Briggs did not comment on it.

"Right you've got it have you, once they get out of the van and go into the cash office, you drive my old wreck across the junction which, hopefully, should trap them." The PC nodded. Briggs left him and returned to the boiler room, wondering as he walked whether the PC would be able to carry out the duties assigned to him.

"You two Okay?" Briggs queried the two shots. The question seemed to spur them both awake. "Yes," grunted one as they both checked their weapons and loaded them in much the same manner that Briggs had done.

"That's a right guvnor you've got there ain't it?" Briggs searching for something to say to relieve the tension.

"He hasn't been up there with us long, a right 22 carat prick I can see him getting one of us killed," the morose one moaned. "But he'll put in a beautiful report which will put it all down to you not him." They both laughed with Briggs.

They all settled their gear and themselves into waiting mode. Jones had been very quiet throughout. He was pale and seemed nervous.

"You alright Ron, not sick or anything?" Briggs asked, concerned for the hero of the valleys.

"Yes fine, absolutely perfect see, the Pringles are going to blow bloody great holes in us and you want to know if I'm alright," Jones sitting in the corner with his head in his hands. The D11 men were embarrassed by this outburst and turned away to an invented task.

"Come on Ron get a grip, we've the drop on them so we should get away with it Then if we're successful, Jack the Hat and Bolton will get great big medals, I'll get disciplined for telling Hollis to fuck off and so will you for being my mate, so it'll all come right in the end." They all laughed at this paraphrase of what usually happened in such cases. Ron seemed a little happier.

"Sorry about that Tel, not used to it see."

"Don't worry Ron, we've all had the same thing, just follow me and do your best and we'll be alright." Ron nodded in agreement.

Briggs checked his watch – 7.55am, they were early and already set up. Briggs decided to do a transmission check and picked up the personal radio. "Hello Mike Tango, Mike Tango, this is Mike Tango Two, Mike Tango Two, request transmission report." The response came in almost as soon as he had finished speaking. "Hello Mike Tango Two, Mike Tango two, this is Mike Tango, Mike Tango, your transmissions are clear strength R5, are you set on the plot?"

Briggs recognised Jack the Hat's voice. "Mike Tango, Mike Tango from Mike Tango Two, Mike Tango Two, all units in position on plot." Jack the Hat then requested situation reports from all units beginning with the one closest to Crystal Palace Park Road. There then commenced about ten minutes' worth of transmissions and situation reports, all of which Briggs logged on his clipboard as he mused, "Mm all seems to be going alright, we're bound to cock up shortly." Briggs checked his watch again – 8.15am. "Right then chaps, we are coming into H hour, let's each check each other's equipment.

Briggs got Ron to check the revolvers and ammunition, thus giving him something to do and maybe taking his mind off what was to come. The D11 guys were checked and correct a long time before Ron. Briggs spoke quietly, "Right then one more time, once the Transit is outside the cash office and they have gone in, the local crime squad seal the road off with my Westminster, then we give the 'off' to the snipers. I reckon they are going to be in the office for a maximum of three minutes. Ron and I go in first and take out the driver. Once we've done that, you two set up on the exit from the cash office. When they come out you take 'em out. I know your guvnor has given you the bit about statutory warnings, whether you do or not is down to you, but I am not going to bother. My view is that by the time you have got all that garbage out you're dead – any problems?" The D11 officers shook their heads. Ron looked decidedly queasy. Briggs poured some coffee into a mug and offered it to Jones. Silently he refused it. The D11 blokes were not interested either. Briggs sat in front of the ventilation slit, watched, drank coffee and munched his sandwiches, pleased both not to be talking or considering Ron and avoiding the puzzled looks of the D11 men.

"Mike Tango Two, Mike Tango Two from Mike Tango Control," Jack the Hat practising his radio voice. "Mike Tango Control, Mike Tango Control from Mike Tango Two receiving you clear strength R5" Briggs responded. "Hello Mike Tango Two from Mike Tango Control, we have reports of the bandit vehicle being on the move in the Crystal Palace Park Road area with three up."

"Mike Tango Control from Mike Tango Two, message received and entered on operation log," Briggs writing as he spoke. He checked the time was now 8.27am. "Strange I would have booked them out earlier than this" muttered Briggs, continuing with his sandwich.

"All units Mike Tango operation from Mike Tango One Four, bandit vehicle plus three, stationary in de Crespigny Park." Briggs grabbed a Geographia from his holdall. "If I remember right that's opposite King's College Hospital – sod it." Reference to the book confirmed his worst fears. They all four sat and waited for another transmission. It reminded Briggs of his youth when only radio was about and people huddled around the set listening to such gems as "Educating Archie" or his favourite "Dick Barton Special Agent."

After what seemed like an eternity "All units Mike Tango operation, vehicle now moved from de Crespigny Park and moving towards Camberwell Green at 25mph, still with three up. No idea why they parked up in the street, out." Briggs busied himself with the operational log. "Right, they're coming back our way."

"All units Mike Tango operation from Mike Tango Eight, bandit vehicle has turned into Albany Road from Camberwell Road, still three up, they seemed to be amused by something Mike Tango Eight out." Briggs again made a note on the log and wondered why the Pringles had been checking on King's College Hospital. Maybe they had been tipped off he pondered. If they had, they'd have been looking for the Robbery Squad. If that was so, no wonder they were amused.

Bringing his mind to the operation before him, he thought about requesting control to push all mobile units onto the other side of the Old Kent Road, but decided against it as they would be doing this on their own volition.

"All units Mike Tango operation from Mike Tango Four, vehicle in Dunton Road, turning right on to Southwark Park Road, still three up, Mike Tango Four out." Again Briggs wrote in the operational log. He checked the time, it was now 8.45am. "Well chaps, better get ready I think we are going to fire some bullets in anger," Briggs as usual trying to lighten the situation. He looked across at Jones in the gloom. "Alright mate?" Jones nodded slowly and said nothing.

Briggs carried on looking out through the ventilation slit. "All units Mike Tango operation from Mike Tango Seven, vehicle has turned right into Gomm Road and is now stationary near the junction with the Lower Road. All three up seem to be paying attention to the entrance to the hospital which is about 100 yards north. We are now leaving the area and will cover the junction by the Surrey Docks Station, Mike Tango Seven out." Briggs noted his log "They've got the right idea, I wish we were covering the Surrey Docks, or wherever – anywhere but here." Jones mumbled almost incoherent and getting more anxious by the second.

"Why have they stopped? What are they waiting for?" asked one of the D11 guys getting twitchy. Briggs checked his watch. "What I think they are waiting for is the security van. They won't take the van as that can cause problems, but once the cash has been delivered and is still in one lump that's when they will go for it. The D11 guy nodded. "Time now 8.59am" Briggs intoned and noted the log.

"Mike Tango Two, Mike Tango Two from Mike Tango Control, we have reports of a security van in Jamaica Road, turning around the roundabout and going down the Lower Road, could be your one," Jack the Hat's voice echoing around the boiler room. "Mike Tango Control from Mike Tango Two message received, out." Briggs put the handset down and noted that his pulse had increased.

Briggs leaned forward. "Here it comes now." They all crowded around the ventilation slit and watched the security van drive up to the cash office area. The uniformed security man got out of the back and walked around to the side and pressed a button. The slide opened revealing a large cash box which he took, pressed the button again, the slide closed and he went up the steps to the office. He returned a few minutes later and collected another box from behind the same slide and returned inside the office with it. He came out again a few minutes later and got back in the van, which then drove forward into the bay in front of the boiler room and reversed back into the road and drove off.

"Shit, it won't work," cried Briggs with sudden realisation. "They'll have to turn around as the security van has. The driver will see the service road get blocked and be on his toes."

Briggs picked up the radio handset. "Delta One One officer, Delta One One officer from Mike Tango Two receiving over." Almost immediately there came back a reply. "Mike Tango Two, Mike Tango Two from Delta One One receiving over."

"Yes er Delta One One from Mike Tango Two, further developments, when and if they arrive, it could be that they react to our presence quicker than we first thought. I may not be able to instruct you. or give you the 'off', so be prepared. I will of course warn you of their approach and it is still current that they will look around when getting out of the vehicle so don't show out. After that, it may be a case of independent action. In other words, you decide. Mike Tango Two over and out."

After a pause there came over the air "Fucking marvellous, absolutely fucking marvellous, I am pissed off."

"Last caller, last caller say again, your call sign Mike Tango Control out." There followed another pause at the end of which a voice said, "I am not that pissed off."

"All units Mike Tango operation from Mike Tango Control, maintain RT discipline or shut the fuck up," Jack the Hat's gritty intonation coming over the airwaves.

Briggs concentrated on the ventilation slit and the view down the service road. He could just see the junction with Lower Road. "Mike Tango Two, Mike Tango Two, from Mike Tango Six, am obbo at bus stop. Van within sight, has just started up and moving off. They're all wearing woolly hats which may be balaclavas. They're coming past me now, turning left into the hospital. Have you got them? The personal radio gave a screech and click as though warning them of something. Briggs looked for Jones who now stood in the corner vomiting.

"Mike Tango Six, Mike Tango Six from Mike Tango Two, yes I can see the bandit Transit entering the hospital and coming towards the plot, all units be ready."

Briggs turned to Jones. "Ron for pity's sake get a grip, we are on shortly." The D11 authorised shots looked embarrassed and checked their weapons to hide their emotions. "Yeah, I'm alright Tel, I'll make it" Jones said, breathing deeply to try and re-establish some bottle.

Briggs watched the Transit cruise slowly up the service road. The occupants seemed very interested in high roofs and buildings around them. They drove past the office entrance and into the bay in front of the boiler house.

The transit then reversed around and pulled forward until it was outside the office entrance and facing the exit. Two passengers got out of the vehicle, one had a long raincoat on, obviously the holder of one of the sawn offs, the other had a donkey jacket on. Briggs could see that this one was Dessie Pringle. They both looked around very cautiously. They leant up against the van and had a whispered conversation, both still looking around. Dessie turned to his colleague and nodded. They then pulled down their woolly hats which immediately became balaclava helmets and walked quickly towards the office; they resolutely entered the office.

"D11 officer from Mike Tango Two, GO.GO.GO." Briggs turned to his three colleagues. "Right, as arranged, Ron and me first, here we go, come on Ron."

Briggs exited from the boiler room, ran up the four steps and turned left. He noticed the van's engine was still running, much as he had expected. He slouched across the back of the van as though going to walk around it and passed along the driver's side. As he came alongside the driver, he held his gun below the window opening. "You going to be long mate, as we're waiting for a delivery of oil?"

Briggs looked idly into the eyes of the driver. Out of the corner of his eye Briggs was aware that the exit was being blocked by his old Westminster.

"Only a few minutes mate," stuttered the driver. Briggs lifted the gun over the window sill. "Get out now, or die," Briggs said quietly but with a great deal of menace bred out of intent.

The van's engine raced and it took off towards the exit and Briggs' Westminster at a great rate of knots. Briggs turned and looked at Jones who stood about twenty feet behind him white faced, holding his gun loosely in his hand. Obviously no help would be forthcoming from that quarter and Briggs ran towards the van which, by that time, had crashed into the Westminster. The driver was trying to open the driver's door but couldn't as it had been buckled by the impact of the crash. The driver transferred his attention to the passenger door. Briggs ran around that side of the vehicle and the driver started to come out of the van, just as Briggs arrived at the rear. Briggs saw, or certainly thought he saw, the barrel of a Browning with the driver. Briggs ran forward and slammed the door on the emerging figure and the Browning clattered to the floor. Briggs kicked the gun under the van and then opened the door slowly. The driver made a movement forward and Briggs slammed the door on him again, this time catching his head with the impact. Briggs opened the door again and the driver poured out of the cab onto the ground, unconscious. Briggs dragged him away from the van and beckoned to the Constable from the Uniform Squad. As he approached, Briggs called to him, "Right mate, get on the radio, get an ambulance for our friend here, but first search him and cuff him to the van. Any problems call me and I'll exit the bastard." Briggs kicked the driver in the ribs as a punctuation mark. The driver moaned and Briggs ran back towards the cash office.

"Right Ron what have you got?" Briggs stood next to Jones at the corner of the boiler house. The D11 men he could see were either side of the cash office door.

Briggs studied Jones closely, he looked pale and frightened. His fear plainly showed. "Don't really know Tel, they came half out to see what the commotion was with the van. We haven't seen them since."

The cash door half opened. "Listen up old bill, I've got a hostage, you go for us and I'll kill her." Briggs thought he recognised the voice as being Dessie. "Call off the gunmen outside the door and come forward so I can see you." Briggs gave his gun to Jones. "Ron, don't screw up, get on the radio and put the snipers on independent action and ignore all orders from Jack the Hat and anything I say." Briggs then walked forward and stood in front of the entrance about twelve feet away from it. He waved the D11 officers away from either side of the door and they walked off so that they could be seen from inside the building.

"Right then, the coast is clear come on out" yelled Briggs, standing on the road in front of the cash office double doors. Briggs could see a balaclava'd man just inside the doors. He was holding a girl closely to him with a gun to her head.

"Right Briggsy get me a car. You're driving us out of this and if we don't get away neither do you or the girl – got it?" Briggs nodded in reply. Briggs calculated the angle between the sniper posts and the inside position of Dessie and decided they would be unlikely to get a clear shot in this position. "Let's see your hands in the air." Briggs put his hands up in the accepted manner and said quietly, "It ain't going to work Dessie, it's off at all meetings. Even if you do her and me you're going to get the same. You'll never see the light of day. Plus my mates are all around, tooled up and waiting. You blow me away and I think they may take a dim view of it." Dessie pulled up his balaclava. Dessie probably did this as Briggs had correctly identified him, and possibly it had become uncomfortable and itchy.

"Fuck you Briggsy, just get me a car and cut the psychology." Dessie popped his head out a bit, enough to check both sides of the door.

"It's alright, the blue berets have been called off, come on out you're quite safe," Briggs with his hands still in the air.

Dessie shouted from his interior position "Get us a car or she's dead." He paused and pushed his hostage and part of himself out in full view. "Want her to die as…" Dessie spoke no more, his voice cut off by the flat crack of a high powered rifle. Dessie recoiled with the force of the impact, a surprised look on his face, all of which initiated screams and hysterics from the hostage.

The other bandit called out, "Dessie's down I want to give up." There followed a clunk as a sawn off shotgun hit the asphalt in front of Briggs. "There are two ways of coming out of there; one is on your knees with your hands on your head, the other is in a body bag – which do you want?" Briggs shouted, well aware that the third bandit could be playing for time. A short time later the bandit appeared at the double doors hobbling on his knees. The bandit completely ignored the screaming hostage and his late partner and paid a great deal of attention to this detective who now held the power of life (his) and death (also his).

Briggs ran forward and picked up the sawn off. He dragged the robber onto the asphalt and laid him face down, kicking his arms and legs into the spread eagle position. He ran his hands over the robber and made sure he was unarmed. "Please don't blow me away guv, I've given up." Briggs noted that the robber was in dire need of a change of underpants.

"Behave yourself and you'll be doing a nice comfortable twenty stretch."

Briggs waved to Jones to come and take over the prisoner. Jones walked over, he was shaking and very pale. "Tel, I've got to tell you I was absolutely terrified."

Briggs grinned "So was I Ron, so was I. Now look after our friend here." He indicated the prostrate prisoner, "And I'll go and see what's going on in there." Briggs took his gun from Jones and placed it in his holster. Jones looked puzzled. Briggs, catching his glance, said "One never knows mate. While you're sitting around, get on to Jack the Hat and give him a situation report and give everyone else the stand down."

Briggs entered the foyer of the cash office. There was a glass partition in front of the door which had a neat hole in it where Dessie's head had been. The partition was splattered with brains, blood and bone fragments. The young girl who had been held hostage was sitting on the floor next to Dessie's body. She was crying and screaming hysterically. Briggs knelt down beside her, "Come on love it's all over you're safe now."

"You bastard, you've killed my brother," she screamed and hit

Briggs full in the face with her clenched fist. Briggs fell from kneeling to lying in one short movement. She stood up screaming, "He was nice he was, he never would have used that gun on you, just had it for show like." During this diatribe she kicked Briggs in the balls as he was endeavouring to get up, and he collapsed in a crumpled heap in agony. The girl reached forward and took Briggs' gun from his shoulder holster. The girl then screamed and Briggs heard her crash into the partition. Briggs looked up, holding his genitals, into the face of a middle aged lady.

"Are you alright officer? I had to hit her hard, I'm sure she was going to kill you," explaining what Briggs knew to be fact. The girl moaned and turned over, her brother's blood on her face. Briggs managed to get up and drag her to her feet. "You're nicked Tracy and so's your husband when I get around to him" Briggs said, still rubbing his sore cobblers.

"Nicked – what for? I ain't done nuffink have I?" Tracy exclaiming that which is the clarion call of most villains who think they are not bang to rights. "I'm not surprised she's involved," sniffed the middle aged matron.

The Aftermath

Rodney Road was in chaos. The canteen and CID office were crowded with those that had been on the operation and those usually of higher rank who came to pontificate. The third bandit and Tracy were in custody. Dessie was lodged at the local mortuary awaiting a post-mortem to ascertain cause of death. The mortuary attendant examined Dessie on arrival at the morgue and opined that, "His demise might have something to do wiv the great hole in the back of his head," indicating the space where the back half of Dessie's head should be.

An ambulance had eventually turned up and carted Mickey Pringle, the driver, off to hospital with a broken arm and jaw, complaining noisily (jaw allowing) of police brutality and how he was really going to get even with Briggsy and his partner for these injuries.

Briggs with Jones in tow entered the CID office. They both sat down, quiet and spent. The office went quiet on their entrance. Officers pretended to be doing something so important that they could fail to notice the entrance of the dynamic duo.

Jones stared at his desk. Briggs sat quietly opposite. "You alright Ron?" asked Briggs eventually, raising some concern about his very silent partner, a burst of advice from the scriptures was more preferable than this morbid silence.

"No, not really, I don't think I will ever come to terms with it." Briggs could tell that Ron was close to tears.

"Come on mate, it could be worse, they could have killed us, or more importantly me," said Briggs, laughing at the prospect. This had quite the reverse effect on Jones who placed his head on his blotter and began to sob uncontrollably. The detectives present ignored him completely. Shrouded in embarrassed silence they got on with what they had to do. Those who had to go out did so, and yet still others disappeared to the canteen. Sid Mills approached Ron and whispered, "Come on Ron, get a grip, others are watching," Sid patting Ron's shoulder in the process.

"I couldn't give a shit," said Ron still sobbing. "It's all Briggsy's fault, why can't we deal with shoplifters and the like. Why do we have to do this sort of nonsense. I'm not ashamed. I wasn't just terrified, I shit myself and threw up – that terrified Now it's all over I don't know what to do or what to think." Jones placed his head on the blotter in front of him and continued sobbing.

Briggs beckoned to Sid to the stairwell outside the office door. Outside Briggs said, "The best thing we can do is put our Ron uncertificated sick. If we call in the Police Surgeon he'll commit him to Maudsley and he don't need that on his AQR." (Annual Qualification Report).

Sid thought for a moment "I agree, who do we know who can help?"

"I suggest that we send him home and get in touch with his GP in a couple of days, when hopefully he should have got a grip. In the meantime, I'll get some valium off a mate, that may do him a bit of good. I'll pop it round to him later," said Briggs.

"Right then Briggsy, I'll run him home. I expect you have some heavy interviewing to get through. Apparently they are not too pleased with the way it went – something about civilian casualties." Briggs looked surprised. "I don't know what they are on about, only one got killed. I could have done another one, but my natural self control and restraint took over." They returned to the office.

Jones was still slumped on his blotter. "Ron come on, Sid is going to run you home. I'll be around later and see how you're doing" Briggs said patting Ron's shoulder.

"Right then," said Jones slowly rising to his feet. He looked distant and had stopped crying, but his eyes were red rimmed.

"See you tonight mate right? Now go and get some rest or get pissed. Try and forget. Do what you like and I'll see you later." Sid led Jones out of the office. As he retired, Briggs could see the backs of his trousers which were stained where he had evacuated his bowels. He felt sorry for Ron.

Briggs considered his position. There were three or four officers present in the office but they all pretended Briggs was invisible. Barking came in through the door at the end of the office. He was red faced and looked thoroughly pissed off. "Briggsy I want a word with you, me and my mates on the Squad waited at KCH and you were doing the business at St Olaves. You led us up the garden path," Barking said accusingly.

"Look John do me favour, I don't need you or this shit at the moment, just fuck off will you?" There was a certain edge to Briggs' voice that impressed Barking that this was not a good time to discuss the matter.

"Right then, but later, definitely later." Barking strode off, slamming the door as he went.

Briggs sat down at his desk and assessed the situation. On the basis of the law, he had no problem as Dessie had been engaged in serious crime and was armed. The problem that Briggs had was that, as Dessie had wound up dead, this gave employment to solicitors, social workers, do-gooders and family, all of whom would be gunning for him and, to a lesser extent, the guy from D11 who had actually ejected Dessie into eternity. He was deep in thought when the telephone rang. Shaking his mind back to the present, Briggs picked it up. It was the station officer. "There's a Mr. Beamish down here, wants to see the prisoners, the ones you let live that is." The sergeant giggled at his attempt at black humour.

"You opened your Christmas crackers early skip? I'll be down in a minute." Briggs got up and went downstairs.

"Ah good morning Mr. Briggs, we meet again. I'm here for Tracy Coker, Ibrahim Hussain, and Michael Pringle. Can I see my clients please?" Mr. Beamish placed his expensive briefcase on the counter as he spoke. "They are, after all, in peril of substantial prison sentences and could benefit from legal counsel as is their right." Beamish looked expectantly at Briggs.

"I'm sorry sir, I cannot allow you to see your clients at the present time, to do so would not serve the ends of justice." Briggs spoke forcefully, the front office staff were impressed.

"Then perhaps we can go to an interview room in order that I may make notes of this and other details on my brief?"

"Certainly Mr. Beamish this way." Briggs ushered the brief into a side room and closed the door behind them.

"Alright Frank, how you doing?" Briggs immediately dropping the official front.

"Not too bad Tel, could have done without this one though. How about you? You've been through the wringer this morning I understand." Briggs nodded. They both sat down. Beamish took out his cigarettes and offered them to Briggs who shook his head.

Beamish lit one of the cigarettes and inhaled deeply, and exhaled, almost with relief, which made Briggs wonder why people bothered with smoking at all. It had been different in the fifties, it had almost been compulsory then. Anyone who didn't smoke was a right prat, and probably a poof.

Beamish studied the end of his cigarette. "Firstly, as you can guess, I'm here at the behest of old man Pringle on a damage limitation exercise. Not so much worried about Hussain – he's just a common soldier, but Tracy and Michael are close family and he wants outers for them. He is prepared to pay the ante as usual." Beamish spread his papers across the table.

Briggs paused before answering. "I think you could be whistling in the wind on that one Frank, she's on for a serious conspiracy and attempted murder of a police officer – me, and I do take the whole thing rather seriously. Michael's on for robbery, possession of a prohibited weapon – the sawn off, and attempted murder, you name it he's there."

"Well just see what you can do. I've already told Pringle he's crying for the moon. If you could get around the attempted murder it would be a help," Beamish said hopefully.

"Well I have yet to have the conference with Jack the Hat, we'll see how we go yes?" Briggs got up indicating that the interview, or more likely the truce, was over.

Beamish did not get up, he played with his cigarette on the ash tray. "Only one other thing and already I know the answer, but as I am being paid to ask I will. Old Man Pringle wants your informant."

Briggs opened the door, and gave Beamish one of his severe looks. "Well Frank you have asked and, as you say, you know the answer." Briggs indicated Beamish's exit.

Beamish got up, gathered his papers and turned to Briggs, wearing just the whisper of a smile. "I can take it that George Harris is not your informant then?"

Briggsy looked Beamish straight in the eye, "No that was put down so that others would see it and believe it." Beamish broke into a broad grin.

"Just what I told old man Pringle, that you wouldn't leave that information just lying around." He left after treating Briggs to a sombre handshake.

Briggs sat in the canteen, for the first time in a long while on his own. Jones was sick and the others were treating him as leper. They didn't even look in his direction. Briggs stared into his tea, thinking of Jones's words, "Who needs this shit, why do we do it?"

"Detective Chief Inspector Parris wants you in his office, like now." The voice was that of a new young duty officer, known to all as the Bramshill Wonder on account of his having been on a twelve month stint at the Bramshill Police College for those selected for rapid promotion. Briggs looked up at this toy soldier who, to Briggs, looked about fourteen, but ever so smart in his immaculate uniform. "Do you understand me Constable, get going, now!" The Bramshill Wonder made to march off down the canteen towards his front office.

"Sir," Briggs called to him, and knew that the toy soldier couldn't resist the "Sir" routine. Briggs beckoned to him as if he wished to speak privately with him. As the Bramshill Wonder got close to him, Briggs stood up and towered over him, which Briggs knew would upset him because it accentuated his diminutive size. "Sir, if you can find an old slapper who will take on all comers, go and get fucked. In the meantime, don't bother me." Briggs sat down and continued drinking his tea.

Bramshill Wonder had a touch of the stutters and said, "I shall report this to your Chief Inspector Briggs." The Bramshill Wonder was flustered and rummaged for his pocket book. Had he been really well versed he would have called for Briggs' pocket book to endorse that. In this case Briggs would have refused to give it. "Sir, my advice is for you to make that report and then roll it into the only paper suppository in this kingdom and then guess what you do with it?" The Bramshill Wonder was speechless and stormed off towards the front office uncertain how to deal with this stroppy Constable.

Briggs finished his tea and went upstairs. He knocked on Jack the Hat's office door. "Enter." It didn't sound like Jack the Hat and it wasn't. When Briggs entered, Jack the Hat was standing in the corner and his desk was occupied by a grey haired man wearing the uniform of Deputy Assistant Commissioner. "Detective Constable Briggs sir, you wanted to see me."

"Ah yes Briggs, obviously about this operation this morning. One dead, one badly injured in hospital and two in custody." Briggs thought, "Ideally I would have liked to make it four dead, less paper work" but didn't, instead he nodded dutifully. The grey head continued, "There are already questions being asked as to whether it was really necessary to kill him." The grey head smiled the Cobra smile of most senior officers from the yard.

"Well sir I cannot speak for the D11 officer, but I expect he followed my instructions for dealing with a hostage situation," Briggs trying to make it sound like an everyday occurrence, maybe even part of some game played on the streets of London according to a set of rules which keep changing.

"I see," the DAC said, making notes. Jack the Hat caught Briggs' eye and shook his head slowly, which Briggs took to mean, "Don't rock the boat." Briggs couldn't see that he could do other than tell the truth, Dessie had taken a hostage and come second, Mickey Pringle had come out of a van with a gun in his hand and had also come second. "I want a report on my desk within one hour" the grey head demanded, not looking at Briggs, but seemingly directing this order at the blotter, almost as though frightened to look Briggs in the eye.

"Can't be done at the moment guv, I have to do my statement first, then I'll do your report," Briggs responded looking down at grey head's bald patch. "You will do my report first, then your statement – understand Briggs?" Briggs could have pointed out that the length of time taken to do the report delayed his compilation of a statement from the operational log which would, in the fullness of time, be examined by some very clever people and made much of to the benefit of Tracy and Michael. However he said, "Yes guv, I understand." Grey head nodded to him from the office. Briggs went back to his desk.

"What the hell's up with you Briggsy?" asked Jack the Hat parking himself in Jones' chair a few minutes later.

Briggs looked up from his papers. "I'll tell you what the matter is guv. I have just come through a bottle testing job, I have half killed someone, my buck is having what is best described as a nervous breakdown and now the parasites from the Yard want me to jump through hoops so they come out lily white." Briggs' voice rose to a crescendo.

"Alright Briggsy alright, calm down, do the report and go home," said Jack the Hat in calming manner.

"No guv, I'll do it the right way, my statement first, then his fucking report. Then if they want me on the dab, be my guest." Briggs carried on writing on a statement form from his pocket book and the operational log.

Jack the Hat nodded sagely, "As always Briggsy down to you. How about interviews, are you going to do them now?" Briggs paused for thought.

"Well guv as far as I can see I only have to accumulate the evidence from the various officers and the evidence is there, technically I don't have to interview anyone."

Jack the Hat said, "I can see that, but for form I think they should be questioned even just to put 'X's' in boxes." Briggs studied the situation.

"I can see something has to be said guv. I'll do it tomorrow, how about that? After all I don't expect anything is going to be given in evidence." Jack the Hat nodded and retreated to his office.

Briggs completed his paper work, including the report for the grey head and booked off duty. On his way home he called into Sammy Fisher's chemist's shop and collected some valium for Ron. Sammy said something about taking it off some depressed housewife's prescription. Briggs didn't laugh but nodded.

Briggs drove to Ron's house in Biggin Hill. The door was opened by Audrey the owner of the hairy mole. She looked severe. Briggs could sense the animosity in her voice. "What do you want Briggs?" Under less serious circumstances Briggs would have laughed, but not now.

"I'd like to see Ron if he's about, and if that's alright." She nodded to the side of the house, not inviting Briggs in.

"He's down the garden in the greenhouse, but I warn you he's not himself." Briggs nodded and went round the side of the bungalow and into the back garden. He walked down the path to the greenhouse at the bottom. Ron was sitting on a wooden box transplanting seedlings. Briggs could see that he had been crying.

"Alright Ron, you feel better now?"

Ron looked up and spoke slowly. "No Briggsy I don't feel any better at all, in fact, a bit worse." Briggs searched for something to say that would help his partner but could find nothing. Ron stared at him blankly.

"Here Ron, Sammy Fisher sent these for you, don't take them all at once now." Ron took the bottle of pills and stared at them.

"That thought has a strange attraction to it." Briggs studied Ron for a second then decided that he was not the type.

However, he did say, "I thought that even the thought of suicide was against the scriptures Ron."

Ron shook his head, "Aye it is, it most definitely is." Briggs decided to leave Ron to the tender mercies of Audrey and left without speaking to her.

Later, at home, Briggs watched the evening news when, in clipped BBC English, an announcer said, "This morning in Rotherhithe a man died in a police operation when marksmen opened fire. There follows an interview with Deputy Assistant Commissioner Smithson."

The picture changed to the Press Suite at New Scotland Yard where the grey head Briggs had spoken to earlier was seated behind a desk with a single sheet of paper on it. He looked up from the paper to the camera. "I regret to announce the death of Mr. Desmond Pringle who was shot dead by armed police this morning during an operation to prevent a robbery at St Olaves Hospital, Rotherhithe. The matter will be considered in depth by the Police Authorities but criminal or disciplinary proceedings are not, at the present time, contemplated against the officers concerned."

The picture changed again and showed Mrs. Pringle in tears. "Oh he was a really lovely boy he was, never a moment's trouble. Always good to me he was. He wouldn't have used that gun, he was just mucking about like." Briggs grinned at the television. "So were we my love, so were we."

The picture changed again and Ms Sally Rodgers, a social worker, came on screen speaking with all the earnest integrity of ignorance, "One good family man has died because the police over-reacted, why did it have to be? Couldn't they have overpowered him or perhaps shot him in the legs? That we have men in the pay of the state who can do such things is insulting to the normal freedoms of society."

Briggs got up and turned Ms Rodgers off in full flow.

Although much happened before the case finally came to court, Mickey Pringle received ten years for attempted armed robbery and Hussein fifteen years. Coker, after pleading guilty, received eighteen months for conspiracy, no charge having been entered against her for attempt murder.

The Arm

"Come on Fabian, your boss wants you at the nick now," Mrs. Briggs shaking life back into Briggs. Briggs came out of slumber slowly, extricating himself from the embrace of his youngest son who, because of nightmares, had taken to transferring beds in the middle of the night.

"Is it time to get up Dad?" asked a bleary eyed pyjamas wrapped little figure.

"No, Tommy, go back to sleep, this is a "Dads only" getting up time. You cuddle up to Mum and I'll see you tonight, I promise." As he mentioned "cuddling up to Mum" Briggs felt a wave of envy. Cuddling up to Mum was one of his favourite bedtime occupations.

"Make sure you keep your promise" muttered Maggie. Briggs crept downstairs, washed and shaved in double quick time and made his way back to the nick. It seemed like only minutes ago that he had left the place.

He entered Jack the Hat's office after the customary knock. Jack the Hat was sitting behind his desk, a bottle of gin and a glass before him and, stretched across the front of the desk, was a human arm. It lay there open-handed and white. It had been severed at the shoulder. Tendons and slivers of flesh could be seen where it had been detached. Jack the Hat contemplated the body part with glass in hand.

"Morning Briggsy, how about that then, found in a dustbin in Camberwell," said Jack the Hat indicating the arm draped across his desk. "The Laboratory Liaison Officer will be here in a minute, but I'm sure we have a murder on our hands – like, where's the rest of the body?"

Briggs examined the arm closely without touching it. "Guv, there's no blood so it looks as though it has been hacked off after death."

"Very interesting Briggsy, but we'll wait for Sergeant Probyn, the lab man. He will enlighten us," said Jack the Hat as he reached for his glass, refilling it with neat gin. He offered the bottle to Briggs who shook his head emphatically.

"Much too early guv, or too late – whatever, wrong time for me."

Jones entered, looking very detached from reality, bleary eyed, tousled hair, shirt buttoned incorrectly. "Alright guv," Jones spoke, eyeing the arm reposed on Jack the Hat's desk.

"Well, I think we could be said to be indulging in an 'armless exercise in investigation." Jack the Hat beamed at his joke. Briggs and Jones groaned as they realised that this would be the start of many jokes and wind-ups. Jack the Hat briefly explained the situation again to Jones and the fact that they were now awaiting the arrival of Detective Sergeant Probyn, the Laboratory Liaison Officer who would, no doubt, throw light on an otherwise cloudy enquiry.

"Got any more troops arriving guv, or is it down to us?" Briggs asked, feeling uncomfortable in the room with this part of human anatomy.

"Down to you and Jonesy for the time being. If the thing looks as though it is going murder squad then we will form one but, of course, you two will be on it as you are now."

A knock at the door announced the arrival of Detective Sergeant Probyn. "Enter" bawled Jack the Hat. Into the room strolled "Doc" the Laboratory Liaison Officer from Four Area, smartly dressed in pinstripe suit and a crisp white starched collar shirt with contrasting pink body. He was wearing an awful old school tie, the colours of which clashed so much with each other and the rest of his attire, that it must be the flag of some really prestigious organisation. The briefcase was of the best leather, as were the shoes. The whole rigout screamed "Detective Chief Superintendent," not "Detective Sergeant."

Jack the Hat was staggered. The contrast was magic; Jack the Hat with yesterday's growth on his chin, his trilby firmly stuck on his head and without the jacket which hung over his office chair. The stark fluorescent light highlighted every crease in yesterday's shirt.

Jack the Hat felt, and looked, unclean.

"Good morning Sir. This is the offending item of which you rang, is it?" Without waiting for an answer and, possibly because it was the only obvious amputated arm in the place, he placed his briefcase on the desk and opened it. By looking over Probyn's shoulder, Briggs could see a number of glass phials with corks, swabs and containers, rubber gloves, a large anal thermometer, forms, notebooks and a large stop watch clipped to a mill board. Probyn clicked the stop watch and it began recording. He took off his jacket, rolled his sleeves up, pulled on a pair of rubber gloves and, once satisfied with their fit, turned to the arm and felt it along its length. "Mm, muscle tone still present, must be fairly recent." Probyn continued to feel it along its length. He flexed it at the elbow and the wrist. "As a preliminary report sir, I would say it's three months old and has been in the ground. Past that I cannot be sure." Probyn pulled the gloves off and threw them in the waste-paper bin. He then replaced his jacket and checked his appearance in Jack the Hat's full length mirror, an article on the inventory of every Detective Chief Inspector's office but seldom, if ever, used by Jack the Hat.

"And any clue as to violence employed?" Jack the Hat asked, keen to drag as much information from this well dressed expert. "I really cannot say sir without laboratory facilities" Probyn said, now standing and closing his expensive briefcase. "Can I enquire sir when the limb will be submitted to the Forensic Science Laboratory for scientific examination? I need to know so that I can liaise and provide the relevant scientist for the job," Probyn at last getting into what was really his job, being the link man between the scientist and the policeman on the street.

"I don't know exactly, but later on today sometime. I have various enquiries before I release it for your department's examination. Thank you for turning out in the middle of the night Sergeant." Jack the Hat said it with as much deference as he ever employed. Briggs looked hopeful, perhaps Jack the Hat was going to thank him for turning out as well, but no such nicety was forthcoming. Jack the Hat looked at his watch. It was about 4.45am, the summer sun could be seen to be coming up over the rooftops on Rodney Road, the market bustle could be heard going into East Lane. "Right then you two. What I want you to do is to go to the flats where this thing was found," indicating the arm, "and turn out the communal dustbin and see if there are any more parts of this body lying around in there." Jack the Hat paused, leaned back in his chair, took a swig of neat gin and continued, "Secondly, do some house-to-house enquiries and as, in my view, we are talking about murder, murder squad rules apply. Anybody you think knows something, drag 'em in."

Briggs nodded and indicated the door to Jones. They left. "Bugger me, that's going to be lovely, emptying that dustbin" Jones said, bemoaning his fate.

"Ours is but to do or die mate and if we are successful, the guvnor will get a good write up. If we are unsuccessful, we get a bad write up, simple innit. Come on, let's get down there." Briggs was just glad to be out and free. "Afterwards we could stop off at Maisie's Cafe for breakfast."

"Yes, that would be lovely, after examining the chute effluent of a South London block of flats, we can then have a nice greasy fry up, sounds delightful," Jones grumbled as they walked along.

They arrived in the deserted backyard of the block of flats. Briggs was reminded of the flats where he grew up in Notting Hill Gate, which were probably designed by the same architect. Much use of steel galvanised window frames, central chute out of precast concrete, usually, and as in this case, painted blue. Between the blocks was the tired playground furniture, long past its best, sited on shiny black tarmac. Around the blocks were once flower beds, which had now been vandalised and become home to old car engines, milk crates and supermarket shopping trolleys. They found the relevant block and tried the chute door, it was locked. On the side of the chute shed was a notice, "Caretaker No. 56 Heron House."

Briggs went to No. 56, checked his watch, it was now 5.45am. "High time an employee of the Council was out of bed and assisting Her Majesty's Constabulary." Briggs knocked loudly on the door. It was answered by a man in a boiler suit.

"I've been waiting for you lot to come, it's about the arm isn't it?"

"Yes it is, we need to look in the dustbin to see if any more bits are in there."

The caretaker shrugged his shoulders and went outside jangling a bunch of keys as he went. He opened the chute shed door and waved them in. "But I'm sure you won't find anything." Jones was already going forward as if on automatic pilot.

"Hang on a minute Ron." Briggs then turned to the caretaker. "How is it that you know we won't find anything?" Briggs looked searchingly at the caretaker. The caretaker sniffed. "Be a good idea if the Council issued this one with handkerchiefs" Briggs thought, observing another dewdrop forming on his nose.

The caretaker sniffed again but this time answered, "Well, just know dun I?" The caretaker looked at the ground and stirred some rubbish with his foot.

Briggs gauged that the caretaker had something to impart, but would not do so until forced, as this would preserve his credibility within the flats. Briggs, apparently in his most patient sounding manner, said, "Listen guv, I think it would be a good idea if you made us a cup of tea and we discuss how it is you know so much. Now that discussion can either be in your flat, or down the nick, where I promise life will get definitely uncomfortable and painful. On the other hand, we can be mates and you tell me all you know. Now you choose."

This proved to be exactly the right amount of force and, mixed with a less confrontational alternative, the caretaker grumbled, "Alright, come in the flat, I'll tell you."

They returned, keys clanking, to the ground floor flat. They entered and were immediately assailed by the smell of a flat that has never been favoured by the opening of windows. The caretaker called out, "Oi, Sally, make us a cup of tea will you." After a few seconds, Mrs. Caretaker appeared. She seemed a female version of her husband, judging from the dewdrop on her nose and by her miserable countenance. She nodded and retired.

The caretaker made himself comfortable beside the kitchen table and, inevitably, sniffed, the caretaker emphatically nodding his head. "S'right ain't it Sall?" He spoke to Sally who was bringing in a tray of none-too-clean cups and saucers, with the teapot and accessories.

"Oh yes, dirty little bleeders, saw 'em last night playing with it in the area, waving it around like a wand they wos." Sally poured the tea. Briggs looked at the cups and realised they had never been cleaned, ever. There was a brown rim around them. "Our best china this is, keep it for special guests" Sally said, as though bestowing some special award.

"How did you know it was a real arm?" asked Jones, voicing that which troubled him.

"Well we didn't know for sure. At first I thought it was part of one of those tailor's dummies, but then I called Sall, she was in the rag trade you know." The caretaker announced it as though they should be impressed" and she said it was too floppy so it must be real."

"And who had the arm?" enquired Jones, pushing the ball along the desired path.

"Young Wilkins from the top floor, nasty bit of work he is, you know, one of those bovver boys, all tattoos and swearing, not a civil word in his head." Sally seemed to know the lad quite well.

"And where does Wilkins come from?" Jones continued, still aiming for the main chance.

"Top floor Ellison House, I forget the number, but it's the one with a horse brass on the door." Sally seemed to enjoy being helpful. "Now drink your tea or it'll get stewed." Briggs looked at Jones, they both grimaced and drank some of their tea, if only to avoid offending the chatting Sally.

"Ever so sorry my love, but must go and have a little word with young Wilkins. You know how it is, duty and all that." Briggs delighted to be away from the acid tea. They left quickly and walked across to Ellison House. They went up in the urinal/lift to the top floor.

The flat on the left had a horse brass screwed to the door. Briggs knocked on the door and it was answered a few moments later by a spotty youth whose flaxen hair was fashioned into a crewcut. The grubby tee-shirt shouted "Screw yer." The jeans were suspended by thin red braces and stopped just below the knee, where the long Dr. Martins started. He was extensively tattooed and, one in particular, was a dotted line across his throat which invited "cut here." Briggs thought, "I might just do that."

"What the fuck do you want?" snarled the spotty youth.

"We are police from Rodney Road Police Station" began Jones, but was interrupted.

"I know that, don't I prick, what the fuck do you want?" Briggs, deciding that no amount of reasonable remonstration was going to achieve very much, grabbed the youth firmly by the soft tissue between his nose and his upper lip, using his thumb and forefinger, and pulled him out of the flat onto the landing.

"Ow, sod off, that hurts, leave orf." Briggs pushed the bell for the lift. The door opened and Briggs pulled the youth into the lift and slammed him up against the back wall. Jones got into the lift and pressed the ground floor button whilst Briggs went though the youth's pockets.

Having found nothing of interest, he said, "You are Wilkins I take it?"

The youth muttered, "Yeah."

Briggs pulled him up hard by his upper lip and asked, "What was that you said you sweaty turd, was that "yes"?

"Yes" screamed the youth, "Yes."

"Oh good, I thought that was what you said," said Briggs.

Once on the ground floor, they walked into the yard, Briggs still leading Wilkins by the upper lip. By this time, Wilkins was streaming from the eyes and moaning. "Shut up you scaly bastard," Briggs grunted, giving the lad just a touch more on the upper lip. The youth screamed.

"Here leave off Tel, you trying to kill the lad" Jones said, showing a bit of concern for the youth.

"If I killed him and burned his body to make sand for egg timers, I bet he would still be useless, probably clog up the bloody works," responded Briggs, giving his best yet impression of Bogart. Briggs opened the rear door of the Hillman, pushed Wilkins inside and slammed the door. Wilkins laid on the back seat and held his upper lip, his eyes watering. He looked as though he had been given six by the headmaster.

"Here you, what are you doing with my son?" an irate woman asked as she approached, dressed in dressing gown but no slippers.

"We have arrested him Madam, on reasonable suspicion that he is involved in an offence of murder," Jones putting what was later accepted as the official view.

"I don't care" she said. "You can't just come round and take him like that, you have to let me know."

Briggs looked closely at the woman and then at Wilkins holding his upper lip. It seemed hard to imagine that anyone could care for such an acne ridden, tattooed yobbo, but obviously this lady did. "Madam, I will let you know later this morning as to what is going on. In the meantime, he will be in custody at Rodney Road." Briggs spoke to her, got in the passenger side and Jones drove off. The woman stood there and waved forlornly at the disappearing car. On the way to the Police Station, Briggs began to have pangs of remorse. Maybe Jones was right, maybe he had been too hard on the lad. Briggs turned and looked over the seat at their prisoner. "Now listen to me very carefully. You're going to be interviewed by the senior detective at Rodney Road; you come the old acid as you have with me and I promise life will become very uncomfortable, got it?" Wilkins looked up from his ministrations on his lip and said, "Sod off you fat prick."

Briggs exploded over the front seat into the back and, grabbing Wilkins around the throat, began to batter him with the back of his other hand. "I'll give you fat prick you slimy shit," Briggs punctuating the words with slaps to the head until Wilkins became or feigned unconsciousness. Briggs stopped slapping the youth.

"Now officer, tell me, when did you first notice your psychotic paranoia and have you stopped beating your wife yet?" Jones mimicking the psycho-analyst's routine. "Do you find you have difficulty relating to the young?"

Briggs answered in more basic form, "Screw you Jones and double screw him, the little shit." Wilkins still feigned unconsciousness, but now with more difficulty.

They drove into the yard of Rodney Road Police Station and, to the amusement of the yard officers, Briggs clambered out of the back, having been let out by Jones.

"Come on you or do you want me to help you?" Briggs growled at the youth. Miraculously he woke up and got out of the car at Briggs' bidding. They ushered him into the charge room and sat him down on the bench which ran across the back of the room. "Now shithead" said Briggs, introducing an element of realism into the conversation, "Before I announce your presence to the almighty, who is much better at the violence routine than me, is there anything you want to tell me about your possession of the human arm last night?"

Wilkins looked sheepish, scratched his nose and said, "Found it din't I," giving Briggs a beaming smile which disclosed broken and discoloured teeth.

"What an ugly little article but he does have one redeeming feature, his mother loves him" thought Briggs.

"Where exactly did you find it?" Briggs asked, leaning close to Wilkins, close enough to suddenly notice his awful bad breath. Briggs pulled away.

"Over the cemetery, down in the crypt like." Wilkins looked almost embarrassed as he studied his calf length Dr. Martens.

"You found it in the crypt? Was it attached to a body when you found it?" Briggs feeling his way gently.

Wilkins shrugged his shoulders in the accepted hard man routine. "Well yeah, of course, we cut it off." Jones was making a face of distaste. "We also cut off a head and used it to play football with outside the church," Wilkins added brightly and almost with pride.

"You did what?" Even Briggs was astounded by what Wilkins was saying.

"Yeah like, did it din't we" Wilkins spoke as though quite made up by what he took to be admiration from Briggs and Jones but which, in fact, was incredulity.

"Let's get this right. You cut off a head to play football with and then you cut off an arm – both from the same body I take it?" Briggs feeling more than a little queasy.

"No, different bodies, they're all across the crypt floor."

"Why did you go into the crypt in the first place?" Briggs asked, now more intrigued than following any designated line of enquiry.

"Well, it was somewhere to go when it rained like, to play, and all that" the spotty youth said, as though explaining the obvious.

"To play!, to bloody play?" Briggs exclaimed, suddenly realising that he and Jones may have made a terrible mistake. "Exactly how old are you?" Wilkins seemed started by the question.

"I was seventeen today, why?"

Briggs got out his pocket book and made a note of the date of birth and silently heaved a sigh of relief. As the spotty shit was an adult today, parents and social workers were a thing of the past for this little lad. Although, to be fair, Briggs had judged him to be twenty without a doubt. "Right then, we'll put you in the detention room and inform the Station Officer and the guv'nor, in that order." After that explanation, Briggs left Wilkins sitting on the bench looking at the not-very-artistic graffiti on the wall opposite.

"Run that past me again Briggsy. You've nicked a bovver boy who admits cutting the arm off a corpse. Is that it?" Jack the Hat asked, still sitting at his desk contemplating the isolated arm before him "And where again did he get it from?"

"The crypt beneath the chapel at the cemetery guv." Briggs was almost sorry to burst Jack the Hat's dream of a celebrated murder enquiry.

"Do we know that this is the truth. How do we corroborate what this turd says?" he queried, looking towards Jones but, realising this was a hopeless cause, at Briggs.

"Well guv, just bouncing it off the wall, what we have to do is to take the arm to the crypt and see if they have broken into it, at which point, we then have to find a body which matches our arm – a bit like Cinderella really" Briggs added, realising as soon as he said it that the Cinderella crack was in very poor taste. Anyway, Jack the Hat started the jokes, so what the hell. Jack the Hat pondered the suggestion for a few moments.

"Right, can't fault it, get yourselves together and get to it."

Briggs nodded and left the office, returning with a large exhibits bag. He gingerly picked up the arm by the hand and fed it into the exhibits bag. Jack the Hat and Jones stood by in silence.

"Right then guv," said Briggs, holding the arm. "We'll get to it." Jack the Hat nodded but Jones did not appear too keen on anything. "Alright if we have tea and toast before we start guv?" – better to ask rather than be found in the canteen without permission. Jack the Hat nodded.

Briggs and Jones, together with the bodiless arm, retired to the canteen. Briggs sat down and Jones went to the counter, got the obligatory two stewed teas and ordered up two breakfasts. While waiting for Jones to join him, Briggs studied his colleagues from the uniform branch. Even at this early hour, a number of them were wildly interested in a game of "Chase the Lady" which was going on at a table on the other side of the canteen. Shouts of "Gotcha yer bastard" and "Go on my son" came from the crowd of spectators. Briggs watched and listened with amusement. Eventually he got up and picked up the arm exhibit with its polythene covering. As he walked across to the table, he exposed the hand part of the arm, wedged himself between the spectators and placed the arm palm upwards on the table.

"How's about this for a hand then chaps?" There was a pregnant silence as all assembled looked at the arm, not being able to believe their eyes.

Eventually one said, "Sod you Briggsy, you're bloody sick you are."

Briggs smiled. "Not at all mate but I do like a bit of quiet while I am having my brekkers." He lifted the arm and placed it palm down on the shoulder of the Constable he was talking to. "Otherwise I shall be forced to finger you, render you 'armless and point you in the right direction" aiming the dead hand towards the exit. Nervous laughter accompanied his performance. Briggs returned to his table, where Jones was sitting with the teas.

"You know Tel, you have got a sick sense of humour," Jones spoke, looking into the depths of his turgid tea.

"Quite probably, but at least we have got a quiet breakfast time," looking across to the sullen card players.

While Jones went back to collect the breakfasts Briggs arranged the arm across the table with the hand showing out of the exhibit bag, palm up, with the salt and pepper pots nestling in it. Jones returned with the breakfasts and sat down. Briggs watched him closely. He took the salt and pepper pots and sprinkled his food and replaced them without noticing they had been in a dead palm. Briggs did the same with all solemnity. Much to the amusement of the uniform officers, they finished their breakfast with their table punctuated by the arm.

Their breakfast finished, they left the table, Briggs with the arm over his shoulder smiling to the uniform officers who, he could tell, thought he was quite mad. As they got into the yard, Jones called to the RT driver. "You got a "seek and search" on board Harry?" Harry nodded and said something, then got out of the Rover and went to the boot to get the large searchlight type spotlamp with its electrical supply coming from a case which contained the battery. Thankfully there was a shoulder carrying strap.

"Let us have it back before I go off duty. It has to be signed for by the new crew coming on," everything seeming to be a problem to the mournful Harry. "Anyway, what do you want a "seek and search" for during the day?" queried the puzzled Harry.

"Ah well you see, special jobs for special men," said Briggs with the arm over his shoulder, imitating Robert Newton's Long John Silver.

"From nine o'clock to Christ knows when," added Jones as he stowed the "seek and search" in the boot of his car. They drove out of the yard to the bemused look of the yard staff and the RT crew.

They arrived outside the cemetery, one of the large South London efforts which came into vogue in the last century when land and space in South London were not so scarce. Now the cemetery was overgrown, the once imposing gates hung off their hinges. They fronted a drive which went uphill to the chapel. Briggs and Jones drove halfway up the drive until their passage was blocked by a fallen tree. They got out of the car and surveyed their surroundings. Briggs noticed a tree growing out of a grave just about where the body should have been. "I bet that tree was started by the old stake in the heart routine" Briggs said, collecting the arm from the rear of the car.

"What?" Jones puzzled. "What are you on about now Briggsy?"

"The Dracula thing you know, catch him during the day and drive a stake through his heart, stopped him leaving the grave in the future." Briggs pointed to the growing tree.

"Briggsy for pity's sake leave off will you. I've got the "eebies" already," Jones said as he was getting the "seek and search" from the boot.

They began to walk up the drive together. Unable to resist the opportunity, Briggs placed the hand of the arm on Jones' shoulder, "Come along with me Officer," Briggs adopting a spooky voice.

Jones jumped and shuddered. "Please Tel, don't muck about, these places give me the horrors."

"I don't see why, your lot are always carping on about the eternal afterlife and all that; you should be used to it, expect it even," Briggs swinging the arm as he walked along. "As for myself, I wouldn't mind a black plastic bin liner alongside the front gate, take me away with the rubbish," Briggs said laughing at the thought.

"They never would allow it, there must be laws about it," said

Jones, indignant at the suggestion that a good funeral be missed.

"I don't know so much old son, you don't see too many lolling about on top. They would have to do something, forcible cremation or whatever. I'm sure I would have no interest in the proceedings at all." Briggs looked up the hill at the chapel. "Where did he say that bush was where he left the head? Round the back wasn't it?" Jones nodded grimly, silently.

They walked up to the chapel, partially broken stained glass windows stared down at them. There was an overgrown path to the left, moss hung from the walls and all the nearby gravestones had been overturned. Some were broken into pieces. Nearby, one ornate statue was of a woman with flimsy dress reaching up with a wreath in her hand. Carved into the plinth was "Mabel Cecilia Simmonds 1814 – 1856. Beloved wife of Horace Waterloo Simmonds – died giving birth. Fell asleep." Underneath, by the use of the cellulose aerosol was written "not asleep but bleeding brown bread."

"I wonder if it was our delightful little chap who wrote that?" Briggs pondered at the aerosol inscription.

"Come on Tel, let's get on. I want to be out of this place soonest" said Jones, with a slight waiver to his voice.

"Ron, it's the living that do you harm, the dead can't hurt you. They just make you feel queasy when they get themselves mangled in the process of shrugging off this mortal coil" Briggs said, whilst trying to give an impression of Richard Burton doing his bit.

"It's alright for you, you don't believe anything," Jones' voice was becoming plaintive and beginning to snivel. Briggs decided to leave it.

They walked around to the rear of the chapel and a small clearing opened up before them. The rear of the chapel was taken up with the grand entrance to the crypt which had a large mock Norman arch around a crescent of steps leading down. Briggs felt there should have been an entrance motto especially for Jones, something like, "Don't look behind you" or, perhaps, "Don't enter without your garlic." They looked around to a number of bushes surrounding the clearing.

"That looks likely" Briggs said, pointing to an area of bushes semi-flattened by feet of some sort. They walked over but Jones seemed reluctant and held back. Briggs picked up a stick and began parting the foliage and, after a few minutes, he said, "That shithead was telling the truth, it's here." Briggs held the branches back so Jones could look in. There, near the roots of a bush, was a head lying face up and the line where it had been severed could be clearly seen. There were various lacerations about the head and, what could be best described as chips of flesh missing from it.

"Little bastards," said Jones, gagging as he spoke and, after a pause, starting to vomit his canteen breakfast.

"Hold up Ron, not over the evidence" yelled Briggs, pushing Jones to the side, where he retched and was violently sick. Briggs looked at Jones closely. "You going to be okay, only I need someone to hold the lamp and sort out things you know, be embarrassing to call someone wouldn't it?"

Jones nodded, "I'll be okay."

"Well, I suggest we leave the head where it is, cover it with the bit of board over there," Briggs said, indicating a piece of hardboard. Jones went and got it and handed it to Briggs, making it obvious that, under no circumstances, was he going to get involved in going near the head. "Ron, get a grip for pity's sake. If what old spotty says is true, there is much worse facing us in there," Briggs indicating the entrance to the crypt.

They both walked silently towards the crypt entrance. Standing at the top of the stairs Briggs said, "Best turn on the "seek and search" Ron." Jones turned it on and shone it towards Briggs who, despite his hard man chat, breathed in deeply and said, "Right, here we go."

They descended the crypt steps together, Ron shining the light before them, even though they were still with daylight. Slowly the gloom began to take over, the torch disclosing coffins which had been pulled out of their holes in the wall and the bodies emptied. There were shrouds, bodies and coffins littering the floor. Jones shone the torch the length of the crypt. It was about one hundred yards long with coffin pigeonholes along the right hand side, where the coffins should have been placed in head first. Most of them were on the floor, empty.

"Best thing Ron is if we go along methodically and check each corpse for missing bits" Briggs said, fighting to keep his voice steady. Jones said nothing and they walked forward checking as they went. Almost immediately, they found the body to which the head belonged. As far as they could make out, it was female. They carried on, Jones sweeping the surreal scene with the "seek and search." Briggs could feel that Jones was becoming more confident by the second. In the far corner they found a body still in a coffin but with the arm missing and, leaning against the wall, was a garden spade which had probably been used to hack it off. "This looks as though it could be the owner of the arm" said Briggs, kneeling down and offering the arm up to the amputation point. "There you are Ron, a perfect mechanical fit" Briggs said and, looking around to Jones, "See if you can find the lid Ron." There were several lying about, all of which Briggs tried for size until he found one which was a perfect fit and therefore assumed it to be the right one. Briggs covered the body with it and took a note of the details on the brass plate on the lid. "Hortense Mary Burroughs 1802 – 1856." So much for it being three months old and having been in the ground," Briggs chuckled.

"Is that it Tel, are we finished, can we get out now?" Jones' voice revealing his fear graphically.

"Yes, all done my old son," Briggs said as they turned to make their way towards the exit. Suddenly the "seek and search" went out. Blackness surrounded them.

Jones screamed, "Bloody thing" and began bashing it on the ground in a quite violent manner. "Come on, light you bastard." Briggs put his hand out to Jones' shoulder.

"Steady now Ron, you're only going to break it doing that," Briggs said trying to calm the terrified Jones but, as he said it, Briggs heard the torch part of the lamp shatter and bits of glass cascaded over both of them.

"Ron get a grip, come on," said Briggs shaking Jones violently. "Come on, hold my hand, we'll head towards the door, you can just see a glimmer of light." So they did, gingerly stepping over coffins and bodies as they made their way towards the light coming down the stairs. Eventually they arrived at the bottom of the steps leading up to full daylight. "Ron, you can let go of my hand now, that is unless you intend to marry me." Briggs laughed and they ascended the stairs.

"Tel, you won't tell any of the others will you? I feel such a fool" whined Jones, talking into the damaged lamp.

"Of course not old son but you do the report on the damaged "seek and search," right. I suggest that you dropped it or something, whatever."

Briggs stowed the arm, together with the damaged "seek and search" in the boot of the car. They sat in the car for a while, mainly because Briggs wanted to give Jones time to recapture his escaped nerve. Eventually, Briggs said, "You alright mate, shall we return to reality at Rodney Road?"

"Yeah, fine now, I'll be okay. What about those dirty little shits, desecrating the last resting place of those poor souls," Jones beginning to look the very epitome of an earnest vicar.

Briggs drove north smiling. "Ron, do leave off, there is nothing there, only the embalmed remains of some people who lived in the last century, nothing else, no feelings, no outrage, no sod all. Now forget it." Briggs spoke with a finality which he hoped would impress itself on Jones. Jones sat quietly, not looking forward but looking down at the floor. Briggs was worried and, thinking that Jones was descending into the trauma which caused his recent breakdown, shouted, "Ron, for pity's sake get a grip."

Jones reacted with a start. "Wassa matter with you, I was just dozing off that's all." Jones looked startled and angry but knew what Briggs was thinking.

They drove back to Rodney Road in silence. They entered the backyard and parked up. The RT car was in for refreshments and Jones took the broken "seek and search" into the canteen to explain the damage, offering to put pen to paper explaining it to the equipment people. It turned out that it was not to be in the interest of the RT crew to allow CID to report on the damage, as this would mean a report from them explaining how equipment came to be loaned in the first place without the benefit of a report between CID and uniform branches requesting the same. Therefore the damage report was completed by the RT driver, Harry, who explained it – somehow.

Briggs took the arm up into the CID office and placed it in his locker and waited for Jones to appear. He sat behind his desk completely knackered. Jones came in and sat down opposite him. "Well, who's going to tell Jack the Hat?"

" Your turn I think Ron, unless you want me to hold your hand on this one too," Briggs hitting where it hurt.

"Yes Tel, but be fair, he knows you better than he does me and he's expecting to be in charge of a celebrated murder case. I would say he is going to be touchy about it all," Jones wriggling for what it was worth.

"And you think I will be able to handle it better than you, is that it?" Briggs pushing Jones into the inevitable corner.

"Well not exactly boyo, you know, 'horses for courses' and all that." Jones was getting more embarrassed by the moment.

"Are you really saying officer," Briggs adopting the courtroom style of Roger Ashburn QC, "That a Welshman, a hero of the valleys, a fine tenor (or even a fiver), a lay preacher in the Methodist Chapel, isn't up to standard compared to a scrawny kid from the back streets of Notting Hill Gate? Is that what you believe? Shame on you for having no national pride – I rest my case."

"Oh alright, if you put it like that. I'll tell him, but will you come with me?" Jones asked timidly.

"There, there, of course Uncle Tel will come with you. What, do you want your hand holding again, is that it?" At that precise moment, Jack the Hat's office door flung open.

"Briggs get your arse in here and bring the preacher with you."

Jones smiled the self-satisfied smile of the victor who has won by default, and they both got up. Briggs picked up the arm and put it under his, with the "I expect this going to come into it somewhere" thought. They entered the office. "Yes guv, what can we do for you?" asked the helpful Briggs.

"What's all this bollocks about that thing (indicating the arm) being over a hundred years old?" Jack the Hat demanded looking, what is known in polite circles as being "slightly miffed" but, where Briggs came from as having "got the rats."

"Yes, I'm afraid so guv, we found a body with an arm missing and our arm was a mechanical fit. The body was interred in 1856, as near as I can make out." Briggs left it to Jack the Hat to react.

"Well, how the hell did Probyn think it was three months old and had been in the ground?" Jack the Hat puzzled.

"Made a mistake, didn't account for embalming I imagine. The Victorians were very good at that, preserved 'em to last a thousand years, or so they said. Anyway, made this last didn't it?"

"Yes, I suppose it did. I really must give Sergeant Probyn a ring." Jack the Hat picked up the telephone. Briggs and Jones made a getaway whilst the going was good.

Spotty Wilkins was eventually reported for the summary offence of "Disturbing interred remains" under the Burial Act of 1870, and was duly fined.

The Hitler Youth and Widow's Mite

"Here, this seems like one for the dynamic duo," Sid Mills said as he was allocating the morning crimes to be investigated. "Seems like some sort of mix up in the old flats in Brandon Street, a blind old lady has mislaid a substantial sum of money." Sid was plainly indicating that he did not want this one to be recorded as a crime – more likely "No crime – lost property," thereby saving the crime figures from a savaging.

"Right Sid, I'll collect Jones and get down there," Briggs stowing his bits and pieces in his desk drawer. "Anything else local whilst we are at it?" Briggs asked innocently, knowing full well that Sid would not be sending them out to investigate a sole crime.

"Er, yes, there's a break-in round the corner in the miltaria shop, something about a Hitler youth dagger and a uniform being nicked." Sid paused for breath, "And oh yes," he added as though it had suddenly come to mind, "There's also a break-in at the sex shop, some dildos and other bits nicked."

Briggs nodded "All sounds a bit weird to me Sid. Uniform, dagger and some sexy bits, whatever is the world coming to," Briggs muttered as he noted the details from the crime sheet.

Briggs stowed the notebook and went to the typists' office where Jones was dictating a short report to the delicious Alison. Briggs entered the office where Alison was perched on her typist's chair showing a large expanse of thigh and the hint of knickers to Jones, who stood beside her taking full advantage of the view of her melon like breasts and creamy thighs. Jones seemed mesmerised by this exposé and was stuttering over his dictation, but not taking his eyes from the sexy bits of Alison. Alison knew, of course, as women always do, exactly what was going on. Jones was fantasising over her luscious body and she was enjoying every minute of her power over him, again as women always do. "Ron come on mate, we've got a couple to look at, one's in the sex shop, so that should be handy." He grinned at Alison. "You might even get a sex maniac's discount."

Jones coughed and stuttered. Alison scowled at Briggs for breaking the silver thread which for the moment tied Jones to her.

"In view of all the circumstances I ask that this report be transmitted to Commander COC1 in order that the subject may be included in the drugs indices held there, signed Ronald Arthur Jones, Detective Constable 'M' Division, Rodney Road Police Station. Do us two plus one and leave it on my desk love, please." Alison smiled sweetly and heaved her ample bosom in the direction of Jones who almost blew her a kiss. Briggs laughed and Jones left with him.

On the way down the stairs Briggs said, "You shag that one and you're on a hiding to nothing." Jones looked offended. "Wouldn't dream of it boyo, not my style, you know" Jones retorted, almost about to start on about purity, celibacy and how God loves you.

"Listen you Welsh ram, in your case, a standing prick knows no conscience, plus I know you'd fuck the crack of dawn if it had fur round it. All I am saying is this, do your thinking with your brain for a change not your bollocks." Briggs sensed that Jones was offended, which he felt was peculiar as all that he had said was true and anyone could see that Jones was on the lust after Alison. "Look mate, she's bad news, she wants a husband not a good screwing, she'll wreck your family mate, leave it well alone."

"I hear what you say," said Jones employing that lawyeristic term which usually means "I intend to ignore all that you've said."

They took the CID car and drove to the first break-in, the miltaria shop. Entry had been effected through the back toilet window, where Briggs could see plenty of small fingerprints all over the glossy paint work. He examined the rest of the shop. The till had been rifled and some small change taken, also a rather elaborate Hitler youth dagger and a black SS uniform, which wasn't genuine but looked good, or bad, depending on your point of view. Briggs recorded the details on his sheet then rang in to Rodney Road and informed the Scenes of Crime Officer of his discovery of fingerprints and requested he attend the burglary.

The sex shop proved more interesting. Again entry had been effected through the rear toilet window and again small fingerprints were visible around the frame and sill. The stolen property was interesting too, four large vibrators and a wholesale pack of French letters. "Looks as though someone is planning some heavy action" mused Briggs, "Maybe he does it for England." Again, Briggs rang back to the nick and requested the Scenes of Crime Officer to attend the sex shop and lift the suspect fingerprints.

Jones and Briggs then moved on to Brandon Street, Flat 4, No 49, where they were greeted by Mrs. Harris a blind and lame octogenarian. "Hello Mrs. Harris, Detective Constables Briggs and Jones about the money you have lost." Briggs touched her shoulder, more in sympathy than anything else.

"Didn't lose it, it was stolen," she snapped, her opaque eyes wandering around but not focusing on anything.

"How exactly was it stolen then mother?" Briggs asked quietly ushering her towards the only chair in the filthy flat, sweet wrappers littered the floor. "Don't you have someone to look after you, clean the place that sort of thing?" Briggs continued, concerned that this old lady could live in such squalor in the so called enlightened seventies.

"No, they offered me home help, but I didn't like the woman who came to clean, bossy and nosey she was, didn't like my dog either." With such terse words she dismissed the efforts of the Southwark Social Services. Almost as if on cue, a nondescript mongrel, vastly overweight, began to sniff around Briggs' feet. Briggs leaned down and stroked the dog, almost immediately realising that the dog, like its owner, was blind, it's coat matted and rough. "Yes, she's like me now, blind and can't get around too well." Mrs. Harris answered the unanswered question whilst easing herself into the chair. The dog came and sat across her feet. Briggs and Jones sat on their haunches.

The invasive smell of the flat seemed to increase from the moment the pair entered the flat and it now seemed to be all around, surrounding and enveloping them. Briggs coughed to clear the smell away from him. "Now, how is it my love that you reckon this money has been nicked?" Briggs asked, pulling his pocket book out of his pocket.

"Well my dear, it's like this" Mrs. Harris started, settling herself deeper into the armchair. Briggs could feel that this was the beginning of an epic tale and poised himself to curtail it when the opportunity arose. "The woman next door was moved by the Council. She went to one of those new one bedroom flats on the Aylesbury, nice they are, fully fitted kitchen and all that, very nice, mind she only got that because her dead husband" – she paused long enough to cross herself – "was a freemason. Mind you she was no better than she ought. You should have seen her during the war with those Americans, at it like knives they were."

Briggs managed to find a space. "Yes mother, now, how did whoever come to nick your money?"

She pondered, "Oh yes, that's what we were on about, why you're here even isn't it? Well anyway, they moved her out next door and after she had gone the Council came round to clear the flat of all the old rubbish, so I asked the men if they would take away an old armchair that I had and include it with her gear, which they did. I bunged them five bob and everyone was happy." She paused, tears could be seen to be welling up in her eyes.

"Don't distress yourself mum. Whatever has happened isn't worthy of your tears." Briggs looked at Jones who had got his handkerchief out and was mopping his eyes in a theatrical fashion, then he silently began to mime applause. Briggs treated his partner to a look which Jones knew meant, "Shortly I am going to kick the ring out of you." Jones composed himself. Mrs. Harris pulled herself together and dried her eyes with Briggs' offered handkerchief.

"Well anyway, the up and down of it is that I'd forgotten my life savings were under the seat cushion of that chair. Now it's gone and they've got it."

"How much are we talking about my love?" Briggs asked with pen poised.

"About fifteen hundred pounds," Mrs. Harris said it slowly as if savouring the amount. "I put a little by each week. I used to say it was for my old age, but really it was to bury me with. Now I will have to have a pauper's grave, unmarked and unloved." She put her head down and sobbed quietly. Briggs looked menacingly at Jones and put his arm around her, pulling her close to him in spite of the odour.

"Look my love don't take on so, firstly we'll see if we can find out who has done this then, if we fail, we'll personally make sure that you don't have a pauper's funeral, alright?"

Mrs. Harris brightened immediately. "Oh thank you, that is kind. Let me feel your face." Briggs sat very still whilst the old lady gently felt his face and touched his hair. Jones suppressed laughter. "I can tell you're a nice man who has to do nasty things, don't let it change you. Your friend however hasn't your depth of character." Jones looked offended.

"Anyway," said Briggs briskly, wishing to change the subject, less for Jones' feelings than because of his own embarrassment. "First off, we'll find out who the Council people were who took the armchair and then go after them to see where we're led. However it's fair to point out that if they don't admit finding the money there is very little we can do, as it will be your word against theirs that it was never there in the first place."

"And, of course, I'm blind and really cannot identify anyone" she added and smiled grimly.

"Unfortunately that is the case, my dear," Briggs sad as he closed his pocket book.

Briggs and Jones left the flat together, bidding farewell to Mrs. Harris and her wheezing, smelly dog. Once in the fresh air Jones said, "Thank God for that, I thought I was going to gag in there. You'd think she'd clean up her act wouldn't you."

"It just may be Ron that she feels there's no point, doubly so since those arseholes have nicked her dough," Briggs said whilst unlocking the CID car.

"I don't think we stand much of a chance, boyo. After all they can't be identified, also we have no evidence at all that they stole it. What do you intend to do?" asked Jones as he settled himself in the passenger seat.

"Well what WE are going to do is to question people and make a nuisance of ourselves. You never know, we could get lucky. What we are not going to do is to give in just like that." Briggs snapped his fingers.

Jones, who had noted the edge to Briggs' voice, responded, "Are you by any chance going to get your white charger out and polish your armour, you know the one with the cross of St George on the front?" Briggs looked into Jones eyes and discovered not a lot there.

"I may well do anything so long as we get within striking distance of the scum who think they've won the pools."

Briggs started the car and they drove off. As they turned into East Lane from Brandon Street, Briggs noted a young man playing with others in the street. What brought him to Briggs' attention was that he was wearing the full dress uniform of an Oberst in the Waffen SS. They drove past him and Briggs noted that he was brandishing a rather flash dagger. Briggs pulled around the corner and stopped.

"Come on Ron, nice easy one for a change." Briggs looked across to Jones, who seemed puzzled.

"What, why, where are we going?" Jones, startled by this sudden change of plan. "The kid back there, in the German uniform, the break-in at the militaria shop. Come on mate get it together." They got out of the car and Jones followed Briggs. Briggs said, "Me first, you be behind me by about three yards, save all that running and chasing won't it?" Briggs made off at a leisurely pace around the corner. The young man who aspired to the Waffen SS was walking towards him surrounded by his cronies and, as he got within arm's reach, Briggs grabbed him. "Gotcha my little Goebbels." His friends ran off at a great rate, but the uniform carrier was held firmly in Briggs' grip.

"Ere 'old on, leave off," came the protestations from the young man who was only in contact with the pavement by the tips of his toes. "I ain't dun nuffink," completely dispensing with, "Who are you sir and what do you want with me?" as the young miscreant knew exactly who they were and why he was being suspended by the scruff of the neck.

"Do you always wear the uniform of one of Hitler's regiments whilst playing in the street?" asked Briggs shaking him by the collar.

"It ain't nicked, my Dad brought it back from Germany at the end of the war" replied the youth, looking earnestly into the disbelieving eyes of Briggs.

"Oh right, did he bring this home as well?" Briggs pulled the ornate Hitler youth dagger from its scabbard on the belt.

"Yus, as matter of fact he did, so what of it cozzer?" The artful dodger was getting confident. Briggs looked up and down the road. There appeared to be no-one looking so, purely in the course of truth and justice, Briggs fetched him a well-timed slap to his right ear, which elicited a response of, "Ere leave orf, I'll get my bruvvers on to you."

"Listen sonny, you're nicked and you're coming along to Rodney Road where, if you were of age, I would personally bounce you off every wall and door. But because you are a baby I will content myself with just giving you a bit of a good hiding." The artful dodger gulped visibly.

"You're not supposed to do that, I can complain." Briggs smiled and moved towards the parked car carrying the elevated artful dodger with him.

"Of course you can complain and after you have complained you had better move off the manor, as I think my mates might have desires on getting even. Now shut up Himmler and get in the car."

Briggs opened the car door and heaved the young thief into the car. "Right Ron take us round to the militaria shop." Jones nodded and drove off in silence. He stopped the car outside the militaria shop which, in fact, was only about one hundred and fifty yards away. Briggs got out of the car and went in. The shop owner approached him and Briggs pulled the knife out of his pocket. "Is this part of the gear stolen from you last night?"

The shop owner examined the knife closely. "Yes, that's the Hitler youth dagger, definitely mine." He handed the knife back to Briggs who continued. "We have a prisoner in the car outside who is wearing what I believe to be the missing uniform. Would you care to step outside and endeavour to identify what I believe to be your property?" The shop owner nodded and followed Briggs out of the shop to the car where he leaned over and peered at the figure seated in the rear.

The shop owner straightened. "That young man is wearing the uniform stolen from me." There seemed to be an air of disappointment in his voice. Briggs did not question him further.

"Thank you sir, both items will be returned to you in due course."

Briggs got into the car and they drove off. Briggs turned around and spoke to the young man. "Well my young gauleiter, the shop owner reckons you're wearing his gear, what have you got to say to that?"

"Well 'eez wrong see, my Dad brought it back from the war." The

Hitler youth remained surly as they drove to Rodney Road in silence. On arrival the juvenile was placed in the detention room whilst Jones got on with contacting the parents.

Briggs, for his part, contacted the Southwark Borough Council and eventually traced the department responsible for removing rubbish from empty flats. After much consultation of records they decided that the work had been carried out by a sub-contractor – Galley Wall Transport, 439, Galley Wall Road, Bermondsey, S.E.19, the contact name was Mr. Boyson. Briggs rang the transport company and spoke with Mr. Boyson who expressed no interest in the theft, but did state the armchair and other bits and pieces had already been off loaded at the Council tip in Erith and gave a time of arrival there. Boyson gave the driver and his mate's name as Ivor Hills and Brian Poole. Briggs replaced the phone and pondered the information he now had before him.

Jones by this time had spoken with the lad's parents who had emphatically denied all knowledge of military uniforms and the dagger. The young man was charged and fed through the myriad system of forms and processes necessary in the case of juveniles at that time, including fingerprints, which later identified the lad as the double burglar. The lad was released to the custody of his father, whose greeting was to slap the lad round the face and enlighten him as to what was going to happen once he arrived home.

Briggs and Jones then drove to Erith and examined South East London's offerings in the rubbish department. The place stank and was infested with rats on the ground and seagulls in the air. On the directions of the supervisor they located the armchair or, at least, it answered the description of the one taken from Mrs. Harris's flat, but no money was found anywhere. "Almost certainly the driver and his mate have swagged it off" Briggs said to Ron, cleaning his shoes off on the side wall of the car.

"Quite probably, but we'll never prove it," said Jones settling himself into the passenger seat, as he always did. He maintained that London traffic unnerved him. They drove back to Rodney Road in silence apart from the tinny voices emanating from the force radio.

Once back in the office, Briggs called in to the collator's office and enquired about Galley Wall Transport which, as he thought, transpired to be a Pringle owned or backed company and thought to be assisting the gangland fraternity by transporting stolen lorry loads. Briggs looked through his personal telephone directory and rang Frank Beamish's private number.

"Hello who's that?" Beamish answered cautiously.

"It's Tel." and, after a pause, Briggs added "Tel from Rodney Road."

"Right gotcha, what can I do for you Tel?" Beamish sounded, as he always did, very amiable.

"What I would like is a meet with Tracy's father, an urgent meet."

There was silence, then Beamish said, "I'll ring you back in two ticks."

Briggs put down the telephone and Jones looked puzzled. "Don't worry, I know what I am doing." Briggs settled down for a return call.

"Why are we bothering with this Tel pleaded Jones? She's an old lady and if they deny it we can't prove anything." We've already had a body off today. Why do you need to go after these people? They know the score, they'll just tell you to piss off." Briggs considered what his partner had said, maybe for as long as a milli second.

"You may be right, or may be not. We'll just have to see old son. But unless we try we'll never know for sure." The telephone rang. Briggs picked it up.

"Tel? it's Frank about the matter we talked about, eight tonight, the Paradise Club. I will not, of course, be there so be careful." The line went dead. No doubt Frank had earned his day's money on that call alone.

"Right then, it's on for tonight, a meet with old man Pringle, and his minders I expect. You on for it or not?" Briggs bluntly putting Jones on the spot.

"Must admit I'm not keen, they're nasty people the Pringles and what with past confrontation being so violent," Jones looking down to avoid eye contact with Briggs.

"Well Ron, it's make your mind up time, you on or off? If it's off, I am in there," Briggs indicating Jack the Hat's office, "asking for a new partner. Suit yourself."

Jones' head went up. "No need to be hasty Tel, I didn't say I wouldn't, did I? Just that it's bleedin' risky. We'd better watch our backs." Jones was obviously not happy with the situation at all but, at the same time realising that the road to promotion was on the back of this surly young man from Notting Hill Gate.

"I see no risk whatsoever. We've used Frank Beamish and if it all goes boss-eyed they've lost the greatest middle ever. Anyway that's the way I book it." Jones laughed sarcastically."

"And we always go with the way you book it." Jones was about to say more when he was cut short.

"Because if we went with your way we would end up nicking old ladies for shoplifting after the store detective had delivered them to us, the same as the rest of these dead legs," Briggs hotly indicating the rest of the office with a sweeping gesture. Barking, who had been listening to this interchange, thought about saying something, but decided against it, realising that Briggs was annoyed and could and probably would do anything, so his silence was more like private health care.

"The Paradise Club" screamed the brassy neon lights, then beneath the sign "Girls, girls, girls," then "Drinking with dining and dancing till 2am."

Briggs and Jones stood before the club examining it. "One thing's for sure, we should be able to get you a shag in there. Not quite up to Alison standard, but it would do to vent your sexual spleen on," Briggs dug Jones in the ribs.

"Looks as if it's patronised by the dregs of society," Jones grumbled in one of his pompous lay preacher moods.

"Then we will be completely at home old son come on." Briggs pulled Jones forward into the club. The bouncer on the door said, "Sorry chaps, members only."

Briggs flashed his tattered warrant. "We are members mate, to see Mr. Pringle on official business." The bouncer nodded and escorted them inside, where everything seemed to be red plush upholstery, matching carpet and polished brass. The bar, over to the left, was open and serving. The sole customer was the resident tart of the night who perched on a stool at the end of the bar, her high necked Suzie Wong dress hiding wrinkles, her eyes betraying her hard trade. The bouncer caught her eye and shook his head at her unspoken question. He led Briggs and Jones towards a corner table and indicated they should sit.

"What would you gentlemen like to drink?"

Briggs looked at Jones and queried "Beer?"

Jones added, "That'll do me" and settled himself into the plush upholstery.

"Two beers mate" said Briggs, sitting in the corner examining the room and its contents. "Watch out for Old Man Pringle," he said in a quiet voice, "He's a big geezer, wears flash gear and plenty of gold." The bouncer brought the beers, half bowed, which Briggs took to be a piss take, and retired from sight.

"The guvnor will see you now." The voice was from a heavy man with a broken nose and, from what Briggs could see, at least one cauliflower ear. They followed the heavy along a hall to a large office where Pringle sat behind a desk.

"Good evening Mr. Briggs and Mr. Jones, so nice of you to call." Pringle was being, sort of, pleasant but Briggs detected a harsh note in his voice. Forcing himself to be well mannered, Pringle said, "Please sit down," indicating two chairs in front of the desk. Briggs and Jones settled themselves in the comfortable armchairs. "Now gentlemen what can I do for you?"

"Well Mr. Pringle, I understand Galley Wall Transport is one of the companies that come under your control," Briggs explained, eyeing the heavy who had parked himself behind Pringle, a comforting sign which meant that the heavy was engaged in protecting Pringle from Briggs and not in the business of offensive operations – well not at the moment anyway.

"Well, let us say I have contact with that company" said Pringle, lapsing straight into his Herbert Lom impression.

"Well, today, two employees of that company took an armchair, with permission from an old lady in Brandon Street. Underneath the cushion of that chair was the old lady's life savings, which I happen to know these employees have now stolen," Briggs said and took a swig of his beer.

"Well then officer, you know who they are, go get them," Pringle laughed.

"Not quite that easy, the old lady is blind and wouldn't be able to pick them out," Briggs explained with open-faced honesty.

"So, you have no evidence and no ID, so what are you doing here?" Pringle puzzled.

"We are here to tell you that unless those two scumbags send the money back to the old dear, or at least what's left of it, we're going to fit them up." Briggs noticed Jones had gone rather pale and, in order to assist his complexion, Briggs added "And get them a straight seven each."

Pringle went quiet and studied his blotter closely, finally asking, "And what is in it for me, and don't tell me the knowledge that I've helped an old lady in distress?"

"Well it could be that it is in the balance whether your Tracy goes on for attempt murder on me," said Briggs slowly.

Briggs knew full well that he couldn't promise anything as she was already charged but what he did know was that the Director's office had put forward the opinion that the indictment for attempt murder did little as the evidence on conspiracy was very strong. They would probably offer no evidence if the accused pleaded. Briggs added, "That is, of course, if she pleads." Old Man Pringle straightened himself in his chair.

"We Pringles never plead, it's not something we are good at."

Briggs laughed. "Don't be daft, of course you plead if it's the difference between ten years and two years, it's a fact of life. Now don't be silly." And remembering where he was and who he was talking to added "Please."

The heavy behind Pringles said, "Watch your tongue filth," cracking his knuckles as he spoke."

Briggs suddenly became very serious and spoke with clipped tones. "Mr. Pringle, I am here to sort out a deal, tell your gorilla there to shut the fuck up while I'm talking, or I might take him seriously. If you don't want the deal just say so and we'll leave."

Pringle waved his minder out of the room, looked Briggs straight in the eye and said deliberately, "Now listen carefully Briggs, you've got bottle coming here when you know your balls are on the block from my two boys and Tracy. I only let you in here out of morbid curiosity as to what you'd try next but I'll tell you this for nowt, Dessie was out of order running wild and bound to come a cropper in the end. Mickey took his chances and got caught but Tracy was plain stupid. She let her brothers talk her into the blagging just to help them out. I can't believe they were all such idiots to think they'd get away with it. Even if it had come off, your lot would soon have tumbled Tracy as a Pringle. anyway I want her out of this as much as possible and I'll deal with you to that end, but don't push your luck. As I understand it, you want these two yobbos to return the money, no questions asked and, providing Tracy pleads, you think she'll only be on for the conspiracy." Briggs nodded. "When's the dough got to be back for?" Pringle asked, sitting back deep in his armchair still trying to weigh up Briggs.

"Next Friday at the latest. Failure for them to do so will earn them a fitting up which will make their eyes water, plus a good kicking, personal, 'cos you don't nick from old dears, not if you want to be respected," Briggs coming out with all the accepted bullshit patter that villains often spout, the truth being that if there's enough in it they would steal the pennies off their mother's eyes and find a way of accommodating the act within their consciences.

Pringle pondered, "I agree, this isn't the behaviour we expect from good villains." Briggs contemplated the contradiction in terms, said nothing, but nodded his agreement.

"Their names are Ivor Hills and Brian Poole" said Briggs, speaking from his pocket book.

"Right, this is the way it is going to be," Pringle spoke with finality, making notes on his blotter, "If the money has not come back by Friday morning, you do what you must."

Briggs got up, Jones followed suit. They nodded to Pringle and left. Outside Jones said as they walked, "What was all that shit about, you might take that heavy seriously if he didn't behave himself? What a load of bollocks, you could have got us a good hiding."

Briggs laughed. "Just because he has a broken nose and a cauliflower ear you think he is hard, right?" Jones nodded. "All those injuries indicate that someone has hit him very hard indeed, all I was saying really was that he didn't impress me."

Jones shook his head. "You've more front than Selfridges you have."

Briggs paused getting the car keys out, "Probably, but the main thing is we got away with it, they are now more impressed with us than we are with them." They drove back to the Station and booked off; Jones to his nocturnal sexual confrontation with Christine and Briggs to home and family, thankful he did not have the complications of his partner's private life.

The following Friday morning, Jones sat in the canteen, waiting for Briggs to arrive and the day's adventures to begin. He studied the contents of his teacup, his mind wandering to the sexual contest with Christine. That was very heavy stuff. Her demands were becoming almost impossible, even for a sexual athlete which was what Jones secretly thought of himself. He was worried as Christine was making very dangerous noises, like demanding protestations of undying love and day dreaming aloud in his presence about how it would be nice to live in a smart house in Biggin Hill or somewhere similar with two children and, obviously, Jones. Jones was at a loss as how to extricate himself from this mess and was unwilling to take advice from Briggs, who would only take the piss anyway.

Briggs came in, nodded to his partner, got his tea and sat down with a sigh. "Friday morning mate, any news?"

Jones awoke from his worried meditation. "No not yet." Briggs took a swig from his tea and wondered why he bothered with such stuff. Mind you it was always of a standard – horrible.

"Right then mate, we've barked so now we are going to bite, at least I am. I am not standing this shit from them or anyone else." Briggs looked at Jones waiting for his contribution but received silence in response.

"Well are you with me, or are you still with the Woolwich?" Jones nodded.

"No, you lead I'll follow," stating the usual.

"But don't let me look over my shoulder and find you gone," Briggs cautioned Jones.

"As if I would Tel, as if I would," but secretly Jones found it comforting to be away from the front of this deal.

The reserve officer entered the canteen, looked around and, locating Briggs, walked towards him. "Briggsy there's an old lady in the front office, a Mrs. Harris, got a smelly old dog with her. She's asking for you. She says you're the best copper for ten streets." Briggs put his teacup and its corrosive contents on the table.

"Oh really" he beamed. "Come on Ron, our fan club has arrived."

They left the canteen and entered the adjacent front office.

There stood Mrs. Harris, replete with scruffy mongrel. Several Constables were milling abut as well as the Duty Sergeant. Briggs touched her arm. "Hello Mrs. Harris, how are you?" She reacted in surprise.

"Oh, Mr. Briggs, you lovely man." The PC's grinned in silence. "I've got all my money back apart from one hundred pounds, but the rest is all there. Wonderful news, I'm so happy. Here, you have a hundred pounds for yourself." The front office froze. The Duty Sergeant waved and caught Briggs' eye, gently shook his head and indicated the office divider behind him, meaning that there was someone of higher rank secreted there. She stood there offering money to an unseen man.

Briggs said, "That's alright Mrs. Harris, you keep your money, my pal and me, were only too pleased to help you," which relieved the tension in the front office. He continued, "Mrs. Harris, why don't you put this money into a bank account. The National Provincial is only over the road. I'll take you over there if you like."

"Don't trust banks, never have," snapped Mrs. Harris becoming a little terse, cranky even. "But Mrs. Harris, the manager over there is a friend of mine. They wouldn't dare upset you. Come with me and we'll get your money deposited." Together they left the station arm in arm.

Barking later put forward the view that Mrs. Harris was the only bird Briggsy would ever pull. Briggs smiled to himself, proud of his involvement with this old lady and knowing that he would certainly rather be seen with her than some of the worn out old slappers, both male and female, that Barking was known to consort with.

The Hitler youth was somewhat less ostentatious when he appeared before the Magistrates' Juvenile Court, and quieter still in voice when he received his two years' probation for burglary. No doubt the two years would be probationary to further wrongs against the local community but one thing's for sure, he would never be a Mr. Big or Brains.

Sid Mills got his heart's desire. The theft of the old lady's money was classified as "No Crime – Money Mislaid Due to Extreme Age." Tracy pleaded and was not sentenced for attempt murder.

Dips in the Elephant

Briggs and Jones settled themselves at the back of the conference room. When Briggs was at school, he used to call it a classroom but now, because the guvnor was going to speak to them, it was a conference room.

"Listen up you lot, less chatter more attention. For Christ's sake Barking put out that evil smelling cigar or I'll throw it out the window with you attached." John hastily put out the cigar. Briggs thought he was secretly relieved as he had previously asked, "Does this cigar give me a sort of air, you know, like Clint Eastwood?" Barking had been serious. Briggs was dying to say, "More like Lassie having a shit," but contented himself by laughing but offending Barking never the less.

"Anyway, listen to me very carefully. We have dips working the Elephant and I'm not going to have it. They can work Knightsbridge all they like, only tourists, mainly yanks there." Briggs had the impression that Jack the Hat didn't have a lot of time for Americans. Perhaps something had happened during the war which had left him with a lasting enmity towards them. Jack the Hat continued, "But they are not working my manor, not ever, no way. They're preying on pensioners and young mums and it's going to stop, right now. We've had ten cases reported in the last four days and, by my reckoning, that means that we've had at least another twenty which haven't been reported. I'm going to put a stop to it and the first thing you are going to do is ALL be out on the street in ALL weathers, ALL the time. Any dips that get nicked go on the sheet for conspiracy to steal, not attempted theft, not suspected person loitering but conspiracy and it's up the Bailey for you my son. Any questions?" They all studied the floorboards. "Right then, who knows any dips?" Briggs and no doubt others did but didn't say anything. "In that case I'll hand you over to Detective Sergeant Hallows of the Flying Squad dip team, who'll enlighten us. Sergeant Hallows."

A small compact man got up from the front row, very well dressed but in the understated non-flamboyant style of the seventies. "Thank you guv, my name as you already know is Hallows, Sergeant. I have been on the dip squad for about five years and have dealt with most of them. That doesn't mean I know it all, it just means that I've seen some of it and maybe know something." Briggs immediately warmed to this man as being whatever, but certainly not a bullshit artist. "Dips run from the very amateurish, the soppy kids who think it's a bit of lark, to the very very professional of the likes of Angel Fingers, a Colombian who could take anything, and I mean anything, off you at any time. We had no way of catching him and his team so we warned them off. They're now plying their trade in Rio, and yes, Interpol have been informed and have passed on their whereabouts. Mind you, in South America, if they can't catch them they tend to bump 'em off, which does have some attraction to it. Imagine the panic if we started exiting our targets.

Anyway, I digress. A dip team usually consists of three people, the whizz, the buzz, and the whisper. The whizz is the actual thief, he takes the goods from the mark, that's what they call the victim, the mark. The whizz passes it to the buzz, who happens to be walking by. The buzz then passes it to the whisper who is going in the opposite direction. The whisper, on the basis that he rarely gets taken, holds the 'hod' which is the accumulation of stolen property. Dips come in all shapes and sizes. Some use disguise, for example, the city gent in pinstripes with a brolly etc, the Sloane Ranger headscarf and twin set routine – obviously you have to be a female to pull that one." The assembled throng erupted in laughter. "We've various sources of information up the Yard about where dips are working and, as far as we can make out, your lot were working the West End and Knightsbridge but things got too hot. They're a local team and live on the manor. This is a broadsheet on them," passing a wad of papers to Jack the Hat. "Their associates and their MO. I suspect from the crime reports I've seen that they are working bus stops and the way I've always worked is from the end of a bus stop watching faces. Most people waiting for a bus are aimless, day dreamers, becoming sort of intense on the arrival of the bus. A dip working the bus stop is almost the other way around. He's alive whilst waiting and part of the crowd when the bus arrives. Once the crowd surges forward, he's at it, taking the mark, working the buzz and, to a lesser extent, the whisper.

"I've arranged for one of our flounders to come and give a hand." Hallows smiled at the puzzled expressions. "Flounder – dab – cab" explained Hallows. "We've our own taxi cabs which travel around looking for dips." Hallows turned to Jack the Hat showing that he'd finished, saying, "I don't think I can assist you any further guv. If any of you have any questions, I'll be pleased to assist if I can." There were no questions. Hallows said, "Thank you gentlemen for your attention" and sat down.

Jack the Hat stood up, "Right then you lot, out on the streets, let's give these shitheads some grief." Everyone got up and left in almost single file.

Briggs and Jones went to Auntie Maisie's café, entered and sat down in the front of the café by the window. Auntie came out from behind the counter. "How's my favourite detective then?" giving Briggs a beaming smile. "Breakfast?"

"Yes please Auntie," he answered like a little boy, as he knew Auntie loved it. "Come out to the back parlour, you'll be more comfortable there." Briggs and Jones followed her to the back of the café.

They sat down either side of the dining table. "Make yourself comfortable and I'll bring you your breakfasts as soon as they are ready" said Auntie Maisie, fussing around Briggs. Auntie Maisie was, in fact, the Auntie of a very close friend and because of this and the fact that she had taken an instant liking to him, Briggs had almost been adopted by her, consequently being treated as one of the family who could be trusted with many tender secrets. Auntie was a strange creature. She wore men's clothing on her top half with sensible skirts and punched brogue shoes on her bottom half. She had never married, but lived with her Gert who was very feminine, almost to the extreme. Today's almost embarrassing interest in an individual's sexual orientation would have demanded that they be pushed out of closet as lesbians, or some other category. In those days it did not matter, the subject never being mentioned, even in gossip. The only thing that might have been said was that perhaps she was a bit strange. She would merely have been accepted as such. This is probably more tolerant than the present day clamour for anyone not conforming to the normal, or whatever is accepted as being normal, being hounded until they conform to some strange category approved by the predator.

Jones, as usual, surveyed his surroundings. Along one wall of the dining room were cases of Beefeater Gin and Bacardi rum, all cases being labelled "for export only." Jones signalled Briggs and indicated a silent question regarding the cases. Briggs smiled and shook his head, indicating the contraband did not exist.

They sat there talking and waiting for their breakfasts to arrive. Jones said, "I thought that DS Hallows was a bit of a star, very impressive." Briggs looked up.

"Yes, so did I, we could do with him on the manor full time. Strange though isn't it, five years on the dip squad, no promotion."

"He's probably happy where he is."

Auntie entered with the teas. "Your breakfasts are on the way, only Gert's got a rush on at the moment."

Briggs beamed, "No problem Auntie, we've plenty of time. Anyway it's nice of you to put up with us." Auntie blushed just a touch and left them to serve in the café.

"We've got to do something about this booze, it's bent" hissed Jones, indicating the crates which lined the wall.

"I don't see anything to worry about Ron. I expect Auntie is going into the import export business, no sweat." Briggs leaned back in his chair and sipped the excellent tea that Auntie had brought. "Anyway, if she has a little bent gear once in a while, so what, it's only in line with what all the other businesses do on the manor, plus of course, she is my Auntie, me being the adopted prodigal so to speak." Briggs beamed with the dazzling simplicity of his logic. "Also if she gets nicked, I would have an attack of the memories."

"Memories, memories?" Jones puzzled, "What do you mean?"

"Well I suddenly remember things like, who Christine really is, where her informant's report dosh really goes. Oh yes, and who didn't deserve that high commendation on that blagging job, which

239

he got because he's up for promotion shortly, whilst his mate had to put up with just 'commended'. Or perhaps, where all the gear went on the Moffat job. In all the circumstances officer, I suggest the safest course for you is to forget all about those boxes, before the memories I have stored in my brain come bubbling to the surface."

"Yes, yes, I quite see and do agree officer," muttered Jones as Auntie came in with the breakfasts.

"There you are, that will keep my little soldiers going all day," cooed Auntie. "Now you eat up or you won't grow up big and strong." Auntie placed two plates of eggs, bacon and other essentials of the English version of breakfast before them. "More tea?" she enquired.

"Yes please Auntie" chirped Briggs. Auntie picked up the tea mugs and left with them.

"Why do you do that?" Jones puzzled over his eggs and bacon.

"Do what?" came the munching query from Briggs,

"Suck up to her so much. It can't be just for the eggs and bacon."

Briggs cleared his mouth. "No it isn't, it's because she enjoys it so much. She's never had children and I feel she likes to think of us as her children, or something like that." Briggs trailed off into silence, embarrassed by his own explanation.

"Mother and child, Freudian is that it?" asked Jones grinning.

"I don't know, but I think it might be. Anyway about that sort of thing, how's things on the Christine front, all happiness love and passion?" Briggs wishing to change the subject and wrong-footing Jones at the same time.

"Not very well actually. She's on about love now, passed the point of just getting laid, now she wants love, undying love. It's getting a bit of a pain actually, if it wasn't for the information I would be out of there." Jones seemed dismal.

"Yeah but she knew the score from day one," said Briggs offering a life line.

"Ah well, the ground rules have changed, she's fallen in love." Jones appeared to be sinking into even greater depression.

"And now you're lusting after Alison, how do you get rid of the thoughts? Cold showers? Long solitary walks with the Bible for company?" Briggs was hitting at the sore spot which became obvious from the moment Jones realised that Alison was having her evil way with Ted Richards who was on the same shift as them.

"How did you know? I never told you?" Jones was now indignant as well as puzzled.

"You didn't have to, you dipstick, you get a hard on every time you see her," Briggs stating his version of the obvious.

"Well let's put it this way, I felt and do feel let down. I expected better from her, almost as though she betrayed me," Jones offered by way of explanation, forlorn and mistily looking into the distance.

"Ron let's have some realism here. You're married, right, and you're screwing the arse off a villain's wife who, incidentally, you put inside, yes?" Jones nodded. "And you've got the rats because the office typist, who looks like a monumental prick teaser to me, has gone off in a direction other than yours, yes?" expounded Briggs, giggling at Jones' discomfort. "Are you addicted to aggravation is that it?"

"Well I just had hopes of better things for her, you know advancement." Jones trailed off into silence, realising that his partner regarded him as a fool. Not only that but he was proving it himself. Auntie entered with yet more tea and toast.

"How are my little chaps getting along then?" she asked whilst cuddling up to Briggs and leaning one of her ample breasts on his shoulder.

"Sorry Auntie you have done me, I couldn't eat anything more," Briggs holding his tummy to emphasize the point. "Just so long as you're full up son, that's the main thing. Perhaps a tincture of the old scotch to finish it off with style." Despite their protests, Auntie produced two tumblers half full of single malt whisky, which Briggs loved, and which Jones detested when sober, yet came to like when in full flow of "Bread of Heaven."

They drank the scotch. Jones snorted "Terrible stuff you know, the elixir of the devil" but held the glass to his lips again.

"If it's so terrible Jonesy, give it here and I will help you out of a spot" as Briggs finished his and reached for Jones' glass. "No that's alright see, I shall save you from yourself," said Jones draining the glass.

The pair left the café bidding farewell to Gert and Auntie. Auntie flushed slightly as she pecked Briggs on the cheek, pulled his coat together and straightened his tie. Briggs felt like asking if he could play with the rough boys down the lane, but didn't. Gert seemed put out by this overt show of affection.

Briggs and Jones wandered along Rodney Road towards their designated bus stop, their greasy breakfast sloshing about inside them and the single malt whisky giving an unusual ingredient to the mix. As they approached the bus stop, Briggs noted one of the faces on the Squad's dips handout – John Joseph Peck, otherwise known as Monkey Face. There were a number of others standing waiting for the bus. Briggs particularly noted a tall man in a pinstripe suit who might or might not be the buzz or the whisper. The pinstriped man seemed aloof and not at all aware of his surroundings. Briggs thought his face familiar and might be on the Squad's dips list but didn't dare get the sheet out to check. They joined the bus queue behind a postman on his way to work, hardly the crowd which demanded the attention of a dip of the rank of Monkey Face. Briggs thought Monkey Face was setting himself up to lift the purse from the top of a shopping bag belonging to the old lady in front of him. As the bus arrived Monkey Face gave the appearance that it was not his bus but, as the old lady went forward to get on, he lifted the purse. Almost immediately, he was lifted by Briggs and Jones.

"Ere leave off, I ain't done nuffink, her purse fell orf and I was going to give it to her weren't I," Monkey Face indicating the old lady, then standing on the platform of the bus. Briggs looked around for the smart man in the pinstripes. He was marching smartly along Rodney towards the police station, going a little bit too quickly. The old lady got off the bus slowly and with difficulty. Briggs judged her to be crippled with arthritis and helped her down onto the pavement.

"Police, Rodney Road," Briggs announced them. "Bit of an incident clippie, hold the bus for the time being." Briggs flashed his warrant card. He turned to the old lady, "Is this your purse my dear?" asked Briggs, indicating the purse he had taken from Monkey Face.

"Yes it is. Did he nick it?" The matron indicated Monkey Face, who was trying hard, but failing, to look innocent. "That's a matter of investigation, but it looks likely," answered Briggs, keeping his hand firmly on the shoulder of Monkey Face. "You're nicked old son and the guvnor's word is that it's not theft from the person, or suspected person loitering etc, it's conspiracy to steal, so it's the Old Bailey next stop for you. I won't caution you as you probably know it better than me." As Jones took the old lady's details, Briggs began to march Monkey Face towards the nick.

As they walked along Monkey Face said, "You ain't serious about that conspiracy thing are you? I mean leave off, it's a straight whiz ain't it?" Monkey Face looked hopefully at Briggs.

"The guvnor isn't standing for it, you're not supposed to be working this manor and, as you are, you get a conspiracy and probably a seven for your cheek, got it?" Briggs explaining the facts of life to Monkey Face.

"Who was I working with? I was on my own," Monkey Face hoping that Briggs had not sussed his accomplice. Briggs smiled.

"The geezer in the pinstripes, much too up market for Rodney Road. He would look more comfortable in Knightsbridge or up West wouldn't he?" Monkey Face looked shocked that his mate had been seen.

"Anyway, who said we're not supposed to be on the manor. It's ours, we live on it." Monkey Face was hurt that someone should treat him as an outsider.

"My guvnor thinks it's his manor and has distinct thoughts about dips doing bus stops on it," Briggs announcing Jack the Hat's policy on dips. They walked the remainder in silence.

On arrival at Rodney Road, Briggs announced Monkey Face's presence to the Station Officer, whose eyebrows shot up at the intended charge of "Conspiracy to Steal."

After charge, Briggs placed Monkey Face in the cells. "Ere guv can we bunny about this or what? I mean a bit strong ain't it, bleedin' conspiracy," Monkey Face pleading as though his life depended on it, which I suppose it did.

Briggs looked at the ceiling. "Well the guvnor might be interested in a meet to explain your promise never to work this manor again" Briggs said, not quite closing the cell door.

"Here, hold up a minute," which just stopped Briggs closing the door on him. "A meet you say, like a council of war sort of?"

Briggs laughed, his mind immediately focused on the film, "Drums along the Mohawk" where just such a council of war took place, but that time, under slightly different circumstances. "Yes a meet on neutral ground" explained Briggs, knowing full well there never is neutral ground anywhere between villain and copper –

officially, but said it anyway.

Monkey Face thought for a moment. "I think I can arrange such a meet, do I get bail on the strength of it?"

Briggs laughed. "Leave it there for the moment and I'll speak to the guvnor, but you can do that can you – arrange the meet?" Monkey Face grinned. "No problem mate, I am the whiz, important guy on the team. Get me on the out and I'll set it up for you." Briggs closed the cell door and walked away towards the stairs to the CID office.

"Er excuse me guv, can I have a minute?" Briggs asked hopefully at the top of Jack the Hat's trilby. "Sit" grunted Jack the Hat. "I'll be a minute." Jack the Hat indicated the easy chair in the corner of his office.

Briggs settled himself in the comfortable armchair and daydreamed that he was the visiting Commander, that, in a moment, he would give Jack the Hat a monumental bollocking and be taken out to an expensive lunch to unruffle his feathers and be shown the correct amount of respect.

Jack the Hat finished his pondering of the report, which Briggs noted with double pleasure was not one of his but Barking's, and looked up. "Well Briggs what do you want this time?" his eyes boring into Briggs' soul.

"Er Jonesy and I have nicked a well known dip – Monkey Face Peck, captured him at it. In accordance with your instructions guv I have charged him with conspiracy to steal from the person, which he is well upset about." Briggs explained the event as quickly as possible. "He states he can arrange a meet with the rest of the team, council of war sort of, and wants to know if you're interested guv."

"Is he sure he can arrange the meet?" asked Jack the Hat, speaking and considering the proposition at the back of his mind.

"He sounds very convincing guv, says he's the main man on the team and that they will do what he says."

Jack the Hat mulled over Briggs' announcement for a few seconds then said, "Right then, get him up here, let's have a chat with the man," Jack the Hat closing the file on Barking's report and stowing it in his drawer.

Briggs left and returned to the cells. He got Monkey Face out of his cell but looked almost upset at being woken up. "Come on, the guv has agreed to see you." As though this was an audience with Royalty, Monkey Face grunted and shrugged on his coat.

"Is he amenable or what?" Then explained, "I mean does he want to deal or what?" Briggs ushered him out of the cell.

"I don't know you'll have to ask him yourself." Briggs then directed him up the stairs, as you never let a prisoner walk behind you.

"Guv this is Monkey Face Peck. I have charged him with conspiracy to steal from the person." Briggs announced the pickpocket with a flourish.

"Yes, and a right bloody liberty that is, bleeding conspiracy, you're taking the piss you are" Monkey Face expostulated, blurting out his protests and injured criminal pride. Briggs dug Monkey Face sharply in the back.

"I would keep a civil tongue in your head, otherwise life could become even more uncomfortable. This is the guvnor you're talking to." Briggs nodded to Jack the Hat.

"Well guvnor or not, it's still a bleeding liberty," Monkey Face sullenly speaking to the floor.

"The straight answer is don't work my manor, don't steal from old ladies, don't even dream of standing at one of my bus stops and you won't find yourself charged with conspiracy - got it?" Jack the Hat snarled with menace. This announcement of Rodney Road policy seemed to have a sobering effect on Monkey Face. He stood before Jack the Hat's desk looking at the floor. "Right then are you going to listen to me?" Monkey Face nodded his head silently.

Jack the Hat continued. "Right then, I want a meet with your team. I will have Briggsy here as my minder, you can have who you like." Briggs shuddered at the concealed challenge contained in this little speech.

"I can arrange that guv, but of course I will need to be on the out" Monkey face said, making his play for freedom, "And, of course, if I'm going to help you out of this problem, I think the least you can do is to drop the charge to 'sus', or 'attempted theft'." Monkey Face paused and then added brightly, "I'll plead then."

"Briggs" roared Jack the Hat, "Take that microbe back downstairs, place him in his cell and for his cheek, kick the ring out of him." Jack the Hat picked up a file from his pile and opened it, signifying that this audience was at an end. Briggs grabbed hold of Monkey Face by the scruff of the neck and started to lead him off to the cells.

"Ere guv, hold up, I didn't mean nuffink, like, you've got to try ain't you, know what I mean." Briggs paused and waited for Jack the Hat's decision on this plea to his non-existent heart.

Jack the Hat took a deep breath. "Now listen to me shithead, very carefully. I say how this deal goes, you merely agree, or disagree, in which case you're back in the bin, got it?" Monkey Face nodded quietly. Jack the Hat continued, "As to what you're charged with or reducing the charge so that you can enjoy more of your life, well now, that's a matter which must be discussed and settled according to established rules, do you understand?" Monkey Face straightened himself into almost the attention position. "Yes guv."

"Right then as regards this meet, you will arrange it. It will be held at the Captain Hardy in Kennington, 9pm tomorrow night, you will make sure that all your team are there – got it?" Jack the Hat at his meanest.

"Yes, but how am I going to achieve that while I am in here?" Monkey Face asked, genuinely puzzled.

"Very simple old son, you're going to be bailed to return to this Police Station under the Magistrates' Courts Act 1952. No doubt you have someone to stand surety for you in the sum of, say, five hundred pounds?"

Monkey Face looked despondent "Fuck me guv, leave off, I am only a dip, not a mail train robber," pleading poverty.

"Too much is it? Well you shouldn't play with the big boys, should you?"

Jack the Hat turned to Briggs. "Put him back, also get onto the other thirty losers and see if they recognise him and, if by chance they do, charge him with those offences as well. All conspiracies, no thefts, should be good to get him a ten stretch." Again, Briggs got hold of Monkey Face by the scruff of the neck and began leading him out of the office.

"Hold up guv, I didn't say I couldn't. Ring Mr. Beamish, we always keep him holding for just such an eventuality. He'll put up the surety as well, no problem. What about dropping the charge to something more friendly?" Monkey Face was now grovelling and hopeful. Jack the Hat waved at Briggs. "Mr. Briggs here will discuss the matter with Mr. Beamish and IF a business like arrangement can be arrived at, the charge will be reduced, but I will not discuss it with you." Jack the Hat dismissed the pair from his presence.

"Shit! He's a bit hard ain't he? Bet he learnt his manners from Attila the Hun." Monkey Face complained bitterly, basically saying that in the confrontation he had come second. Briggs opened the cell door and ushered Monkey Face into his alternative address.

"I'll ring Mr. Beamish and let you know."

Briggs returned to the office and sat down before a disconsolate Jones. Briggs grabbed his telephone index and looked up Frank Beamish's number. "What's the matter with you, you look as though you've lost a fiver and found a tanner?" said Briggs dialling the number.

"She's got engaged to Ted Richards – you know, Alison." Jones seemed genuinely upset.

Briggs waited for the number to ring. "You're well out of that one old son."

"I am not supposed to know, it's all supposed to be secret squirrel." Jones seemed very miserable.

"Why, because Ted's already married? I told you she was grief didn't I?" Briggs grinning at this partner's sex fuelled misery.

"Hello?" the cultured tone of Frank Beamish.

"Hello Mr. Beamish, DC Briggs from Rodney Road. We've an old client of yours here and he thinks you can help him by coming up with a surety, thereby assisting him to get bail," Briggs noting the time on the outside of the case file.

"I see, who is it you have in custody?" Beamish inquired.

"John Joseph Peck, otherwise known as Monkey Face."

"Ah yes Mr. Peck, know him well, he is part of a syndicate who have retained me for just such an eventuality. How much is the surety for?"

"Five hundred pounds." Briggs waited while Beamish paused and rustled papers.

"Yes Mr. Briggs, I shall be there immediately with the necessary surety."

Briggs put the telephone down and was immediately confronted by Jones' miserable countenance. "For fuck's sake Ron, get a grip,

247

she's only a prick teaser. You watch, she'll break old Ted's marriage and cause him no end of grief, you'll see. Briggs noted that Alison was then leaving the typists' office and going downstairs for lunch. She could have gone down the stairs next to the office, in which case, no-one would have known that she had left. However, she always sauntered along the main office in front of the assembled detectives, swinging her body around in that exaggerated manner of fashion models, hips swinging like John Wayne's saddlebags. "Come on Ron I'll buy you a tea," said Briggs getting up.

"No thanks Tel, I'm still full from Auntie's breakfast see." Jones looked glumly at his paperwork.

"Ron this is important, come and have a cup of tea with me now." Briggs was quietly insistent.

"Oh alright," Jones realising something was afoot.

They left the office and went downstairs to the canteen. On entering, Briggs noted that the delicious Alison was perched on a chair in the centre row of tables and that the table on the next row to her was empty. Briggs smiled as he observed Alison playing up to the twenty or so lecherous eyes which were undressing her at that moment. She sat back from the table showing her thighs as she crossed her legs, holding her tea up to her lips and sipping, dropping her eyes to her knees and looking sideways occasionally just to make sure everyone was watching her. She wriggled, allegedly, to make herself more comfortable, but really to cause her breasts to jiggle about, which forced gasps of desire from the watching throng. Alison sipped from the cup through delicately pursed lips, her little finger extended, as per the upper classes. She put her cup down and smoothed the hair out of her eyes with an action so sensuous that, almost in unison, there were twenty erections in the canteen. Briggs got two teas and sat down with Jones at the table next to Alison. She was still playing ardently to the crowd, moving about on her chair with exaggerated actions which made her breasts rise and fall. Briggs watched this performance with amusement as he turned to Jones. "Shame about Ted Richards isn't it?" loud enough so that Alison could not fail to hear.

"What, what's happened to him?" queried Jones, genuinely puzzled. The erotic performance being put out by Alison stopped immediately and, although she looked resolutely ahead, Briggs knew she was listening.

"Well" continued Briggs. "He got a bad result down at the seaman's hospital in Greenwich," Briggs talking into his tea cup as he raised it to his lips. He was aware that Alison was leaning sideways to hear what he was saying.

"What, you mean the Dreadnought, has he caught clap then?" Jones asked aghast almost believing but half knowing it to be a wind-up.

"Not clap mate, the other one, syphilis" said Briggs, speaking slowly and quietly. He could tell Alison was in receipt of the message.

"They can cure that now you know, massive doses of something or other," Jones reciting part of an article about venereal disease he had read in a Sunday supplement.

"Not this strain they can't mate, it's the tropical variety, it is so virulent it can even burn its way through a French letter." Briggs spoke noncommittally to Allison's rushed exit from the canteen. All pretence at erotic posing dispensed with, this was straightforward running to the door, with tits and bum wobbling in a very unattractive manner, and up the stairs to check this new information with Ted Richards.

Briggs watched this performance with amusement. "There you are old son, that gets you even doesn't it?" Briggs was grinning at his achievements.

"I feel you were a bit cruel, there's no need to treat the poor girl in such a manner, but yes you're right – even." Jones grinned as he drank his tea.

"Tel there's a Mr. Beamish in the front office for you." The communications reserve announced Beamish's presence.

"Be right there mate, come on Ron." Briggs left his tea and the canteen in expectation.

Mr. Beamish waited in the front office, looking very legal, expensive briefcase, pinstripe suit and an old school tie, which some time later he admitted was left behind in a pub after a stag party. "Good morning Mr. Briggs, I am here to see Mr. Peck. I understand he is here in custody. Our surety will arrive shortly and I am sure you will find him acceptable." Beamish smiled the curt business smile that most briefs have as their stock-in-trade.

"Yes fine Mr. Beamish, perhaps we should wait in the interview room." Briggs indicated a nearby door. They entered, Jones bringing up the rear. Once the door was closed, Beamish reached into his briefcase and pulled out an envelope.

"I think you will find our surety's credentials are impeccable." Briggs took the envelope and placed it in his inside pocket.

"I am sure we will find no fault with him at all." Briggs glanced at Jones, who appeared to be in the early stages of strangulation. "Steady Ron." Ron coughed and grunted a non-committal reply.

A uniform head appeared around the door. "A surety here for Peck, is he one of yours?"

Briggs nodded, "Yes he's down to us" and with Beamish they left the room. Monkey Face was released on bail with a surety and, as he left, Briggs caught hold of his arm and in best Humphrey Bogart said, "Don't forget sweetheart we have a date for tomorrow night."

"How could I ever forget?" Monkey Face left the station with surety and brief in tow.

Briggs and Jones then attended Jack the Hat's office where the surety was divided. Jack the Hat grabbed the lion's share. Briggs allowed himself a protest. "If we get a capture on this one guv and they hand down the bird in the same proportions you dished out the dosh, Jonesy and me will get a conditional discharge." Jack the Hat did not smile and did not part up with any more of his 'surety' either.

The Meet

The Captain Hardy at the rear of Kennington Park Road, a small nondescript sort of pub, seemed to be squeezed between large blocks of flats and offices. "Drive round again," Jack the Hat muttered, insisting they tour the block again looking for the A10 rubber heel mob. At last after another circuit and satisfied that maybe everything was in order, Jack the Hat ordered Jones to park the car. They got out of the car and walked towards the pub.

"Jones, as soon as we get inside, you go to the loo and check that there are no nasty surprises in there, right?" Jack the Hat looked closely at Jones who grunted a reply.

They entered the small pub which had only one bar. Not too crowded, maybe it didn't get crowded – ever. Briggs beckoned to the barmaid. "Three light and bitters please love." All three of them were studying the bar customers closely. The barmaid brought the drinks. Briggs noted the barman, who might also be the licensee, making a phone call, speaking very quietly into the receiver. Briggs assumed he was giving Monkey Face the high sign that they had arrived in the pub. Jack the Hat, Briggs and Jones, stood there quietly, backs to the bar, with drinks unattended behind them, warily watching the customers.

"Jonesy, I thought you had an urgent call of nature to attend to?" Jack the Hat indicated the Gents' Toilet at the end of the bar. Jones sloped off quietly to the toilet.

"I think they've informed of our arrival guv" Briggs said, still looking around the bar.

"Who do you mean the team or…?" Jack the Hat's voice trailed off.

Briggs was unsure. "I don't know guv, to be honest it could be either." The street door opened and Monkey Face entered followed by two men and a woman.

One of the men Briggs immediately recognised as the Whisper who had been on the bus stop plot when Monkey Face was arrested. This recognition might become a matter of operational action if the meet tonight was a failure but, for the moment, it was just a matter of Briggs noting points and storing away useful knowledge. The Whisper was, as before, extremely well dressed. The three-piece suit was obviously a product of Savile Row and the shoes screamed 'hand made'. His expensive striped shirt would not be out of place in Jermyn Street. He looked so expensive and so superior that, at first, Briggs took him to be a stockbroker who had lost his way. The other man was nondescript, of middle height, and dressed in clothes that would be difficult to describe later. The most apt description for him was 'grey'. Briggs racked his memory but, in all honesty, could not remember him being on the plot when Monkey Face was lifted. However, that did not mean that he was not. The woman looked as though she had come straight from a shop counter, leaving her apron and putting on the dowdy top coat, again she would be difficult to describe.

"Wotcha guv, see we are on time," Monkey Face showing his watch. "We are reliable, that's what we are," Monkey Face trying to placate any fears that Jack the Hat might have.

"So I see." Jack the Hat spoke quietly, surveying the occupants of the bar to see if anyone was showing any undue interest in their conversation. "Are we going to talk here?" Jack the Hat indicated the bar.

"Nah out the back, much more private." Monkey Face nodded to the barmaid for a drinks order. "Two light ales and a vodka and dry martini please love." The barmaid nodded and went away to get the drinks.

"Jesus, whose drinking vodka and martini?" Briggs asked unable to control his curiosity.

"I am mate. I like it dun I." The misplaced stockbroker spoke with an accent which was pure Elephant and Castle.

"And how many of those do you normally put away?" Briggs was amazed that anyone could possibly drink such a combination.

"Depends on how I feel, happy, I suppose ten or twelve" said Harry, as he was latterly introduced.

Jack the Hat prodded him in the chest. "You keep working my manor old son and I promise you that you are going to be permanently unhappy," growled Jack the Hat. "In fact, where you will end up, they don't have a bar and you'll be able to find God whilst you practice abstinence."

Harry the Whisper blanched visibly. "Ere hold up, that's what we're here for innit to sort it out. Anyway I'm only the small fry not the whizz, nor the buzz, only the whisper, that's where I get my name from Harry the Whisper." This address seemed to have little effect on Jack the Hat; he just grinned and nodded at Harry.

The drinks arrived and were collected by the team. Monkey Face turned to Jack the Hat and inclined his head. "Alright guv?" Jack the Hat nodded and they all went to the back room.

As he entered, he noted that the big round table had been set up as if for a conference, pens paper and carafes of water. Briggs was impressed.

Jack the Hat sat down at one of the chairs, settled himself in and placed his light and bitter on the table in front of him. "Right then, let's get started" he announced. Monkey Face looked pained and pleading.

"Can we have a few minutes guv, we are expecting another one. He won't be long." Monkey Face plonked himself down in a chair opposite Jack the Hat.

Jack the Hat nodded and drank some of his beer. About two minutes later the doorknob rattled and all present straightened in their chairs. The door opened and Old Man Pringle entered. Briggs could see Jack the Hat was uncomfortable with this new situation and Briggs was none too pleased either, as he knew Pringle would never forgive them for Dessie and would do his best to set them up. "Hello Jack, didn't expect to see me is that it?" Pringle sat opposite Jack the Hat.

"Just here to mediate so to speak, to make sure that Monkey Face and his friends don't get cut to pieces by our bold Jack." Pringle glanced around the table. His permanent heavy came in with two drinks, recognised Briggs and nodded in his direction, put one drink before Pringle and sat down.

"Right then ladies and gentlemen, I call this meeting to order, no violence will be tolerated, no abusive language either and definitely no minutes will be taken. Also we'll have no paying back old scores starting with, 'Do you remember when?' Do we all agree?" The assembled coppers and villains nodded and muttered. "Then lets begin." Pringle turned towards Jack the Hat. "Jack?" nodding for him to begin.

"Well as I see it, it's like this, they're working the bus stops around the Elephant and Castle and nicking off old dears and young mums and it ain't on. Therefore everyone what gets nicked goes on the sheet for conspiracy." This pronouncement by Jack the Hat was greeted with muttered insults from the villains. "It's our manor if we decide to work it, it's down to us ain't it?" Harry the Whisper adding his not-too-intelligent contribution. "And it's down to us to catch you old son and when we do, expect no favours," Jack the Hat snapped a reply.

"Gentlemen, gentlemen we are here to negotiate, not to start another war, fighting each other is counter-productive. What's the bottom line with you Jack?" asked Old Man Pringle, trying to mediate.

Jack the Hat paused for thought, then said, "Well we know they were working the West End and Knightsbridge 'cos the Squad told us. What I suggest is that they go back there and face the music."

"Yeah and get nicked every other day. It's costing us a fortune buying off the squad," Monkey Face moaned. "Bugger me are they expensive or what?" Jack the Hat doodled on his pad of paper.

"Well, as it happens, you have one more week to go before they are off to Ascot for the races, so take a week's holiday then the West End is your oyster."

"Yes but for how long, there's the rub, how long will they be away?" mumbled Harry the Whisper mournfully.

"Well old son that's for me to know and you to wonder about, but certainly until they start nicking you again." Jack the Hat's attempt at humour was not appreciated, well not at least by the other side. Jones dutifully giggled, but Briggs concentrated on watching the other side. "Well, a week's no problem, we'll take a holiday, all agreed?" All nodded at Monkey Face's suggestion. "Right then agreed, let's have a drink to celebrate."

"Before you dash off and get silly drunk" said Jack the Hat studying the opposition, "Lets have it what you are agreeing to. Not working my manor again is that it?" Jack the Hat looked to Monkey Face for an answer.

"Well not for the foreseeable future let's put it that way." Monkey Face was doing his politician bit and avoiding the question.

"No let's put it my way, nicking off old dears and young mums is out as far as I am concerned." Jack the Hat was getting – well – ugly, but in this department he did have a head start on most. "Nick off each other, rob banks even, but old ladies and young mums are not fair game ever."

Old Man Pringle nodded his assent. "I am constrained to agree with Jack. You lot are not really on. Work the West End or whatever but don't nick off your own, that's bad news." Pringle pronounced his judgement, after which there was universal agreement. "I can see that we're all agreed so let's join the customers in the bar and have a right good drink to seal our agreement." They all filed out into the bar, where the other customers studied their faces to try and gauge what might transpire, relief was evident on their faces.

"What'll you have then Briggs?" asked Pringle parking himself on a stool at the bar. "What's your poison?" Pringle chuckled at the implication.

"I'll just top up with a light ale thanks" Briggs replied, watching Jones chatting up the barmaid, then turned to Pringle and added, "Turned out alright didn't it?"

Pringle nodded "Yes, no problem they'll keep to their word, old time thieves always do, it's these young tearaways, doing all these muggings I can't stand. They couldn't give a shit about the amount of damage and injury they cause, no finesse, comes down to no training, really, no guidance in the home, know what I mean." Pringle handed Briggs the light ale bottle with the cap off.

"Yes indeed I do," Briggs somberly, but secretly amused, at Pringle's little homily.

The landlord came from behind the bar, opened up an old piano and began to play. One of the customers gave a rendition of "If you were the only girl in the world" and the assembled crowd joined in. A few more drinks and Jack the Hat got up and, accompanied by boos from the dips and cheers from the coppers, gave a George

Formby impression of "When I'm cleaning windows', at the end of which he went down under a shower of beer mats and applause.

Briggs noticed that Harry the Whisper was putting away his vodka and martini with regularity and seemed very red faced and jolly. Jones, being Welsh, could not resist the opportunity of singing "Men of Harlech," which went down very well, and closed to much cheering and stamping of feet.

Closing time came and went and the party went on. Eventually Briggs was winkled out of his corner by the lady dip wearing the head scarf and curlers. "Come on darling there must be somefink you can sing." Her voice was slurred, she breathed beer and stale tobacco over him as she spoke. "Oh alright" and to cheers and shouts Briggs mounted the small stage and sang an off-key version of "My way" – not quite Frank Sinatra, but at that time of night, it did not matter.

About 2am, the landlord called "Come on lads and lassies, time to go home to someone's bed, if not your own" and amid much banter they left the bar. As Briggs was the one least worse for wear he volunteered to drive. They got into the CID car, Jack the Hat and Jones burping and farting in the back. Briggs turned the car around and was driving back past the pub when he noticed Harry the Whisper, now looking very dishevelled, red-faced and staggering, singing 'Rule Britannia' at the top of his voice. Without asking Jack the Hat, Briggs pulled over and called to Harry, "Oi, come on Harry, we'll give you a lift home."

Harry stopped mid chorus and tried to focus his eyes, and then with a bow said, "You sod off Briggsy, I get in there and I'll be fitted up, I'm only drunk not silly" and lurched off. Briggs pulled alongside him as he staggered.

"Come on Harry, armistice tonight, I'll nick you another day. If I don't give you a lift home some young copper is going to snaffle you." Harry wavered about trying to focus and stay upright at the same time "Leave off Briggsy, I know you'll fit me up, you can't help yourself." Harry then evacuated his stomach over the wing of the police car.

"That's it" snorted Briggs. "I have had enough of being the good Samaritan." Briggs drove off leaving Harry to his devices.

Next morning, Briggs looked across at Jones and decided that he was lacking in colour. "Great night last night wasn't it?" Briggs said with more verve than he actually possessed.

"Yes, very good, but I do need a rest this morning though." Jones looked as though he was about to throw up.

"I have some very good advice for you preacher." boomed Jack the Hat from across the office, looking as fresh as a daisy, sprightly even. "If you can't handle it, don't drink it." Jones nodded at either the sense of this pronouncement or in an effort to stop his tea and toast from blurting out over his corres. "Briggs I want you in my office now." Jack the Hat marched away from the crime book table towards his office. Briggs got up wearily, thinking that maybe this could be a bollocking about a report that he had been expecting to be pulled up about.

Briggs entered Jack the Hat's office "Yes guv." Briggs stood in front of Jack the Hat's desk, sincerely wishing the thumping inside his head would go away. "Pringle passed these to me last night." Jack the Hat handed Briggs a small cardboard box. Briggs opened it, and saw that it contained number of high value gambling chips.

"Yes guv and?" Briggs could guess what was coming next.

"Well you and Jones are going to spend Friday night at Pringles Club, doing a little bit of gambling, say three rounds of blackjack, then you will cash these and bring me the proceeds."

"Oh that's a surprise guv," Briggs allowing himself a degree of sarcasm.

"Don't take the piss Tel, you're coming up for promotion and you'll need my recommendation and this is the way to make sure it's a good one." Jack the Hat sat back in his chair and studied his man.

"Do I get anything else out of it, other than the road to the stars that is?" Briggs asked studying the chips closely.

"Well, Pringle has agreed that you will win three hands at blackjack to make it look right, more than three hands and you're taking the piss, say a tenner a hand got it?" Jack the Hat indicating the conversation over.

"Right guv." Briggs left the office. He locked the cardboard box in his drawer, saying nothing to Jones as this would only cause unnecessary drama.

Briggs booked out to court as he had a burglar to deal with for the uniform. He was standing in the underground part of the cells and watching the drunks being led out to be dealt with first. The third man in the line was Harry the Whisper. Briggs tapped him on the shoulder. "Harry I told you this would happen, you should have taken that lift home," Briggs amused at Harry's predicament.

"Yes I suppose so, but you would have fitted me, I know you would you couldn't have been off of it." Harry seemed to be suffering from pangs of alcoholic remorse. "A ten pound fine is much better than twelve moon any day of the week." He shuffled off with the drunks and derelicts.

Friday evening Briggs and Jones booked out to Pringle's gambling club. On entering, Pringle's personal heavy nodded to them. Briggs made his way to the bar and bought a drink for both of them. They then made their way to the blackjack table and sat down. Briggs gave Jones two of the gambling chips that Jack the Hat had given them. They placed their bets and the first hand was dealt. Briggs had nineteen and Jones had sixteen. Jones was about to twist but Briggs indicated him not to. The dealer ran up his hand and busted. They were paid out in chips. They then played a further two hands with the same result. Briggs picked up his chips and made to leave. "Ere hold on Tel, I'm on a winning streak." Briggs pulled Jones over into a corner.

"Listen Ron, they're letting us win three hands, any more than that is bad manners and quite liable to earn you a good kicking." Jones had many questions most of which were unanswered. They left the club after cashing in their chips.

On receipt of the cash, Jack the Hat counted it and said, "Right then, an alternative charge can now be preferred against Monkey Face, make it 'attempted theft'." Jack the Hat put the cash in his top drawer. "How much did you earn at blackjack?"

"I can't remember guv" said Briggs, stone-faced. "That is the best way old son."

Pat's Arrest

"Briggsy you're a time served mechanic aren't you?" queried Sid Mills, still looking at the crime book and, without waiting for a reply, "only there's a job here about engines that's got me. One of the Trafpol cars has stopped a geezer and they're not happy with the engine in his car. They know what they are on about, but to be honest I haven't a clue. Go and have a word with them downstairs will you?"

Briggs put down his Moffatt. "I am a bit busy at the moment skip with the other crap that's been lumbered on me," Briggs sounding as plaintive as his pride would allow plus, of course, hinting that Sid had already lumbered him up to the Plimsoll line, but then no-one ever took any notice of that.

"That's as maybe Tel, but you are the only one who would understand what they are on about, engines and all that." Sid waved his hand at 'all that' thereby dismissing all mechanics and their services etc. Feeling that he was turkey-tied ready for the oven Briggs shrugged, got up and went downstairs to the canteen. He surveyed the occupants and spotted the 'Trafpol' guys in the corner. On his way over to them he reminded himself that because 'Trafpol' were known almost universally as the 'white filth' this would be a good time to forget that nickname.

"Ello chaps, you the blokes with the funny engine job?" Briggs addressed his question to the older officer who was nursing his tobacco tin whilst rolling a cigarette. They both looked up.

The older officer spoke with an almost surly snarl. "Yes that's us, you been told to help us?" The older Trafpol officer certainly had an unkind edge to his voice, which Briggs thought was

259

maybe just his way.

"That's me mate, I've been selected because many years ago I served my time as a mechanic." Briggs smiled and waited for a response.

The older officer sniffed disdainfully. "That don't mean nuffink do it, it don't mean you know anything about motors do it?" Briggs was stunned, the older officer continued, "I mean you ain't done the nuts and bolts course have you?" intent on establishing his superiority. Briggs was exasperated, the thought of all those files and cases on his desk upstairs and he was standing here being given the bum's rush by this prick.

After a suitable pause, during which his temper would not be controlled, Briggs said, "Listen mate, I couldn't give a toss what you or your soapy mate think of me, got that? Now do you want my help or not, as if you don't, I have lots of work upstairs to get on with." Briggs was irritated more than anything else and made to walk away.

"Here hold on mate," the younger officer deciding that maybe they needed the help of this detective. "We really need a bit of help on this one, we deal mainly with traffic law and the few times we deal with a bit of crime we tend to get a bit lost, know what I mean?" Briggs sat down and paid attention.

"Right then tell me about it," speaking to the younger officer who was the one with the brain cell.

"Well it's like this, me and my mate here," indicating the older officer, "were on patrol when we pulled this bloke in his Cortina and decided to have a look at his engine, chassis plate and all that." The younger officer drew a breath and looked to his older colleague for confirmation. The older officer said nothing but carried on drawing on his wafer thin roll up. He inhaled so ferociously that Briggs was sure his shirt would be sucked up into him at the other end. "Anyway, the Cortina should be fitted with a 1300cc overhead valve jobby and it's got the 1600 overhead cam motor you know the Pinto. Given a closer look we note that the engine is brand new and so is everything on it, the starter motor, alternator, the carburretor and both inlet and exhaust manifolds. There's no way that such an engine should be in an old dog of a Cortina. We question the driver and he says he bought it but won't say where, so we swifted him in here." The young Trafpol officer pushed his notes across the table to

Briggs. Briggs read them without comment and passed them back to the officer.

"Right, the best thing we can do is this. First we have a look at the motor and second I, or we if you like, have a word with the Ford Motor Co's arch enemy that you have lifted." The younger officer smiled and seemed relieved. The older one stared at Briggs impassively. Briggs could just feel that there was grief coming from this one. As they walked towards the station yard, Briggs was trying desperately to remember what a Ford engine, overhead valve or whatever, looked like.

The sagging Cortina was parked in the corner of the yard. There wasn't a straight panel on the car and it was two-tone – blue and rust. The young Trafpol officer got the bonnet up with a resounding creak and Briggs could see that the engine reposing in the car was in distinct contrast to the rest of the vehicle. He made a note accordingly. "Right then, let's go and have a word with our mate." They went back into the Police Station. Briggs went to the interview room. A short while later the Trafpol officers brought in their prisoner.

"Mr. Guest, this is Detective Sergeant Briggs of Rodney Road. He will interview you about the engine in your vehicle." The elder Trafpol officer ground out the introduction.

Briggs sat behind the desk, smiled and said, "Yes Mr. Guest, it's Detective Constable actually, but in the future who knows? Anyway about the engine." Guest looked blank. Briggs continued. "The one in your car that these officers were so interested in – where did you buy it?" Briggs was trying hard to be pleasant as the Commissioner had ordered that one must be nice and pleasant at all times. Guest was sullen and surly, "I bought it off a geezer in a pub din I?"

The police trio burst into laughter. "So, let me see," Briggs continuing the joke "You were standing in the Temple Bar having a light ale, when this bloke idly saunters in carrying a Ford 1600 engine under his arm. You fancy it and buy it off of him right there and then?" Briggs and the other officers still laughing.

"Yeah well he didn't have the engine with him did he, know what I mean." Guest was studying the floor.

"Chaps, we might as well perform the script to its logical conclusion," Briggs addressing the Trafpol officers. "And how much did you pay for this engine?"

After a pause, "Er it was a hundred and fifty quid fitted." Guest looked as though he was dragging the answers from his boots.

"So we can assume that it was one hundred pounds for the engine and the rest for labour – yes?" Briggs asked, making notes.

"Yes I suppose so, sumfink like that," Guest showing an interest in Briggs' notes.

"Why did you need a new engine? Was the original one knackered?"

"Knackered that wasn't the word for it, white smoke everywhere every time I used it. I was dot on the cards to be nicked everytime I used it." Guest smiled in remembrance.

"And presumably you made inquiries on the cost of a reconditioned engine?" Briggs asked and looked expectantly at Guest.

"Well yeah it was a good hundred quid more, just for the engine alone." Guest looked please with his deal.

"And you would still have the old 1300cc engine, just an ordinary overhead valve, not the super 1600cc overhead cam you have got now – right?" Briggs nodded and Guest followed suit. "So you were having an excellent deal, one that you couldn't turn down?" Briggs nodded but Guest didn't seem to keen to follow suit, perhaps realizing where this conversation was leading.

"Well it wasn't that good, just like, well, a bit above average, know what I mean?" Guest was squirming in his chair.

"Did that man in the pub give you a receipt for your money, any guarantee, or anything like that?" Briggs was still taking notes, head down.

"Well no, it was strictly cash, no questions asked, you know, no Vodka and Tonic and all that game," Guest shrugging his shoulders to express the point.

"Vodka and Tonic?" the younger Trafpol officer enquired, mystified. Briggs smiled at his confusion "VAT – Value Added Tax."

"So let's summarise shall we? You buy an engine, which is obviously brand new, not a recon, straight off the line at Dagenham, for one hundred pounds from a man in a pub who you don't know. Lo and behold, this engine, even without its added bits and pieces, is worth about three hundred and fifty pounds when you buy it across the counter at Ford Motor Spares and you don't think there is anything wrong in that?" Briggs waited whilst Guest's thought processes ranged over the various topics put to him.

Eventually he said, "Well I thought it a bit strange, but it's the way round here, know what I mean," Guest pleading to be understood.

"I know exactly what you mean old son. You're nicked for dishonestly handling the engine and you'll go on the sheet shortly. You might get bail – maybe." Briggs left the 'maybe' hanging in the air, working on Guest's brain.

"So what do I have to do for bail?" Guest all of a sudden becoming ever so sharp.

"Well, we need to know where you bought the engine, who from like. Briggs was still head down taking notes. Guest paused, thinking of the implications of this conversation.

"If I told you where, would it help me when I appear in court?" Guest spoke slowly and awaited a reply from Briggs with almost baited breath.

"Yes, providing of course that we get a guilty plea in a statement before you get anything." Briggs let the words settle.

"And what else do I get?" Guest looked a touch pugnacious. Briggs and the other officers were beginning to lose their patience.

"Well I'll tell you, we'll give the Commissioner and his Deputy a ring. I'm sure they will be delighted to come down here and kiss your arse and possibly a blow job as well. Now where did this engine come from shithead?" obviously said before the advent of tape-recorded interviews. Guest looked startled, almost though doused with ice cold water. He flinched as though Briggs was about to belt him. "Ryan's Garridge, John Ruskin Street, he's got loads of them out the back, all new like mine," he blurted out quickly, in case irritation turned into violence.

Briggs sat back in his chair and studied Guest. "If you're pulling my plonker, I will kick the ring out of you," Briggs with that hard edge to his voice that so impressed the villains.

"No honest guv, Ryan's Garridge, that's the place," Guest pleaded like a little boy.

"Right then chaps, put him back in his little hole in the wall, let's go and see Mr. Ryan," said Briggs getting up from the table.

"Ere hold up, don't I get bail or somfink like?" Having given his all, Guest believed he was due some preferential treatment.

"Not just yet mate, we'll see if your information is any good first shall we?" The Trafpol officers led Guest back to his cell.

"I'll get my buck, won't be a minute" called Briggs, making his way upstairs. Jones was almost asleep over some case files. "Come on, the old grey fox is needed to solve some dirty deeds on the ground," Briggs using the nickname of that legendary thief taker Tommy Butler to refer to his buck. The old grey fox who came later and who hi-jacked the nickname was pure plastic by comparison.

They all drove to John Ruskin Street in the Trafpol patrol car. Briggs told them to stop some fifty yards from the garage whilst he went in. There were two ramps in the garage and only one mechanic working, which Briggs found strange. "Hello guv," said Briggs talking directly to the mechanic. "I've got an old Cortina what badly needs a new engine, what's your price for a recon?" Briggs was idly looking around the garage, noting that most of the equipment was past its best and the place generally scruffy.

"What you got, OHV or OHC?" The mechanic's thick brogue surprised Briggs who desperately tried to place the accent, and concluded it was Southern Irish. "I think it's OHV, it's the old woman's and I'm no mechanic anyhow, so I'm not sure really" replied Briggs, as casually as he could manage.

"Come with me." Paddy indicated the rear of the garage to a side room. Briggs entered and when his eyes had accustomed themselves to the gloom, he saw six brand new engines of the OHC variety, all with their plastic sealers in place and, as such, directly out of Fords of Dagenham.

"How much would one of these be then Paddy?" Briggs queried looking closely at the engines.

"One hundred and fifty pounds fitted and don't call me Paddy my name's Pat." Pat was curt but Briggs felt he was probably peeved at always being called 'Paddy'.

"Right then, I'll have one of them." Briggs fished out his wallet and gave Pat a ten pound note. "Take this as deposit and I'll bring the motor around straight away. "Is that OK?" Pat pocketed the tenner with a flourish.

"Yeah fine but there'll be no receipts or anything strange like that, also no VAT, so can't be bad." Briggs nodded and walked to the entrance of the garage and into the street. He waved to the patrol car. They drove up to the garage and into the entrance. "What's occurring here then?" Pat approached the car as Jones and the Trafpol officers got out.

Briggs cut him short. "I am a Police Officer and you are under arrest on suspicion of dishonestly handling stolen engines." Briggs got out his warrant card and displayed it, a totally unnecessary action due to the presence of the Trafpol officers and the 'jam sandwich' patrol car. "While we are doing the thing I will have my tenner back." Pat quietly opened his wallet and gave Briggs his much travelled ten pound note.

"I'm nicked then?" Pat seemed crestfallen.

"Yes I'm afraid so mate" Briggs said, thinking that Pat looked almost suicidal.

"I only did it so I could get the business going, would have been alright except I got caught."

Briggs laughed. "That's the problem with most things unlawful old son, the offence isn't doing it, it's getting caught doing it."

Pat shook his head. "Yes I suppose so, the problem is I can't stand a nick at the present, got things to do, can we talk about this?" Pat indicated his little garage but really meant his involvement with bent engines.

"Sorry old son, but that's the way it is, nothing can be done." Briggs indicated the Trafpol officers with his eyebrows.

"The only thing is that I have a good mate, who would like to help me I'm sure. His name is…" Briggs cut him short.

"Look, not at the moment, you'll have plenty of time to talk at the nick, right?" Briggs turned to the Trafpol officers. "Get on to Rodney Road would you? Get them to send the van round here." The older Trafpol officer looked puzzled. "Do it on your radio, you know, in the car." Briggs decided that this one was definitely eleven plus failed, or, as his dad would say 'tuppence short of a shilling.' The Trafpol officer went to the car and transmitted the message on the force radio. Briggs noted that he had the surly attitude of a spoilt child and was probably the prima donna of his section of Trafpol. He left the patrol car and came back to Briggs. "I've done that. The van is on its way. Can we leave now – I mean hand over to you – you've got it sorted haven't you? We have our patrol to think of." Briggs listened intently to this presentation of prime bullshit.

"I see, you would like to leave now, yes? You're now fed up with playing CID officers, is that it? I am afraid not old son, we have those engines to load onto the van, together with anything else we might find and, as you're the arresting officers for Guest and the assisting officer of this gink here" (Pat looked offended at the description), "We are entitled to demand that you stay and assist us in those endeavours. Who knows, your nuts and bolts course might come in handy yet." Briggs spoke in that condescending manner of one who is firmly in charge. The Trafpol officer slouched away to join his mate where he stood and muttered discontentedly.

The van arrived with one extra PC and the three uniformed men began loading the engines onto the van. Whilst this was going, on Briggs and Jones wandered around the garage looking in storerooms and cubby holes. Jones found some oil paintings which looked a bit dodgy and put them ready to go in the van with the rest of the contraband. Briggs, in his wanderings, noted the roof was covered by a lorry tarpaulin. He struggled and, with the help of Ron, pulled it down into the yard. It was blue plasticised on its covering and bore the oval insignia in white of "Ford." It was fairly new and had not been on the roof very long. They folded it up and dragged it over to the van where, with the aid of the van driver, they put it on top of the engines.

"What do you want to bother with that for?" asked an inquisitive Pat. "I only put it up there to seal the leaking roof."

"Really and where did it come from originally?" Briggs almost speaking to himself as he really did not expect an answer from Pat and was not disappointed. They had to do two trips to get all the engines to Rodney Road, after which Briggs turned to Pat and said, "You might as well get on board and keep the engines company. Don't worry, I'll lock up for you." Pat got into the van reluctantly. "Make sure you lock the office door won't you?" Pat said as he sat down next to an engine. "There's the day's takings in there."

Jones got into the van with Pat. When Briggs thought about it, this and the oil paintings were his only contribution to this operation and mollified himself on the basis of the excellent information coming from his sexual efforts. Briggs got into the Trafpol car and they drove to Rodney Road, Briggs feeling that he had well and truly upset the Trafpol officers. This gave him a morsel of satisfaction as they had done the same to him earlier. They arrived at the yard at Rodney Road and parked, when the older Trafpol officer broke the ice, "Well, having got you back here with the evidence and the body, can we go and get on with our job now?" He said it with the truculent attitude of a four year old who has been castigated for bad manners. "Well old son, there is still the interview of Pat and the statement under caution to be done. Do you want to be part of that, finishes the job off really," Briggs giving them the opportunity of being out but really telling them that they were not finished yet.

"We don't do statements under caution, don't know how." The older Trafpol officer was going for freedom. Briggs was sure he knew how to do the statement but wasn't bothered either way. In fact, of the two options, he felt more comfortable with the Trafpol out of the way, especially the older sulky one.

"Righto then, off you go, like the Lone Ranger and Tonto riding off into the sunset righting wrongs and all that." Briggs waved them away. Jones and Briggs cajoled all available troops to assist with the unloading of the van and transferred the engines into the property store. Pat was placed in the detention room and locked away whilst the property was sorted.

Briggs and Jones entered the detention room where Pat was asleep, or feigning the same, on a rough bedboard. Jones shook him. "Come on Pat, day of reckoning is upon us, time to account for your naughty deeds." Pat sat up and made an elaborate display of rubbing sleep from his eyes.

"What do you want now, you've ruined my business what more do you want?"

Briggs laughed "Well, we could put you away for few years as well. How does that grab you? Don't fancy it? Well pay attention." Once Briggs was happy that Pat was paying the correct amount of attention and also that Jones was ready with pen poised, "Right then, I am going to keep these questions nice and simple, so you can't get confused or complain afterwards that you didn't know what I was on about. Is that alright?" Pat nodded and looked at the floor. "OK here we go – where did you get those engines from?" Briggs waited for a reply.

"What engines are those?" muttered Pat from beneath his bowed head.

Briggs gave a sigh, "I just knew it was going to be one of those days." You remember the engine you were going to sell me for one hundred and fifty pounds?"

Pat looked up. "Nah I don't remember that at all, never happened." Pat allowed himself a sidelong glance at Briggs to assess how angry the detectives were getting.

"So where do the six engines come from that we have in the property store and what about the paintings?" Briggs was being almost even tempered.

"You planted them didn't you?" Pat said it ever so quietly, perhaps so that Briggs and Jones wouldn't notice and maybe not take offence.

"We planted them, you dumb arse bog trotting shithead, do you really think we are going to lug that sort of gear around to plant on you," Briggs was red faced and roaring. "Ron forget the question and answer routine, we'll book him and let him get on with it, he'll find Brixton will give him a lovely feeling of imminent truth, especially when he realises that he could be spending the next few years there." Briggs got up from the bed and made for the door.

"Here, hold up a minute, don't I get bail or nothing, do I have stay here all night?" Pat seemed genuinely worried.

"You will be charged and go to court in the morning. You might get bail then, but I doubt it as I will object and I haven't lost one yet." Briggs grinned as the implications settled on Pat's brain.

Pat gulped. "That's a bit hard guv, my wife will suffer you know." He said it quietly.

"What's the matter with her then Pat?" Briggs suddenly paying attention. "Well she's got cancer. If I don't see her tonight she will get, well, you know, agitated and it won't do her any good." Pat seemed crestfallen having imparted this information, tears were welling up in his eyes, which Briggs took to be genuine.

Briggs thought for a few moments, then sat down on the bed again. "Listen Pat, you stop playing the Irish shithead who don't know nuffink and I'll try to help – carry on as you are and I see no reason to change my view of things." Pat nodded quietly. "Now let's start again. Where do the engines and oil paintings come from?"

Briggs asked quietly and slowly. Pat nodded his head.

"The paintings I bought from a bloke who was hard up and I thought I might be able to make a few pounds. As for the engines, you know already they're out of Fords, they come to me by the lorry load," Pat now seeming to tell the truth.

"And how much do you pay for them?" Briggs checked that Jones was taking notes.

"I buy them in tens, I pay six hundred pounds for ten." Pat answering slowly.

"And the tarpaulin over the roof was part of a load was it?" Briggs suddenly remembering that he had seized that as well.

"Well yeah, the roof was leaking wasn't' it," Pat stating the obvious.

"Do you want to make a statement about all this?" Briggs broaching the most difficult subject – getting them to put it into writing.

"I might as well, I've told you about it now haven't I?" Pat said, smiling for the first time.

Briggs began writing the statement under caution. He wrote the script as far as he could remember it, and consulted Pat for additional detail when necessary. When he had finished, he read it to Pat and got him to write the certificate at the end. Pat then signed it.

"I've a friend who will help me, be pleased to he will." Pat spoke in a matter of fact manner.

"Really! and who might that be?" Briggs showing a passing interest.

"Detective Sergeant Sayers of Tower Bridge CID," said Pat, naming an officer who, having served on both the regional crime squad and the flying squad, was much respected as having a number of active informants.

"Are you saying this officer might owe you a favour on the basis of things you have done for him in the past?" Pat smiled and nodded. Jones looked bewildered and Briggs expected nothing more.

"Right you will be bailed later on in your own recognizance to appear at Camberwell Green Magistrates' Court. If your mate wants to talk, tell him to make a meet with me." Briggs and Jones left the detention room and briefed the station officer about Pat's presence in the police station.

Subsequently Pat was charged with dishonest handling the engines and bailed to appear at Camberwell Green Magistrates' Court the next day.

Briggs was sitting at his desk the next day, going over the various papers he had and considering a complaint from the uniform that he was using all the spare space in the property store. They were considering transferring his property to a central store, which was the last thing Briggs wanted, as it meant he would have to travel to restore or check his property. The phone rang and Briggs picked it up. "Hello Rodney Road CID. Can I help you?"

"Yeah, DC Briggs please." The caller spoke as though he was familiar with Briggs. "Yes that's me what can I do for you." Briggs picked up his pen and addressed it to paper just in case.

"DS Sayers here, Tower Bridge, you've nicked one of my little helpers." The caller sounded amused by the situation. Briggs did not answer. "I was wondering if we could have a meet sometime."

"Yes of course Sarge, whenever or wherever," Briggs answered, writing like mad on his scrap of paper.

"Well how about tonight at the Tankard in Walworth Road, do you know it?" Sayers paused for an answer.

"Yes I know the place, it's where they have all the retirement and transfer do's."

"Tonight at nine be OK?" Briggs tried to sound offhand.

"Fine see you then." The final click of the phone seemed heavy and unnatural to Briggs, maybe they were working on the system.

"Got a meet tonight at nine with the DS who runs Pat as a snout, you up for it?" Briggs throwing the invitation at Jones, but really knowing the answer before it came. "Can't tonight, it's special see, at the Chapel" Jones said in a mournful pleading voice.

"Oh right, what are you doing at the chapel then?" Briggs was curious and genuinely interested as he couldn't understand an organised religion that would accept Jones as one of its leading lights. Certainly not if they knew the full story. Briggs expected Jones would never let his petticoat show in that quarter. "Bible classes for the converts to the faith, and I'm lecturing on the Bible see." Jones said it with a trace of pride.

"What, do you take it all literally, the Bible that is?" Briggs asked, still interested, but Jones was suspicious, well knowing Briggs' capacity to construct an elaborate wind-up.

"Well, more that I try to give an interpretation that's likely to be more acceptable in modern times" explained Jones, with a trace of pomposity, repeating what the Pastor had said to him. "You know, help the heathen along the way."

"How do you explain to your ex-heathens that the Bible has been edited at least four times and in the King James' edition alone they left out a complete gospel, probably forgot it I expect?" Briggs laughing and exposing his limited knowledge of the scriptures.

"It has never been edited, it is the word of God," Jones blurted out in crusading mood.

"Oh right" smiled Briggs, "That answers everything doesn't it, makes it nice and cosy, all wrapped up in dogma which flies in the face of scholarly research, as I understand it, but never mind. How do you manage the commandments, when it comes to the bit about adultery, you know, you bashing your bishop into strange churches. Or is it the case that you mustn't lecture on a subject in which you are truly expert?" Briggs teased, smiling at the prospect and knowing that Ron hated being reproached in this way.

"We are all sinners, it is trying to be perfect where the faith really lies you know." Jones was obviously upset by Briggs' irreverence.

"Perfect at what though" thought Briggs, heaving sweating bodies flew through his mind but he said, "Right Ron, you would know old son." He could feel Ron becoming evangelical and decided to leave that wind-up for another day. Briggs wondered if Christine and Ron indulged in a bout of prayer before they joined in the terrible sin of fornication and, if they did, what did they pray for – thunderous orgasms perhaps, not to pot the eight ball this time (get pregnant). Briggs smiled to himself at the prospect. "Anyway, bottom line, you will not be there tonight, in the forefront of the white hot war against crime," Briggs closing the conversation and the subject for the time being.

"No I will not," responded Jones hotly and Briggs could tell he had made Jones prickly with his leg pulling.

Briggs entered the saloon bar alone and surveyed the scene, hoping that DS Sayers might be obvious for he didn't know him, although he couldn't fail to be aware of, and be impressed by, the man's reputation. The man standing in the corner of the bar, big, with Prince of Wales check suit and expensive shoes might be him. Briggs went to the bar.

"Light and Bitter please Dan," Briggs leaning up against the corner of the bar. Danny nodded and went and got Briggs' pint. Briggs put his hand in his pocket intending to pay for the drink but Danny said, "No, have this one on me Tel, the wife's birthday." Danny smiled and continued. "Mind you, I would prefer to drink to the funeral of my mother-in-law." They laughed together. "Why, is she a problem?" Briggs was interested as Danny was a nice man who didn't deserve the hell of a pub in the Elephant and Castle. "Well being Irish, she does tend to think she's still the senior lady about the place and because of that she can give me a hard time." Danny took a swig from his glass. "Why don't you tell her to go forth and multiply," Briggs threw in helpfully. Danny laughed "You would I know, but if I did, it would cause more problems than it would solve." Briggs decided that poor Danny was well and truly under the thumb. Breaking the moment Briggs said, "Anyway, I'm here to meet DS Sayers do you know him?"

"I do, he's over by the toilets looking at the back of you." Danny spoke quietly into Briggs' ear. "Oh, right" said Briggs, realising that the chap in the Prince of Wales outfit was not his man. Briggs turned around and saw a smallish man looking very upmarket in leather jacket and jeans, smoking a 'Clint Eastwood' cheroot. He was leaning up against the one-arm bandit next to the gents' toilet. Sayers was looking at Briggs with a sardonic smile. Briggs approached him.

Briggs stood quite close to the man and, speaking in an almost whisper, asked "You DS Sayers from Tower Bridge?"

"I wondered when you would get around to giving me a tug, Danny had to tee me up for you did he?" Sayers asked, laughing at Briggs' discomfort.

"Sorry skip, but I've never met you and I had to find out somehow didn't I? Anyway, you want a drink?" Briggs nodded at Danny and the bar.

"No, no thanks I have another meet to keep and I've already got one. I am here about Pat you know, Ryan and the bent engine job. I've spoken to Jack the Hat, apparently you're sound to be spoken to."

Briggs grinned. "Well I haven't let anyone down – yet."

"Right then, our little man with the engines, he wants help, large dollops of it and is prepared to pay for the privilege. What can be done?" Sayers looked hopefully into Briggs' eyes.

"Not a lot really, he's already charged and is going to stay that way." Briggs said it quickly as though staking his claim to the high ground. "If he puts up the source of the engines I would let the court know that he has been helpful." Briggs let the statement hang in the air, aware that what he was saying was not quite what was expected.

"Fuck me, is that the best you can do, bear in mind this Pat is a steady snout. I want him out and working, not branded as some sort of receiver." Briggs perceived Sayers to be a little annoyed.

"But that's exactly what he is, a receiver of stolen goods, you must surely see that," Briggs showing himself to be just a shade naïve.

Sayers was annoyed, "We all know what he is, but there are wider issues here. You don't know who he's involved with." Sayers said it quietly out of the side of his mouth. Briggs felt like laughing at this performance, but didn't.

"Listen skip, I don't care who he's connected with, he's on the sheet and he ain't going to walk away." Briggs said it with finality, and refreshed himself by taking a swig from his beer.

Sayers fell silent for a few moments thinking, then said. "How about if?" he began slowly, thinking on the way "we had a small hiccup in the evidence, a little door left open so our little bird can escape. Would that suit you, plus two grand cash, can't be fairer than that?" Sayers was speaking as though selling a car, or maybe buying one.

"Listen skip, I don't want to upset you, your reputation precedes you. However, the evidence is already in, the 'Trafpol' lot have it in their books, so he's on fair and square. If we alter it all now, which I wouldn't do anyway, we'll have the traffic lot screaming and quite honestly it's not worth it."

Sayers looked disgruntled "So what's on offer for my little helper?"

Briggs took a deep breath, knowing that what he was going to say was not what was acceptable, or which would make Sayers his bosom buddy. "He pleads and if he puts up the source of the Ford gear, he can have as much help as he wants, outside that no deal." Briggs shrugged his shoulders to indicate that that was it.

Sayers lit another evil-smelling cheroot. "It's not so much him, it's the lot behind him. They want to preserve his credibility for some reason." Sayers took a drag on his cheroot and blew the smoke away from Briggs. "Anyway I'll let you know, what do you want to see for help?"

Briggs shook his head, "Not bothered really, if he's happy with the result say thank you after the event. If he's not happy, say nothing." Briggs nodded to Danny for another drink and looked quizzically at Sayers.

"Not for me I have to be going, I'll keep in touch but I have to tell you that the people behind Pat are not going to be pleased, they're not where the gear comes from, they are where it's going to," Sayers looked apologetically.

Briggs spoke firmly, "Look skip, they can please themselves, but definitely no outers." Sayers nodded, avoided eye contact and left the pub.

Briggs went over to the bar, picked up his beer and paid Danny for it. "I would watch yourself with that one if I were you Tel, he has a bad name with the villains, know what I mean?" Danny gave Briggs a knowing look.

"Oh really, I'm sure he's worried about that, but I'll bear it in mind thanks." Briggs stood in the corner and finished his second pint whilst thinking deeply.

Briggs left the pub and made his way back to Rodney Road. As he strolled along he considered what DS Sayers had said and the offer he had made. It wasn't that Briggs was saintly, because he was not, but there were certain things he would not get involved in and opening a door in evidence so a villain could walk away was one of them. Obviously DS Sayers felt completely at home with this arrangement and Briggs wondered just what might be going on outside of what he was being told.

Being in Mid Air

Briggs sat at his desk, refreshed by a night's sleep, but still puzzled by his meet with Sayers. Briggs searched the crime book in case Sid had put him down for one or two break-ins, which would be against the grain as he was late turn and only there to clear up paperwork. "You alright Briggs, how did you get on with our super Tec?" Jones asked from behind his Telegraph.

"Oh alright I suppose, works to a different set of rules though, must be the squad influence," said Briggs getting the engine file out and preparing it for court.

"Different, how do you mean, different?" Jones asked as he put down his paper and started to pay attention.

Briggs mouthed the words "Bent."

"Oh I see, leave me out then," Jones picking up his paper again.

"Oh certainly guv, you can be in while it's raining and out when the sun shines, all down to your buck." Briggs gritted the words out, pissed off with Jones. "I don't think."

"Ere Tel," Barking approached Briggs.

"Which one do you want, left, right or the one in the middle?" Briggs grunted.

"What?" Barking questioned, mystified, as he always was by most conversations which were not childlike.

"What do you want John?" Briggs spoke in an exaggerated slow manner.

"Er yeah, can I borrow your handcuffs mate?" Briggs noted he was always a 'mate' whenever John wanted something.

"I suppose so, but why do you want them, you've got your own set." Briggs was puzzled by the need for two sets for one officer, perhaps he was going in for nicking werewolves or something that needed shackling fore and aft.

Barking leaned on Briggs' desk and whispered in Briggs' ear. "Got this bird see, needs to be chained, loves it she does, so I need yours to chain up the other arm see." Briggs unlocked his desk drawer and took out his ratchet cuffs and handed them to Barking.

"Now clean them before you bring them back. I don't want my cuffs coming back in a dissolute and debauched manner." Briggs said it straight-faced.

"Of course Tel, could I do anything else." Briggs was unsure whether Barking was joking or was aware that he was, but passed it off as another confusing conversation with Barking.

Briggs carried on at this desk, completing the file apart from some small points on property. He considered the paintings which Jones had seized from the back room at the garage. Briggs had examined them but, being uneducated, could see no particular value in them. Just in case, he formulated a telex message to the Arts and Antique Squad up the Yard, giving a description of the paintings and the perceived name of the artist on the canvas, requesting they send an officer to examine them and to run them through the indices. Briggs went downstairs and sent the telex and then adjourned to the canteen. He got his tea and joined Ted Richards at a table near the door.

"You alright Ted?" Briggs wheezed as he sat down.

"Yes I am now, but you didn't intend that did you?" Richards replied in a matter-of-fact accusative tone.

"What! Do you mean that thing with Alison? Only a wind-up old son, nothing meant by it – mind you she was posing like hell. Anyway if it caused you grief I'm sorry." Briggs looked earnestly into Ted's eyes.

"No problem, blessing in disguise really, she was turning into a right homewrecker. When she fronted me about the syphilis thing I didn't deny it. Didn't confirm it mind, but she got the hump and dumped me, thank God." Richards grinned. "Also for all that posing she's a rotten shag." Briggs was relieved.

"Doesn't surprise me Ted, she always seems to make an act out of everything" Briggs said, staring into the turgid depths of his tea. After a minute's thought he said, "Ted while I think on it, will you do me favour?"

"Of course if I can. What do you want?" Ted thinking he's off on another tack.

"Don't tell Jonesy it's all off, else he'll be up her like a rat up a drainpipe." They both laughed at the truth of this statement.

After several hours Briggs was still at his desk. He had been working at files for what seemed an age and he was demoralised as he surveyed the scattered paperwork. It always struck him that the ones who were active got snowed under with paper and complaints and were always getting attacked in the Old Bailey by super briefs like Ashburn. The really clever ones, instead of causing aggravation by nicking real villains, were coasting to their promotions with very neat desks and uncompromised consciences. He looked across at Roger Ainsley's desk. He was known as the 'Grey Ghost', not because of any gift for secret squirrel operations, but because most of the time no-one knew where he was. Ainsley was famous in the Met as the officer who, when his house was being broken into, had hidden behind the kitchen door and told the breaker that if he didn't go away he would call the police.

Briggs looked at Ainsley's desk. It was immaculate, all the files were in line, the blotter had a nice new piece of blotting paper on it, no odd messages tucked in the corner here. The pens, including a Charlie Moffat, were arranged with the ruler along the top edge of the blotter and the obligatory photo of mum and sprogs stared out at the empty office. Briggs made a mental note to tell him that to compete the picture he needed a specimen glass with a single rose, then and only then would he be destined for the top. In contrast, Briggs' own disaster area of a desk had pieces of paper all over the place, unfinished files wedged under file boxes and result sheets tucked into Criminal Record Office files awaiting his attention. He decided that he would never have enough time to become a career planner. A voice interrupted his thoughts.

"Detective Sergeant Gillender, Arts and Antique's Squad, come about the paintings you've got." Briggs looked up at a very nattily dressed young sergeant, pinstripe suit, pink shirt, the full set, plus of course the false plummy accent that Bolton would have been proud of. Rumour had it that this one went to elocution lessons to hide his East London accent. Now, with his hair parted in the middle and smarmed down with Brylcreem, he looked the full art expert.

Briggs was tempted to say "Know what I mean my old, son," or perhaps "Come on the two dog," but resisted the temptation and instead said, "Yeah right, I'll take you down to the property store so you can have a gander like," inverted snobbery forcing Briggs to accentuate his cockney accent for this pseudo art expert.

Together they went to the property store. Briggs got the paintings out from the rack and put them upright so the sergeant could see them.

"No not there, over here in the natural light." The sergeant indicated a large window at the end of the store. Wishing to be rid of this idiot, Briggs obeyed quietly and placed the paintings as directed. The sergeant stood back and lit a cigarette, not one of your ordinary fags but one of those with a black paper covering and a gold stripe around it, and which smells strongly of rotting socks. He stood there and gazed at the paintings.

"No I don't really think so" he said, his other hand cradling his expensive cigarette.

"Er skip I only want to know if they're nicked, I don't need an appraisal," Briggs trying to cut short this irritating performance.

The sergeant turned and looked at Briggs as though he was some horrible animal come up from the sewers. The sergeant spoke condescendingly. "Before you do anything with art you must have a feeling for it, you must realise the statement the artist is trying to make." Loftily he indicated the paintings with a flourish.

"How's about putting the name and description through your indices to see if they're reported stolen" snorted Briggs, irritated.

"I have already done that and they're not, on the face of it, stolen. I just wanted to see them and assess them for myself. The sergeant waved the paintings away. Briggs took them down from the window.

"From that, can I assume it's alright to restore them to their owner" asked Briggs, replacing the paintings on the shelving.

"Yes of course, unless you have any reason to hold on to them." The sergeant swept out of the store, not bothering to wait for Briggs, got into his car, which just had to be an MGB Roadster, and drove out of the yard with much revving of the engine and skidding wheels. Briggs returned to the office. He sat down opposite Jones who was busy on the phone, from the sound of it, placating Christine over some missed duty or unfulfilled promise.

Briggs picked up the phone and rang Ryan's Garage. "Hello, Pat here," said the voice with the unmistakable Southern Irish accent.

"Hello Pat, Briggs here at the station, you can come and pick up your valuable oil paintings." Briggs doodled on the front of a case file.

"So they're not nicked then?" Pat sounded almost disappointed that he was missing out on a further charge of dishonest handling.

Briggs trying to sound helpful replied, "Not according to our Arts and Antiques Squad, they can't find them on their lost or stolen, 'cos if they are nicked they don't know about it and it can't have been a big job."

"Did he give you a value on them?" asked Pat, hopeful in the extreme, and trying to get a free valuation out of being nicked.

"No he didn't and if he had I wouldn't have taken any notice of it. From my own enquiries I can say they are both late Victorian copies of an earlier medieval theme, which is quite often the case. Worth, I should think, a couple of hundred pounds each – no more." Briggs was trying to let Pat down gently.

"Jesus!" said Pat, making it sound like 'Jasus', "I gave a lot for those because I thought that they had been pinched and were valuable," giving a fairly good impression of one who is in love with a pound note.

"Sorry Pat, but you've been taken, happens to us all at one time or another," a strangely prophetic emotion from Briggs. "Anyway when are you going to come and get them?"

There was pause. "Er could you bring them back for me? Only I haven't got a car or a van I can use."

Briggs groaned inwardly as he already had too much to do but said "Okay, I'll be around in a minute."

Briggs put down the phone. Jones was still uttering protestations of undying love to Christine. Briggs waited for him to finish, admiring his style in the meantime. Eventually he put the phone down with a groan. "Tel what am I going to do? She now wants to go on holiday, her and me together. Paris in the Spring or something." Jones sat moaning, head in hands. "What am I going to do?" Briggs was amused at his colleague's discomfort.

"I have absolutely no idea. As you say, I'm not attractive to women, so I really wouldn't know. In the meantime, Casanova, would you give me a hand to get the paintings back to Pat?" Jones nodded, got up and followed Briggs to the property store. They got the pictures and placed them in the back of the police van. Briggs went and winkled the van diver out of the canteen where he was in the middle of an involved game of 'chase the lady'. He stacked his hand, moaning about "Bleedin' CID."

They drove the short distance to the garage in silence. On arrival, Briggs and Jones got the paintings out of the back and took them to the garage.

Briggs said, "Ere you are Pat, your artistic heirlooms delivered back to you." Pat nodded and came out from under the ramp. He came over and examined the paintings in detail.

"They seem alright" he said.

"Good! Then sign the receipt and we'll see you at court on the 15th – don't be late." Briggs dug him playfully in the ribs.

Pat smiled. "Don't be silly, I'm in enough trouble without being late for court," adding in a softer voice, "Can I have a word with you Mr. Briggs?" indicating the rear of the garage. Briggs followed to the indicated area and Jones returned to the van and waited.

"I've come up with a grand which you and Dick Sayers can share. I have it here in the back of the office. You can take it with you now." Pat looked hopefully at Briggs.

"Look Pat I'll tell you what I told Sayers, what I am after is the supplier of the engines. If you're pleased with the way you have been treated you can bung me a drink after the hearing, right have you got that? So keep your dough in your sky and, as I said, if afterwards you're happy we'll have a drink together." Briggs walked briskly away, got into the van and was driven back to Rodney Road in silence, satisfied that he had put Pat on the right road.

Briggs and Jones carried on their individual and joint activities. Briggs had decided to conduct the prosecution of Pat himself, as it seemed likely that he would plead guilty. He did, however, compile statements of evidence from Jones and himself and obtained copies of the Trafpol officers' notes. Fords at Dagenham identified the engines as being their property and were adamant that they could not come from any other source but them because of the sealing bungs all over the engine and carburettor etc. Apparently these bungs were put on during manufacture and taken off just before the engine was fitted in the chassis, the bungs then being returned to the beginning of the production line. Fords, however, could not yet say where the engines came from within their organisation as any loss would not become evident for a number of weeks.

Feeling himself prepared for either a plea or a remand, Briggs attended court on the 15th. Pat was waiting in the ante-room. "Good Jesus, you had me sweating" he exclaimed.

Briggs was puzzled. "What do you mean, you knew I was going to be here today, what's the fuss?"

Pat became conspiratorial, he whispered, "Sayers said he was going to be here for the grand. I have it in my pocket now. Do you want me to hand it over to you now or later?" Briggs was stunned, it appeared that events were being arranged behind his back.

"Pat, I've already told you twice that I don't want your money. Keep it, give me information. I want to know who supplied the engines, shouldn't be too difficult. I understand from Sayers that you're a very successful snout and you've worked for him in the past." As he was in the waiting room surrounded by a number of petty villains he laid stress on the word 'snout'. Almost everyone in the room sat up and looked at Pat. He became red and subsided into silence.

Briggs left Pat in the waiting room and went into court. He announced himself to the court inspector who told him that Pat was represented by counsel. Briggs approached the designated counsel, a red-haired lady with an Irish sounding name. "Should get on well with Pat I should think" thought Briggs.

The lady brief was very professional and very cool towards Briggs but he dismissed this as being just her manner. She informed Briggs that they would be applying for a remand on that day for about six weeks. Briggs nodded and gave her a copy of her client's statement.

As remands are dealt with second on court lists, drunk and disorderly being the first, Briggs got Pat into the cell corridor before entering court.

As they stood there waiting Pat said, "Go on, I have the dough, take it, share it with Sayers later."

Briggs laughed, "I would sooner open the box Pat. I thought we had all this sorted. I told you to keep the money."

Pat looked pained and pleading. "But I can't, it's for Sayers, I've promised it to him." Briggs looked at him closely.

"I don't know what the deal is with Sayers, but it's nothing to do with me or this job, got it?" Pat flinched at this hard tone and looked at his boots.

"But Sayers said…"

Briggs became even more angry. "I don't care what bleedin' Sayers said, this is my job. Listen to me, not him. Keep the dough, I don't want it and you'd be a fool to give it to Sayers – click."

"Call the case of Ryan."

Briggs ushered Pat into court and told him where to stand. He was duly remanded for a period of six weeks.

Briggs made his way back to Rodney Road and took lunch alone in the canteen as Jones was out attending to the carnal needs of Christine. Briggs wasn't surprised that Jones was as skinny as a rake and that he, Briggs, conversely had a weight problem. Only continual exercise of the non-sexual nature kept him trim, well trimish. Briggs was upset about Sayers' continual involvement in the engine job and his meddling about in the enquiry. He resolved to warn him off, bearing in mind that Sayers was the police equivalent of a 'face' – heavy, he had a reputation and was connected to the hierarchy. "No time like the present," thought Briggs. He went back to his office, picked up the phone and rang the internal number for Tower Bridge CID.

"Hello, Tower Bridge CID, Office Manager speaking." Briggs knew the office manager at Tower Bridge and thought that he sounded a lot more efficient than he actually was.

"Yes, Terry Briggs at Rodney Road. Is DS Sayers there?" Briggs thinking that his voice sounded ever so tinny on the line.

"No he's out at the moment. Expected back whenever." The office manager laughed.

"Oh I see, put a message in the book for him to ring me ASAP, and tell him it's urgent. Also that I am not best pleased, not that that will have much effect on him, but still say it." Briggs replaced the phone still feeling that there was something wrong with the line. It was almost as though he was hearing an echo of himself talking.

"Tel" Sid called, waiting for Briggs' attention before continuing, "the Guvnor wants to see you in his office." Sid nodded towards

Jack the Hat's office.

"Right" said Briggs, got up, walked down the office and knocked on the great man's door.

"Enter," bellowed Jack the Hat. Briggs opened the door and went in. Jack the Hat was behind his desk as usual, his trilby hat clamped firmly on his head, his suit jacket hanging over his chair, exposing his bright red braces.

"Come in Tel sit down," Jack the Hat indicating a chair in the corner. Briggs sat down warily. Jack the Hat finished writing on the report attached to the file. "Another squib for Barking, his English is terrible, he'd be better sticking to 'the cat sat on the mat'" Jack the Hat closed the file and put it on one side. Briggs gauged that he was unsettled and maybe a bit nervous. "Now young Tel, just a word in your shell like. About this business with DS Sayers, I understand you've given him the bum's rush over the Ryan job."

Briggs spoke slowly. "Well yes guv, I think it's all a bit dangerous. Ryan's on the sheet, all the evidence has been written up and I can't see how to change it now, nor do I feel inclined to do so." Jack the Hat could tell from previous experience that Briggs was about to explode and knew that after such explosion there would be no discussion, only total war.

"Come on Tel, I can think of five thousand reasons why you should see it our way, plus of course I am not feeling two grand at the moment." Jack the Hat grinned, hoping to amuse Briggs into seeing the situation in a different light.

"Listen guv, it can't be done, do you understand?" Briggs spoke forcefully. "It can't be done. If I do anything that shows out the 'Trafpol' will go absolutely ape." Briggs shook his head, "Can't be done. Plus I don't agree with letting villains out at all, goes against the grain with me and this isn't just a bit of pilfering you know, it's big stuff. Sooner or later Fords will complete their inventory and find themselves dozens of engines short. We don't know how many but Ryan admits they come in loads of ten. When Ford's security get involved the shit will really go fanwise. There must be big organisation to get the engines away and, by the sound of it, another one that Ryan sends them on to. It's not fucking possible to sweep that under the carpet." Briggs made for the door.

"Alright, alright Tel, just thought I would mention it, there's a golden opportunity going begging, that's all. Come on Tel, do it out of respect for your guvnor, why not?" Jack the Hat was pleading, which was unusual for him.

Briggs stood with his hand on the door knob. "If it went boss-eyed and I was lumbered, would you stand up for me – out of respect?" Briggs grimaced at this unlikely outcome.

"Of course I would, I have never been known to run out on my men," Jack the Hat replied hotly and quickly.

"I'll bear that in mind," Briggs said but thought, "I won't hold my breath waiting." He left the office and went back to his desk.

Several days passed in uneventful boredom, shoplifters, suspected persons "loitering with intent" captured by the Aids Squad, numerous burglary and housebreaking investigations etc. etc. passed under the pen of Briggs and Jones, but mostly Briggs. Odd officers kept coming up and pleading the case of Ryan to Briggs, some more senior than Jack the Hat. Briggs gave them all the same answer – "He can have help but not outers." This attitude seemed to upset the very senior ones, who regarded this refusal as some sort of insubordination and got quite huffy about it all. Briggs, once he had stated his case, always stood his ground. The more he was leaned on, the less likely he would be to bend to the wishes of others. Even Jones, who could see the chances of passing the imminent promotion board flying out of the window, tried to get Briggs to see it the way of the majority. These conversations usually ended with Briggs saying to Jones, "Tell em to go and get fucked."

The telephone rang. Briggs picked it up. "CID Rodney Road."

"Tel is that you?" Briggs could not mistake the Wiltshire whine of John Barking.

"Yes John it's me. What do you want?"

"Thank God I've found you. I need your handcuff key and I need it now." Barking sounded almost manic. Briggs laughed. "But you've got one that fits, yours, they're all the same" Briggs said, as though explaining to a four year old how to tie shoe laces.

"Wrong assumption Tel, they do not all fit and I need yours now, ten minutes ago." Barking paused and Briggs thought he sobbed.

"Right then my old Wiltshire moonraker, where do we meet? It's fair to warn you that I must see the licentious purpose to which my handcuffs have been put," Briggs laughing to himself at the thought of one of Barking's old trouts being trussed up long after the heat had gone out of the action.

"Tel, please, don't sod about, her old man is a heavy and is expected home in about an hour, maybe less. He's not going to be too pleased to find his missus chained up with some old bill's handcuffs. Meet me in East Lane outside St Vincents Villas, now!" The phone went dead with a heavy click.

The click was unusual, Briggs wondered idly whether it could be hooked up on the tinkerbell system, but for what purpose? He dismissed it from his mind and concentrated on getting out and running down the lane with his handcuff key. As he trotted along the road, he spotted John some hundred yards ahead who waved as enthusiastically as he might if Briggs were an approaching lover. John took the key with a gruff, "Thanks Tel see you in a minute." He then disappeared quickly into the tenement building, leaving Briggs standing on the kerb pondering his good luck in being almost totally faithful. Briggs wandered back towards the nick and, as he approached, a car passed him in the opposite direction and he immediately recognised DS Sayers at the wheel. The car didn't stop and the driver stared to the front as he passed. "Shit!" said Briggs to himself, but it came out aloud. "I've only been gone twenty minutes and that sod knows I want to talk to him. He must have come over to see me, as nothing else is going on that involves him. Why couldn't he wait and why didn't he stop just now, he must have known it was me?" Puzzled, Briggs made his way back to Rodney Road.

Next day, Briggs and Jones were sitting at their respective desks, Briggs writing furiously, Jones day-dreaming or perhaps exhausted from his supreme efforts in the cause of information gathering. The phone rang and Briggs picked it up on the first ring. "CID Rodney Road," Briggs talking but still looking at the report he was working on.

"Yes Mr. Briggs it's Ryan here. Can we talk?" Ryan whispered as though being overheard by others.

"Yes of course Pat, but why are you whispering?" Briggs' mind was still on the report on his desk.

"I don't know, all this cloak and dagger stuff has got to me I suppose," Pat resuming a normal sort of voice. "Anyway I've got what you want. You know the information." Pat said it slowly for whatever reason.

"Right then Pat, spill the beans old son, I am all ears," Briggs nodding to Jones to pick up the extension.

"Not on the phone Mr. Briggs, come round and I'll explain, only I don't trust telephones." Ryan sounded hunted and in fear which would be in order as, if he was about to grass on the lot who were nicking the engines out of Ford, he was about to put some very heavy people away.

"Fine, Ron and I will be around straight away." Briggs put the phone down on its cradle. "Come on Jonesy, we have to meet an informant on bail."

Briggs and Jones went downstairs to the front office and told the duty officer that they were about to go and meet an informant on bail and requested that the duty officer make an entry in the occurrence book to that effect. Briggs stood and watched as the Inspector wrote in the book and gave the name of his informant as Charles Kent, it being usual to give a pseudonym in such circumstances.

Jones and Briggs drove to Ryan's Garage and parked outside. Briggs looked up and down the road, but could see no obvious evidence of the Cambridge Road mob (A10) as they had became known. They entered the garage. Pat was working underneath a ramp. "Be with you in a second," he called out from under a car. Briggs and Jones wandered around the garage looking at odds and ends whilst Pat completed his task. After a few minutes Pat emerged from beneath the car and approached them. "Sorry about that but I had a gearbox balancing on one stud and had to get it bolted in properly."

"Alright Pat no sweat. Now what have you got for us?" Briggs wishing to get it over with and get on.

"I have it written down in the office." Ryan indicated the side office.

"Won't be a second Ron," said Briggs and followed Ryan into the office. Ryan pulled open a drawer and took a very large brown paper bag out. "This is for you and Mr. Sayers" said Ryan, louder than was strictly necessary. Briggs opened the bag and looked in. It was full of five pound notes.

"I thought we agreed that I was after information not money," Briggs annoyed that Ryan had not taken his instructions on board.

"You've got to have that instead, there is no way I can grass on the people where the gear comes from, or where it's going to. I'll end up dead."

"Look Pat do yourself a favour. Put the money away and we'll forget all about it. Take your chances at court." Briggs offered the money to Ryan.

"No way, it's your money now. I don't know nuthin about it." Ryan folded his arms to accentuate the situation.

"You realise that, if I take this money, I will have to arrest you again on a charge of attempted bribery," Briggs hoping against hope that Ryan would back down, as with an arrest of this nature in the back of his book, none of the villains would ever talk to him again.

"You must do as you like," Ryan mumbled with his head down, avoiding eye contact.

"Right then you're nicked, come on." Briggs took him out of the office and was about to call Jones when several men in plain clothes appeared from the backyard of the garage. One of them, older than the rest, said "Detective Constable Briggs I am arresting you for corruptly accepting this money from Ryan here." He snatched the bag from Briggs.

Briggs was stunned. "Here hold up I've just nicked him." The older officer said, "I must caution you that you are not obliged to say anything unless you wish to do so, but what you say may be put into writing and given in evidence."

"I have just told you dickhead I've just nicked him." Briggs raised his voice, annoyed and, if truth be told, frightened.

"Save it for the interrogation you bent bastard," a small tubby officer with cold clammy hands said as he grabbed hold of Briggs. He was bundled outside the garage and put into a car. He could see Jones in another car and could gauge from his face that he was frightened.

They drove in silence to Rodney Road Police Station where Briggs was placed in one of the men's cells and Jones he thought was in one of the women's.

The Station Sergeant came into the cell accompanied by the little fat sergeant. The Station Sergeant spoke apologetically. "Sorry about this Tel, but I have to ask you to turn out your pockets." The Sergeant seemed genuinely sorry.

"Don't apologise to him, he's bent," said the little fat sergeant full of messianic zeal and hope of promotion. Briggs hit him as hard as he could and immediately felt a lot better. The A10 man fell in a crumpled heap in the corner. "Right that's another charge. Assault on police" he screamed.

"I never saw a thing and in any case you were begging for it" the Station Sergeant murmured, pleased to be on the side of Briggs. "I wish I had done it myself. Now Tel please turn out your pockets and I think we can dispense with the violent responses, seeing as how I asked politely." Briggs turned out his pockets as directed and the Sergeant noted the times on the detention book. He signed at the bottom and Briggs countersigned it as being correct.

The A10 officer stood in the doorway of the cell, shrugging his shoulders and giving Briggs the Reggie Kray look. "We'll be questioning you later and just make sure you give us straight answers else we might have to bend a few rules," which caused Briggs to smile. He was here for allegedly bending the rules. Briggs was sitting on the bench. He looked up at the A10 man and said coldly, "Fatty, I would fuck off if I were you else I might just take you seriously, go home to your Mum and have nice cuddle."

The door slammed and Briggs was left to his thoughts. He tried and tried to analyse the situation but, in the end, feeling that such thoughts were too confused, he got the mattress, unfolded and got on it. He covered himself with a smelly blanket and tried to sleep. He largely failed but, through the exhaustion of gut retching concern dozed fitfully.

However, long after, the door burst open and two A10 officers entered, one was the older who'd arrested him. "We are going to put some questions to you. You are still under caution." The younger one, presumably a Sergeant, began to write.

"Save yourself the trouble, I am answering no questions at all," Briggs speaking to the older one who braced himself. "I, being your senior officer am entitled to call for a duty report on this incident from you, which I am now doing."

"And," said Briggs, "being an official report, it's admissible in evidence, correct?"

The older officer hesitated, "Correct, but it is your first duty to obey your senior officer." The older officer pulled himself up to his full height.

"Go fuck yourself you slimy bastard," mumbled Briggs as he turned over and pulled the blanket over his head. "Get up and show some respect." The note taker barked. The words acted as a goad.

Briggs got up quickly and in so doing, frightened the interrogator and his note taker both of whom moved out of harm's way. "Respect you prick, you talk to me of respect, you go and earn some and I'll give you some," roared Briggs. "Now sod off and leave me alone. Go and talk to Jones, I'm sure he'll be impressed by you."

"Interview terminated 5.30pm" intoned the interrogator. The sergeant wrote furiously. "Hang on, I'll read and sign your notes. Briggs got up and walked towards the Sergeant, who backed away.

"No, no that's not allowed, we don't allow prisoners to sign our notes." The interrogator expounded policy, smug in his little world. Briggs pressed the bell push to call the custody sergeant, who arrived very quickly – almost before the bell finished ringing.

"Yes DC Briggs what can I do for you?" The skipper, well known to Briggs, was deadpan and serious. "Sergeant, I have requested to sign the notes of interrogation made by these officers and they have refused. I would like you to enter this conversation between you and me in the occurrence book, including the fact that I have requested to sign their notes and that they have refused. Will you do that for me?" Briggs looked hopefully at the Sergeant.

"I am duty bound to record all requests made by prisoners, which is what you are at present. I should record it on your charge sheet, but as you do not have one I will enter it in the occurrence book, you have my word." The Sergeant almost bowed as he retired.

"Now the best thing you can do is clear off, I am saying nothing more to you, or to anyone else at the moment." Briggs sat down on the cell bed.

The sergeant put his millboard on the end of the bed. He tried to muster a menacing look but was much too young to achieve it. "I should keep a civil tongue in your head Briggs or life could get painful." Briggs felt that what the young Sergeant meant to say was, "Look at me Guvnor, I am doing the business for you." Briggs smiled, certainly not in fear of this gentle young man with a strange view of career planing.

"Look mate, don't be silly, honour is satisfied, your guvnor here has heard it and no doubt you will go to the top, now leave or you might get hurt." Briggs laid down on the bed and ignored them. After a few moments they left the cell.

Briggs laid on his hard bed and considered his predicament. Thank God he had not told Jones anything about what Sayers had said or Jack the Hat's overtures about 'Golden Opportunities', so all Jones could do was cry and protest his innocence. Briggs mulled over the operation in its entirety and decided that, altogether, he had been far too confident of himself, a recurring failure which he managed to carry off on most occasions and this one was still to be decided.

The cell door was flung open and the little fat Sergeant entered, accompanied by a tall, heavy built officer that Briggs didn't know. "Come on Briggs the guvnor wants to see you." Briggs got up from his bench and stood before the little fat Sergeant.

"That eye is bluing up nicely, did you walk into a door or something?" Briggs doing his best to smile.

The heavy built officer snapped, "Watch it smart arse or else."

Briggs turned on him, "Or else what? Your mouth is writing cheques your body can't honour – fuck off." The heavy built officer made a move towards Briggs.

The little fat Sergeant spoke to both of them, "Behave yourselves the pair of you, and you Briggs do as you're told," little fatty giving a fair impression of a military sergeant. Once he was content that order had been re-established the little fat Sergeant took Briggs by the elbow and led him out of the cell. The heavy built officer treated Briggs to a hard man's stare, whether he was a real one or not Briggs couldn't establish, but in case he wasn't, Briggs blew him a kiss.

All three together, they walked through the canteen, where all conversation ceased and the assembled occupants stared horrified as Briggs was led through their company. Absolute silence reigned. Briggs felt inclined to drop his head, not in shame, but through embarrassment. "Come on Tel, keep your head up, your worth ten of those turds," called Albert Hendry. By way of support from the back of the assembled PC's came, "Yeah go on Tel show 'em the way home."

They trudged up the stairs in silence, walking the length of the

CID office. The officers still on duty studied their desks and paperwork as though they had never seen Briggs before – ever. The escorts and prisoner halted outside the guvnor's office, where they waited in the hallway. Briggs could hear raised voices from within Jack the Hat's office but couldn't make out what was being said. A few minutes later, they were joined by Jones and his escort.

"You alright Ron?" Briggs asked, genuinely concerned as Ron looked decidedly seedy.

"I think so," said Ron "No thanks to you," Jones showing how upset he was with his buck. "Be quiet you two" snapped the little fat Sergeant, pushing the military impersonation to the hilt. "Arseholes," Briggs not at all entering into the spirit engendered by the little fat Sergeant. The office door opened "Detective Constables Briggs and Jones, come in please." Jack the Hat invited them into the office.

They both entered the office and stood before the desk, behind which was seated Detective Chief Superintendent Bolton and on the desk before him were two type-written sheets. He sat there exposing his bald patch and read both sheets with his Charlie Moffat pen poised in his hand.

Eventually he said, "Serious allegations have been made against you two, including various tape recordings of conversations between you (indicating Briggs) and a suspect on remand. It is my unfortunate duty to suspend you both from duty. Have you anything to say before I serve these notices on you?"

"Yes sir," said Briggs forcibly, "I would. I'd like to hear more about these bleedin' tapes, which incidentally have now been mentioned for the first time, and to ask for copies and transcripts of the conversations." Bolton looked up from the notices.

"In due time Briggs, in due time" said Bolton, reacting to Briggs' accusing tone.

"There is considerably more investigation to be carried out before such information is released. However I have heard extracts from those tapes and have seen the money. I have to say that I believe the evidence to be most damning and more than justifies your suspension and that of DS Sayers. I should add that I find it unforgivable that you should exhibit such belligerence under the circumstances surrounding your suspension, but that of course is what we have come to expect from you Briggs."

"In that case," continued Briggs with undiminished animosity, "I'd like to say how admirable it is that senior officers stand up for their troops against pressure from the dirty tricks department and also sir, I would like to say that is a very nice pen you have there as befits a man of your high rank." Jack the Hat was annoyed but said nothing.

Bolton looked embarrassed and said, "That's enough of that Briggs."

But Briggs continued, "I don't think that's nearly enough, but more of that later, I would ask you sir (looking directly at Jack the Hat) to remember that you have never been known to run out on your officers." Jack the Hat could not hold the stare and his head went down. Jones made a sniffing sound and as Briggs looked at him, he spoke, somewhat waveringly, for the first time. "Sir, I have done nothing wrong, why should I be suspended? I am innocent." Jones began to cry, great tears welling up in his eyes and falling down his cheeks. The entire population of that office, Jones apart, fell into embarrassed silence.

Eventually Bolton broke the spell and gave them each a copy of the suspension notice saying, "I advise you both to go home and stay there. Do not contact any police officer or anyone connected with this case. Do you understand?" Briggs nodded.

"Of course. But where is the presumption of innocence in our case?" knowing the answer before it came but wanting to expose the nonsense of what Bolton had said.

"Don't worry about that," replied Bolton. "It doesn't apply in these cases. Hand over your warrant cards."

Briggs hesitated, tempted to tell Bolton what he thought and felt. Jones had his warrant card out in a flash and Briggs reluctantly followed suit by throwing it on the desk. Jack the Hat was about to say something but changed his mind. Bolton shook his head and waved them both out of his presence.

Briggs and Jones left the office and walked down the yard together, Jones still drying his tears by pretending he had something in his eye. His voice betrayed the pretence. "Well Tel, you've finally done it, pushed the system too far. We're now deep in the shit and it's official."

"Sorry mate" offered Briggs. "I tried hard to avoid it but there's more to this than just a bit of bunging and I'm not even guilty of that. I bet that Sayers fits in this somewhere."

Briggs was hoping against hope that there was more to it and his mind was racing at the possible implications. Who was behind it all? Sayers, certainly, but it sounded as though he was being suspended as well. Why had he been set up? Why were so many senior officers keen to see Pat Ryan walk away? Jones interrupted his thoughts "Anyway it's done now, how am I ever going to explain it to the church?" Jones was obviously contemplating his destiny.

Briggs would have none of that. "Why not explain it to the wife first and see how you get on in that direction before worrying about the sky pilots."

"That's okay if you're not involved with them, but I am," whined Jones, "I feel gutted and it's all your fault." Jones was secretly disgusted with himself at his own acquiescence throughout the affair. He would liked to have been more like Briggs and fought back, but he knew he would never have the bottle to attempt such a thing. Anyway it WAS Briggs' fault, he always had to buck the system and now it had bitten them both.

Briggs voiced his resignation aloud, "The best I can tell you Ron is that, in a strange way, I feel relieved, like I just got off the merry-go-round. It's still whizzing around but at least I'm not on it any more."

They parted for the very last time as almost friends. They went with their own thoughts to their own cars and each drove home alone.

Coming to Earth

Briggs stood at the bar of the public house, contemplating his pint. He'd phoned Ron, suggesting a meet to discuss their problems, at the very least, to share a friendly drink. Jones in turn had suggested this pub in the Mile End Road, it being well away from their ground. As he stood with his drink, Briggs mulled over the circumstances of yesterday, he couldn't follow the sequence of events at all and surmised that, as his suspension went on, things would become clearer. At least he fervently hoped they would become clearer.

"You Briggs?" the barman asked from the end of the bar and speaking directly to him.

"Yes that's me," Briggs surprised and wondering what was next on the agenda.

"Phone call for you." The barman nodded towards the back office.

Briggs walked around the bar, entered the office and picked up the telephone which was off the hook. "Hello," Briggs said tentatively into the handset.

"Tel it's me," Jones' Welsh accent was unmistakable.

"Ron you're supposed to be here meeting me, where the hell are you?" Briggs in a not-too-gentle voice, being perplexed at the need for a phone call instead of meeting face to face and yet another example of things going awry.

"At home mate, I had a word with Jack the Hat and he advised me not to come. He said it would jeopardise my defence and all that. Sorry mate." Jones' shame came through in the conversation.

"Ron my fucking cat has got more bottle than you and he's scared

294

of his own shadow," Briggs exclaimed as he slammed the phone down without waiting for a response.

On re-entering the bar, he noticed a man, standing at the bar with a woman, whom he recognised as a copper he'd seen on a course at Hendon once. He didn't want to talk to anyone but he looked into their eyes for some sign of recognition but received none as they deliberately averted their gaze and avoided looking directly at him. Briggs returned to his drink and finished it slowly, not looking at the couple, who he was now sure were from A10, or some other such organisation. He pondered that if Jones had told Jack the Hat then maybe other interested colleagues had been informed.

Once he finished his drink, he walked over to them in spiteful mood and said, "I'm now going home through the Blackwall Tunnel and will stay there until tomorrow morning when I will leave at 9am or thereabouts. Will that be alright?" The woman turned her back on him and the bloke smiled and put his glass down.

"I don't know you do I?" He said it pleasantly but without conviction.

"You do know me, I was on the Detective Training Course when you were on the skipper's make up course. Now do you remember me? You ought to be ashamed of yourself." Briggs spat the words out, turned on his heel and walked out of the pub, relieved to be in the fresh air. He could see that the rubber heel pair who claimed they didn't know him, left by another door and were scurrying towards a car parked in the side road. Briggs got into his old Austin Cambridge, started it up and waited until, eventually, the rubber heeled pair came slowly along the road in their white Volvo, probably expecting to see his tail lights receding in the distance. As they passed he pulled out and followed them closely behind. The cars drove slowly down the Mile End Road towards the Blackwall Tunnel with Briggs twenty yards behind. Suddenly the woman passenger looked behind and, recognising Briggs, said something to the driver who pulled over to the side of the road. It seemed to him that they had to have been told of his presence and, looking into his rear view mirror, he noticed a dark coloured Hillman Hunter with one occupant following him. Briggs couldn't see if it had two aerials or not but decided to treat it with suspicion anyway.

As he passed the white Volvo he treated the occupants to what can only be described as a Queen Mother wave and drove on towards the Blackwall Tunnel, the Hillman staying with him but about twenty yards behind. Briggs increased speed and the Hillman stayed with him. Briggs went on to the approach road to the tunnel and pulled up behind a line of waiting traffic, the Hillman still with him. The inactivity of waiting in traffic gave him an opportunity to study the driver of the Hillman and in the stark electric light of the tunnel approach, he appeared about forty years of age, with a dark moustache, fairly small build and dressed in dark clothing. Briggs moved off with the traffic and the Hillman followed, now closely. Briggs pulled on to the roundabout and about halfway around, gunned the ageing Austin to new heights of acceleration entering the approach road to the tunnel at increasing speed.

Briggs could see in his rear view mirror that the Hillman was increasing speed in an effort to catch up with him, indicating without doubt that he was being tailed home. Briggs drove along the approach road at a fairly fast rate and as Stepney High Street loomed up, without decreasing speed, he suddenly turned into the exit, causing the Austin to roll violently but, thankfully, staying on the road. Briggs checked the Hillman and noticed with amusement that it had just about managed to follow his car into the exit.

Briggs drove as fast as his old machinery would allow him, entering the main Stepney High Street by turning right into it and promptly turning left again, back on to the tunnel approach. Not expecting such a quick change the Hillman screeched a warning but managed to negotiate the corner and get on to the tunnel approach behind Briggs.

The lights turned to green and Briggs drove through the tunnel, not trying now to 'shake his tail'. They carried on through the tunnel at a law abiding rate and Briggs noticed the occupant of the Hillman pick up a radio handset and speak into it. Briggs smiled at the probable lack of success he would experience attempting to transmit whilst in the tunnel.

Once on the other side, Briggs suddenly increased his speed, hoping that, in so doing, he might stop his follower from transmitting his latest efforts at tracker avoidance. He drove furiously towards the Tunnel Approach exit for Greenwich and turned down on to it, not braking as he entered the roundabout at the bottom but steaming straight across the traffic, causing an oncoming motorist to swerve and hoot in annoyance. He was gaining slightly on the Hillman as he turned off the roundabout towards Greenwich but almost immediately turned into a small cul-de-sac (which Jones had mentioned as being used for some of his illicit trysts with Christine), drove about halfway along and parked in the line of cars. Some seconds later, the Hillman came hurtling into the cul-de-sac, passed Briggs round the slight bend ahead and screeched to a halt. Briggs pulled out, drove behind the Hillman, got out quickly and ran to the driver's side. He wrenched open the driver's door in time to snatch the radio handset from his opponent's grasp.

"You, out," ordered Briggs and the other driver obeyed quietly. Briggs threw the handset back inside the car. "Now shithead, what's the bottom line on this then?" Briggs treated the driver to his meanest look as he spoke with his face closer to the other.

"I don't know what you mean, I was on my way home," spluttered the driver who Briggs could see clearly now was terrified. Briggs pushed him up against the Hillman and went through his pockets, the driver not resisting. Briggs felt him tremble under his hand which he took to be fear, as under the present circumstances sexual excitement seemed unlikely. Briggs threw the contents of the driver's pocket onto the roof of the Hillman and in a fold over wallet, found a plastic covered identification card which looked vaguely like a warrant card, but not quite. Examining it closely he discovered it to be the identification card of Warrant Officer Second Class Hollowell of the RMP, which Briggs knew quite well to be the Corps of Military Police. Briggs also noted that the regimental number of Hollowell was almost contemporary to his own old army number.

"What's a squaddy old bill doing following a real old bill?" Briggs asked quietly, whilst going through the other contents of the wallet. "We're seconded to the Met for training in surveillance duties. I was told to follow you that's all." Hollowell looked like a little boy about to get the cane.

"You must think I came down the Clyde on a water biscuit you dope," Briggs said as he clumped Hollowell and enjoyed it.

Just then the car radio squawked, "Oscar Papa one, one are you still in contact with the subject?" Oscar Papa control over."

Briggs smiled at Hollowell and queried, "Is he talking about me dipstick?" As Hollowell nodded, Briggs picked up the handset, clicked the transmission button and said "Oscar Papa Control, Oscar Papa control from Oscar Papa one one, this is Detective Constable Briggs brackets suspended. WO2Hollowell is being interviewed by me at the present time regarding his suspicious behaviour."

Briggs clicked off and the radio was quiet for a few seconds until it erupted, "Last caller say again, last caller say again."

Briggs switched the radio off and took the ignition keys from the steering lock. He looked at the dejected Hollowell as he took the man's wallet with identification card and, together with the ignition keys, threw them over a garden wall. Briggs got into his car, reversed out of the cul-de-sac and drove towards home by a circuitous route. About half a mile from his house, Briggs pulled over, parked the Cambridge in a side road and made his way home over the walls of back gardens until almost next to his home, when he laid down under a neighbour's hedge listening for developments, for about three quarters of an hour. Apart from cars coming in and out of the cul-de-sac, which he presumed to be the rubber heel mob checking on his address, there was little activity, so it appeared there were no 'on foot' observations going on. He climbed out of his hide and went indoors and, almost immediately, went to bed to sleep the unsound sleep of the very worried.

One morning a few days later, and still idling his time with his mind in turmoil, Briggs was reading the Telegraph with his youngest, Tommy to whom breakfast had become a secondary consideration. "Why doesn't it have lots of pictures?" queried young Tommy, interested in the strange comic that Dad was reading.

"Well, the writing is like pictures when you can read it," Briggs said turning to the sports page.

"When will I be able read it?" asked Tommy with innocent mischief all over his face.

"When you have been to school and they've taught you how," said Briggs noticing that the Met Police Rugby Club had been stuffed by Maesteg.

"But I go to school now and I still can't read."

Briggs was about to offer some further implausible answer but luckily, was saved from further difficulty by the ringing telephone. Briggs went into the hall, picked up the strident instrument with, "Hello!"

"That's you isn't it Tel?" Briggs' mind raced to identify the voice. It was familiar but he couldn't place it and, under the present circumstances, being suspended, playing guessing games on the phone was not on.

"Yes it's me" Briggs answered slowly.

"No names no usual, old son. I met you at your caravan last year in Whitstable, I am the boy friend of your old girl friend, have you got me?" The voice paused.

"Yes I know who you are," replied Briggs, remembering the flash Detective Sergeant who had shacked up in is caravan with one of his boyhood sweethearts.

"Do you remember discussing a game of cricket played on a village green. We were laughing about the antics of the vicar?"

"Yes I remember," Briggs picturing the Chislehurst Common ground as he last saw it.

"Meet me there soonest and be careful you're not followed. Oh and by the way, if you don't know, your phone is on the tinkerbell." The phone went dead as the Sergeant rang off.

Briggs went next door where his friend agreed his request and, being such a friend, did so without asking for explanations. Briggs exited from the house by the bottom of the garden and into the lane that ran along the back. For a few minutes he stood inside a hawthorn bush and ignored the prickles. Being satisfied no observation was being kept in this area he hurried along the path and waited in the shade of an elderflower bush. After a short while there was a toot of a car horn just loud enough to catch his attention and Briggs came out. Approaching the car, the neighbour got out and Briggs got in the driver's seat. "Be lucky Tel" said the neighbour as he closed the door, to which Briggs smiled grimly and drove off.

Briggs kept to the back streets as far as possible, keeping a wary watch for following vehicles. He arrived at Chislehurst Common, drove round it for few minutes and being satisfied, or as satisfied as he could be expected to be, parked near the Tiger's Head Pub and wandered towards the cricket pitch. Passing the boundary nearest the pub, he saw the Sergeant in the distance throwing sticks for a brown and white Springer Spaniel, Briggs approached him, looking around all the time, "Alright mate?" the Sergeant asked. He stopped throwing the stick so that the dog sat and panted with expectation at his feet.

"Well, no, as you mention it, I have felt better, but at least I'm alive." Briggs grimaced at his own ironic words and the Sergeant joined in with, "They say that about you, 'never say die'."

The Sergeant came closer to him and patted him down paying particular attention to the inside of his jacket and trouser pockets "Just the formalities. If you'd done the same thing you would have been alright."

Briggs snorted, "Do you know skip, I've always considered hindsight to be a wonderful thing. It can make you appear really clever you know."

The Sergeant nodded, continued his search and said, "Right then, the message is "Keep your bottle intact and you will be okay." There's something moody about the tapes, some think they've been tampered with, bits cut out and all that. Also the Sayers' suspension doesn't seem to fit all that well." The Sergeant examined the boundary as they spoke.

"How come you know this?" asked the puzzled Briggs. Puzzled not only by the message, but also by the involvement of this Sergeant, whom he had never rated as anything special and didn't really know that well.

"My buck from aiding days is, or rather was, the investigating officer in this lot. He asked to be relieved as he says it's a fit up, too dirty for him, some heavy people have got it in for you I'm afraid my old son." The Sergeant shrugged his shoulders. "The other thing that he said was, "Will you stop pissing about with the tails on you, just go about your business. No more stopping them, or rather trapping them and generally making everyone look pricks. It's not regarded as friendly, plus of course it makes them suspect you're up to something, whereas no doubt, you are merely exercising your bloody strange sense of humour." The Sergeant nodded expecting Briggs to follow suit, but he didn't.

"Tel me skip, how comes a WO out of the Red Caps is detailed to follow me? What's that all about?" Briggs was still mystified by the dopey Hollowell.

"I told you some heavy people are after your blood and I shouldn't be surprised if they don't get a taste of it in the end." The

Sergeant threw the stick for the now excited spaniel as he spoke. "If I call again, I'll arrange for us to meet at our local, which will be the Director General pub on the corner of Whitefoot Lane. We'll change thereafter as we go ok?" Briggs nodded and the Sergeant made off towards Eltham. He obviously had a car somewhere but Briggs never saw it.

Briggs wandered back to his neighbour's car. He looked around but no-one seemed to be showing any interest in him or the Sergeant so he got in and drove home. He gave the keys back to his friend and retired to his front room to think deeply. Several hours later the jangle of the phone interrupted his worried thoughts.

"Hello Tel, it's Hymie remember?" said the voice on the phone, which Briggs recognised straight away, stopping himself from saying Hymie's real name.

"I do indeed, the owner of the beat up Paris Ambulance." Briggs was buoyed up by contact with an old friend, a still serving member of the Police Force.

"You remember doing that bit of welding on my old car?" Hymie referred to an afternoon they had spent in Briggs' garage trying to weld good metal to rust flakes.

"Yes I do and I still have the scars" Briggs responded, laughing and pleased to be talking to someone who didn't behave as though Briggs was a pariah.

"Do me a favour will you, get it ready so that I can drive the old heap in this afternoon, there's something wrong with the brakes." Hymie rang off.

Briggs would do as Hymie asked but was a little puzzled as he knew that Hymie was unlikely to drive to his house in his car or anyone else's for that matter. He considered he might turn up on a motor bike as he had two old Vincents and a Japanese bike, the make of which Hymie could never remember or pronounce therefore he called it his "Yamahonduki."

Briggs went outside and reversed his old Cambridge onto the road outside his house, leaving the driveway clear. He looked up and down the road, but there were no signs of observation vans and the like. He then lifted the up and over doors of his garage and went and sat on the bench and waited developments. Some minutes later he heard the monotonous beat of a large single cylinder motor cycle.

Briggs got off the bench as he felt that Hymie was quite close. Another few seconds and Hymie turned into his drive and drove directly into the garage, when Briggs dropped the up and over door behind him. Hymie cut the large engine of the Vincent, it stopped with a hesitant wheeze and remained ticking whilst Hymie disrobed. He took his large English crash helmet off, unwound the college scarf that his facial features and eventually climbed out of his ex Army 'all in ones'. He stood before Briggs tubby and smiling. "How you doing Briggsy, you found God yet and told the truth?"

"I'm withstanding the temptation at the moment but if the urge ever becomes too much, I'll put you in the frame first. I could start with that job where we kept obbo from the church, that would do for a start." They laughed in remembrance. Hymie left his gear in the garage with his hot ticking Vincent and they walked together across the garden into the house where Briggs plugged the kettle in asking, "Tea or coffee?" and looking to Hymie for a decision.

"Either mate, if my memory serves me right, whichever you make it all tastes the same."

"Then coffee it is," Briggs said as he busied himself making the drink while Hymie sprawled out on the easy chair near the window.

"They're well watching you, you know. I passed two motors, each one covering an approach to your cul-de-sac. Mind you, they were both crewed by dipsticks and didn't seem to take any notice of me at all, very odd." Hymie seemed puzzled, "Could it be that they're not experienced in the subject of surveillance?" Briggs pondered a recurring thought while waiting for the kettle to boil.

"Unlikely mate. If they're from A10, they must know what they are on about. Mind you I didn't recognise any of them which seems strange. I've seen most of A10 at one time or another." Hymie seemed puzzled by it all.

"I was tailed the other night by a WO2 from the redcaps," said Briggs, dropping the bombshell.

"Get off, how do you know? You sure you weren't on the turps, tired and emotional like?" Hymie smiled at the prospect.

"No way, I pulled him out of the motor and scanned his ID. Anyway he admitted it, definitely the Military Police." Briggs handed Hymie a hot cup of coffee.

"So that's what they were on about," mused Hymie. "Apparently the other night there was a tailing job that went badly wrong and the mark pulls the tail and whacks him – you?" Briggs nodded without answering. "I might have known it" said Hymie shaking his head. "So what's the SP on this lot then. Have they got you or what? Is it a fit up?"

"It's a fit up yes, but I don't know why. As to have they got me? I don't know, remains to be seen." Briggs was determined to remain silent about his inner feelings of the situation, even to a tried and trusted friend such as Hymie.

"Anyway, I'm really here to say, 'Keep your chin up'. If you ring me, use the public phone and the first meet will be Hall Place at Bexley, twenty minutes after the phone call okay?" Hymie said sipping his coffee and smiling into his mug as he continued, "One thing that doesn't change is that your coffee is as awful as ever. Seriously, something you should know is that they've circulated everyone who knows or has served with you. They've warned them off from contacting you. So, old son, apart from me, because I'm too stupid to obey, you are strictly on your own, forget what good works you've done in the past, that's history and means nothing when the shit hits the fan."

Briggs nodded, the facts coming home to him, "Thanks for taking the risk mate, you're the only one," Briggs meaning every word.

"That's alright mate, as I say I'm just too stupid," Hymie mumbled into his cup, embarrassed that he couldn't do more than offer friendship. He grinned, as he raised his head, "Any brandy about to make this coffee almost drinkable?" Briggs laughed and got out the brandy bottle and two glasses.

They spent the rest of the afternoon gossiping and emptying Briggs' brandy bottle. Eventually Hymie got unsteadily to his feet. He insisted on getting dressed and taking his ancient Vincent Motor cycle from the garage to drive home, even after assurances that Briggs didn't have any designs on the rusty heap of scrap metal. Briggs watched Hymie ride off down the road from his front room window and fervently thanked the Almighty for the calibre of this one good friend.

Life for Briggs became very family orientated as none of those formerly regarded as friends would have anything to do with him, with the notable exception of Hymie who seemed to enquire daily through his neighbour as to his state of health and spirits. Briggs occupied his time with decorating and gardening. After about two months, the house was completely redecorated and the garden looked as though it came from a page of 'Gardener's World'.

Terry Briggs sat in his front room, not admiring his handiwork but just contemplating his next time-consuming endeavour. Police Regulations forbade him from getting involved in any secondary occupation for money, the insistence being that he had to stay at home and sweat it out. As Briggs studied his surroundings, it seemed to him that the front room had begun to move. Ever so slightly, things were definitely on the move. Briggs blinked his eyes to re-clear them, thinking that something had upset the focus of his eyes but when he refocused, the room was getting bigger and bigger whilst he seemed to be getting smaller and smaller, until he felt as though he was in a huge dark cavern. He was frightened and ran out into the garden but, although he was relieved to be in the open air he still felt enclosed.

He put a lead on the family pooch and treated him to a fast march of some six miles, forcing himself to sweat and the dog to wheeze with surprise. On his return home the dog collapsed on the hall mat and Briggs went back into the front room. Although he still felt strange, things had at least re-established themselves normally in terms of size.

Briggs felt sick and went to the kitchen for water, which he drank in fast gulps, Briggs tried to consider his predicament in another light. Having been very active, he had been forced into idleness. His mental condition was rebelling against inactivity and, at the same time, the pressure of his predicament. He had to do something, anything, to preserve his sanity.

Sometime later that same day, Briggs went next door and rang an old mate who ran a lorry driver's agency, arranging to start work next morning driving a nineteen ton Arctic between Barking and Dover, taking one down and bringing another back. The money offered was derisory but Briggs wasn't interested in money, he was frightened at the inactivity and the mind bending events that had occurred in his front room and so, at 7.30am the next morning Briggs walked into the yard of Swordsman Transport in River Road, Barking.

The yard foreman did not look up from his Daily Mirror but

grunted, "Agency driver?" Briggs mumbled the affirmative reply. "The Volvo over there, it's hooked up and ready to go. Take it to Dover, meet one of our Continental drivers there and bring his rig back, simple innit?" Briggs took the offered manifest and walked out of the office without comment.

He climbed up into the cab of the artic, hoping against hope that he could get the thing started and going, but he needn't have worried, it was simplicity itself. Briggs quickly got the Volvo started, checked the air brake pressure and fuel levels and was on his way. He drove into the East End rush hour and through the Blackwall Tunnel going south. He had no problem in traffic, as the trailer was lightly loaded, but once on the open road it took him a few attempts to get used to the complicated splitter box. Having mastered that, he settled down and drove to Dover where he handed over the vehicle in the lorry park and exchanged it for an ERF and trailer. He immediately drove back to Barking where he reversed the unit back against the loading bay and, having felt it touch lightly, he put the handbrake on and left the vehicle in gear.

Climbing down from the cab he was confronted by the yard foreman, "You made good time, you looking for promotion or somfink?" The foreman sniffed a dewdrop back to its origins. "Got your union card, we're all strict union here like." Briggs was flummoxed.

"Nah ain't got it with me have I brother."

The yard foreman made a note on his millboard. "You should have your union card with you at all times, in the rules ain't it. Bring it with you tomorrow. anyway, why are you so early?" Briggs thought for a moment and couldn't work out why but he concluded that everyone else had a kip in a layby.

"Well I never had a break at Dover, you know, should've really but I wanted to get back before the traffic. Perhaps I can take my break now at the end of my journey like."

The yard foreman took a sharp intake of breath. "Many brothers have suffered many strikes and privations so that you young drivers could have a break in the middle of their journeys and now you're ignoring their sacrifices. Unity Brother unity, that's the way forward."

Briggs felt like issuing one of his customary greetings such as 'get stuffed' but decided against it as he really had to take rubbish from the Transport Section of Militant Tendency. "Sorry about that Brother, I'll bear it in mind in future."

The yard foreman nodded sagely "Just make sure you do." The yard foreman took his manifest and clipped it to his millboard. "You might as well catch a flyer." He tossed the words over his shoulder as he walked away towards his office.

Briggs left the yard and headed for his friend's drivers' agency where he met up with him in his office, explaining his predicament of not being a member of any recognised union. "No problem." muttered his friend as he rummaged though the desk drawer, eventually producing what looked like an old fashioned driving licence. "Here you are Tel, you are now Mr. J.P. McGuiness of the Transport and General Workers Union, don't worry it's fully paid up, for just such an eventuality you see." Briggs looked closely at the union card, memorising his new name. "And here's your HGV 1 licence to match, now go and earn me a fortune." Briggs thanked him and stumbled out into the sunshine, still feeling very Briggsish and not at all McGuiness like.

The next morning Briggs presented himself at the transport yard at 6.30am, early so that he could show his credentials. He found the yard foreman sitting on his perch in the office. "Here you go guv, my union card and my HGV1." Briggs put the documents on his desk. The yard foreman sniffed and picked them up. He opened the union card and sniffed derisively.

"Wrong fucking union ain't it, we're the Highways Section of the Road Haulage Association, you'll have to join our union. Closed shop see." The foreman explained it as though it was eminently sensible, but if so, it was completely lost on Briggs.

"You go fuck yourself, I'm fully paid up on that one and if you're an example of your union I don't want to join, and you know full well I don't have to." Briggs took his documents from his foreman and looked fiercely into his eyes.

"Well if you put it like that young man." The foreman sniffed again, "The Scania in the corner, it's got a right load on, I just hope the motorway police don't give you a tug. Keep your speed down and perhaps they won't notice eh?" Briggs nodded, walked out into the yard, climbed up into the Scania and started it up. He checked the gauges and went to drive away but it felt as though the handbrake was still on. The foreman was right it was overloaded and if he was caught with this lot on the motorway he would be disqualified, or rather McGuiness would. He drove cautiously out of town and onto the A2, keeping a very tight rein on his speed and resisting the temptation to join the wacky races that seemed to be the norm on the way to Dover. Thankfully, he turned into the lorry park at Dover and was immediately flagged down by another driver, who indicated another Swordsman lorry where Briggs parked alongside and got out. He swapped manifests with the other driver and climbed up into this new lorry almost without a word and drove off, deciding that he didn't want to get involved in the transport section of café society.

Briggs got back to the yard and had reversed the lorry onto the bank when he saw a dark haired heavy built man about his own age hovering about. Briggs put on the handbrake and switched off. The engine stopped with a wheeze and a sigh. Briggs climbed out of the cab, the heavy man walked purposely towards him. Sensing trouble Briggs walked out into a clear area of the car park, just in case. "Oi, you, I want a word" said the heavy, who shook his shoulders in menace as he came forward.

"Yes, what's the problem mate?" Briggs asked, forcing himself to be pleasant, and crouching in the accepted servile manner

Encouraged the heavy said, "You dealt some shit out to our foreman this morning like and we don't like that see." The heavy punctuated his little speech with jabbing Briggs in the chest with his forefinger. Briggs reeled back feigning alarm.

"Here hold up, I didn't mean nothing like." Briggs cringed, holding his hands up and outwardly pleading forgiveness, but really waiting for the moment he hoped would come.

Supremely confident the heavy said, "And we don't take none of that from the likes of you, see turd." The heavy swung a ponderous blow at the head of Briggs but he stepped forward and the blow landed on the back of his shoulder with almost no force. Briggs heaved an uppercut into the heavy's solar plexus and was satisfied to hear him gasp with pain. Briggs grasped the heavy's belt and held him up. A split second later the heavy's head came up and Briggs struck him a sharp blow with his forehead. The heavy cried out in pain and Briggs let go of his belt and let him fall to the floor. Briggs looked at him lying there, blood was flowing from his eye area where he been 'nutted'. Obviously a case of split lid. Briggs kicked him hard in the balls, the heavy screamed in agony.

Briggs knelt down beside him and spoke into his ear. "The next time you come for me I'll kill you got it?" The heavy nodded with the urgency of one truly frightened. Briggs left him groaning on the concrete and walked to the office where he could see the transport manager and foreman looking out of the window.

Briggs entered the office, ignored the manager and spoke to the foreman. "Guv, anyone who needs a 'minder' is by definition a wanker and that's what you are. If you have something to say to me, say it, don't send silly boys to get hurt, got it? See you tomorrow." Briggs took the manifest out of his back pocket and placed it on the counter, turned on his heel and walked out.

Having set the seal on his albeit temporary employment, Briggs continued working for Swordsman Transport for about six months. He was always shown the utmost consideration and respect by the other employees, his work rotas were never too hard and usually consisted of driving back and forth between Dover and London. Any overtime he performed was always doubled or trebled by the foreman, who took to calling him "my son," which made Briggs' skin creep.

Eventually, and much later than he had expected it to be if he were to be honest, Briggs received a telephone call from some faceless Chief Inspector, warning him that it was a disciplinary offence to take other employment whilst suspended. Because of his fraudulent identity and the problems it could engender for the owner of the agency, Briggs called it a day, having earnt a considerable amount of money in cash and gaining some valuable experience. Most of all, the work had been beneficial in saving his sanity.

Having left lorry driving behind him, Briggs embarked on a period of self-employment as an itinerant mechanic, using his garage at home for repairs and servicing of vehicles. To his surprise this quickly became a roaring success for, as well as servicing and repairing vehicles, Briggs began buying non-runners from the auctions, repairing them and then selling them, not always for a profit. This occupation became so busy that Briggs was booked up for weeks ahead. So much so that when A10 rang him to attend Scotland Yard to be interviewed and, by inference, charged, Briggs told them he was much too busy as he had a Triumph gearbox on the bench in pieces and would attend once he had got it back together and in the car again as he really could not let his customer down. The Chief Inspector delivering the message became ever so upset, saying things like, "The job comes first" and "it's your duty to attend" and more of the same, none of which cut any ice with Briggs who kept saying, "I will be there tomorrow. Shall we say about 9.30am?" Eventually the Chief Inspector agreed and Briggs attended at the appointed time walking in under the famous revolving sign.

Being without warrant card, the requisite to drift past the back hall Police Constable, he walked up to the reception desk. Behind the desk was a fat and forty, busty reception clerk, who was obviously in the habit of wearing brightly coloured large pattern clothes thinking no doubt that this diminished her size and made her more attractive. If this was so, Briggs felt she was mistaken.

Briggs coughed to attract the receptionist's attention. "Yes!" she said, unparking her pointed end glasses from her large strange nose, "Can I help you?"

"Definitely not sexually," thought Briggs but said "Yes you can. Detective Constable Briggs to see Detective Chief Inspector Dodge and/or Detective Inspector Sparrow."

Miss Fat and Forty sniffed and regarded him with disdain, "Your warrant card please officer." At this point Briggs knew that she knew who he was and that he was suspended.

"I ain't got one any more. They suspended me and took it away," Briggs said brightly as though without a care.

"Suspended eh? What for? Something exciting?" she asked making it sound as though she had a sense of humour. In reality she was being malicious, speaking as she was in a loud voice such that civilians and police officers in the entrance hall turned and looked at this poor suspended officer. There was not, however, a lot of sympathy in their looks.

"That's right darling, got suspended for raping a civilian employee, but I've got a perfect defence, as I thought she was a dog and shagging dogs is my weakness." Briggs was amused by the shocked look from Miss Fat and Forty and added for further effect, "Didn't you find that blouse made a nasty hole in the curtains?"

Miss Fat and Forty huffed and rang a number, which Briggs supposed was the reserve for A10. In her poshest voice she said, "There's an objectionable suspended officer by the name of Briggs to see DCI Dodge. Thank you." She put the phone down. "Somebody will be with you shortly," she said icily. Briggs turned on his heel and sat down on one of the settees.

Briggs was daydreaming, deliberately trying to keep his mind free from the trauma which no doubt awaited him. He looked out from the Yard reception area into the Broadway and watched as men often do, the female staff entering the Yard. Briggs wondered how it was that they all managed to bounce their breasts on entering the building, perhaps it was his imagination? "Mr. Briggs, DI Sparrow, will you come with me please?" Briggs looked up into the friendly eyes of DI Sparrow, got up and followed him into the lift. Once the doors closed and they were on their own the DI whispered, "Be shrewd my old son, say nothing not a thing. By the way Jones and Sayers are also being charged. Okay?" The DI looked expectantly at Briggs, who nodded silently. They entered an office on the fifth floor of the Yard where, seated behind a desk, was Detective Chief Inspector Dodge.

"Sit down Briggs" he said curtly, impersonal and with a touch of disdain, indicating the chair in front of his desk. Briggs sat down without comment.

"Firstly," he continued, not bothering with any courtesies of greeting or introductions. "I must caution you that you are not obliged to say anything unless you wish to do so, but what you say may be put into writing and given in evidence, do you understand?" Dodge looked expectantly at Briggs.

"Yes." said Briggs, watching the DI writing on his clipboard.

"Yes what?" Dodge prompted sharply and obviously intimating that a 'sir' here and there would not be out of place.

"Yes I understand," Briggs growled and Dodge decided the point was not worth pursuing or was completely lost on this oaf in front of him.

"I am now going to ask you some questions about the circumstances under which you were suspended." Dodge waited for the Inspector's pen to catch up.

"Look guv, you're wasting your time, I will answer no questions at this interview. I have already sworn an affidavit to my side of this incident and my intention of not answering any questions put to me by you or any other senior officer. No offence meant, but that's the way it is." Briggs shrugged his shoulders.

"I do not understand the relevance of the affidavit," queried Dodge. Briggs understood Dodge to be a uniform plodder and he was now proving it.

"Well guv," explained Briggs slowly, "it is sworn before a Commissioner of Oaths, one of my choosing and it gives my side of the story. It may be produced at my trial if there is to be such a thing." Briggs watched the Inspector's pen catch up.

"I am offended," said Dodge. "I can't see the difference between a solicitor and your interviewing officers, myself and the Inspector here," indicating the owner of the racing pen.

"Well I can and that's what counts, not what you think, but what I think. Therefore I will answer no questions at this stage and you guv, can think what you like." Briggs said it in a matter-of-fact tone, putting the situation as he saw it.

"Constable Briggs, do not be impertinent," Dodge said hotly, obviously upset.

"I am not being, as you say, impertinent, I am saying what I am going to do and that's it," Briggs explained, making it as plain as he could but still feeling he hadn't communicated his lack of trust for members of A10. Perhaps it was because Dodge came from a different planet than Briggs, one where villains didn't have to be dealt with by the likes of Briggs and where Dixon of Dock Green was a real copper.

Dodge stopped the conversation with, "Inspector, take Briggs here to Canon Row where I will charge him as per the charge sheet we prepared earlier." The Inspector put his clipboard away and got up. He nodded towards the door and Briggs got up and went with him. Together they went downstairs to the reception hall and waited for a car to take them to Canon Row. Neither spoke.

After a few minutes a Hillman General Purposes car and a civilian driver arrived and they drove the short distance to Canon Row, where Briggs was placed in a cell. The inspector peered through the cell flap but spoke without malice, "Your mate Jones is in the next cell, but he doesn't want to talk to you, in tears most of the time."

Briggs laughed, "That's a surprise, never seen him in tears before. What about Sayers where's he?" Briggs asked, trying to get some information about what was going on. "Sergeant Sayers is being charged at another station. He should be out on bail by now." The Inspector left Briggs with his thoughts.

About half an hour later the cell door rattled as it was opened. The custody sergeant poked his head in and said, "Oi come on Briggs," as he indicated the corridor towards the charge room. Briggs walked out and stood in the charge room in front of the desk behind which was Detective Chief Inspector Dodge. A few moments later Briggs was joined by Jones, who avoided any eye contact with Briggs and, as he arrived, the custody sergeant sat down and took the charge board and read from it. "You are charged together with Detective Sergeant Sayers that you did conspire to pervert the course of justice, contrary to Common Law. You are both further charged, together with Detective Sergeant Sayers, that you accepted from one Pat Ryan, a prisoner on remand, five hundred pounds as a bribe to induce you to corruptly pervert the course of justice in his favour Contrary to the Prevention of Corruption Act 1906. You are not obliged to say anything unless you wish to do so, but what you say may be taken down in writing and given in evidence." The sergeant looked at both Briggs and Jones but neither said anything. Briggs looked at Jones and saw him quietly weeping.

On Remand

After spending a night in the cells and hearing at first and close hand the wailings and moanings of life's unfortunates, Briggs and Jones appeared before Bow Street Magistrates' Court. As they waited in the cell corridor to be called, with Jones looking haggard and worried, Briggs drew close to him and whispered, "No worries blue." Ron Jones turned and looked him straight in the eye but apparently without comprehension. Briggs felt he could be looking directly into Jones' pain racked soul and he added, "Don't worry Ron, you'll walk at Committal I should think. You haven't got a thing to worry about. I'll make sure you walk, now snap out of it my old son."

Jones, for the first time ever, snarled at Briggs, his red-rimmed eyes gave him a manic appearance as he spat out his response to the kindly meant words. "I couldn't give two shits about you Briggs, if I get a chance to sink you I will."

Briggs was shocked at this response and, feeling the need to hit back, he said with all kindness in his heart vanishing in the process, "Does that include Christine as well? Does she want to put me down as well? Or perhaps we shouldn't discuss her and the dosh you signed for on her behalf and spent on yourself. The only thing she saw was the end of your dick, you sanctimonious prick."

Briggs turned and noticed that his escort from A10 was busily trying to get his pocket book out. Briggs waited until he had completed the manoeuvre then grabbed the pocket book and tore it into tiny pieces.

The escort looked decidedly upset, "I shall nick you for criminal damage" he squawked, trying to salvage the pieces from the floor.

"You twenty two carat prick you, I'm already nicked, just add it to the list," said Briggs as he kicked the pieces of paper about with his foot.

"Quiet in the cell corridor," bellowed the gaoler sergeant, knowing what had gone on and winking at Briggs.

They were called onwards and upwards into the court where they both appeared in the dock. The assembled coppers and clerks showed interest in the strange pair of gamekeepers who had been charged as poachers.

The court clerk recited the charges to the bowed heads of Jones and Briggs after which a pimply faced barrister rose from the prosecution bench and said, "On behalf of the Director of Public Prosecutions, I respectfully request a remand in this case. There is no objection to bail in the case of Detective Constable Jones, but a strong objection in the case of Briggs." A strange hush descended on the court. Briggs had expected something to be said but was dumbfounded to be singled out.

Frank Beamish had seen Briggs in the cells before the remand and warned him that the prosecution might try to keep him in custody. However Briggs had been relieved to hear that some of his old, less law-abiding friends had offered to foot the bill for pre-trial advocacy, or at least until Briggs was properly represented. It seemed more likely to Briggs that Frank was intending to wave the costs but would never say so, hiding behind the so-called friends instead. Briggs had instructed Frank to strenuously apply for bail, as there was no way he relished the prospect of being on remand in Brixton. Briggs also told Frank that if the going got rough he would dismiss him and carry on, on his own, as it could get nasty and would do Frank's relationship with the upper echelons of the police no good at all.

Frank got slowly to his feet. "Your worships, I wonder if we might be acquainted with the objections to bail and, of course, any supporting evidence there might be." Frank sat down.

The young barrister got up, ever so important in his wig and gown but seeming to be little older than fourteen. He shrugged his gown and adjusted his wig in time honoured fashion. "Your worships, this officer is a past member of the British Army's Special Forces, the Special Air Service Regiment to be exact. In that regiment he learnt skills which it is now feared could be turned against the prosecution in this case. More importantly he was being followed recently by a member of a surveillance team when he effectively took that tailing member prisoner and struck him several blows to the head. It is feared that if he is allowed his freedom, he will interfere with witnesses in this case." The barrister sat down.

Frank got up and smiled at the young barrister and addressed the bench. "I really cannot believe that the prosecution has put forward such flimsy objections. Firstly this officer has ten years service in the Metropolitan Police and there are several times in that service, to my personal knowledge, when he has put his learnt skills to use in the course of his duty and been commended by the learned Judge for that valuable assistance. Secondly, presumably the member of the surveillance team is going to be called to show his injuries and give evidence." Frank looked across at the young barrister who shook his head vigorously. "My learned friend seems to be indicating that he is unwilling to call this so called injured surveillance team member to court to give evidence, in which case I will call officer Briggs to the witness box to account for his strange behaviour."

The Chairman of the Bench interrupted. "There is no need Mr. Beamish, no evidence of the interference with witnesses has been given and therefore Mr. Briggs has nothing to answer at this stage." The Chairman paused to take advice from the magistrates on either side of him. "We are going to allow bail to both defendants in their own recognizance of five hundred pounds. The objection about Briggs' service in the army is really not acceptable. Presumably the Metropolitan Police knew that he had such service behind him when he enlisted in the Police Force?" Briggs noted that the young brief nodded. "Therefore, it cannot be a credible objection to bail. Surely it is to his credit that he has satisfactorily met the selection processes and been badged into such a select and fine band of soldiers?"

Briggs looked closely at the magistrate and thought he recognised the regimental tie he wore as being that of the 22nd Artists Rifles, the Territorial Army outfit of the SAS. He also thought the magistrate half smiled in encouragement.

Briggs and Jones left the dock and went downstairs to the gaoler's office where they both signed the form which admitted them to bail. Jones was still not speaking and signed in silence.

They left the court without a word between them. On the steps outside, Jones was enveloped in body crushing hug from Audrey, the owner of the hairy mole. She was crying and speaking in some strange language which Briggs took to be Welsh, could have been Swahili for all he knew, but she certainly seemed animated about something, hugging Jones in the process. Briggs assumed she must have some quality as outward attractiveness did not seem to be her forte. Briggs wandered over to the underground station, quietly vowing that if anyone was following him they could do it in peace and quiet and without interference.

Briggs arrived home to find his wife and children very upset, tears and sobbing. It transpired that a neighbour on the other side of the cul-de-sac had dished the eldest Briggs boy a megaton telling off about playing football in the cul-de-sac. Apparently young David had followed his Dad's example and retorted some cheek in response. The neigbour happened to be a uniform sergeant stationed at Woolwich, dealing with local and minor complaints against the police and whose stated ambition was to be posted to the Yard as a bag carrying sergeant for some aspiring Chief Inspector on A10. As a reply to the cheek from David the sergeant had made some spiteful remarks about his old man being bent and a thief to boot. David had come home and told Mum and they all sat down and howled. It was at this point that Briggs arrived home, in less than jaunty mood, to family uproar. Briggs listened carefully to what young David had to say, but Maggie was distraught. "I know you, you'll go after him and we'll be in even more trouble. Leave it alone, please leave it alone," she said, but as always, her tears had a definite effect on him. He stormed out of the house and across the road to where the Sergeant was in the drive working on his car. Briggs noted this with disgust as he had recently helped the skipper to repair this very car after a scrape.

The Sergeant turned around as Briggs approached. "Alright Tel?" he said it with a slight waver in his voice that said, "I'm afraid." Briggs didn't reply. He hit the Sergeant a full bodied blow to the face, not caring where or what he damaged. The skipper fell against his car and held his face, blood creeping from behind his hand. Briggs fetched him another blow to the side of his head and the skipper fell to the ground. "You spiteful shit, fancy saying such a thing to a kid." Mrs. Sergeant appeared from the rear of the house and started screeching as she cradled her husband in her arms and helped him to his feet.

"You animal look what you've done now."

"Missus don't bother about that," Briggs said red faced and annoyed. "that's nothing compared to what will happen if shit face here decides to make another such remark to my kids – got it?" Briggs turned and walked away.

"You won't be happy until they put you away for ten years will you" Maggie said, as he returned, upset at the performance she had seen in the street. Briggs thought this was not a good time to mention that if he went down on the conspiracy, ten years was not beyond the pale. After the event, as always, Briggs felt sorry and ashamed but knowing there was little else he could do.

"Sorry love, but I'd rather have them worry about what I am going to do, than me worry about them. Anyway what a turd saying that to a boy." The saving aspect was that young David regarded his father with admiration, so much so that Briggs later had a meaningful talk with his son about solving life's problems with violence, and how really clever people didn't need to do that and how it was generally not a good idea. All of which young David listened to with attention, after which he asked, "After all that, do I bash 'em Dad?"

Committal

Suspended life continued with Briggs working himself to the point of exhaustion, concentrating on today, blocking out tomorrow with hard work. Eventually, after some six months and many more car repairs, he was notified of the date of Committal. Frank Beamish had by this time dropped out of the case as it was obviously going to become a fight between Briggs and the upper echelons of the police, A10 in particular. As such, it would do Frank Beamish's reputation as a safe middle man no good at all. He had passed Briggs on to a young solicitor Simon Cantwell, who Frank rated as being competent and upwardly mobile.

The statements of witnesses in the Committal were served on Simon Cantwell and later passed on to Briggs for him to construct his defence and to suggest lines of attack. Briggs spent many hours reading and rereading transcripts of the tapes and the witnesses' statements. For the life of him, Briggs could not understand why his final meeting with Ryan had not been recorded. According to the transcripts, Ryan had an active body tape on for the previous nineteen days, starting at 9am and finishing at 7pm. An active body tape meant that the recorder was on all the time and required no action from the wearer, but, on that last day, nothing had been recorded, or so the transcripts maintained. He could not countenance that Ryan was involved in a conspiracy with Dodge and the others to fit him up, as being a normal member of society he could not be trusted to carry it through and not to wilt under pressure. So it either had to be that he switched the tape on and off at Court when he was engaged in hostile conversations with Briggs, or on the final day it must have been a malfunction and the tape just did not work; whichever, Briggs was confused. Briggs noted this down as something that had to be thrashed out with Chief Inspector Dodge and Pat Ryan and decided to have both of them give personal evidence at the Magistrates' Court.

It was during the run up to the committal proceedings that Briggs began to hear rumours of Sayers and illness. Apparently he was suffering from cancer. Hymie imparted this intelligence on one of their frequent meets and the fact that a collection was being put round for Sayers; the inference taken by both Hymie and Briggs was that Sayers was not long for this world. Briggs gave Hymie a five pound note for the collection. Not that he had any regard for Sayers, but more with the thought of, "There but for the grace of God go I." As he gave it to Hymie, Briggs said, "I hope the slimy shit doesn't exit before trial."

Committal was notified for three days in August at Old Street Magistrates' Court and, as the start date loomed, Briggs became more gloomy, realising that it was going to be an extremely testing time.

On the morning of the Committal, Briggs walked up the front steps of the court. Almost immediately, he met Simon Cantwell. Past him he saw Ron Jones and a young woman in black, who Briggs took to be Jones' brief. He couldn't help thinking, "I wonder if he has." Jones made no effort to speak.

"Sayers is in the side room over there," Simon said as he indicated a door in the corner. "He really is quite ill."

Briggs grimaced and asked, "Are you sure? I wouldn't put it past him to try and get out on a sick note." Simon merely shrugged his shoulders. Briggs sat with Simon discussing tactics, the order in which witnesses were likely to be called and whether they would be conditionally bound, i.e. unlikely to be called to give their evidence personally at the higher court, or whether they would be fully bound, in which case their presence would be definitely required at the higher court.

After about ten minutes of discussion with Simon, Sayers came out of the side room with his own brief. Briggs was shocked. Sayers was walking with the aid of arm crutches, his left foot was swathed in bandages and encased by some form of shell, which Briggs presumed prevented it from getting knocked. He had the pallor of a dead man, stark and white lines of pain were etched on his face as he struggled along. He sat down with an effort at the end of the benches. Simon tried to indicate that he shouldn't, but Briggs went up to Sayers and stood before him. Sayers looked up.

Briggs said, "I'm ever so sorry skip." Sayers asked, "About what? My illness or the fact that we have both been fitted up?" Briggs paused for a moment and considered what this desperately sick man had said.

"For all of it skip." Briggs could sense the pain coursing through Sayers' body. "Can't they give you something for the pain?"

Sayers smiled. "I came off medication yesterday, wanted my faculties about me today. So for the sake of being sharp, I have to stand the pain. Anyway Briggsy, I hope it goes well for both of us, but at least you have one advantage over me, you will at least live to see it through." Briggs nodded, unable to speak and rejoined Simon. There was much he could ask Sayers to do for him, much that Sayers could say, but for once Briggs didn't have the heart. How could he possibly say, "Well anyway, sorry to hear about your illness and that you are due to die soon, but before you go could you sort out one or two points for me?" He didn't doubt that there were some who could encompass such actions within their consciences – those who fitted him up for sure – the fat Sergeant from A10 who seemed to encapsulate the lot of them, for one.

The Committal got under way. The only witnesses Briggs particularly wanted to hear were Chief Inspector Dodge, Detective Inspector Sparrow and Pat Ryan himself. Briggs instructed Simon Cantwell to make the others the subject of a conditional witness order, and, accordingly, proceedings were whisked through until they arrived at Chief Inspector Dodge. Dodge ran through his evidence-in-chief, being prompted this way and that, at the end of which the prosecution brief said, "Wait there please." Simon Cantwell rose and, as best he could, fixed Dodge with a stony stare, which was particularly difficult for Simon as he was a nice man without a malevolent bone in his body. That said, he did his best to look fierce.

"Tell me officer" Simon opened, "With regard to operational plans, are they ever changed along the way?"

Cantwell paused and waited.

Dodge chewed the question over and eventually he said, "Yes sometimes, as the need arises."

Cantwell smiled pleasantly. "I see, and does there have to be a cogent reason for the change of plan once it has commenced in operation?"

Again Dodge mulled the question over before answering, "Usually sir yes."

Simon looked at his brief "So what was the reason for altering the operational plans relating to this case?" Dodge looked surprised.

"How do you mean exactly?" Simon pursued his subject.

"Well officer, it would appear that Mr. Ryan was body taped for some nineteen days and we have transcripts of those days. Such a body tape means that it is recording all the time, is that correct?"

"That is correct" said Dodge.

"However," continued Simon, "the last day when my client called for a pre-arranged visit, Ryan wasn't fitted with a running body tape but, apparently, with one for him to operate as he felt necessary. Why did you change the operational order for that day?"

Dodge coloured slightly, not enough to make Briggs leap in the air, but enough to indicate that they were pressing the right button. "I don't know exactly, it was just decided that he would turn it on himself. Simon looked directly into Dodge's eyes. Dodge could not hold the confrontation as Simon said, "Are you the officer in charge of this case or not?" Simon barked.

"Yes, yes of course," blurted out Dodge.

"Then tell me if it wasn't you, who was it who changed the operational order of the day?" Dodge looked at the floor of the witness box.

"I don't know, it was sort of decided that he would turn it on himself, as and when Briggs came in."

Briggs scribbled a note. "We are there. Leave it for the moment, it's all grist to the mill at trial." Simon read the note, turned to Briggs and nodded before continuing with the cross-examination of Dodge.

"Now Chief Inspector, perhaps you can tell us if there are any pieces missing from these tapes which have been submitted in evidence. Has any editing been done that you know of?" Simon indicated the piles of tape transcripts, which lay on the court bench. Dodge coughed. Briggs thought he showed a touch of embarrassment as he answered, "No sir, the tapes are a complete record of what went on – as far as I know. Mind you, they were not in my direct possession twenty four hours a day." Briggs scribbled another note. "The bastard's left himself an exit. He means, 'they are edited but prove it and I will say I was upstairs collecting fares' – leave the subject for trial." Simon allowed Dodge to leave the box and as he did so Dodge treated Briggs to his version of a hard man stare. Briggs grinned broadly.

Detective Inspector Sparrow entered the box and went through his evidence, which basically backed up Dodge's, known in the trade as a 'ditto' statement. He was cross-examined by the various briefs present and adopted the same line as Dodge on the tape questions. Briggs got the very distinct impression that they had discussed the business about tape evidence and their responses to the various questions had the sameness that makes one suspect that they had discussed the subject together in some depth.

Briggs waited with bated breath for the arrival of Pat Ryan, who eventually walked into court and gave the appearance of being overawed with his surroundings. Briggs thought that his accent on taking the oath had become thicker, almost to the point where he could not be understood. He ran through his evidence with the assistance of the prosecution brief. There was only one question to which Briggs wanted an answer and he asked Simon to put it straight away. "Between your arrest and the return of the paintings, who did you discuss this matter with?" Ryan looked worried. He looked left and right and gave a good impression of a meek man being hassled.

"Well sorr, I discussed it with my wife."

Simon was making a note. "Anyone else?"

"Well sorr I discussed it with the father." Cantwell smiled the smile reserved for those who are not that clever.

"Your father you mean?"

Ryan looked puzzled. "No sorr, the priest, when I was in confessional."

Unable to help himself, Briggs said in a louder voice than he had wished, "I wouldn't mind a tape recording of that one, if he told the truth."

The stipendiary magistrate looked over his glasses. "Mr. Cantwell will you please instruct your client that if the court is subjected to any

more remarks of that nature I shall review the subject of his bail."
The message was not lost on Briggs. Simon looked annoyed at Briggs
then turned to the Magistrate. "Of course your worship."

After a short pause Simon continued, "Now Mr. Ryan, who else
did you discuss this matter with?" Ryan looked around the court but
his A10 friends were deep behind their defences.

"I discussed it with a lady from the Security Services." There was
complete silence throughout the court and everyone was staring at
this idiot Irishman.

Eventually the Magistrate broke the spell, "I don't know if this is
relevant or not, but if the subject of national security comes into this
Committal I shall suspend it and take advice." Briggs wrote another
note, "I don't believe it, but we'll take it up at trial." Simon read the
note and indicated his agreement.

"Now Mr. Ryan, it would appear from the tape transcripts that it
was Sergeant Sayers who kept asking you for money and Detective
Constable Briggs who kept asking you for information. Is that the
situation?"

Ryan thought for a moment, "Yes sorr that's the situation."

Simon pressed on. "Did you ever see Sergeant Sayers and
Detective Constable Briggs together?"

Ryan looked down at this feet and answered, "No sorr." Briggs
gave Simon the cutthroat sign, to finish it at that point.

The other briefs both gave Ryan a severe savaging. Jones' lady
brief was particularly effective, hammering into Ryan like he was fox
cornered by the pack, until Ryan agreed that he had not seen Jones
do anything, say anything, or even look objectionable, and it was all
down to that nasty Sergeant Sayers, and even nastier, Constable
Briggs. From this Briggs surmised that Jones was going for
"Dismissed due to lack of evidence" and he was pleased, for there
was no way he wanted to stand in the dock at the Old Bailey
accompanied by the hero of the valleys. If this did happen he would
have to wade through puddles of tears and recriminations, so it was
better that he was out of it altogether.

At the end of the Committal, both Sayers and Briggs were
committed for trial and Jones was released due to lack of evidence.
Ron left the dock without a single word to either Sayers or Briggs.

After Committal, Briggs resumed his tedious life on suspension.

One of the subjects he broached was the matter of legal representation. He raised it first with the Police Federation, the so called coppers' trade union. Every policeman and woman in England and Wales subscribes to the Police Federation and supports its efforts to gain and maintain their living standards. The Federation was formed after the Police Strike of 1919, when it was declared an offence for the police to go on strike, or to incite any police officer to do so. From the very start, the Federation was regarded by rank and file as a toothless tiger. However, within the Federation subscriptions, there was a percentage which went towards legal representation of the individual members, should he or she ever get into trouble. Briggs was curtly informed that this fighting fund was for the defence of officers in the civil court, not for officers facing criminal charges. Briggs, feeling that a mistake had been made, contacted his Federation representative regarding the matter but was told quite forcibly that he was lucky not to be in custody awaiting trial and that there was no way Federation funds would be used to defend a bent officer. Briggs wanted to take the matter further and demanded to know where the authority came from to make such an exclusion, but never received a satisfactory answer.

Without the assistance of Federation funds, Briggs went to work on car repairs, buying and selling the same with almost manic vengeance to lay up a supply of cash that could be utilised in the event that he had to find money for a brief. In the event, this money was not needed as Simon Cantwell approached the court with a view to obtaining legal aid and, much to Briggs' surprise, this was granted. This legal aid included the briefing of a Queen's Counsel (QC) and, consequently, a junior counsel to hold his hand and briefs. Briggs thought at the time of this grant that this softening of the official line was a melting of the hard heart of the establishment. It never crossed his mind that the appointment of a QC could be the establishment's method of keeping tabs on, and control over, both the prosecution and defence. Such a thought occurred to Briggs some time later, especially after his first briefing meeting and, particularly, when he later heard that an eminent QC had refused to accept his brief, stating, "There's been too much dirty work in the background for my liking."

Some two months after Committal, Briggs was called to barrister's chambers in Lincoln's Inn for a case conference with his appointed barrister. Briggs travelled up on the suburban train from New Eltham, for the first time in months dressed in a suit and tie and feeling very uncomfortable. In the same carriage he noticed Brian Perry, who had been a Temporary Detective Constable on the same division as him. It was rumoured that Perry was a flyer and had connections. Certainly, he had come out of aiding, gone Detective Constable for a year and almost immediately made Sergeant. Briggs let a few stations fly by, watching Perry all the time, being sure he had seen him, but Perry was studying the view whizzing past the window with almost scholarly intent. Feeling the need for light relief and being irked by the rebuff from a one time colleague, Briggs got up and sat on the seat in front of Perry.

"Wotcha Brian, had it off lately?" Briggs said it only to make the career conscious Perry squirm but, without taking his eyes from the scenery. Briggs laughed, "Do you remember that job when we were aids at Lewisham, you know, when the safe breaker parted up with large dollops of cash to get his explosives back? You were on that with the first class weren't you? How's about if, when I get up the Bailey, I play a marathon game of 'do you remember when', what about that then?" Perry looked uncomfortable, reddened slightly but not a lot, as befits a prospective senior officer, got up and went to another seat, again studying the fast moving scenery with rapt attention. Briggs let him go and sat watching him until they arrived at Charing Cross, when Perry scuttled off up the platform with manner of one who just had to get somewhere, anywhere, as long as it was away from this infected officer.

Briggs caught a taxi to Lincoln's Inn, finding the chambers without difficulty. He stood in the general office and waited to be noticed by the staff rushing hither and thither. Around him were plummy accents, with plenty of Nigels and Simons. All the women seemed to be called Samantha or Hortense. Briggs stood and let this maelstrom whirl around until, eventually, a middle aged woman with large horn-rimmed glasses enquired, "Yes?" with just that trace of haughtiness that gets one noticed, usually for nothing other than the fact that the voice is sharper than anyone else's. "Terry Briggs to see Miss Cotterill QC, a case conference." Briggs waited for this information to seep into the mind of this twinset wearing clerk.

"Ah, yes the, er, officer charged with corruption and conspiracy." Briggs felt she wanted to say, "The corrupt copper" but she did say, "If you would wait in the ante-room, Miss Cotterill's clerk will call you." Briggs went into the waiting room and sat, feeling almost as though he was going to give evidence at the Bailey. The ante-room was expensively furnished in leather and mahogany. "Not bad on other people's misfortunes," thought Briggs, weighing up his expensive surroundings against his perceived intelligence of counsels he had seen operating. With few notable exceptions, he considered them to be a bunch of freeloaders, with no actual experience of anything. However, they do talk a good job.

"Miss Cotterill will see you now." Briggs followed the young spotty faced clerk into an even more expensively furnished room where behind a desk sat Miss Cotterill, a lady of around fifty five years but very well preserved. She beamed Briggs the standard issue smile.

"Officer Briggs we meet at last, Janet Cotterill. This is my junior, Miles Bannister." Briggs shook hands with the young man who grasped Briggs' hand like a damp rag. "Typical young officer type," thought Briggs. "Like a lighthouse in the desert, very pretty, but not a lot of use."

The young Miles grinned warmly. "A pleasure officer, I have heard lots about you." Briggs nodded. "Good or bad?" wondered Briggs. Not that anything this gown carrier thinks is going to affect anything. Briggs then noticed his solicitor, Simon Cantwell, sitting in the corner behind him.

"Morning Simon, you alright?" Simon looked up from his pad, "Fine Tel, nice to see you."

"Well, shall we get on," said Miss Cotterill, all brisk and business like. "As you can see, Miles, Simon and myself have already had a preliminary conference and, as far as we can see, your defence is one of, 'I had already arrested him and was taking him to Jones, then to the car and then to Rodney Road.' Is that right?" Miss Cotterill looked quizzically at Briggs.

"Yes that's right" replied Briggs, uncomfortable not only in this skimpy antique chair, but also with the fact that they had been chatting about the case before he arrived, almost as if his defence was being decided behind his back. He dismissed the thought as all these people were surely on his side, weren't they?

"Well the only fly in the ointment is that Ryan says he gave you cash to get you and Sayers off his back. How do you answer that?" Miss Cotterill posed the question over her glasses.

"Well bottom line, he had already been charged with the engine job, he couldn't get out of that, he had already appeared before a court. I told Sayers that if Ryan helped me to arrest the people stealing from Fords, I would help Ryan by letting the court know that he had supplied helpful information. Sayers was very interested in money but I kept telling him it was not on." Briggs explained in a rush, "It was Ryan and Sayers, all the talk about money came from them."

"Well we have a problem with Sayers, it would appear that he is going to be given a nolle prosequi," Miss Cotterill announcing the latin phrase as if everyone present understood, which Briggs was sure none, including himself, did.

"A what?" Briggs asked, expressing the puzzlement that all of them felt.

"Oh yes, of course Mr. Briggs you would not be conversant with the term. It basically means that Sergeant Sayers is so ill that he is unlikely to survive and that, to put him through the agony of a trial, would be inhumane."

"So can we get him to give a deposition?" Briggs almost said, 'Dying deposition', which he supposed is what it would be really. "As far as I can make out from my sources" (Miss Cotterill hinting darkly at what she had been told by a man from the Director of Public Prosecutions' office but, of course, under a cloak of confidentiality) "the deal Sayers has is that being so ill, he can walk from the case on the understanding that he leaves no evidence either way."

Briggs was stunned. "So it's down to me. What about Jones? We can call him to give evidence can't we?"

"Again we have a difficulty. Jones is unwilling to give evidence for you and will be hostile if called by us." Miss Cotterill said it softly, so that maybe the impact would not be so crushing. Briggs thought deeply for a moment.

Eventually he said, "Miss Cotterill, inform the Director's Office that we will be calling Jones in defence. We have no alternative. I assure you that he will give evidence for me and will not be hostile." Briggs thought it would be shrewd to leave it there.

"I hear what you say," again, lawyer speak for 'no comment'.

"Also what about Jack the Hat, er I mean Detective Chief Inspector Parris? Will he be giving evidence for the defence?" asked Briggs hopefully.

"Again, he has indicated that he will not willingly appear and will be hostile," Miss Cotterill said in a manner that appeared apologetic.

Briggs had by now guessed that both Jones and Jack the Hat would hang him out to dry if given the chance.

"Miss Cotterill, take it from me that Mr. Parris will give evidence for the defence and most definitely will not be hostile." Miss Cotterill nodded. "I will request the Director of Public Prosecutions to make sure those officers are available for the defence." Miss Cotterill and the other two wrote furiously on their pads.

"What's this nonsense Ryan came out with about him speaking to the Security Services on this?" Briggs asked, speaking directly to Miss Cotterill. She raised her head and seemed to speak past Briggs and not to him.

"Yes, I have studied this aspect and discussed it with Simon and we will definitely be pursuing this matter during cross-examination." Miss Cotterill's head went down and she made a note.

"Well just to top and tail it, why not ask the Director whether Ryan is involved in Security Service matters, get it formally that he is not so, so when he prattles on we will be in a position to slaughter him?" Briggs suggested, appealing to all three.

Miss Cotterill shook her head. "Wouldn't do any good, they would neither confirm nor deny his employment with the firm. I personally do not believe he is anything to do with any of the Security Services. We would have been told," Miss Cotterill giving a fair impression of someone being positive.

Briggs thought for a moment. "Then why don't we ask anyway, it can do no harm and at least puts them on notice that we are going to delve into this aspect. It might just shake the tree."

Miss Cotterill smiled, thin and wispish, probably because she was not used to the pose. "It is not my policy to 'shake trees' as you say but to proceed on the basis of evidence or lack of it." Briggs was a little stunned by this pronouncement.

"Miss Cotterill you proceed on the basis of others producing the evidence for you, the ammunition to fire if you like, and if my memory serves me well, as based on the case of Regina v Kruma 1955, you couldn't care less how that evidence is produced, just that it is." (R v Kruma 1955 a Mau Mau terrorist found in possession of live ammunition and sentenced to death appealed on the basis that the ammunition was found as the result of an illegal search, conviction upheld = swift end for Mr. Kruma). Miss Cotterill looked down at her notes, a little surprised that this oafish officer had the temerity to quote case law at her.

"I shall look into the matter and we will discuss it at the our next case conference" she replied, knowing full well that there would not be one before the Court appearance. Feeling that he could not affect the matter much further at this stage, Briggs let it drop, but was not happy with these superior legal people who were supposed to be on his side.

Briggs continued, "What about the change of operational plan?" They all looked blank. "You know, Ryan is body taped for nineteen days and on the twentieth I appear and he does not have his body tape running. He's left to switch it on himself when he decides." Briggs looked round at the three blank faces. They appeared not to understand.

Eventually Miss Cotterill said, "Ah yes officer, I have taken this point up with a contact in the upper echelons of the Metropolitan Police, and he informs me that they can change operational plans as often as they like. There is nothing hanging on that particular point, evidentially it's a non starter." Briggs noted that she did not look him in the eye and he responded more forcibly than he intended.

"Really? I'm not surprised you were fed that line. As one who has been on these little operations I can tell you, and I can call evidence on the point if it is disputed, that operational plans are not altered unless there is a cogent reason for doing so. It has to do with the continuity of evidence, in other words, not giving you people any ammunition. I assure you this is unusual and I instruct you to cross-examine on this point."

Briggs noted that the Queen's Counsel was not particularly

happy about this his forceful attitude to her instructions. After a moment or two she recovered her composure.

"Again I hear what you say," accompanied by the ice cold smile of superiority. Briggs could feel his temper rising and strove to control it.

With as much of an even manner as he could muster he said, "Miss Cotterill you can hear what you like, but you will confirm to me here and now that you will cross-examine on this point." Real novelists, unlike the writer, would describe what followed as a pregnant pause, but for Briggs it was a period when everyone else sat and contemplated anything in the room other than him. "Well?" Briggs asked, pushing the matter along the course he intended it to take.

After a short pause Miss Cotterill said, "Of course officer, you're in charge."

Briggs smiled and added, "And the one who has to do the bird when it all goes boss-eyed."

Miss. Cotterill grimaced and said in an embarrassed voice, "Well we obviously hope that that does not happen."

"That is also my fervent wish," said Briggs." Now, what about tape evidence? It is my assertion that these tapes do not contain a true record of what was said between Ryan and myself. It is my belief that they have been edited," Briggs feeling that he is not believed, also that he is pulling a heavy weight, without wheels, uphill.

"Oh come on Mr. Briggs, why should the police fabricate evidence against you? It doesn't add up. I can see no cogent reason why the police would wish to edit those tapes."

Briggs mulled it over for a moment then said, "Neither can I, but that doesn't mean it hasn't happened. Therefore, I would like the tapes examined for manual interference, i.e. Ryan mucking about with the recorder, and also editing after the event."

Miss Cotterill examined her brief in great detail. "We can have the tapes examined, but it has to be done by a Home Office accredited expert and the base maxim is that 'a perfect edit is undetectable.' In addition I don't think the legal aid fund would be too happy to foot the bill for the examination." Briggs became animated on this input.

"Oh, I see, it's different for old bill is it? What about all those dead legs you see in court with expensive experts giving evidence for them on all sorts of subjects? Do they end up getting a bill for it all then?" Briggs getting decidedly pugnacious. Miss Cotterill looked to the other two for assistance, but they were both studying their briefs, or the ceiling or whatever.

"Well of course you may be right, I'll contact Mr. Austin and get the tapes examined before trial."

Briggs sat in his expensive antique chair and studied his surroundings. He could feel the other three studying him and eventually said, "Maybe it's only because I am the accused in this case, but I feel there is something very odd about it." He looked at Miss Cotterill and noticed she reddened slightly, maybe she was tired, or annoyed with him perhaps. Whilst considering this unlikely aspect, Briggs suddenly returned to his most consuming subject and felt the need to discuss it further. "I realise that we have talked about changes to operational plans but I want to know why Ryan wasn't apparently wearing a running body tape when I called on the last occasion. He knew I was coming, he asked me there himself. They needed those tapes Miss Cotterill, to support the allegations against me and they should, surely, have kept to the operational plan to ensure they got them. Furthermore, if tape recordings had been made, they would have supported my contention that Ryan had been arrested by me for trying to bribe me and, therefore, I would have no case to answer. Remember, I stated the fact even before the use of body tapes was declared. It would clearly be most strange if they changed the plans and risked the loss of evidence through the incompetence of an untrained operator, but not so strange if the plans were changed after the event when the evidence didn't sit too well with them."

Miss Cotterill glanced at Simon to see if she could call any support there, but he was studying the floor with concentration. "Well as I understand it, from the senior police officer in charge, the day you called was going to be the last day of the observation, obbos I believe you call them, and it was decided that he would switch it on if you came in."

Briggs stared at Miss Cotterill in amazement. "Miss Cotterill, there was no 'if I came in' – I was invited. Do you mean to tell me that you have consulted with Chief Inspector Dodge before speaking to me, your client? Don't you think that a bit irregular?" Briggs was getting more annoyed by the second.

Miss Cotterill responded quickly in the hope of smoothing the situation. "I did happen to speak to him at court one day and I thought I might elicit some useful information from him."

Briggs stared into the open face of Miss Cotterill and demanded, "And did you?" Miss Cotterill looked confused. "Get any useful information that is."

She brightened up immediately. "Oh no, the officer was unable to assist us."

Briggs laughed. "As a QC, are you really surprised that the officer was unable to assist?" Miss Cotterill's complexion became slightly redder. Briggs was pleased that she had some semblance of conscience left.

Briggs spent the rest of the conference looking at his notebook. When his ordeal was over he got up and grudgingly shook hands with everyone before leaving. Simon Cantwell wanted to walk him to the underground but Briggs made an excuse and went on his own. On his way home, Briggs mulled over the conversations he had had. It seemed so obvious to him that everyone was playing their own game, with little interest for his welfare. Were they against him or was he just being paranoid? Could he again be close to losing his marbles.

Up the Bailey – Again

Briggs sat in his kitchen, drinking coffee and thinking about the conference with counsel. He actually had the local baker's van in the garage, the engine of which was strewn across the bench awaiting measurement and decision as how best to rebuild the thing, but that could wait while he thought about the eventual decision on his future. He kept thinking about what Miss Cotterill had said about 'consulting' her contacts on the prosecution team. Briggs could accept that it was possible that over the years Miss Cotterill might gain a large number of contacts, which would assist her in her profession, but what worried Briggs was the question, "Was she for or against him?" Had she been chosen as one who would see the prosecution's point of view and, indeed, help that view to conviction – his. The ringing telephone annoyingly interrupted his thoughts and he demonstrated his impatience. "Yes" he grunted, his mind still trying to fathom Miss Cotterill and her upper class twit of a junior.

"Tel, it's the guy who still owes you a bottle of scotch."

Briggs, after a moment's thought, remembered the day that a lorry load of stolen whisky had come into Rodney Road and eventually been written down that only a half load had been recovered, the other half being distributed around the various offices, particularly to senior officers, who didn't talk in bottles but complete cases. Briggs and Jones had been left out by the distributing officer, mainly by oversight, and Briggs had taken to pulling that officer's leg about the oversight. It was his First Class Sergeant, Sid Mills.

"Yes, I know who you are. What do you want?" There was a pause, as though Sid was put off, possibly by the gruff answer.

"Just wanted to know how you are, how you are managing and all that." Briggs thought deeply before answering. Sid was a nice man, there was no side with him and therefore this must be him kicking over the traces and getting in touch with someone who has been outlawed.

"Yeah, not bad, not bad, everything seems to be alright, looking forward to getting it over with." Sid almost let the conversation die, probably through embarrassment, having not spoken to Briggs for nearly two years.

"I am sure you are Tel. Do you remember, in happier times, shinning up a pole in a pub and signing your name on the ceiling?" Briggs didn't have to stop and think, Sid was talking about the Prince Alfred in Albany Road, just off Rodney Road's ground.

"Yes I remember it well, we had a good night that night." Briggs smiled, recalling the high jinks of the evening.

"Can you meet me there in an hour, I need to talk to you?" Briggs' mind raced. He could not countenance the very straight Sid Mills leading him astray.

"Yes, of course, if I'm a bit late hang on for me."

Briggs replaced the receiver and went upstairs to change into jeans and jumper. He took money out of his secret car dealer's hoard, went out and drove to the meet in an old Mini van he had taken in part exchange for a nearly new Ford Capri the week before. As he came to Clifton's Roundabout on the A20, which leads on to the South Circular Road, Briggs could not be sure whether he was being tailed or not and watched his rear view mirror. Being uncertain about one particular car, he drove around the roundabout three times and watched the consternation of the driver of the suspect Ford, as he endeavoured to transmit radio messages whilst driving furiously. Briggs stopped the Mini van halfway round the roundabout and the Ford overtook him on the inside. Briggs immediately moved forward and crowded the Ford onto the road for Eltham, whilst he himself continued round and took the road for Lewisham at a very fast rate, well for a clapped out Mini van anyway.

Briggs drove through Lewisham, Peckham and Camberwell, keeping a sharp eye on the rear view mirror for the tailing vehicle. Being fairly sure he had given the tail the slip, he headed for the Aylesbury Estate, where he parked the Mini van almost hoping that some enterprising thief would steal it. He walked off towards the pub. He stood at the bus stop opposite and watched the pub for about ten minutes and, being almost satisfied that there were no mysteries about, crossed the road and entered the pub.

Sid was standing at the bar, looking towards the door. He smiled a welcome as Briggs walked over to him. "Tel it's good to see you, how are you doing?" Briggs took his hand and shook it.

"As well as can be expected under the circumstances. That's what they say on the telly isn't it?" Briggs smiling at his own half joke. Sid looked him up and down.

"You're looking well, a bit skinnier if anything. Mind you, you could do with losing a few pounds. How's the car business going?" asked Sid. Briggs hesitated and stammered. "Oh come on Tel, everyone knows about you and the gearbox you were repairing so you couldn't attend the Yard to be nicked."

Briggs laughed. "That has gone down as legend has it?" Sid nodded as he caught the eye of the barmaid.

"Still light and bitter is it?" Briggs nodded. "and yes that story has been told around the Met. I actually heard it was put down to a skipper suspended off the Flying Squad and, of course, knowing the truth I had to put them right." The drinks arrived and Briggs took a swig, waiting for the real reason for this meet to emerge. After all, he had been suspended for two years and had not had anyone from Rodney Road contact him and so, to Briggs' mind, there had to be a reason. Something had driven Sid to contact him.

"Tel, the word is that your trial is listed for the 3rd July. Are you up for it?" Sid not speaking to him, but muttering into the glass.

"Yes as ready as I will ever be. We all know it's a fit up, but the trouble is proving it."

Sid nodded. "But you have some on your side. The top brass at the Yard have insisted that I come and talk to you, mainly about not rocking the boat." Sid seemed a bit shamefaced, and Briggs decided to rub it in.

"Well I didn't think it was your idea to come Sid, what did they offer you, the DI's job at last?" Sid was hurt, and Briggs laughed to try and make it into a half-hearted joke.

"Well anyway," Sid charged on "the message is, don't change anything, everyone is talking to everyone else behind closed doors and a deal has been sorted that will let you out and have a sting in the tail for little Paddy."

Briggs mulled over Sid's suggestion for a few moments. "But that's exactly it Sid, my brief's been talking to the other side and I am not sure that it's all to my benefit." Sid became ever so earnest.

"Stand on me Tel, this comes from the very highest. They know you've been fitted and the good guys are going to help out. Stand on me." Briggs stared into his glass thinking deeply. He trusted Sid and knew he wouldn't mislead him and was obviously here to assist him.

"I'll think on it Sid," Briggs almost apologetic for his half-hearted manner.

"Look Tel, I am not here to get on, you know me better than that surely. The word is, leave it as it is and you will be okay." Briggs stared into the earnest eyes of Sid Mills and decided that he believed what he had been told to do, which didn't mean that Briggs would obey, just that he was thinking on it.

On the 3rd July, Briggs stood in the dock alone, a strange place for a copper to be. Briggs had often wondered what it felt like, now he knew – not very pleasant. The prison officer escort stood next to him and regarded him with scorn. "You must be part of the brothers grim," said Briggs endeavouring to get the screw to smile, but was unsuccessful. The clerk stood up and the humpy screw indicated that Briggs should do the same. "Terence Andrew Briggs you are indicted that on or before the 16th May 1975, at Camberwell in the County of London, you did conspire with Richard Ashley Sayers to pervert the course of common justice, contrary to common law. How do you plead, guilty or not guilty?" Briggs replied in his deepest brown voice.

"Not guilty my lord."

The clerk continued, "You are further indicted that at Camberwell in the County of London, you accepted five hundred pounds to act contrary to the interests of your masters the Metropolitan Police, contrary to the Prevention of Corruption Act 1906. How do you plead, guilty or not guilty?"

Again Briggs said, "Not guilty my lord."

The court then empanelled the jury. Briggs watched closely. He objected to two who he thought were looking at him in a menacing manner and, eventually, they all sat there, twelve good men and women true, who according to the Judge would try the case on the evidence, and not on their personal feelings or prejudices. Briggs felt they were unlikely to be able to attain such a level of distanced reasoning. After all, how many of them had been nicked for speeding, parking, or letting their dog crap on the pavement?

The prosecution brief rose and began to open the case against Briggs. He explained that Sergeant Sayers would not be appearing because he was terminally ill but that the jury would still hear evidence against Sayers in respect of the conspiracy with Briggs. He also pointed out that such evidence would not be offered against Sayers as he had been excused from appearing due to his illness. The brief left the court in no doubt that Sayers would be best advised not to buy any long playing records, or start watching soap operas.

Briggs sat in isolation in the dock, taking comfort from the loving smile from his wife whilst the scowling screw said nothing and smiled not at all. Briggs listened intently to the prosecution brief as he outlined the case against him. What struck Briggs as strange was that, in his conversation with Sayers and, indeed, Jack the Hat, he had been strenuously against accepting anything from Paddy, but here and now, this strange brief was putting it all down to him. The scenario seemed to be that he was a clever mastermind who devised the whole thing and that everyone else was just a pawn in his game.

The brief called the first witness, Detective Chief Inspector Dodge. Briggs watched and listened with interest as Dodge took the oath, adding as he finished, "I ask the court's permission not to give my exact occupation." The red coat Judge looked up and said, "Granted" Briggs got the very distinct impression that this little snippet had been discussed somewhere, but certainly not with him.

Briggs tapped the side of the dock to attract the attention of Simon Cantwell who was in the well of the court. Simon looked up and nodded. Briggs beckoned him towards the dock. Simon got up and sauntered over to the dock. "Yes Tel what's up?" he asked smiling insincerely. "What's his correct occupation then?" Simon looked embarrassed. "He's in Special Branch." Briggs was stunned as he had always believed that Dodge was a prime example of the A10 special, maybe that was the part he played to mollify Briggs. "What section of Special Branch exactly?" Simon looked at the floor, intent on avoiding eye contact. "I really can't tell you, you'll have to ask Miss Cotterill she knows." Briggs hissed at Cantwell. "So do you, now tell me and stop fucking about." Cantwell nodded and looked Briggs in the eye, "Irish Affairs Section." He almost whispered the words. "But a deal has been sorted with the court and you will walk."

Briggs was furious, obviously he should have been told earlier. "Tell Miss Cotterill I want a conference at the earliest moment and I want to know the ins and outs of this deal that allegedly has been sorted. Tell her I have got the distinct impression that I am being turkey-tied for the oven." Simon walked away shaking his head. Briggs' insistent stage whispers had caught the attention of the Judge, who glared at Briggs, such as to demand silence.

Dodge ran through his evidence; how he came to arrest Briggs and later Sayers. Dodge also gave the evidence about tapes and how Paddy was fitted with a body tape each morning, except the last morning when it was decided to fit the tape and let Paddy switch it on as, and when, Briggs appeared. Dodge then gave details of the interviews and the charges preferred.

The court adjourned for the day. Miss Cotterill, her junior and Simon arranged a conference in a side room. Briggs and his wife were called in by Simon. Briggs was furious and demanded to know how it was they had managed to secrete the real occupation of Dodge from him. Miss Cotterill made a note but did not say anything. Her junior, the bold Miles, replied in a voice clearly showing his embarrassment. If truth be known, he was more than a little frightened by this large officer. "We have an arrangement with the prosecution and the Director's office which, if carried to fruition, will ensure you suffer a mere inconvenience and not the full weight of the law." Briggs was stunned.

"Are you saying that whatever the evidence disclosed, I am going down? I am speaking to you Miss Cotterill." She looked up as though wakened from a deep sleep.

"Oh yes, quite, well as far as I can see, you have the best of both worlds. If you get acquitted I am assured your career will not suffer and, if convicted, you will suffer a mere eighteen months' imprisonment, a mere trifle." She waved her hand dismissively.

Briggs exploded. "A mere trifle, you stupid bitch, who the fuck do you think you are kidding? This is a fit up, they have it on tape three times, twice me refusing the dosh and the one meet where I nick him. As they don't have a recording of that, isn't it obvious they have binned the tape, or do you still believe in Father Christmas?" There followed a drama laden pause where everyone waited, not sure what Briggs was going to do next – this included Briggs. Miss Cotterill was the first to break this awkward silence.

"I can quite understand you being upset Mr. Briggs. However, there are special circumstances in this case, circumstances which involve national security." Briggs felt his anger rising but his wife put her hand on his arm and smiled that special smile and said,

"Love, let's get it over with and get on with the rest of our lives. They are not going to let you win and they have all the cards."

Briggs could feel tears welling up, tears of frustration and anger. He took out his handkerchief and made out he was blowing his nose, but really he was hiding tears from this cynical bunch. His wife squeezed his arm, but he continued, not yet giving up but becoming calmer with her touch. "And what about Paddy talking to the lady from the Security Services, when do we mention that, or don't we?" The three looked at each other, almost as though deciding who was going to answer.

Eventually Miss Cotterill coughed and said, "Well the real situation is that we have been told that we must not mention anything at all about the Security Services because Ryan is now working for them in Southern Ireland, cipher clerk I believe, and any mention could endanger his life and the cause of national security." Miss Cotterill paused, as though waiting for this to sink in.

Briggs thought she gave the impression that Paddy was the holder of the Holy Grail as he replied. "So the real situation is that I have got to fight this trial with one hand tied behind my back and if I do that successfully and get acquitted I can return to be a time serving copper, and if I lose, as surely I will if I do as you bid me, I get eighteen months. What if I blow the gaff on Paddy and the Security Services, tell the court what really went on?" Miss Cotterill paused, maybe collecting her thoughts.

"Well Mr. Briggs, the situation is that if you go down, the learned Judge will endeavour to make sure you go down on the conspiracy as well and, in those circumstances, has promised you twelve years and more if he can manage it. See things their way and you will not have punishment for the conspiracy, and only eighteen months on the other charge." Briggs laughed without humour.

"Like most things, eighteen months is easy to talk about, how much of it are you going to do?" Miss Cotterill smiled resignedly.

"You are quite right officer, nothing at all, it is for you to decide, but I feel it fair to warn you that if you decide to disclose Ryan's Security Service connections I must drop the brief immediately. I just cannot represent you."

Briggs burst into laughter, he roared, more to relieve his nervous tension than anything else, "What is it? Would it affect your career? Would it mean that you would not be the first female red coat Judge?" Miss Cotterill looked Briggs in the eye, plainly hurt by his jibe.

"I can understand your feelings. However, that apart, I want to know how you are going to play it." Briggs held her gaze.

"I can't answer you at the moment, I'll think on it overnight. I'll see how I feel in the morning and give you my decision then." Miss Cotterill smiled the smile of one who is comfortably out of everything.

"Of course officer but, in your deliberations, do bear in mind that you are dealing with an extremely amoral organisation who stop at nothing, and I mean nothing, to get their way." Briggs nodded soberly, looked at his wife who was near to tears and hugged her.

Speaking from the heart and with hope he said, "Don't worry love I'll make sure it's alright." Miss Cotterill closed the case file and Briggs noted the act of finality.

"What about the situation where I disclose who he is and what they've done and I get acquitted, what then?" Miss Cotterill sat down heavily, and wearily said, "Well then officer Briggs, that is an extremely unlikely scenario. However, having said that, you will have made some very powerful enemies indeed and I doubt you will ever be forgiven, if you follow my drift." Briggs didn't but didn't say so. He got up and left with his wife holding his hand.

Briggs and his wife travelled home on the train, 'the rattler' as he called it. Briggs was on edge. He felt trapped and also that everyone was looking at him. Someone must be following he thought and was tense and ready. He surveyed his fellow travellers. One in particular struck him, a very fit looking young man, very well groomed, well dressed, the very epitome of the Security Services, or so Briggs imagined. Briggs noted that the young man kept looking at him in the reflection in the window and eventually Briggs caught him looking a him full face. The young man smiled a thin smile, which Briggs took to be knowing. Briggs got up, grabbed the young man by the collar and pulled him to his feet. "Who the hell do you people think you are, following me everywhere," shaking the young man as he said it. Maggie Briggs clutched his arm and pleaded, "Terry please don't, please don't." Briggs ignored her, now in some private world where fear dictated action. He slapped the young man who then subsided back into his seat.

"Oh, what did you have to do that for?" whined the young man, in the camp tone of some homosexuals. Briggs saw the situation for what it was and realised he had made a terrible mistake.

"I am terribly sorry mate, I mistook you for someone else" he said, straightening the young man's clothing as he spoke.

"Oh that's alright, it happens to me all the time, I'm used to it."

He got out a small mirror and rearranged his hairstyle. Briggs returned to his seat with his wife, who he could sense was not too pleased by his display of paranoia. "You couldn't leave it could you, just had to have a go." She hissed the words out of the side of her mouth. The rest of the passengers regarded him with distaste.

In the evening Briggs sat watching television. The Briggs family had eaten the evening meal but very limited conversation had passed between them. The telephone rang and Briggs picked it up almost immediately. "Yes?" he snapped and waited for a response. It was delayed.

"Oh dear, what did you want to do that for?" Briggs immediately recognised the camp intonation of the train homosexual. Briggs was forced to laugh.

"So you really were, weren't you?" There was another pause and a distinct change of voice.

"Yes I was and I am. I am ringing you to make sure you make the right decision, remember if you go down, and without doubt you will, your family will be on the out and strange things can happen old son. Play it sensibly and both the family and you will be looked after. Do it the other way and life could become tragic, very tragic." The telephone clicked dead.

"Who was that dear?" Maggie looked up from the television. "No-one really, only someone from the Yard wishing me well, taking a bit of a chance really." Briggs sat down and pondered.

Reality

Together with Maggie, Briggs walked along the landing outside court. Almost immediately he saw Miss Cotterill and nodded. She waved him to the same side room they had used the night before. They entered and sat down. "Well Mr. Briggs, do I still hold a brief in the case?" she asked, with her case file open on the desk.

"Yes, you do," the words of the pseudo-homosexual ringing in his ears. "As I understand it, any mention of the Security Services is forbidden." Miss Cotterill nodded. "Can we make some waves about the changing of the operational plans?" Miss Cotterill thought for a moment.

"I will enquire about that," she responded, making a note on her brief.

"Surely you mean you will take instructions on that." Briggs was at his most sarcastic.

"Mr. Briggs," said Miss Cotterill in exasperated tone. "We are doing the best we can under very difficult conditions." Briggs could tell his jibe had hit hard but he wasn't at all concerned for her feelings, believing that she had violated the trust he had placed in her.

"What about the bits missing from the tapes? Are we allowed to mention them, or will that upset the real guvnors?" Briggs continued, not comfortable with the constraints placed upon him.

Again she made a note, saying offhandedly, "I will include that with the operational plan."

Briggs braced himself for the coming storm and said, "And finally Miss Cotterill I shall, of course, be canvassing this matter before the Appeal Court." Miss Cotterill frowned.

"I do not think that is a good idea, definitely not a good idea."

Briggs looked her straight in the eye and responded.

"That's as maybe, but I think it's arrogant to assume that I will swallow all this shit. They have screwed me, wiped their cocks on the curtains and now they want me to touch my forelock and say, 'Thank you sir'."

Miss Cotterill grimaced, "Not very pretty language Mr. Briggs, but I get your drift." Briggs felt his anger rising. He had to make this self-indulgent woman understand.

Exasperated he said, "What do you really expect? I have given my life to nicking villains. I am not saying I have never crossed the line, but whenever I have, a villain has fallen. Now the establishment wants to throw away the rule book just because little Paddy is important. What is so important that he can't be nicked?" Miss Cotterill shrugged her shoulders in resignation.

"The truth is I don't really know. As I understand the whispers, he's involved in sending some merchandise to Southern Ireland, and they are financing something with the result of the sale but, what that is, I don't know."

Briggs was thoughtful. "So we don't even know which side this is for?" Miss Cotterill looked blank.

"Which side?" she asked.

Briggs became even more exasperated. "IRA or the Loyalists – which side?"

Miss Cotterill became frosty. "I do not know and I don't want to, it's a messy business all round."

Briggs shrugged, "Except, of course, you are representing someone who is caught in the middle and, don't forget Miss Cotterill, in the fullness of time this could rear its head again." She look puzzled.

"What if the skill of the tape editor is overtaken by the technical advances of the future? If that happens, you are all going to look very foolish. Don't think for one moment I will ever be able to forget this case, or these conferences." Briggs got up. Miss Cotterill seemed surprised at his anger.

"I understand all that, but we do have agreement, we do what the prosecution want?"

Briggs sneered. "Not just what the prosecution want, but what the Special Branch and the Security Services want and what Scotland

Yard want and what the legal profession want. Yes we have agreement. I would not put my family in danger over such a small thing as my going to prison." Maggie squeezed his hand as she finally understood the predicament in his mind.

Briggs stood outside the court and watched Paddy Ryan reading the Financial Times. Briggs was amused, as this was contrary to the character he portrayed at Committal. He was musing at the implications when the court usher came out and beckoned to Briggs that he should enter the court and surrender to his bail. Briggs entered the court and joined the grumpy screw in the dock. He sat down and got out the Daily Telegraph. The screw peered over his shoulder endeavouring to read the copy. Briggs waited until he thought the screw had read all that he wanted and said, "Can I turn the page now?" The screw grunted and Briggs turned to the sports page, passing the paper to the Screw. The court was called to order.

Dodge was waiting by the witness box ready to be cross-examined when he entered, took out his pocket book and waited. Miss Cotterill rose slowly, looking at her brief and began cross-examining Dodge. Briggs paid close attention to the questions and answers, but Dodge was not giving anything away and Miss Cotterill was being careful not to cross the agreed line. Miss Cotterill smiled sweetly. "Mr. Dodge, can you explain why it was that for nineteen days, I think it was, Mr. Ryan was body taped, i.e. fitted with a running tape, and on the twentieth day, when Mr. Briggs appears by appointment he is not fitted with such a tape, and therefore there is no recording of that last meeting?" Dodge looked aimlessly about the court.

"It was deemed a good idea at the time that Ryan should switch the recorder on as, and when, Briggs came in." Miss Cotterill nodded her head.

"I see," she said, unwilling to accuse Dodge of lying, for to do so would inevitably disclose the involvement of the Security Services. She continued to cross-examine.

Dodge did agree with Briggs' commendation record and that he had recently been recommended for promotion. Dodge also mentioned that Briggs had been a badged member of the SAS but that his record of service was subject to the Official Secrets Act and, as such, could not be produced before the court. Briggs was amused when this information caused some members of the jury to sit up and pay a bit more attention. The female member of the jury went decidedly dreamy. Briggs thought, "If that is what it takes, you have got it," smiling at the absurdity of his private obscene thoughts. There was no re-examination. Detective Inspector Sparrow got into the box and backed up Dodge. He was asked much the same questions as Dodge and answered them as he and Dodge had obviously agreed. Miss Cotterill was at pains not to kick over the sacred traces and trod cautiously throughout.

Ryan got into the box and gave his evidence as the idiot Irishman who did not understand anything too well. He was adamant that Briggs had bent his ear trying to get money out of him, stating that information meant money, so that, when Briggs asked for information, he really meant money. He was at a loss to explain how it was that, when he offered Briggs money, it was refused on three separate occasions. Was he talking about information or money when he was talking about money?" Ryan made out he was totally confused and didn't understand any of this, but he did know that Briggs was hounding him for money to get him off. Miss Cotterill asked, "How, when you were already charged, was Mr. Briggs going to get you off?"

Ryan thought for a moment and then said, "Ah well Mr. Sayers said that Briggs was very clever and could get anyone off, he knows someone in the court like."

Miss Cotterill nodded, almost as though she was agreeing with the outlandish assertion, asking "And Mr. Sayers, where did he fit into this case?"

Ryan paused and then said, "He didn't fit into it at all, he was a friend just helping me out."

Miss Cotterill looked closely at Ryan's statement. "But you say here that Sayers was hounding you for money and Briggs was hounding you for information. Is that the way it was?" Ryan looked at the Judge who did not meet his eye.

"It was Briggs who was on about money. Mr. Sayers was just trying to be a good friend." Much to Briggs' surprise Miss Cotterill left it there.

"When Mr. Briggs came to see you on the day he was arrested, why didn't you switch on the tape recorder, as instructed by Mr. Dodge?"

Ryan stammered and flustered, "Well he came in too fast and I didn't have a chance. The switch was on my leg, I couldn't get to it." Miss Cotterill nodded.

"Very convenient. Basically you say Mr. Briggs said, "Give me the money." Mr. Briggs, in effect, says you offered the money and he arrested you. What do you say to that?"

Ryan smiled, "He's lying of course." Miss Cotterill, still looking at his statement, continued "I understand you have brought the accounts of your company to court with you today. May I see them please?"

The prosecution brief jumped to his feet. "We claim Crown privilege in respect of these accounts." Before Miss Cotterill had a chance to address the Judge on the subject, the Judge said "Granted." Miss Cotterill feigned amazement and sat down.

The prosecution barrister got up. "No re-examination my lord." Ryan left the witness box and treated Briggs to a cheeky grin. "That is the case for the prosecution my lord," said the man for the prosecution.

Miss Cotterill sat down heavily behind the side room desk. "Well Mr. Briggs, how do you think we are doing?" she asked, knowing what his attitude would be. "Well I think we have done the best we could without disclosing the real reason for all this and, to be quite honest, what has gone on in that courtroom is more corrupt than anything I have ever been involved in."

Miles Bannister made a face. He was obviously quite terrified by Miss Cotterill and rightly so. Compared to him, she possessed a mighty intellect.

"Have we secured the attendance of Detective Chief Inspector Parris and Detective Constable Jones?" Briggs ushered his wife to sit down. He remained standing.

"The Director and the Commissioner have both agreed to the attendance of both officers. However they have both indicated they will not be helpful to the defence."

Briggs laughed. "They can be what they like, one of them at least is lucky not to be in the dock, both of them if the truth be known."

Miss Cotterill winced, "I do not wish to know that officer" she said primly.

"Oh do come on, after what you have been involved in in this case, impeding the case for the defence, or rather helping the other side to do it, you can hardly come the reluctant virgin routine. After all, if you look at what's gone on it could be best described as a conspiracy to pervert the course of justice between the lot of you, the Judge included." The corners of her mouth turned down, with a frown to match. For one awful moment, Briggs thought she was going to burst into tears. He could never handle women who weep, but Miss Cotterill was of sterner stuff.

She coughed to hide her emotions and said, "I deeply resent that." Briggs, who was studying his notes, looked up.

"I expect you do Miss Cotterill and if you have a shred of conscience I hope you are ashamed as well." Miss Cotterill got up and flounced out of the conference room. Simon Cantwell looked mournful.

"You have really upset her now. I wouldn't be surprised if she dropped the brief and withdraws from the case." Briggs was shuffling his papers into some sort of order.

"She would never do that and leave me a loose cannon in the court. I would probably have to make motion to recall little Paddy, so just pass that on to the soppy tart will you." Maggie put her hand on his arm and gave him a look that said "Enough."

The next morning. Briggs sat in the dock and watched the sunlight stream over the court well. The grey wigs looked very dusty and dirty and the faces beneath them had a parchment quality. The Judge seemed remote on his high platform. "Call Detective Chief Parris." The call was repeated in time-honoured fashion and eventually Jack the Hat appeared in the well of the court and was ushered into the witness box. For the first time Briggs saw him without his hat, he seemed strangely vulnerable without it. He had a fair head of hair, although greying, thus dispelling the rumour that he was almost completely bald. He took the oath and announced himself. "Jack William Parris, Detective Chief Inspector stationed at Rodney Road my lord." Jack the Hat looked down at Miss Cotterill, waiting for the dreaded questions to begin to try and trip him up.

"Now Chief Inspector, dealing with the present circumstances, did you authorise Detective Constable Briggs to meet Patrick Ryan, knowing full well that he was a person on bail?"

Jack the Hat paused, looked at Briggs, and replied with a bright grin. "No my lord" intoned Jack the Hat. Miss Cotterril shrugged her cloak about her and pursued her quarry.

"Did you authorise Detective Constable Briggs to go and meet someone using the nom de plume of Charles Kent, for the purposes of gathering information and assisting with the current crime?" Jack the Hat pondered the question for a few moments. "No I did not my lord."

Miss Cotterill looked closely at the typed sheet before her. "Are you absolutely sure Chief Inspector?" Her voice rang round the court, almost clanging off the walls. Briggs could see Jack the Hat was shaken. He may well have forgotten that he authorised Briggs to see Ryan, and the fact that this was recorded in the station occurrence book. "I think you described this likely information as a golden opportunity. Do you remember now?" Briggs had fed Miss Cotterill this line before court in order to focus Jack the Hat's attention to his side of the case and to remind him that if he, Briggs, decided to cleanse his mind of all corruption, Jack the Hat would spend an eternity looking at four walls. Jack the Hat flushed slightly and looked across at Briggs. "No my lord, I do not remember doing that." Miss Cotterill picked up the piece of paper from the bench.

"I have here a copy of an entry in the station occurrence book, which appears to indicate that you authorised Detective Constable Briggs to meet a prisoner on bail for the purposes of returning paintings and gathering information. I can have the original book produced if you wish." Jack the Hat looked crestfallen.

"I am sorry my lord I forgot," Jack the Hat answered with bowed head. Miss Cotterill began to look very white and spiteful.

"Are you telling the court Chief Inspector that you now acknowledge that you gave Officer Briggs permission to go and see Mr. Ryan?"

Jack the Hat looked sheepish at being caught out. "Yes my lord I do." Miss Cotterill wrapped her gown around herself in a theatrical pose.

"And what advice did you give this officer about meeting a prisoner on bail?" Jack the Hat looked puzzled. "Or perhaps you have forgotten that also?" remarked Miss Cotterill waspishly.

"Hrumph." His Honour cleared his throat, about to get into the act. "I feel you are being a touch unfair to the Chief Inspector. He is after all only human and can forget things, small details in the midst of the everyday bustle." His Honour smiled benignly at Jack the Hat and added, "Even Judges forget things." The court laughed obediently. Miss Cotterill finished her obligatory chuckle.

"Yes my lord, that is true and such lapses of memory are usually corrected by the Court of Appeal." His Lordship did not look pleased with his sudden bringing down to earth.

"Quite," he said and returned to his notes.

"Now Chief Inspector, perhaps you would be kind enough to riffle through that rag bag of past experiences you call a memory and tell us what advice you gave this officer about meeting a prisoner on bail."

Jack the Hat still looked perplexed. "I didn't give him any advice. As a qualified detective, he knows how far to go and what to do," Jack the Hat pleading his innocence to the court.

"So you being his Senior Officer, to whom he came for permission to see a prisoner on bail, you didn't feel called upon to make sure he knew what he was doing and what he might be up against?" Jack the Hat spluttered and stammered. "Well no, Ryan was his prisoner, I left him to it."

Miss Cotterill left a theatrical pause in her onslaught, during which she surveyed the jury and the public gallery. "You left him to it, I see. Chief Inspector are you aware of the disciplinary offence committed by Senior Police Officers, that of allowing their charges to go about their duties when under insufficient supervision, as in this case?" Miss Cotterill spat the words at Jack the Hat.

Jack the Hat looked pleading. "I didn't think of it in that light. After all he's experienced, served in the forces and all that. I can't be expected to oversee his every move," Jack the Hat flustered.

Miss Cotterill laughed as she continued, "But Chief Inspector, surely that is your duty, to oversee his every move and every move of the officers under you? Are you saying you are not up to your duties?"

Jack the Hat snapped, "Of course I am able to perform my duties but I don't see how I can supervise what an officer does out of my direct presence." Miss Cotterill smiled the smile of a hunter who has her prey helpless.

"That is certainly what I am saying. You could surely supervise by ascertaining that he is aware of the dangers of meeting a prisoner on bail. However, you didn't feel that was necessary. Not only that, but you dismissed the incident completely from your mind, so much so, that you couldn't recall it for this court."

Briggs noticed with amusement that she didn't accuse Jack the Hat of lying, which Briggs felt was the course she should be on, but only of defective memory. Briggs was trying not to get unduly wound up about anything that went on in the court, as the eventual outcome was already decided. He was either going to prison for eighteen months or he was going to walk away scot free. Either way, they were just going through the motions dictated by Special Branch and the Security Services.

Miss Cotterill picked up a piece of paper from the bench. "I will now ask you some questions about Briggs' annual qualification report. Can I ask you Chief Inspector to cajole your memory on this matter?"

The Judge erupted into action. "Miss Cotterill, it was Oscar Wilde who said that sarcasm is the sharp tool of a blunt mind. I think you have just illustrated the point." Miss Cotterill looked contrite.

"I do apologise my lord." After a suitable pause, which advertised her contrition, she proceeded, "Now Chief Inspector, it is true, is it not, that officer Briggs was recommended for promotion by you?"

Jack the Hat paused and, seeing no way out, said "That is correct my lord." Miss Cotterill pursued Jack the Hat relentlessly.

"And, therefore, presumably you had no cause for concern regarding his behaviour?"

Again, Jack the Hat was constrained to say "That is so my lord." Miss Cotterill obviously decided to chance her arm.

"And as only the top ten per cent of any organisation get promotion, or are recommended for it, it ought to be said that Mr. Briggs was exemplary as a police officer, yes?" Miss Cotterill waited. Jack the Hat looked confused and worried.

"Except, of course, Miss Cotterill, he ended up here charged with a serious offence or two" interjected His Honour with a half-hearted attempt at humour. Miss Cotterill looked exasperated.

"Apart from these matters." She said the words slowly and loudly. His Honour resumed his note taking quickly. "Would you say he was exemplary Chief Inspector?" Jack the Hat looked at the floor of the witness box for inspiration.

"Yes, my lord I would say that Detective Constable Briggs was exemplary." Miss Cotterill treated Jack the Hat to a thin smile.

"And therefore, it must have been a surprise when Mr. Briggs was arrested?"

Jack the Hat looked wary but was unable to think of any answer other than, "Yes my lord."

"One further thing Chief Inspector, when Mr. Briggs and Mr. Jones were arrested they were brought to Rodney Road."

Jack the Hat looked around the court hoping for divine inspiration. Receiving none, he said, "Yes my lord."

Miss Cotterill pressed on. "And you had a conversation mainly with Mr. Briggs?"

Again, Jack the Hat nodded, "Yes my lord."

Miss Cotterill leaned on her lectern. "During that conversation, did Mr. Briggs say to you, "I had nicked him and was on the way here when they jumped me?" Jack the Hat looked as though he had been connected to the mains.

"No, my lord I do not remember that."

Miss Cotterill fixed him with a steely stare. "Are you sure Chief Inspector?" Jack the Hat seemed flustered.

"I am my lord."

Miss Cotterill adjusted her wig. "Or is this another matter you can't remember unless it is written down for you?" Jack the Hat could remember, but knew that if he didn't toe the party line his chances of ever being a superintendent or above were extremely remote.

"No my lord, he never said that."

Briggs laughed and was aware that the jury heard him. "Any minute now a cock will crow three times" and stared at Jack the Hat. "Miss Cotterill, any further outburst from your client will cause me to more than show my displeasure."

Miss Cotterill nodded, turned and looked at Briggs, and winked. "So it was never said?" Miss Cotterill waited.

"No my lord."

Miss Cotterill shook her head in resignation. "Thank you Chief Inspector." Jack the Hat left the box, relieved that he had not suddenly transferred to the dock.

Miss Cotterill straightened herself. She muttered something to Miles Bannister. "My lord, I wonder if we might have a short adjournment whilst I take my client's instructions on a small matter?" The Judge nodded and returned to his notes. Miles Bannister came to the side of the dock. "Are we going to call Jones?"

Briggs was surprised. "Yes, of course, why?"

Bannister leaned closer to Briggs, "Well medical opinion has it that he is on the brink of a nervous breakdown, keeps crying all the time, and if he gives evidence it might push him over the top."

Briggs laughed. "What would it do to him if he stood where I am, what then? No! Call the idiot and he can take his chances."

Miles shook his head. "He might give you irrational answers that might put you deeper in it" Miles said, trying to emulate Briggs' manner.

Briggs spoke slowly. "He can do what he likes, but he stands the chance that all of a sudden I might find God and be constrained to tell the truth. Then he really would have a worry" Briggs snapped, irritated by this foppish brief. Bannister looked as though he had been slapped in the face and returned quickly to Miss Cotterill, who nodded receipt of the information.

"Call Detective Constable Jones." After a number of repeats of the name, Ron appeared in the well of the court. Briggs was surprised by his appearance and suddenly realised that the opinion that he was on the brink of a nervous breakdown could be true. Jones had never been heavy, not like Briggs, "lean and lithe" was how Jones described himself, but he now looked emaciated, almost an advert for Auschwitz. He climbed painfully into the witness box. He took the testament in his right hand and stroked it lovingly with his left. He had a manic, almost crazed, expression. From where he was, some distance away, Briggs could see that Jones' eyes were red rimmed. Briggs felt that Jones was about to burst into tears. He read the oath off the card held by the usher and, in a faltering manner, gave his name and occupation.

Jones looked at Miss Cotterill standing at the bench beneath him. There was a pause and Miss Cotterill coughed lightly. "Mr. Jones, it is true, is it not, that you and Mr. Briggs here," indicating Briggs in the dock, "were partners, bucks I believe you call it, working from Rodney Road CID office?" Miss Cotterill held her brief in front of her.

"Yes my lord, that is true," Jones replied in an almost inaudible whisper.

"And how long had you been partnered with Mr. Briggs?" Miss Cotterill cocked her head, hoping to hear the answer clearly. Jones mumbled something. "I am sorry Mr. Jones I did not catch your answer."

Jones' head went up. "I said, too long, I worked with him too long."

Miss Cotterill cast Briggs a meaningful glance, which Briggs took to mean "He's off his crust and will do you harm." Briggs nodded receipt of the information.

"Exactly how long Mr. Jones?" Miss Cotterill spoke clearly and concisely. Jones looked down. Briggs thought he was about to burst into tears – again.

"About two years" he muttered. Miss Cotterill looked across to Briggs. Briggs nodded his assent to the period.

"And you were with Mr. Briggs when he called at Ryan's Garage, the day he was arrested?" Jones looked vacant.

"I was with him all the time." Jones spoke in a low monotone.

"Mr. Jones, are you receiving medical attention for any ailment at the moment?" It seemed an age before Jones began to answer.

"Yes, I am under Doctor Hillier at the Maudsley." Miss Cotterill made a note.

"That is a psychiatric hospital I believe?" She smiled the false smile that counsel reserve for those who they perceive as idiots.

"Yes," he muttered. This was certainly not the Jones that Briggs knew.

"And what treatment are you are receiving from Doctor Hillier?" Jones looked around the courtroom as though he suddenly realised where he was.

He paused and stuttered, "He talks to me about him," indicating Briggs in the dock, "and he gives me tablets to make me feel better about myself."

Miss Cotterill took a deep breath. "My lord, I wonder if I might have a short recess in order that I can confer with my client?" His Honour looked up from his notes.

"I think that is an excellent idea Miss Cotterill and, as it is now 3.45pm, perhaps we should adjourn for the day." The assembled briefs rose and bowed. "All rise," intoned the court usher. His Honour rose, bowed to the assembled throng and made his way out.

Briggs climbed down from the dock, took Maggie's hand and made his way towards Miss Cotterill. She smiled. "He really is on the verge of a nervous breakdown, or perhaps you feel differently Mr. Briggs?" Briggs looked to his wife.

"I just feel sorry for him, really, really sorry, he seems terrified," she announced to Miss Cotterill and Briggs.

Miss Cotterill became thoughtful. "I think we ought to retire to our private committee room." They all three walked off and into the side office. Miss Cotterill settled herself behind the desk. Simon Cantwell followed them in. "Now Mr. and Mrs. Briggs what do we do now?" Briggs sat pensive, waiting for his wife Maggie who seemed better able to call the shots – most of the time.

Eventually she said, "We let him go. He isn't going to give a good impression and will try and do us harm. We do not need him."

Miss Cotterill smiled. "Of course, as always, it takes a lady to bring some sense to the proceedings. I agree. What do you think?" She aimed the question directly at Briggs.

"I think we should try to wring out of the prosecution the fact that, apart from Paddy's evidence, there was nothing against Jones at all. Also that he was present when I told Jack the Hat, er Chief Inspector Parris, that I had already nicked Ryan before the A10 lot got hold of me. That being stated, we let him go and let the jury know that we have been merciful." She finished making her note and closed the brief. They all left together and walked along the gallery outside the court.

Dick Harris, who had been an aid at Rodney Road, was standing with other officers near the lifts. He saw Briggs and turned his back. Briggs walked past him fairly close and, as he passed, whispered "Wanker" in Harris's ear.

Again they travelled by the rattler to New Eltham. Briggs felt he was being followed, but he didn't bother to try and sort out who, what and how. They walked along from the station at New Eltham, hand in hand past the green suburban gardens. For two in such dire states, and under such pressure, they were very happy.

Briggs entered the double doors of the Old Bailey, holding his wife's hand as she came through and up the steps towards the court's foyer, knowing full well that today he would be giving his evidence – what little evidence there was left after all the editing and falsehoods. But he was tired, tired of the case, Ryan, the Security Services and Special Branch; tired of looking over his shoulder when he was out, tired of watching what he said to friends on the telephone. He was now only looking forward to getting it over with and, if that meant prison, well so be it. He had discussed this with Maggie and they were sure their love could stand eighteen months apart, twelve if he kept his remission. It might even make it stronger. The only thing that bothered him to any great extent was that the kids might suffer from the jibes of unkind neighbours, but he really could not think of too many who would stoop so low. The complaints sergeant perhaps, but he would be aware of what Briggs might do to him in return and would, hopefully, become more diplomatic.

As he walked along the gallery, Sid Mills came out of an alcove and fell in step with them. "Wotcha Tel, you okay?" Briggs was startled.

"Er hello Sid, nice to see you, you know Maggie don't you?" They nodded to each other.

"How's it going?" chirped Sid, cheerful, obviously not aware that things had not panned out exactly as he had foretold.

"It's going as well as can be expected." Briggs was non-committal and hoping to not upset Sid with the truth."

But Sid killed that when he said, "The deal the fifth floor talked to me about, that is on the cards yes?" Briggs stopped, as did his wife in unison.

"Look Sid." Briggs was thinking how to let him down gently, but couldn't think of anything that would work. "I'm sorry mate that's bullshit they gave you. They just wanted to keep me with the same brief, so that all ends could be folded against the middle." Sid looked crestfallen. Briggs thought he was about to burst into tears.

"But they promised me, my old mate put it to me, it was definite from the Commissioner and above." Briggs put his hand on Sid's arm.

"Don't worry mate, it's alright. The way it's going to work, if I don't say he's well connected with the Irish Affairs Section and working for them in Southern Ireland, cipher clerk or something…"

Sid butted in, "That means agent basically, nothing else."

Briggs continued, "Well whatever, and if I get convicted they will dole me out eighteen months and no conviction on the conspiracy. If, however, I rock the boat and insult the court with the truth, they will endeavour to get me twelve years and more if they can manage it."

Sid sat down on a bench, put his head in his hands. "Bastards, bastards, they have had me over." Briggs put his hand on Sid's shoulder.

"Don't get too upset old chap it's not worth it, it's the fifth floor, they are almost duty bound to betray you, it's part of the base qualifications."

Sid was almost in tears. "They promised me, they promised. Tel I'm really sorry."

Briggs tried to comfort Sid. "They probably had your mate over as well. I shouldn't get too upset about it. To be honest, the way I feel now, I am almost happy to be getting eighteen months and be out of the pressure cooker." Briggs got up, joined his wife and they went together to the court and waited outside. Briggs watched Sid get up and go towards the exit, his shoulders hunched, almost like a whipped dog.

Briggs was called into the court with his wife. He climbed wearily into the dock, the grumpy screw grunted a welcome. "You might be joining us today Briggsy, then we'll see just how hard you are." Briggs grinned. "As may be mate, but I doubt if you will have a lot to do with it." The screw scowled and sat down. Briggs sat reading his paper. The briefs started to file into court like cockroaches after food. Simon Cantwell came over and talked up to him in the dock. "They've agreed everything except that they won't have it that you told Jones and Parris about nicking him before you were nicked." Simon waited expectantly.

"There's a surprise." Briggs thought for a moment. "Okay let him go without that admission." Simon nodded and returned to his place at the bar.

The court usher got up.

"All those having business before his Honour the Recorder of London draw near and give your attendance." The usher turned to his right and stood to attention. His Honour entered from his usual door and proceeded with due pomp to his high chair. He turned left and faced the court, bowed to the assembled throng, who dutifully returned the compliment and sat down.

Briggs noticed Jones skulk into court and sit down on a chair near the usher, his head bared and bowed. Miss Cotterill rose, shrugged her gown about her and adjusted her wig. "My lord, my client has given me instructions not to interview this witness any further, this being due to his obvious mental condition. The prosecution have agreed to state that there never was any evidence against Jones, neither was there any discussion between Jones and Briggs as regards any corrupt payment of money." His Honour stared down at the court. "I am quite sure that that is a very wise decision Miss Cotterill." Miss Cotterill bowed. "I will now call Detective Constable Briggs."

Briggs felt his stomach heave and thought he was going to break wind at this most important moment. He stood up, looked down and, as Maggie smiled encouragement, he walked across the dock and down into the well of the court, all eyes upon him. He climbed up into the witness box and settled himself by looking slowly around the court. The usher held the testament which he took in his right hand and read from the oath card held in his left. "I swear by Almighty God that the evidence I shall give shall be the truth, the whole truth and nothing but the truth." Just as he finished the oath, his stomach gave another heave and he broke wind. He tried desperately to hang on to it, and clenched his buttocks against it, but was unsuccessful and the eruption of wind presented itself to the world as a high pitched whine. The usher who was standing next to the box smiled and coughed to hide her amusement. Briggs was well aware that he was surrounded by the smell of his own effluent but he continued on as though unaware. "Terence Andrew Briggs, Detective Constable M Division, stationed at Rodney Road, my lord." Miss Cotterill gave her customary thin smile. "Did she know?" wondered Briggs but decided that he didn't care if she did. He couldn't call the wind back and re-encompass it within his body and wouldn't want to. "Better out than in" as his father always declared after an ear splitting explosion.

"Now officer," Miss Cotterill began to lead him through the

evidence they had decided upon; how he had first come to arrest Pat with the aid of the Trafpol officers and how Sayers had come to be involved in the job and the fact that he had met Sayers in a public house, where Sayers had propositioned him to alter the evidence to let Ryan out. Briggs was careful not to mention the amount that Sayers had offered, but stressed how he had refused Sayers' advances. He denied that anyone else had spoken to him on the matter of Ryan and a bribe. Briggs smiled to himself. He suspected that that part had raised Jack the Hat's spirits and had been conducive to curing his diarrhoea. Also, that a large body of Senior Officers had breathed a communal sigh of relief that their fifteen minutes of fame, or infamy, had not arrived. Briggs gave his version of what happened in that back room when Ryan gave him the money, also that Ryan had said at Committal that it was definitely Sayers who was after money and Briggs who was after information. Whilst at trial, he had suddenly invented the story that 'information meant money'. He also said that he had refused Ryan's offer of money three times, when the money had been present in Ryan's possession. He had, at all times, sought information relating to the source of the engines and had not at any time intimated that information meant money. Miss Cotterill said "Wait there officer" and went to sit down.

Briggs said, "Er excuse me, I haven't finished my evidence-in-chief."

Miss Cotterill straightened herself into the usual brief questioning mode. "I am sorry officer, I thought you had." The learned Judge sat up a little straighter for this impromptu addition to the agreed evidence. "The tapes are not complete, there are pieces missing from them." Briggs thought Miss Cotterill looked a bit white and spiteful at the inclusion of this gem. "Are you saying officer that the tapes have been edited?" Briggs looked her straight in the eye.

"I don't know, have they?"

Miss Cotterill smarted, "How should I know?" Briggs treated her to a broad grin, which displayed how much he was enjoying her discomfort.

"Also, my lord, there is an 'x' factor in this case which has yet to be discovered or discussed." Miss Cotterill sat down quickly, any attempt by Briggs to discuss the 'x' factor silenced. Briggs looked to the Judge, in the hope that maybe he might help out, but the Judge was studying his notes with great attention to detail.

The prosecution barrister rose. For once he looked unsure. "Tell me officer, what was the arrangement with Ryan? Was it information, or money, or did information mean money, or did it mean information and money?"

Briggs laughed. The Judge snapped. "Mr. Briggs you do not realise the peril in which you stand."

Briggs snapped back, "Oh yes I do my lord." His Honour was unable to hold eye contact. The prosecution brief continued with much the same line that had been agreed, almost like pushing raw material through a sausage machine. He took care not to challenge Briggs on his assertion that the tapes had been tampered with and left the subject of whether money meant information or the other way round strictly alone. Eventually, satisfied that he had kicked the ball around enough for the jury, he sat down. Miss Cotterill stood up. "That concludes the case for the defence my lord." Briggs thought he noticed a trace of satisfaction in the look the Judge gave Miss Cotterill.

The prosecution brief got up, fixed the jury with a sweet smile and proceeded to outline the case for the prosecution, how this officer was devious and, with the unfortunate Mr. Sayers, had conspired to together to (a) separate the unfortunate Mr. Ryan from his hard earned cash, and (b) pervert the course of common justice. He said that the jury must take full account of what the uneducated Mr. Ryan had to say about the arrangement between him and the officers and, in all the circumstances, the jury should convict.

Miss Cotterill rose and paused. "Ladies and gentlemen of the jury, this officer survives in the strange atmosphere of criminals and policemen, where codes of practice are rather different than the normal state of intercourse in society and where consciences invariably have to be strangled in the pursuit of criminals. It is inevitable that to shine the light of day on some of these dealings you would come up with a strange sight to the normal person, the man on the upper floor of the Clapham omnibus in fact." Briggs thought, "The way she's going on I would be better off pleading guilty," realising that what she was doing was to ensure he was fully in the frame and unlikely to get out. Briggs had refused to give her details of his Army service, with a statement which upset her and made her tighten her lips to a thin disapproving line. "If the business about the Security Service cannot be mentioned, neither can the Special Air Service." Miss Cotterill then went off in a diatribe about 'benefit of the doubt'.

The grumpy screw leaned over to Briggs and whispered, "If there's a doubt mate, you can be bleedin' sure the benefit of it ain't coming your way." Briggs laughed at the obvious. Eventually, after an age, Miss Cotterill sat down. Briggs was relieved and could see the end of his ordeal, the one in court anyway.

The Judge began his summing up and, although Briggs was expecting a biased summing up, he was surprised at the extent that the Judge went to. According to him, Briggs was after 'money and information' and, although Ryan could be regarded as a 'man who lied like smoke' when it suited him, the tapes however corroborated what he says." This caused a snort of laughter from Briggs. The Judge glared his disapproval and Briggs immediately stifled his mutinous thoughts. The Judge mentioned all the evidence that goes to conspiracy; how the officers had agreed to meet and discussed Ryan. Briggs almost expected him to go into a 'nod nod, wink wink routine'. He mentioned that "Briggs asserts that the tapes are not complete and said he may be right." Briggs sat up, suddenly interested, as the Judge continued. "There may some parts obscured by background noise, as, in some cases, they do not make entire sense." The grumpy screw leaned across to Briggs' ear. "Neat eh?" Briggs nodded. The Judge came to the end of the summing up with the words, "With regards to the conspiracy count, if you have any doubt that these two officers acted together in this manner to pervert the course of justice, just dismiss it from your mind, for I shall not be calling for a verdict on the conspiracy count." Then, leaving a few words for the morning, he adjourned for the night.

Briggs and his wife went home that night, not so happy as they had been before, realising that this was probably the last time they would be together for about a year. As might be expected, Briggs was unable to settle, he was well aware of the aggravation that awaited him at Wormwood Scrubs or wherever they decided to send him. He sat in his garden, a warm summer's night, close by was a honeysuckle climber in full bloom. In later years the scent of honeysuckle always depressed him, remembering this moment. He sat there and looked at the stars, a bright clear night and, no doubt, the last one in his own garden for some time.

The next morning Briggs stood next to the grumpy Screw. "Nice day for it." Briggs looked him in the eye. "Bollocks" he said quietly. The grumpy screw looked away.

The Judge came in, bowed and sat down. They all followed suit. The Judge finished his summing up and ordered the jury to retire to consider their verdict. They filed out of the court and Briggs noticed that none of them looked at him as they left. Briggs and his wife went to the gallery outside the court where they sat, not speaking, for about half an hour, Briggs reading his 'Daily Telegraph', or pretending to. After about thirty minutes, the usher came out and said 'Jury's coming back." Briggs was surprised as such a short retirement usually meant 'not guilty'.

They all trooped back into court, Briggs climbing up into his dock, which by now was almost home to him. He faced the Judge as he came back into court, bowed to all and sundry and sat down. The court clerk addressed the foreman of the jury. "Have you reached a verdict on which you all agree?" The foreman looked confused. "No, we do not know what we are trying this man for, what indictment. There are two, is it both, or one and, if so, which one?" The Judge looked slightly embarrassed, realising that his structured bias had come unstuck. He then instructed them to consider the corruption indictment only, summed up on that count again in some depth and instructed them to retire and consider their verdict. They all trooped out again and into the jury room.

Again Briggs and Maggie waited outside the court on the gallery. As time went on, they adjourned to the canteen and drank tea. After about an hour they returned to the court, but still no news of the jury. Briggs took Maggie for a walk around the outside of the court where they did some window shopping and Briggs bought a pack of playing cards. All the while Briggs felt his wife was close to tears. She didn't say a great deal and the harder he tried to please her, the quieter she got. They returned to the court and sat in silence on the gallery outside. Briggs amused himself by looking every passing Detective in the eye and smiling brightly at his embarrassment.

Together they whiled away the afternoon playing their own game called jacks and sevens, and, later gin rummy and, still later, pontoon for pennies.

Eventually the usher came over. "The Judge is going to call the jury back and tell them about majority verdicts." Briggs nodded. He, in turn, explained to Maggie that after a jury has been out for a long time the Judge can call for a majority verdict, on which at least ten must agree.

The jury were already sitting in their box and the Judge returned along his ledge, bowed to everyone again and sat down. Briggs thought he looked a bit testy. "You ought to try sitting here old son, then you would really have the hump," thought Briggs.

"Ladies and gentlemen of the jury, it is around this point in your deliberations that I am entitled to inform you of the availability of majority verdicts. You are now able to bring in a verdict on which at least ten of you are agreed. Now, will you please retire and endeavour to bring in a verdict under those circumstances." They all trooped out once again and the young woman on the bottom left of the jury box looked at Briggs and smiled, Briggs thought, in a comforting way. Perhaps she was one of the ones who were convinced of his innocence, or not convinced of his guilt, whichever way.

Briggs and his wife sat outside the court and resumed a game of gin rummy. Briggs accused Maggie of cheating as she wiped his score off and doubled hers with a complete gin rummy. "Not cheating love, it's just that you have your mind on other things." She smiled and squeezed his arm.

The usher came out again. "It's on this time, they have a verdict, best of luck mate."

Briggs got up, took his expensive watch off and took his wallet from his back pocket, giving them both to his wife. She smiled, "I might be giving them both back in a minute." Briggs took strength from her smile.

"I think this was all cut and dried from the moment we came into the court. I wouldn't be surprised if their people are on the jury." Briggs could see the beginnings of a tear in her eye and tried to comfort her. "Anyway love, look we have more than most, we can waste a year, it will teach us what it is like to be alone." He lifted her chin and kissed her. They hugged and went into court. Briggs climbed wearily into the dock. The grumpy screw nodded to him. Briggs didn't feel like saying anything.

The Judge came in and bowed yet again. The court clerk adddressed the foreman. "Have you reached a verdict on which at least ten of you agree?"

The foreman stood up, he looked ill at ease in such surroundings. "Yes, my lord we have, ten of us are agreed." The court clerk paused. "What is your verdict on the sole indictment against this man?"

The foreman looked briefly at Briggs and said, "Guilty."

There was silence, broken only by Maggie's sniffing as she tried to hold back a flood of tears. Miss Cotterill rose. "My lord, my client has instructed me that he does not wish one word of mitigation given in this court" and sat down. The prosecution gave details of Briggs' service, the fact that he had ten commendations and had served in the British Army before joining the Police Force, also that he was married with three children. The officer who had taken the antecedents from him had wanted more information but Briggs had told him 'mind your own business'. The Judge fixed him with a steady stare. "Have you anything to say before sentence is passed on you?"

Briggs smiled sweetly, "No my lord" he replied.

"I shall not waste words on you. You have betrayed a glorious service and you shall go to prison for a period of eighteen months. Take him down officer." The grumpy screw took hold of Briggs' arm and aimed him towards the door at the side of the dock.

Maggie Briggs stood outside the court, holding back the flood of tears pressing for their release. She stood and waited despite Detective Inspector Sparrow's invitation to go and see her husband in the cells below the court. Eventually after about thirty minutes, the jury came out of the court, the twelve good men and woman true. Maggie positioned herself before them as they appeared. "Just a minute" she called, with as much authority in her voice as she could manage.

"I have something to tell you and I am sure you will be interested." The jury stopped and formed a half circle around her. "You have been duped, you might as well not have been here. The main witness Ryan was, and still is, a member of the Security Services. He is currently serving in Southern Ireland. The tapes have been tampered with, edited professionally in fact. The final tape was recorded, but after hearing it, the powers that be decided to ditch it. If my husband had dared to open this before you, he was told that he would almost certainly get twelve years or maybe more. He might have risked this for himself but, more importantly for him, he was afraid for his family. Lastly, I don't expect you to believe this, but he is an honest man trying to do a very difficult job. I hope you all sleep well with this knowledge." The lady member of the jury burst into tears and rushed off down the gallery.

Maggie Briggs turned away from them, tears streaming down her cheeks. She went to the ladies' toilet and straightened her make up, after which she felt better and more able to face the world. As she was doing this, Miss Cotterill came into the toilet. "I hear you have made an impassioned speech to the jury, well done."

Maggie Briggs bristled. "At least what I said was the truth and from the heart. You should be ashamed of yourself Miss Cotterill, having risen so high to sell you're your principles so cheaply." Maggie turned and left the toilet to go home alone, her husband's watch and wallet clutched to her breast as though trying to protect him from what lay ahead and hoping that she might still see him before he left the court building.

A Wing North

Briggs sat in the dank windowless cell. The door was open. A tall senior screw came in and demanded, "You Briggs?" Briggs looked him up and down.

"That's me," he said.

The screw smiled. "Not everyone's against you, let me give you a bit of advice. When you get to the Scrubs ask for Rule 43 segregation, otherwise you'll get a hell of good hiding."

Briggs considered the advice for a moment then in a somewhat resigned voice said, "And when I come out of segregation I get a good hiding then, so what's the difference."

The senior screw became earnest. "No! You don't understand you'll be kept away from the others, relatively safe from harm." Rule 43 prisoners were those at risk from other prisoners and consisted mainly of child molesters and sex offenders and, although he might now be a pariah in the eyes of both his former colleagues and the villains he had spent years trying to lock up in the very prisons he was now destined for, he didn't want to be labelled with the people he most detested in life. He answered, without exposing his real feelings.

"I'll have to do the best I possibly can."

The screw shrugged his shoulders. "Your decision mate. Anyway, your wife is outside, do you want to see her?"

Briggs brightened, "Of course, always."

Briggs sat there on the hard bench in this dismal cell and composed himself as best he could. Being here beaten and with the thought of the fate which lay before him, he could feel the emotion of the moment sweeping over him. Maggie came into the cell accompanied by the senior screw. They kissed, the senior screw stood outside the door.

"Love I'm so sorry," Briggs said as he felt the hot tears streaming down his cheeks. "I wouldn't have had this for the world." She cuddled up to him.

"Try not to worry love, we've built a strong family, and it will survive twelve months, no problems keep your chin up love." Now she was in tears as well.

"That's not the problem love, it's being away from you and the kids that will upset me." They sat down on the bench and tried to be as practical as emotion would allow. "Now listen love, I've left you money in the Building Society account. Use it as you wish, I've also spoken to the Building Society about the mortgage while I am away. They seemed very understanding, part of life I suppose, all this." She smiled, the love obvious in her eyes. The senior screw entered the cell and nodded to Briggs. "I think they want me to start my sentence straight away" said Briggs, desperately trying to make a joke of the whole affair. They kissed again and she left in tears. Briggs watched her leave and sat on the bench feeling very lonely.

The senior screw returned. "There's a couple of very senior cozzers here to see. You can tell them to piss off if you like."

Briggs thought for a moment and said, "No I'll see them, it can't make the day any worse," and a few minutes later, two soberly dressed men came into the cell. The older of the two said, "I am Detective Chief Inspector Cork of the Complaints Investigation. It would appear that you have committed the serious offence of being convicted of a criminal offence under the discipline code. If you admit this now, you'll avoid the necessity of a discipline hearing." Briggs couldn't believe his ears, they were still after him.

Briggs looked at the floor and with the vestige of obstinacy and from his knowledge of the hypocrisy involved in this affair said, "Record this in your little book. Tell them I am a member of the Security Services and can do what I like. Now fuck off and let me get on with what I have to do." Cork reacted startled.

Eventually he said, "If that's your attitude we might as well go and leave you to stew." Cork nodded to his companion and they left.

Minutes later, Briggs was called out to the central hall, where other prisoners had been assembled. He was handcuffed to a young effeminate man. Briggs resisted the temptation to ask him what he was in for. Together with about ten others they were ushered to the rear entrance where they were placed in a large green bus. Briggs and his chained companion sat on the nearside of the bus which departed out into the London Traffic. Briggs looked round in case he could catch a last glimpse of his wife, but she had obviously gone home. Even with all these people around, without Maggie he felt extremely alone. The bus drove along through central London towards Wormwood Scrubs and along the way they passed the council flats he had lived in as a youngster. Briggs smiled in remembrance of all the friends he had in those flats and the scrapes they had got into. It was while living there that Briggs had lost his virginity, not that it was unintentional, and was not really taken from him, more discarded as some piece of useless junk that the priests prattle on about. They passed the fruit and vegetable shop where he had helped out on Saturdays. He felt nostalgic for the place and for the people he'd known in happier times. The shop had been owned by a Jew called Marcus, someone who Briggs admired greatly. Marcus had been a Warrant Officer, second class in the Middlesex Regiment and had been captured by the Japanese on the fall of Singapore. He had spent three years on the Railway of Death in Burma, nearly losing his life in the process, but Marcus reckoned he had done well out of the deal. "After all, with my name and religion, I could have gone up in smoke if I'd been captured by the Germans." They had often laughed together at this very Jewish view of good luck. As the bus went past the shop Briggs craned his neck to see if there was anyone in there that he recognised, but there wasn't.

They turned into Du Cane Road, where Briggs could immediately see the prison in the distance, the Victorian towers rising above all else. They turned into the courtyard in front of the prison gate which opened wide to welcome them. One of the others said, "Well here we are, home for the next seven years." Briggs was glad at that moment that he had avoided confrontation with the Security Services and now he had only twelve months to push – hardly worth unpacking his kit. The gate clanged shut behind the bus, then there were shouts of "over to you Mr. Tucker" and "Received this end Mr. Brown." Briggs found this strange, especially as they hadn't moved an inch. Eventually after the outside gate had fully closed, the inner gate opened, and they were driven into the prison proper. The bus stopped in front of a large imposing Victorian block, which Briggs later realised was the reception block. All the prisoners were ordered out and were ushered inside the building where they stood in front of a large bench, on which bundles of clothing were stacked. The scene struck a chord with Briggs. "QM stores," he thought. "If it runs true to form, some dipstick is going to come out and lecture us about 'Hands off cocks, get on socks.'

Sure enough, a fat little screw came out from behind the jump, his hat seemed taller than he was. As with a lot of small men, he seemed acutely conscious of being, well, shorter than average, and made up for it by being plain nasty. Briggs pulled himself erect, to his full six foot two, that way this shitty dwarf would be unlikely to front him or give him any grief. The dwarf went on about how, "when the bell sounds you stand outside of your cell and be counted. You do not go back inside your cell until the bell sounds again. All prison officers are to be called staff, and sir if they are of senior rank." The dwarf then enunciated Prison Regulations, or that part that could be explained quickly. Briggs switched off.

A red band 'trusty' came out of a side office. "Form a line and pick up your gear," he said, indicating the bundles of clothing which lay on the counter. They filed past and were given toilet articles, underclothes, shirts, jeans, jumpers, socks, boots and a towel." If they don't fit, swop 'em with another prisoner until you get a good fit. Now into the next room, out of your civvies and into your prison uniforms."

They trooped into the room where another trusty looked at Briggs and said, "You come from Sidcup don't you?" Briggs didn't answer. The trusty came closer. "Oi dollop o' shit I'm talking to you." Briggs waited with baited breath. He guessed why he was being fronted and didn't particularly want a violent exchange this early in his sentence, but if it had to be… The dwarf came into the room. "What's the hold up. You! Why aren't you getting changed?" He spoke directly to Briggs. "Sorry staff just day dreaming, bit puzzled." The dwarf erupted at Briggs' chest. "Well get unfucking puzzled you dozy bastard." Briggs began to get changed. "Right away staff," he said. The trusty smirked from behind the dwarf's back.

Briggs managed to get into the prison clothing. The only problem he had was with the jeans, they were too short in the leg. Briggs didn't think this was a problem. He could let the hems down and go all beatnik and have frayed bottom jeans, but he really couldn't care less what he looked like. He was hardly likely to be going to any dinner parties whilst here. He packed his civilian clothes into the cardboard case supplied. He was supposed to hand in his cash and valuables, but this was unnecessary as he had already handed them to his boss at court.

Briggs stood in line to hand his gear over to the trusty at the end of the counter. As he arrived in front of him the trusty said, "You've got it coming Briggs."

Briggs smiled as he spoke quietly. "You fancy the job then fatso?" poking the large belly hanging over the counter.

The trusty backed off, shocked, but recovering said, "We're going to have some fun with you shithead."

Briggs responded with a more macho stance than he felt. "I hope you all enjoy pain. I certainly enjoy dishing it out," treating the trusty to one of his Grade A manic grins. He could see the trusty was scared of him and the madman grin had the effect of unsettling the prisoner-cum-screw immensely. The dwarf marched out in front of them.

"Now you are going to be inducted into A Wing North. There are some very hard people incarcerated there, so be careful, especially if you're an ex copper." The dwarf was becoming a poison specimen.

The new batch of prisoners marched along under covered ways towards the famous A Wing North, where they entered the main entrance, and the gate clanged shut behind the last man. There they stood in a huddled group in the centre of the ground floor, watched by the incumbent prisoners who were hanging over the balustrades on each landing. Later Briggs came to realise that this was evening association in full swing and the old prisoners studied the new arrivals with interest. Then one shouted, "That's him, the big un with the black hair. I know him, that's Briggs, the bastard." Briggs looked up for the one who shouted, but couldn't make out which one it was. Then another shouted, "Oi Briggsy, we are going to screw your arse, one after another. By the time you come out of here, you will have an arse like the Grand Canyon." They all laughed. Briggs scowled. The dwarf screw seemed amused, as did the assembled landing screws. The chant 'bent copper, bent copper' was taken up by the various landings, the inmates keeping time with their tin mugs on the railings. Soon they were all roaring in unison.

The screws made no effort to stop this harassment and Briggs was frightened. He felt his anus begin to leak. He breathed deeply, stepped forward away from the crowd of newcomers and looked up at his tormentors. "Alright you bastards," he shouted at the assembled throng and they stopped chanting immediately."Which one of you cunts wants to be the first down these stairs then?" Briggs indicated the narrow stairs which led down from the first landing. "I may come second, but I'll be the best fucking second you cunts have ever seen." Briggs was faced by a stunned silence. "Come on, what's the matter? Was your bottle left dribbling down your mum's leg?"

Briggs was not just frightened, he was terrified, and the only release was to make a lot of noise, which is what he was doing now. One of the screws, with two pips on his shoulders, pushed Briggs towards a side cell. Briggs made to hit him, as he could not see who was pushing him. The screw said, "Don't do it, you'll end up getting the shit kicked out of you every morning," as he ushered Briggs into the side cell. Briggs was shaking. He knew he had made a mess of his new, well new to him, underpants as he could feel the mess of his soil in them. The screw seemed half friendly. "Get a grip Briggsy," he said and Briggs nodded quietly. "You've taken the place by storm mate, never seen anything like it," the screw said and offered him a cigarette. Briggs shook his head as the man continued, "Now listen, you have to behave, otherwise there will be a riot."

Briggs nodded again but said with measured voice, "Maybe, but listen to me for just one minute. If they do for me, I know I'll come out after a year like Royal Jelly, therefore, I'll do the best I can the minute any one of those cunts takes a poke at me."

The screw lit his cigarette. "What about Rule 43? Go on that and all this stops straight away."

Briggs shook his head, "No thanks mate, I'll take my chances."

The screw shrugged. "You alright now?" Briggs nodded but couldn't bring himself to tell this stranger that he had messed his trolleys in fear. "Right come on, lets get you a bed for the night. I'll get you some hot water, you can have a bit of a wash." Briggs thought the screw must know what he'd done but was too kind to say anything. Briggs followed the screw up to the third landing and then along to a cell. Briggs entered and slung his kit up on the top bunk. He later found out that he was now known as being 'Up on the threes.' A black man came into the cell and regarded Briggs with admiration.

"You made a right impression down there. What are you, a superman?! Briggs scowled, still unsettled. "Want a fag mate, I've got the makings?"

Briggs shook his head. "No, I don't smoke but thanks anyway." The black man treated him to a broad grin, "Best way in here, no one can get a handle on you that way." Briggs made his bed up, in much the same way as when he was in the army. "What you in for anyway?" The black man asked. Briggs continued making his bed.

"Getting caught, the same as everyone else," he grunted. The black man subsided into silence.

Briggs climbed up onto his bunk and, as he looked up at the barrel vaulted ceiling, for the only time, wished part of his life away. He earnestly wished he was a year forward and all this was behind him.

"Room service for Mr. Briggs." A trusty stood in the open door with a bucket in front of him. A cover was over the contents. Briggs jumped down and took the bucket and placed it in the corner. The cell door slammed as Briggs lifted the cover. Inside was hot water, on which was floating a large piece of human excrement. Briggs stared in amazement. He took a magazine and lifted out the turd and put it in one of the chamber pots in the corner and covered it. He stripped off and cleaned himself as best he could, then he washed his underpants, wrung them almost dry, then he put them on the end of the bed to dry for the morning.

Briggs slept very soundly. In fact probably the best night's sleep he had ever experienced. He woke up looking at the ceiling, which was covered in graffiti. One which caught Briggs' eye was, 'Only pinkies get parole.' "Luckily I don't qualify for parole," thought Briggs. He got up and brushed his teeth, spitting the toothpaste mixture into the chamber pot and urinating on top of it. He got dressed quickly, feeling vulnerable, naked. His underpants were almost dry, well not wet enough to make it uncomfortable. He made his bed up into a bedpack, army style. Having done it, he decided it was too smart for the Scrubs, took it to pieces and did it again with uneven edges.

The morning screw came round and unlocked their cell. As the bell rang, they all stood out on the landing with their chamber pots in their hands. In this respect Briggs copied the black man incarcerated with him. Another screw came along and counted them and, on getting to the end of the landing, called out, "All correct on the threes." This call was repeated on the ones, twos, and fours. Briggs was relieved nobody had escaped during the night.

The landing screw then bawled, "Slop out." Briggs and company turned to their left and started to shuffle round towards the opening into the slop out point, which was in the opposite corner of the building. Briggs was in the queue moving slowly towards the opening into the slop out area and, as he shuffled along, he studied his companions. They avoided his gaze. It was difficult to categorise people in there, they all dressed the same. It could be that the guy next to him was in for company fraud or theft of milk from front doorsteps. They shuffled on, waiting in line for the opportunity to ditch their overnight droppings down the sewers.

Eventually Briggs stepped into the slop out area, a large corner room with urinals down one side. The floor was wet, the red quarry tiles slippery with spilt urine. The so-called slop out was in the corner. It looked very much like a funnel connected to a six inch sewer downpipe. The over-powering smell was of stale urine. Someone to Briggs' left shouted "Oi." and, as Briggs turned towards the call, he caught a full face of chamber pot contents. The urine made his eyes sting and as he put his hands up, he was kicked in the balls and went down on the slippery floor. He tried to get up but the pain in his testicles was too much. They were kicking him and emptying their chamber pots over him. One unkind soul stamped on his fingers as he tried to rise and he went down yet again, to receive more kicking. Briggs was never sure, but later thought he must have been out for a few seconds. "Oi come on, behave, let me through." Briggs guessed it was the landing screw, who, surmising something of the sort was on the cards had stationed himself at the other end of the landing. Hearing the start of the fracas, he had sauntered down the landing, hoping not to arrive too quickly, grinning at the inmates on the way. As the screw entered the slop out, Briggs was getting to his feet groggily, he was soaked in urine with additional nuggets of shit and smelt to high heaven. "What happened here then?" the screw asked, grinning like a Cheshire cat.

Briggs regarded him with scorn. "I slipped on the wet floor staff," he said, as he scraped some of the less ingrained lumps from himself with the lid of his chamber pot.

"Right you, back to your cell," and Briggs turned and marched back to his cell with the screw behind him.

"I shall need some water to clean myself," Briggs pleaded, well, as much as his pride would allow.

The screw snarled, "Bent coppers get nothing from me, stink you bastard." Briggs shrugged and said nothing as he stood in the corner and tried to clean himself as best he could. Last night's bucket of water had been removed already by the 'room service' trusty. He shook the uniform so as to dislodge as much of the offending material as possible, but really felt it was a token gesture. The black man came back into the cell.

"Are you alright man? They sure gave you one hell of a kicking." The black guy rummaged in his pockets and came out with the crumpled makings of a cigarette. "Here man, have a fag, you need it."

Briggs, despite the pain smiled. "Thanks mate, but I don't smoke I told you."

"Oh yeah right, I forgot." Briggs warmed to the black man. "Anyway what's your name?" he asked. The black man treated him to a broad grin. "My name am Percy Justinian Williams, fine name ain't it?" Briggs grinned and shook his hand.

"Surely is, who chose it?"

Percy sat on his bed. "My mother, she had a fling with a Percy and called me by that name to remind her of her big black man." Percy roared at the concept.

Briggs took off his uniform and underclothes and put them at the other end of the cell away from him, thus distancing himself from the smell, "What happens next?"

Percy laid on his bunk, the one beneath Briggs. "Well the next thing am breakfast, but don't get wound up it ain't worth it. They'll ring when they want us out."

The cell door opened and a trusty came in. "You enjoy that this morning. Nice was it copper?"

Briggs pushed himself off his bunk, slowly and painfully, more so than it actually warranted, giving the impression of severe disability, mumbling slowly, "You guys are really the business you know, you gave me a right good kicking. How many did it take?" As he said 'take', Briggs launched himself at the trusty, grabbing the front of his uniform and nutting him as hard as he could. The trusty's eyebrow burst like a ripe melon and the man cried out in pain, blood streaming down his face. Briggs threw him up against the wall and hit him hard on the rebound. The trusty collapsed on the floor. Briggs picked him up by his lapels and dragged him out onto the landing. He heaved the trusty over the balustrade so that he hung over the side, dripping blood down into the well of the prison.

A screw came running along, calling out, "What's going on here?" He was out of breath from his short run. Briggs now felt conscious, being as how he was stark naked and attracting wolf whistles from the other side of the landing. Percy brought him a towel and Briggs placed it around his active parts.

"I don't really know staff. He came in to see how we were and sort of collapsed, maybe he's got family problems." Briggs and Percy treated the screw to beaming grins.

The bell rang. Briggs climbed into his smelly gear and, reverting to Army routine, he took his mug and eating irons. "Man, just take your mug, you'll be bringing the grub back here to eat." Briggs put the eating irons back on the shelf.

They walked together along the landing and down the narrow staircase to the ground floor, joining the queue for breakfast. As they moved along towards the hotplate, Briggs noticed that their morning fare was beans and toast and decided that the Army similarity thing was becoming ever so close. He wondered if they were all going on parade later to march up and down for a couple of hours. He moved along the line and collected a metal tray with shallow depressions pressed into it. A trusty along the line dropped two pieces of toast on the tray. The next one doled out some beans onto the toast and the one at the end filled his mug with tea.

Percy and Briggs made their way back to their cell without incident and Briggs demolished his toast and beans and gulped his tea like a starving man. With the constant tension, he had forgotten how hungry he was. They placed the trays outside the cell door and Briggs sat at the cell table playing patience. Percy laid on his bed and was shortly snoring again.

A screw stuck his head in the door. "Briggs?" It was more of an accusation than a question really.

"That's me!" Briggs said as he stood up and faced the screw.

"Come on, the Wing governor wants to see you." Briggs followed the screw down to the ground floor, where he was told to stand outside what was obviously a cell converted into an office. "Right Briggs, in you come, stand with your feet on the line, do not move towards the governor and do not raise your hands above waist height." Briggs walked into the office and toed the line in front of the Governor, who was a very small man with large horn-rimmed spectacles and a bald head in the Bobby Charlton style, a wisp of hair stretching from one side to the other.

"You are Briggs?" Briggs nodded.

The screw dug him in the back. "Do not nod, say "Yes sir." Briggs looked behind him at the screw.

"Yes sir." The governor's nose wrinkled. "What on earth is that smell?" The screw straightened.

"Briggs had a slight accident in the slop out this morning sir." Briggs nodded agreement at this lie.

"I see, well accidents do happen don't they?" Briggs didn't reply but looked blankly at the Govenor. "I have had a verbal report that you threatened prisoners on arrival in this establishment last night." Briggs was stunned and his mind raced.

After a pause, he straightened himself and said, "Yes sir all five hundred, all at once."

The screw dug him in the back. "Keep a civil tongue in your head."

Briggs turned and towered above the screw. "Oh I'm sorry, I thought this was Alice in Wonderland time, where the fuck is the looking glass?" The screw stepped back, appearing frightened, his lower lip trembling as he stepped back.

"Now calm down Briggs," said the Governor trying to placate him. "You don't understand the system in here. What they did to you last night was a sort of initiation ceremony. I wouldn't take too much notice, it's a bit like constipation really, it'll pass in time." The dopey Governor smiled at his attempt at humour.

"And what about what they said about screwing my arse, all of them. Was that just jolly japes as well?" The Governor flushed, embarrassed.

"Let me enlighten you on my view of life at this point in time." Briggs smiled his 'you are a prick smile.'

"I aim to survive in here or anywhere you put me and I have been trained to survive in hostile environments. Therefore, I shall do the best I possibly can and, if accidents in the slop out continue, I should book extra beds in the hospital wing." The Governor looked at Briggs – stunned.

Eventually he said. "March him out Mr. Hunt."

Outside the office Mr. Hunt said "Wait here" and Briggs backed up to the wall and waited. A few minutes later another screw came along and enquired "Briggs?"

"Right first time staff" Briggs grinned.

"Don't be a smart arse – follow me." The screw led Briggs out of the wing and into the showers. "Here you are Briggsy get yourself cleaned. There will be a trusty along in a minute who will bring you some clean gear."

The screw turned on his heels and marched back towards the Wing. Briggs quickly stripped off and examined himself. He had bruises on just about every part of his torso, but no broken bones, except of course for his fingers where they had been stamped on. These were either broken or just very sore. He'd been lucky. Briggs luxuriated under the shower and scrubbed every part more than once. Even though there was only carbolic soap available he washed his hair, pubic and otherwise. An old trusty came into the shower with a pile of clean clothing. He collected Briggs' soiled clothing with the words, "Now, flash bastard, try and keep these clean." The old lag grinned. He sat down on the bench and watched Briggs dry himself and get dressed. "You open for a bit of advice mate?" Briggs looked up and nodded. "I heard your speech from the floor last night. I was impressed, so were the plastics and nonces." Briggs was puzzled.

"Plastics and nonces?"

The old lag laughed. "Anyone who is not rated as a villain is a plastic, soppy villain if you like, a nonce is similar with sexual overtones. The real villains will do you no harm. Truth be known, they will respect you. What I was going to say is keep going the way you are and don't lose your bottle." Briggs looked and smiled ruefully.

"The truth is that I lost my bottle last night."

The old lag laughed. "I expect you did, but you didn't let it show, that's the secret. Keep going as you are and take no notice of the screws or the others, you'll be okay." So saying, he picked up the dirty gear and trundled off down the showers towards reception. Briggs got dressed, noting with a small amount of pleasure that the jeans fitted perfectly. The shirt was too small but he couldn't expect too much out of life. He put his jumper on top of the small shirt

The same screw who had brought him into the showers returned. He looked Briggs up and down saying, "There that's better isn't it?" in the manner of a nanny looking after a young charge.

They marched back to the Wing, where Briggs went up to the threes and entered the cell. Percy was still snoring. The bell rang, at which Briggs shook Percy and they both stood out on the landing for the count. The screw came past, counting. He conferred with his counterpart on the opposite landing. Then he stood on the cross landing calling, "All correct on the threes." As usual, this call was repeated for the other landings and they retired to their cells.

Briggs resumed his game of patience. "Here man," said Percy "Come on, I'll teach you a real prison game" getting out a large pack of cards. "This game is called kaluki. It is like gin rummy, but is played with two packs together." Percy then explained the game and they tried a few hands before Percy said. "Now comes the real test. You want to have a bet on the outcome?" Briggs was not averse to the idea. "I could be interested but I haven't got any money." Percy laughed, "Not with money. None of us have got any real money, the tobacco barons maybe, but the rest of us are like the Queen we don't carry money. No, we bet in press-ups and we pay our debts before lights out. That way you sleep better. One other thing, debts are not carried over to the next day, so if you owe two hundred press ups, you are duty bound to do the accumulated press-ups before lights out." Briggs considered the deal. As he was a novice, he was bound to accumulate press-ups but, on the plus side, at least he would sleep well. "Right, you're on let's go for it." They played for about an hour, at the end of which Briggs was ten press-ups down, but Percy was twenty five. Briggs smirked. At this rate, they would both be performing press-ups, which is probably not the way that Percy meant it to end.

The bell rang for another count and lunch and again they stood outside the cell waiting to be counted. From the other landing one of his assailants from the slop out called to Briggs, "Oi copper, are we going to give you some or what?" He pointed to his backside in a stabbing manner.

Briggs laughed, which seemed to upset the heckler. "You really are a hard bastard you. How many was it, three or four? You fancy your chances on a one-to-one straightener?" Briggs was still laughing but the heckler didn't reply. This time his companions laughed with Briggs, which he took to be an encouraging sign. The screw came bustling past, counting as always, and sang out the now usual catechism. They then filed to lunch, the heckler from the other landing keeping well out of his way. Briggs and Percy stood in the line just before the hotplate. The prisoner in front of Percy said to him, "You ought to be ashamed of yourself associating with an ex old bill." Percy laughed. "Man it don't count, I am, as you can perceive, black, and therefore have no standards." Percy and Briggs laughed at the discomfort of the prisoner.

They shuffled up to the hotplate and picked up their metal trays. In the first indentation was slopped a sort of stew, complete with dumplings and carrots. "The last time time I saw anything like that it was sliding down a tree in the jungle. Still ate it mind." Percy laughed and nodded. In the next hollow, the hotplate trusty dumped a slurry of apple something. The next trusty doled out custard, this he did onto Briggs' hand, which burned. Briggs did not flinch, or shout "Fucking hell," as was his inclination, but looked deadpan into the trusty's eyes.

"Now do it again sunshine. Only this time don't put it on me, else you will be wearing this tray." The trusty looked down, unable to hold the confrontation and, picking up the ladle, carefully poured the custard onto the apple something. Briggs changed hands and shook the custard into the face of the trusty together with the word "Arsehole." They returned to their little cell on the threes.

They sat and ate their lunch on Percy's bunk. "Tell me Perce, why don't they come after me in the cell?"

Percy swallowed his mouthful. "Strange to relate, that's not the done thing old chap. The cell is safe ground if you like. They don't encroach on it, mainly I suppose because if they do, you might come after them and they like somewhere safe to hide."

Briggs concentrated on his meal. "But the trusty this morning, he came in here."

"Ah yes, but he was on official business, supposed to give you a message, but you never gave him a chance."

Briggs was puzzled, "What business?" he asked.

Perce pondered, "I suspect he was supposed to tell you to be ready and go and see the Governor."

Briggs grinned. "Oh I see. More kaluki?" Percy got his cards, "Why not."

They spent the afternoon playing kaluki and, at the end, they were very nearly on even terms, both having to do fifty press-ups, or thereabouts.

Teatime was a complete non-event. Briggs munched his way through a cheese salad and noticed, with interest, that he had a maggot in the salad. He supposed he had better not complain as everyone might want one. The tea without sugar was strong and refreshing.

After tea Briggs laid back on his bunk. "Only three hundred and sixty four to do," he smiled to himself, remembering the National Servicemen who cried 'days to do very few, much less than you.' His mind wandered back down the years to those early days in the Army. He became quite wistful about his time as a recruit in 7th Training Regiment Royal Engineers at Cove, and wondered what the rest of his intake were up to now. He doubted if any of them were in prison like him. Although, later in his prison sentence, he did meet a fellow prisoner who alleged he was in the SAS at the same time as Briggs.

They whiled away the evening playing kaluki. Percy had advised against going out onto the landing on association as this would only give the plastics and nonces a chance to have a go at him. At last roll-call they stood outside the cell and were counted yet again, after which they were locked away again for the night and the time for card game bets to be paid. Briggs had amassed a debt of one hundred and twenty five press-ups, whilst Percy owed seventy five. Percy suggested that he cancel his seventy five against Briggs' bill, leaving Briggs to cope with fifty press-ups. Briggs objected, having a fairly good idea that he could manage one hundred and twenty five press-ups, given that he might need a break in the middle, but he doubted that Percy could manage the seventy five. He therefore pressed Percy to perform his debt, whilst Briggs supervised. Percy was upset at his suggestion and it had not met with agreement. "Man, whichever way you look at it, I am de winnah, I am the man."

Briggs got down from his bunk. "As you may be, my black friend, but to reinforce your superiority you have to do seventy five press-ups. Now away you go," Briggs indicated the floor.

Percy got down on the floor scowling and began to perform the press-ups. After about twenty he began to get breathless and at twenty five he collapsed on the cell floor. "Man, this is nonsense, I am de winnah, you should be doing this." Percy laid back and gasped on the cell floor.

"Now listen carefully Percy, you incurred the debt, and as it is less than mine you pay first."

Percy whined in mock protest. "It am always de same. De white man him have the black man over all de time and rub the Negro's face in the dust." Briggs laughed and nudged him with his foot.

"Cut the racial crap and put up the press-ups." Percy groaned and turned over and carried on with his task. After a couple of breaks, Percy completed his seventy five and sat on his bunk almost unable to speak.

Eventually he said, "Now de black man has paid his debt of honour with honour, it am now your time honky." Briggs jumped down from his bunk.

"Is it the same as you? Can I take a break every twenty five or so?" Percy nodded.

Briggs started on his press-ups, took a break at twenty five and carried on. Soon he was passing seventy five. At ninety, he felt as though his arms were coming to pieces and his lungs were bursting, but he managed to get to a hundred and took another break, laying on his back on the cold floor, the sweat trickling down his face. "Give us a couple of minutes and I'll finish it off." Percy nodded, not really believing what he had just seen. After about five minutes Briggs turned over and completed another twenty five press-ups.

Percy was impressed. "I will not be playing cards with you ever again, cos if you win, this black man am going to disintegrate."

They both laughed.

The cell door spy hole flicked open and after a moment flicked back. "It's the screws, they like to check every so often to see if we are screwing each other."

Briggs looked deadpan at Percy. "Sounds like a pain in the arse to me." They both laughed together. "Seriously though Percy, you hear that these things go on in nick. How much of it is true?"

Percy became very serious. "Most of it man, so be careful. You remember this morning when you thumped the trusty?" Briggs nodded. "Well, you noticed that I gave you a towel with which to cover yourself?" Briggs nodded again. "Well there's a very good reason for that. You wander round a nick stark bollock naked and it's a message that you're a woofter and open for business."

Briggs was amazed. "So the wolf whistles were for real then?" Percy was amused at Briggs naïvety.

"Absolutely my son, what you don't realise is there are people called prison poofs. They only become turd burglars when they come into these places."

Briggs became serious. "So how does one handle an approach from the poofs, apart from decking them?"

Percy whistled, "Don't even think about decking them. There are some very hard people in here who are poofs, so whatever you do be careful. But say you get an approach from a raving iron, just tell him you don"t get it off that way. They will not be offended, so long as you are not offensive." Percy spoke slowly and carefully, "After all it's a fact of life in these places." Briggs climbed up onto his bunk.

"Thanks Perce." Percy still sat on his bunk. "While we are having this induction chat for rooky prisoners, tomorrow morning in the slop out, they are bound to have another go. They've got to, and that screw will wind them up to it. I can't help you, cos if I do, after you're gone they will come after me." Briggs lay on his bunk and stared at the curved ceiling.

"Thanks Perce, I had already worked that out for myself. I have decided to do the best I can."

"If it gets too tasty I will wade in on your side, but be aware I don't want to." Briggs resisted the temptation to write 'sod em all' on the ceiling.

"Thanks Perce, I can see your problem." Briggs jumped down and got undressed. The last bell sounded and he climbed back up onto his bunk. "Night Perce." He fell asleep almost immediately. It seemed only moments later that the bell rang to get up.

Briggs got up and had a piddle in his chamber pot and noticed that Percy's was nearly full, no doubt a result of the press-ups. "When we go to the slop out, can I empty your pot?"

Percy, who was in the process of getting up, asked incredulously, "Tell me, are you really saying that you, a white boy, wants to empty a black man's pooh pot for him?"

Briggs nodded, "Well it's really that you are more full of shit than I am, being black and all that, also I might have a need for quantity this morning." Percy laughed at it all. "Sure man anything to help."

The next bell rang and the door was unlocked for the first count. They stood outside with their chamber pots in their left hands and the screw came past counting. Briggs was amazed that he could walk and count and hold all these figures in his head. Eventually the inevitable "All correct on the threes," rang out, to be followed by the other landings. The screw shouted 'slop out' and then marched resolutely and quickly down the landing away from the slop out. Briggs, with Percy in tow, turned left and shuffled towards the slop out. Percy's pot weighed heavily in his hand. "Hell" thought Briggs, "a farmer would keep him for his manure alone." They shuffled on, the slop out coming slowly nearer. Finally they turned the corner and shuffled onto the cross landing with the slop out in the corner.

Briggs looked over the shoulder of the guy in front of him. Inside the slop out, on the right, he could see the prisoner who had shouted across the landing at him yesterday. He thought he detected a sardonic smile on the bloke waiting, and guessed that his little helpers would be to his left as he entered the slop out ready for 'good hiding Mk2'. As he was a couple of paces away from the entrance to the slop out, Briggs grabbed hold of the trouser crotch of the prisoner in front of him and elevated him onto his toes. "Oi, what the hell," exclaimed the man, as Briggs propelled him forward into the face of the one he could see waiting. Briggs emptied Percy's pot with great effect to his left, where he could now see the other two, maybe three, were waiting for him. Briggs moved in close to the filth covered prisoners and hit the first one with a heavy blow to the eye area. The prisoner snorted and went down in front of Briggs, almost like a sack of shit, which is what Briggs thought him to be. The prisoner who Briggs had forced to collide with the dummy in front, now came from behind. Briggs hit him a sharp hard blow under his nose with his elbow on return from the first blow. The prisoner screamed in agony, Briggs sensing that he was now holding his face. The third prisoner was now standing open mouthed as his main support had been negated. "Ere hold up guv, only a bit of fun like." In reply Briggs kicked him hard in the nuts, showing exactly the same amount of mercy that he had been shown yesterday. The prisoner held his nuts and was moaning. Briggs caught him a short right hook to the side of his head. The prisoner went down like a felled tree. The guy who had caught one in the eye was endeavouring to get up. He was swearing. Briggs kicked him hard in the face, spewing teeth and blood across the slop out floor. All three lay on the floor and wallowed in the urine, in much the same way as he had been forced to do the day before, the only difference being they didn't seem too keen to get up in the presence of this now very angry and fired up Briggs.

"What's occurring here?" The screw made his way into the slop out. He seemed surprised to see Briggs on his feet and his pet hard men moaning and groaning on the floor. "They all slipped on the wet floor staff," Briggs deadpan and straightening his uniform.

"You, back into your cell, now." The screw marched behind Briggs and put him in his cell. Percy followed the screw and managed to get into the cell before the screw slammed the door.

"Christ man, that was some heavy shit you handed out in the slop out." Briggs climbed onto his bunk. "Only what they gave me yesterday, seemed fair to me." Briggs examined his fingers which were damaged yesterday and, although painful, they seemed alright; anyway he didn't fancy going on sick parade here.

They waited for something to happen, and eventually Perce broke the silence. "You realise they won't let you get away with this."

Briggs was puzzled. "Who won't?" he asked.

Percy looked up at Briggs. "The establishment, they will have you out of here like greased lightning."

"To where?" asked Briggs half hopeful that he, by accident, had got himself a posting.

"Well if they think you are a violent and disorderly prisoner it's off to Parkhurst with you my son." Percy shook his right hand to indicate extreme heat. "On the other hand, they might take the view that you are just misunderstood and not a troublemaker at all. In which case, off to Ford you go and do your bird with all the barristers and solicitors who got caught. Oh and by the way, convicted peers of the realm go there. Thinking on it, you might be too low class to even sit the entrance exam." They both laughed at Percy's jaundiced view of the establishment at work.

"Briggs!" The landing screw who had studiously ignored Briggs' beating the day before poked his head in the cell. "Briggs" he called.

"Here staff" said Briggs, jumping down from his bunk.

"The Wing Governor wants to see you now, like yesterday. Oh and by the way, he's pissed off." Briggs followed the landing screw down to the ground floor and waited outside the same office as he had been in the day before.

The office door opened. A chief screw appeared. "Briggs in here, toe the line, keep your hands below waist height." Briggs entered the office and stood before the same dopey Governor who had the Bobby Charlton hairstyle. He looked up at Briggs. "I hope you realise you have nearly started a riot."

"Oh good," thought Briggs, "I enjoy a good party." The Governor continued, "Plus, of course, three prisoners are now in the hospital wing. This is not the behaviour we expect from a police officer." Briggs stood rigidly to attention.

"I was a police officer until the day before yesterday sir. I am now a prisoner and, as such, I am entitled to protect myself, which is what I did, sir. Anyway, yesterday you swallowed all this crap about 'accidents do happen in the slop out'. Well, those three dipsticks had an accident and the next three will get the same if they try it on. I aim to come out of this place after a year in one piece." The Wing Governor sat open mouthed.

Eventually he said, "I see." He motioned to the chief screw to march him out. Briggs stood outside the office and watched the inmates filing down to breakfast. Percy signalled to him with a thumbs up question. Briggs shrugged his shoulders. The screw came up to Briggs. "Go and get your breakfast, you're being shipped out after that." Briggs joined the queue for grub, collected his beans on toast and tea and climbed up to the threes to eat in silence with Percy.

Eventually he told Percy that he was being shipped out, but he didn't know where to.

The cell door opened. "Briggs get your kit. you're on the move." Briggs shook hands with Percy.

"Thanks mate, I owe you." Percy treated Briggs to his broadest grin.

"A pleasure honky, a real pleasure." They laughed.

Briggs handed his kit in to reception and drew his civvies out and got dressed. The fat reception trusty kept well out of Briggs' arm's reach. Briggs caught his eye and blew him a kiss. He was led out to the courtyard by a screw and chained to a young prison officer. They got into a taxi of the mini cab variety. Briggs sat in the back with the young screw. "Where are we going staff?" he asked, knowing full well according to Perce that it was either Parkhurst or Ford. The screw looked at him, surprised. "HMP Ford, I thought you knew that." Briggs shook his head, and contented himself for the rest of the journey by looking out of the window at the passing scenery and smiling to himself at his good luck.

The Sussex Hilton

They drove into the prison through the main gate, which was fully open. They turned right and stopped outside the building marked 'Reception'. Briggs got out, still shackled to the young screw, who then took the large handcuffs off him. "We don't believe in these things at Ford," he remarked, taking Briggs by the elbow and leading him into the Reception building. As with the Scrubs, there was a pile of clothing topped by a pair of boots on the counter, but this time only one – his.

The big reception trusty looked him in the eye, cold and unblinking. "I understand you are ex old bill. Is that right?" Briggs squared up and paused, sizing up the opposition, same build, same hard eyes. If it came to it, he would be hard pressed here with this one, but no point in backing down.

"Yes that's right, what of it?"

The big trusty smiled, "Nothing at all, just seeing if you had the balls to front it out, and you have. I am ex myself, City of London, long weary tale, not worth telling, got six months left to push."

Briggs was stunned, he had gone from fronting up for a scrap, to having a friend. "If you take my advice, you will keep to your friends. There are currently sixteen ex old bill in here and we run the place. The Screws are happy with that." The big man took the pile of uniform from the bench and replaced it with another pile, all brand new. "Anything that doesn't fit let me know and I'll change it, no problem." The big man smiled. "My name is Bill Smillie, by the way, and I know yours is Terry Briggs." They shook hands. "I'll see you across to the induction wing, bit pointless really as I can tell you where you will end up, – B Wing, with all the plastics and nonces."

Briggs changed into his prison clothing and placed his civvies into a cardboard box. Bill locked the Reception building and they walked across the large playing field. "Seems very pleasant, nice and airy," said Briggs.

Bill Smillie laughed. "It's the best kept secret in the prison system. On the out, you would pay about seven hundred quid a week for the treatment you get in this health farm." Briggs walked alongside the big man. The sun was shining, a couple of inmates were flying boomerangs.

"Watch out mate," one of them called.

"Don't worry, he didn't mean it, just an accident." They arrived at the induction block and reported to the screw on duty.

"You are?" asked the screw, looking down his list.

Bill Smillie tapped him on the shoulder and mouthed the words, "See you later."

Briggs nodded. "Er Briggs staff."

"Ah yes, here we are, Mr. Briggs. I understand you had an accident in the slop out at the Scrubs this morning?" Briggs nodded, accepting this euphemism for the out and out scrap he had indulged himself in.

"That's correct staff."

The screw hmmd, "Let me warn you Mr. Briggs we take a dim view of violence in this establishment, any of that and you will be sent to Parkhurst, got it?"

Briggs stood to attention. "Yes staff."

The screw continued, "Having said that, we quite understand that a prisoner with your antecedents is likely to have difficulty with his fellow inmates, call it a settling down period." The screw smiled pleasantly. Briggs thought he meant it.

The screw issued him with a mug, knife, fork and spoon and led him to a dormitory where there were six beds, all very chummy, light and airy. "Here you are Briggs. You have a week's holiday while we assess what you can do. Have you got a trade, apart from copper that is?"

Briggs nodded. "I served my time as a mechanic, made a few quid at it while suspended." The screw made a note on his clipboard.

"Well here's your bed, lunch is in an hour, so you have time to get settled in." The screw left him. Briggs sorted his meagre amount of kit into a large bedside locker and laid down on his bed, where he stayed until the bell rang for lunch.

The next few days whizzed by. The other inmates in the induction wing were surly but left it at that, which suited Briggs. At mealtimes he met the other ex old bill. They seemed a motley bunch but they had one thing in common – coppering and, therefore they stuck together. All ranks were present from Assistant Chief Constable down. Briggs was pleasantly surprised with ex Assistant Chief Constable Dalton. He had known him vaguely in the job, where he was universally regarded as an arsewipe. Now, without his rank and supposedly the stresses of high rank, he was quite a pleasant fellow. After three days, his assessment came through. He was posted to work in the laundry, where no doubt his mechanical ability would be of absolutely no use whatsoever. Briggs was not unduly upset about this. He had a year to do, and doing it in the laundry would be no problem. At least he would have something to do and, hopefully, the time would pass quickly.

Whilst in induction, the letters that had been sent to him at the Scrubs caught up with him. Most were expected, Maggie and his Mum, but one which surprised him was from Sid, the First Class at Rodney Road. His letter was very short. He apologised for letting Briggs down and informed him that he, Sid, had resigned from the job in disgust. Enclosed was a copy of a letter he had sent to the Commissioner, outlining the double dealing of the fifth floor. Briggs was surprised that he bothered to resign and felt that beneath his front was a naïve person who believed in fairytales, along with the concepts of truth and justice. However it did show that he had integrity and for that he could be forgiven many things.

Having got his assessment, he was posted to B Wing, which Bill Smillie aptly described as the home of the plastics and nonces. His bunk was designated as being in S hut, right by the perimeter fence. Briggs moved his gear across to the other wing and found S Hut without difficulty. He entered, it was mid morning and the hut cleaner was mopping the central aisle of the hut.

Briggs found an empty bed space. As in the army, it is always the one with the mattress folded back over the bedpack. He stowed his gear in the bedside cabinet. "You the new man in?" the hut cleaner asking the obvious.

"Well yes, as I am putting my gear away I suppose I must be." The hut cleaner nodded vacantly. "My name is Briggs, Terry Briggs."

The hut cleaner sparked recognition. "You're an ex old bill you are." Briggs carried on arranging his gear. "They won't like that they won't." Briggs treated him to his hard man stare.

"Who won't like what?" he grated.

"You being ex old bill and posted in here. The lads won't be happy about that" the hut cleaner said and shook his head mournfully. "No not at all, not at all."

Briggs felt the time had come to stamp his personality on the proceedings. "Listen dingbat, I couldn't care less what they like or don't like, got it?" The hut cleaner nodded. "How many in this billet then?" Briggs showing out on his army training. The hut cleaner looked at the floor, not even wanting to look at this brusque hard man.

"Er, sixteen, counting you that is." Briggs contemplated this information momentarily.

"Now listen carefully sunshine, you tell 'em, all fifteen of them, or in multiples of two, three, four or five, or if they have the bottle on their own, they come to my bed space tonight and I take on all comers. Make it tonight so I can get on with my bird okay, got that?" The hut cleaner nodded dumbly.

"They won't like it," he said morosely.

"Then they can lump it," Briggs said to the departing back of the cleaner.

Briggs laid on his bed all afternoon and waited for teatime. The rest of the billet came in, in drib and drabs. Most of them noticed him but none of them showed any sign of friendship or made any attempt to speak. Briggs was reading a book he had found in the locker. "The Throne of Saturn" by Allen Drury. He concentrated on the book and ignored what was going on around him. The bell rang. Everybody studiously ignored it. Some minutes later he heard, "Stand by your beds." Briggs stood up and stood at the end of his bed space. There was a screw standing at the end of the billet in the doorway. He counted, then nodded. "Carry on" he said.

They all started getting ready to go for tea, mug and eating irons were got out of lockers with Briggs following suit. They all filed out of the hut and towards the mess hall and Briggs trooped along with them, but didn't speak to anyone. After three years on suspension he had got used to being a pariah. The mess hall betrayed Ford's previous service as a military establishment, being an exact replica of many mess halls Briggs had been in whilst in the Army and, judging by the food, the cooks were trained by the Army Catering Corps, or the Aldershot Cement Company as they became known. Briggs smiled to himself. The Army Catering Corps or ACC had long been petitioning for the right to call themselves the Royal Army Catering Corps but so far had been unsuccessful. Briggs felt that if a referendum was called of all the personnel who had been served by Andy Clyde Commandos, they had more chance of being shot for treason. Tea was the usual, fried something and beans but, tonight, was special as they had chips on the menu as well – whoopee.

Briggs collected his grub and made his way over to the ex old bill's table. He joined Derek Ridgeman, who had been a Detective Sergeant at Rotherhithe and had got involved in a bit of 'you do that and I'll do this' with a villain and it had gone horribly wrong. As a result, he was doing seven years. Derek had laughed at Briggs' sentence. "That's not a sentence, you must have been not guilty. Old bill doesn't get eighteen months, he gets seven years. Come on, where's your self respect?"

Briggs retorted. "Waiting at the gate for me to join it." They laughed as the rest of the table joined in.

Briggs found this business of teams a little unsettling, as for the last three years he had been on his own. Now he was accepted on a team again. The other teams which were pointed out to him were the burglars, (five years' imprisonment to qualify and it had to be accepted as a tasty burglary) the fraudsmen and Department of Health and Social Security do not qualify, the solicitors and barristers, who were universally despised by just about everyone and when they got grief, they usually came to the old bill section to sort it out for them. The queers had their own table as well and could be made up of just about anyone convicted of anything, so long as they were homosexual. Among the queers were some who were known as prossies, who would perform for half an ounce of tobacco or thereabouts, that is if sexual pressure became too much. Briggs decided he would find another method of relieving himself. There was also a section of the robbery offenders. Being very few, most being in closed prisons, they had just half a table. Some of them Briggs knew and they nodded when he passed by. They were an evil looking bunch and Briggs knew they were as hard as they looked. The rest were lumped into a general category with the nonces and plastics who occupied about half the hall. Anyone who was 'anyone' sat at the other end of the hall with the 'teams.'

"How's your billet? S Hut isn't it?" asked Derek, head up from fried something and chips.

"Yes, well, as they say full of plastics and nonces."

"Any grief?" Derek enquired over his tea.

"I don't know. I have told the hut cleaner that if they want to go for it after last bell, I am up for it and I hope I can get it sorted tonight and get on with my bird in peace, sort of."

Derek giggled, "They'll take that the wrong way."

Briggs was puzzled. "They'll have heard how you put three in the hospital wing and they'll think you want to take them all on. A professional hard man, that's what you are in their eyes."

Briggs was still puzzled, "I don't see how. That business in the Scrubs I was lucky, I wouldn't try it on with the robbery team over there." Briggs nodded towards the next table of heavy muscle and broken noses.

Derek nodded agreement, "But I still reckon you have frightened the shit out of them. You'll see."

They finished their teas and went to Derek's single cell on A wing. Derek's cell had many touches of home, curtains, scatter cushions and a bedspread. But for all the comforts of home, Briggs would not swap his sentence for Derek's. They sat and talked about old times, the people they both knew and about the future. It was all very rosy until Briggs touched upon how lucky he was with is family and how strong Maggie was and, from the tone of his chat, how proud he was of her. Derek became more morose and didn't seem as happy as he had been earlier. "What's up mate?" Briggs asked, concerned that he had upset his friend.

"Nothing really, it's just that the old woman's decided to divorce me, can't stand the ignominy of being married to a con." Briggs was crestfallen and ashamed he had walked straight into it, without a thought for Derek's feelings or situation.

"I'm sorry mate, I didn't know. Anything that can be done?"

Derek hesitated and said slowly, "No I don't think so. I think she is having it off with my best mate, anyway. A right mess all round." Briggs looked at his watch involuntarily. The passage of time was always never far from the front of his mind.

"It's getting close to last bell before lights out, I'd better make my way back to the plastics' park." Derek smiled and nodded, but Briggs could see he had opened an old wound and felt sorry. Briggs got up and left, pleased to be out of his friend's company for the moment.

Briggs walked across to B Wing. Various other prisoners were walking the same path. None came near him or spoke to him. Either they didn't know who he was, or had been, or they didn't care. Possibly they did know and were avoiding him. Either way, Briggs told himself that he didn't give a damn. As he approached S Hut, he saw or thought he saw, a sentry silhouetted at the door, waiting for him maybe. Briggs steadied himself. Maybe they were waiting for him behind the door, maybe they were all in the small kitchen waiting to jump out on him. Maybe, maybe, maybe.

Briggs opened the door to the hut and walked inside in what he hoped was a cool manner. He got through the foyer and into the dormitory proper and was pleased to note that most of the inmates were standing by their beds. He went into his bed space, which was really like a small cubicle which opened out onto the central aisle. He sat down on the bed and checked the hair he had put across the join of his locker. It was still there. No-one had touched his gear or, if they had, they were shrewd and had put the marker back afterwards, which Briggs doubted. He sat and waited for the call.

"Stand by your beds," came at last from a screw who stood at the end of the dormitory. Briggs stood by the end of his bedspace as ordered. The screw counted, nodded, about turned and marched away, his steel tips clacking as he went.

Briggs was alone. If they were going to bash him, now was the time. He sat on his bed tense, waiting. He heard them whispering. They could only be whispering to exclude him from their conversations and he decided they were coming for him, and he forced himself to relax. One of the blokes from down the hut rapped smartly on his locker. Briggs sat bolt upright. "Yes" he snapped. The prisoner looked surprised and stepped back.

"Nothing really, only we're having pilchard sandwiches tonight and we wondered if you would like some, and of course coffee?" Briggs considered the question.

"Yes fine," he said, still considering the implications of this latest development.

"How do you like your coffee?" Briggs smiled, not believing for one minute that he was ever going to get any coffee, he might get it all over him, but not any to actually drink.

"White, one sugar will be fine." The prisoner almost bowed and retired to the kitchen, allegedly to prepare sandwiches and coffee. He was accompanied by another prisoner. Briggs sat and waited for his good hiding to arrive. They were whispering down the other end of the billet. He thought he heard the words "fucking hard bastard." Obviously they were talking about the bloke who was going to kick the shit out of him. Eventually, the original prisoner returned with a plate and a steaming mug. He put them on the end of the locker, nodded to Briggs and backed away. Briggs knew what was up. They had put a turd in the sandwich and had pissed in the coffee. He leaned forward and picked up the plate. He looked at the sandwich – it seemed normal. He smelt it – nothing untoward in the smell. He opened the sandwich and examined the contents. It seemed like pilchard with no lavatorial additives. He tasted it and was certain there was nothing wrong with it. The coffee smelt exactly right. He tasted it. It was right, in fact, it was quite an expensive coffee. Briggs devoured the sandwich and drank the coffee, all the while thinking that they were softening him up for the sucker punch, therefore, he was ready at all times to receive his good hiding and go down fighting if he had to.

They were whispering again. They were coming for him now, now was the time. He had had his coffee and his sandwich, now they were going to make him pay for it. After a few minutes the original prisoner who had offered the sandwich and coffee returned and cleared the plate and the mug. A few minutes later in complete silence he returned. The others were no longer whispering, having decided how to take him. They were now ready, or so Briggs thought. The prisoner coughed politely, almost like a head waiter Briggs once knew. "Er excuse me." He looked apologetic.

"Yes! What do you want?" Tense, ready to take the face off the first one who came for him.

"No guv you've got it wrong, we only want to talk to you. Be reasonable now, no offence meant." Briggs sat and waited. Another two prisoners appeared at this shoulders. "This has got to be it," thought Briggs. "We were wondering if you could help us." Briggs was stunned. A new approach, not a signal to drop your guard.

"If I can," Briggs muttered, still waiting to fight.

"Well it's like this, I am the hut leader and it's a pain; the lads and me think you would be a much better leader, and l agree." This little speech came out in a rush, the other two prisoners nodding enthusiastically. "Yeah go on guv, do it," they enthused. Briggs was befuddled. "And everyone here has a nickname so we have decided to call you sarge." The original prisoner beamed as though bestowing some great honour. "Alright sarge?"

Briggs nodded, bemused. Once he had consented to be their leader, the atmosphere in the hut lightened and he found everyone laughing with relief, including himself.

Lights out came and Briggs climbed into bed feeling quite safe for the first time since joining the prison population and slept soundly, until the ex hut leader woke him with a mug of tea. At breakfast Derek had forgotten about his wife, or had stowed her away in a secret locker in his mind. "Alright Briggsy?" Derek asked as Briggs plonked his tray down on the table.

"Very much as you said it, I was surprised. I am now, would you believe, hut leader, the guvnor if you like."

Derek laughed. "That is probably the only promotion you are ever, or were ever, going to get." They all laughed at Briggs' good fortune if that is what it was. From that day on he was universally known as 'Sarge'.

Briggs stood on parade outside the gymnasium and was counted before marching to work. The screw counted the laundry party and cried out, "All present and correct for the laundry sah." Briggs' impression was that this was very like being in the Army without the drill and bullshit. Maybe that was coming, but he didn't somehow think so. Once everyone was satisfied that no-one had run away since the first count, they marched off to work. The screw tried to keep everyone in step, but it was an impossible task and Briggs in particular made it look as though he had never drilled before. The two screws were going ballistic. "Keep in step, left right left right."

Briggs fell into swinging his left leg with his left arm and the same for the right, something very difficult to do unless it comes naturally, but Briggs had mastered this as a joke in the mob. Then the baaing started. The ones at the other end of the column started making sheep noises, much to the annoyance of the screws who hurtled up and down the column shouting for the bleating to stop, which actually had the effect of making it worse. They arrived at the laundry to be met by the laundry screw who stood at the door. As Briggs entered, the screw shoved him to one side. "You wait there." Briggs stood and waited patiently.

Eventually after everyone had been counted in the screw turned to Briggs. "You, into the office." Briggs obeyed. Briggs studied this screw closely. A big man, quite old, near retirement he guessed. In the office, which looked out over the laundry the screw spoke, "A brand new prisoner, fluff still on your denims eh?" Briggs nodded, uncomfortable at being described as a rookie.

"That's correct staff," Briggs expressionless.

"Well let me give you some advice that will enable you to get your bird over without grief." The old screw smiled but it appeared malicious. Briggs nodded, not that there was anything to agree with, but more because it seemed to punctuate the screw's monologue. "Firstly don't upset me, otherwise I become petty and upset you, got it?" Briggs nodded. "I shout shit, you jump on the shovel right?"

Briggs, deadpan, "Yes staff."

"Secondly do your bit in the laundry and you will find time passes quickly. Don't get involved in drugs or any silly conspiracies." Briggs nodded. "Right go and see Ali over there. He's the laundry No. 1, he'll give you a job to do. I shall be watching you."

Briggs went out into the laundry, the indicated Pakistani, Ali was leaning up against a big spin dryer. "The screw says you are going to give me something to do," Briggs said sullenly.

"Yes old chap, Briggs isn't it?" The Pakistani spoke with the fruity accent of a public schoolboy. "Nice to have you aboard. I'm sure we will get on very well indeed. I am Ali and before you ask, I am in for mortgage fraud, silly misunderstanding except of course they ended up without their money," he cackled gleefully. "Now to work. I am going to put you on the calendar machine with some other nice chaps. All you have to do is to put the pillowcases or sheets or whatever in one end and they come out dry and ironed, the full bit. All that then has to be done is to fold them and stack them." Ali stepped forward and began feeding wet pillowcases into the machine. The pillowcases went underneath a roller and onto another roller which Briggs surmised was heated by internal heat source, either gas or electric. Then it was picked up by another roller and spewed out onto the platform at the other end, where his opposite number received it and folded it. Ali nodded to Briggs who took this to mean that he was now in charge of putting wet pillowcases into the machine. Briggs carried on placing the pillowcases in the machine until tea break. After that he was put on placing sheets in the machine, which was a two man operation. His new partner was a big Yorkshireman who kept sneering at Briggs, and muttering, "Fooking filth' in a broad Yorkshire accent. As they placed the sheets onto the calendar, Yorky kept making life difficult for Briggs by putting the sheet in before Briggs was ready, therefore, the sheet came out the other end dry but crinkled, plus Briggs became flustered by the abuse dished out by the other operators. After a few such incidents, Briggs had had enough. He watched the screw's office and waited until his back was turned. Briggs caught hold of the Yorky and nutted him hard on the forehead. Yorky collapsed on the floor. Briggs knelt beside him. "Now listen my old Yorkshire pudding, don't fuck me about, cos I'm not up for it." Briggs put his thumb inside Yorky's cheek and jerked his head towards him. "I don't think I have broken anything this time, but next time who knows?" Yorky nodded quietly. The screw came out of his office.

"What's up here, what's happened?" Briggs smiled brightly.

"I think Yorky has trouble with heat staff, he has come over all faint." Yorky, who was now on his feet nodded. The screw, noticing the fast approaching bruise on Yorky's forehead, examined it closely. "I tripped staff and fell over, knocking my head on the machine as I fell." The screw nodded and gave Briggs a look which indicated he did not believe a word of it. Briggs and Yorky carried on putting the sheets into the machine in perfect harmony. At lunchtime Yorky even smiled at him.

Having settled in among the prisoners in the hut and the laundry during the day, Briggs had another more trying test to face – his first visit from his family. He knew they would be here on Saturday afternoon – the full bit, Maggie, three kids and mother. He was not relishing the prospect for he knew the kids would be upset and his mother would be distraught. The saving grace was that Maggie, as usual, would hold everything together. He could already hear his mother threatening the screw. "You harm my boy and I'll come looking for you," a statement which had come down over the years. Briggs was aching to see them, to have some contact with the family he loved so dearly, but at the same time, he knew he would be in pain from the visit, more pain than the plastics and nonces could inflict on him, as he missed them all so terribly.

Saturday after lunch, Briggs dressed in his grey flannels and crisp blue and white striped shirt and black shoes bulled to a fine finish. He looked in the full length mirror and decided he looked half smart. He waited in the wing office with the others waiting for a visit. Briggs noticed an unusual bit of graffiti above the door. It read 'get the abbey habit' referring to saving with the Abbey National Building Society. Then it continued in the same hand "Trunk a monk."

They all stood around in their grey flannels the same as Briggs. He smiled to himself. Each rigout represented a quarter of an ounce of tobacco to the No. 1 Hoffman press operator in the laundry. Briggs decided that when the present incumbent was released to further villainy, he would endeavour to get that job. They called three names at a time, maybe they were trying to heighten the suspense. After three groups, his name was included. He strode across to the visiting hut which was next to the main gate. The screw on the door demanded, "Name and number?"

Briggs looked over him to see if they were here or in sight maybe. "Er Briggs L19266, staff."

"Right stand behind that table over there" he instructed, indicating a table and four chairs. Briggs hurried across to the table and stood as directed, as if by obeying quickly he could hurry the procedure along. Other prisoners came in and stood as directed. Briggs' eyes were riveted on the entrance. Eventually it was all set, each table had a prisoner behind it. The visitors' entrance opened and they started coming in.

Briggs was looking for his little tribe and eventually he caught sight of Tommy with his big brother Dave holding his hand. Tommy cried "Dad, Dad" and pulled his brother towards the table. Not that

David was unwilling, more surprised by his sudden acceleration. Tommy jumped into his Dad's arms, crying and cuddling. "Dad I've missed you so much." Briggs was crying and trying hard to camouflage the fact. Briggs' tears had an effect on David. Briggs got chairs for them all. Tommy could not be unglued from his Dad and Briggs knew that the end of visiting was going to be traumatic. They all kissed and cuddled, tears were forthcoming from Maggie, Veronica, Sally and Tom, only David remained with stoically dry eyes. But closer examination revealed him to be close to tears as well.

Tom sat up. "Dad are you coming home with us?" Briggs gulped back the lump in his throat.

"No sorry Tom, I have got to stay here for a while." Tom was crestfallen.

"But why, there's only those two old men at the end of the room." He indicated the two screws now sitting at a table drinking coffee. "You could bash them and we would be away, nothing could stop us."

Briggs laughed. "Tom it's not them we have to worry about, it's the twenty thousand who would be looking for me afterwards. Anyway, it's better to get this over than be hiding under the stairs for the rest of my life." Tom seemed crestfallen. "Come on now mate, bear up, Mum and the rest need your help, so you must do your best, always do your best." Briggs' voice faltered, he could feel the tears welling up again behind his eyes. He looked into his son's eyes and was wounded by the hurt he saw there. "Tom, I love you, you know that, there is no-one in the whole world I would rather be with than you, Mum, David and Sally, but the court has ordered me to stay here just for a little while, then I can come home. Then I promise I'll never go away again and we will do all the things you want and get into trouble together, like before." Tom showed a trace of a smile. His Dad tickled him as he always did, he laughed and the moment passed.

Briggs dreaded the end of the visit but, in the meantime, they sat and discussed things that had happened. Veronica, Briggs' Mum asked, "How were things in the Scrubs, everyone said you had a hard time?" Briggs squeezed her arm.

"No worries Mum, they were all very nice chaps in there, they looked after me really well," thinking of his gratitude to Percy.

Veronica nodded sagely not believing a word of it.

"Any bruises? Broken bones?" She said it quietly so, hopefully, Maggie and the kids would not hear.

"Not on me, Mum, others maybe." Veronica smiled knowing that her boy, even he had taken a hiding, had maybe done it the right way.

"Time's up." The old screw that Tom had aptly described got up and began walking up and down. Another screw, one which Briggs had not seen before, a stern-faced one pipper stationed himself at the exit from the visiting hall. Tom began to cry, tears streaming down his cheeks.

"Dad, can I stay here with you. I won't be a problem honest." The straightforward logic of a six year old.

"No, come on mate, it's difficult enough for everyone, you'll make the old man cry in a minute."

"Come on, time's up." The patrolling screw interrupted the conversation. Briggs turned and looked at him. The screw, unable to hold the confrontation, walked away.

"Look Tom, behave or they won't let me out when I should come home, so if you get up tight with them they will just keep me here longer. I'm relying on you, please mate." Tom nodded, holding back the tears as best as a six year old can.

Briggs stood and watched his little brood going out of the visiting hall, at the end of which they all turned and waved. Briggs waved back. It struck Briggs at this point that if there was a punishment part of his sentence, this was it. Others maybe would have welcomed being apart from their family but not him. Briggs stood and waited. The screw by the door called, "over here and form a queue, fivers to the left and tenners to the right." Briggs didn't cotton on to this waggish reference to the visitors handing money over on visits. Briggs wandered over and stood in the queue. Another screw walked along the line. He tapped Briggs on the shoulder. "First visit?" Briggs nodded, almost unable to speak. "Over there." Briggs was jumped to the front of the queue and let back into the prison first without being searched.

As Briggs walked back behind "A" wing, he found Derek standing on the fire escape. "Oi want a cup of tea officer?" Briggs nodded and climbed the fire escape and onto Derek's landing where Derek's cell was right at the end. Briggs entered and sat on the bed. Derek had already got the kettle on and the makings ready. "Rough visit mate?" Briggs nodded again, not sure that he would ever regain control over his vocal chords. "First one usually is. Don't worry they do get better, you'll soon get used to it." Briggs felt drained.

"I hope not." Briggs contemplated the floor. Derek served up the tea and after a while Briggs felt a little better.

"Tell you what, there are three of us in here who can play bridge, we'll teach you and you can make the fourth." So started Briggs lifelong interest in the game.

As the months passed, Briggs got almost used to the unreal atmosphere of the visiting hall, but he never ever got used to Tom's insistent questions. "When are you coming home Dad? When?" and the tears that came with the end of each visit. Briggs never got involved in the business of having money passed to him by his visitors as some of the other prisoners did. Like Royalty, he did not need money.

Having sorted himself out with his fellow prisoners and with his work, Briggs settled down to, as the old lags say, 'do his bird.' His coveted job in the laundry became vacant on the release of the prisoner who held it, and after blandishments to Ali he was promoted to No 1 Hoffman presser. Because of this elevation his pay went from £1.87 to £2.50 per week. Not enough to go mad on, but enough to survive on in nick. He earned extra by preparing prisoners' gear for visits. He had learnt earlier that the going rate was a quarter of an ounce per kit and, although Briggs did not smoke, he used this extra tobacco to buy letters, coffee, soap, and other articles to ease his existence.

Briggs found his sentence conformed in his mind to a hill or to a mountain perhaps, the apex being the halfway mark around Christmas. It was hard going getting there, but once Christmas came and went he began to feel quite chirpy, and looked forward with optimism to the end of his sentence.

Briggs became accepted as a universally respected member of prison society and was rarely referred to as 'ex old bill', but usually as 'Sarge' or 'Big Tel', neither of which bothered him. He had been propositioned by a homosexual, who had told him, "I think I am in love with you."

Briggs had borne in mind the advice given to him by Percy in the

Scrubs and resisted the urge to laugh, and told the young man, "I am sorry I don't get it off that way."

The homosexual had been very nice about it and said, "Well, I shall just have to admire you from afar and maybe have wet dreams about you" and minced off down the laundry. Briggs never mentioned this encounter to anyone in the prison lest it got back to the ardent prisoner's ears.

One of the strange customs which Briggs fell foul of was the unwritten rule that you did not attend the cinema on Wednesday nights, unless you were confirmed in the homosexual creed. The cinema was open on four nights a week Monday through to Thursday, Two nights each to A wing and B Wing, which were alternated each week. Therefore, if it was your week to be there on a Wednesday night you swopped the ticket with a poof who wanted to be there. Fairly simple, except that Briggs didn't know and attended on a Wednesday night and happened to notice that almost everyone was engaged in some form of sexual congress, obviously except him. He approached the supervising screw and demanded to be let out. The screw, incidentally, had to extricate himself from the arms of his male lover before unlocking the door. Briggs never again attended the cinema on a Wednesday night.

In about the February Briggs began to get messages from Wandsworth through the grapevine that Ibrahim Hussein, one of the Pringles' soldiers who had gone down on the hospital blag was due to be transferred to Ford on the event of coming towards his last year inside. The gist of the messages was that Hussein and his mates were going to give Briggs the going over of his life, which didn't really bother Briggs. However, what did concern him was that the senior members of the teams came to him and pledged support 'should it go orf at all meetings.' The team that surprised him was the robbery firm. Briggs would have thought they would fall in behind Hussein. However it was explained to him that Hussein was a 'gofor' i.e. "go for this and go for that" and, as such, was a lower form of life and would not be allowed on the robbery team. Briggs pondered this situation and he could see quite plainly that in the event of Hussein causing trouble, a lot of prisoners, himself included, would lose remission.

On the day of Hussein's arrival Briggs waited outside the

reception block. He arranged with the reception trusty that Hussein would be processed first. Eventually Hussein emerged from the reception block to be immediately grabbed by Briggs who whisked him around the back. "Now shithead what's this about you going to do for me? If everyone else gets involved there is going to be a riot and a lot of blokes will lose remission, so let's do it now, you and me." Briggs noted that Hussein couldn't stand still, and refused to look Briggs in the eye.

"Hold up Mr. Briggs, me and my mates were only mucking about, a wind-up see." Briggs hit him and he collapsed up against a corrugated iron wall and subsided to the floor.

"You prat," Briggs was relieved, he really couldn't see this going anywhere.

"You get round and tell your plastic friends that this was your idea of a joke, cos if you don't I can see a massacre taking place with your lot at the business end." Hussein nodded, not wanting to speak or look at Briggs.

Having got used to being in prison and having the parameters laid out for him, Briggs found that doing bird was not as difficult as some had made it out to be. He could begin to understand the old lags wanting to return to the prison gate. At least there they were clean and reasonably well fed. They had someone to talk to and a cigarette or two to smoke. To them it really was not that bad, but the punishment for Briggs was being away from his family. Every visit was torture, but becoming less so, as the end was now firmly in sight, as the National Servicemen had said, "Days to do, very few. Much less than you."

Briggs very quickly became the chief scribe for his hut so that any letters that needed to be answered, or appeals that had to be submitted were all put before "Sarge." He would compose them all in his own style and of course be paid in tobacco. One of the inmates in his hut had a difficulty in writing to his girlfriend, mainly because he could not read or write. Briggs started off by reading letters from the girlfriend to him, and later, at the man's request, writing replies. Briggs became quite literary and in one memorable letter, Briggs referred adroitly to a sexual encounter they had both enjoyed, mentioning it as 'our place', and describing it as the 'exchange of tenderness and love', which Briggs thought was better than the inmate's description of 'well we always have a shag round the back of the reccy after the boozer'. Briggs' letters ignited a flame in the young girl's heart and it soon became obvious that she had fallen in love with the writer of the letters, much to Briggs' embarrassment.

One of the occupants of the hut, had the badge of the SAS on the wall of his bedspace and on occasions took to bragging about his exploits whilst a member of that regiment. Briggs asked in wonder when he had been in the regiment. From his replies, it transpired that he and Briggs should know each other but clearly did not. The other chap was obviously a daydreamer but Briggs did not expose him as dreams are sometimes better left undisturbed.

Almost as soon as Briggs had arrived at Ford he had submitted appeal forms. Appealing not against sentence but against conviction. Briggs could not understand why he did not hear anything at first and the months had gone by almost to the end of his sentence before any real movement took place. He had had a telephone call from a lady in the appeals office of the High Court of Justice who invited him to apply for legal aid, and intimated that this would be granted again, rather than represent himself. Briggs refused legal aid, stating absolutely that he was not going to be fitted up again. His appeals took an age to get to the first Judge who had merely refused to grant him leave to appeal. Briggs was stunned and pushed his appeal on to the full court stating his desire of appearing before the Court and presenting his application for leave to appeal.

One of the grounds for his appeal was that his defence had been impeded by the involvement of the Security Services and Ryan's covert employment. To this end, he wrote to his brief, Miss Cotterill, asking her to confirm that conversation he and his wife had had with her about Ryan's involvement in Security Service matters. He was astounded by the reply, to the effect that Miss Cotterill "could not recall that particular conversation" – not that it did or did not occur – just that it couldn't be recalled.

After this process had been going on for some considerable time, and about a month before he was due for release, Briggs was called before an obnoxious two pipper who informed him that it was within the appeal court's powers to start his sentence again from the date of his failed appeal, and fail it certainly would. Briggs nodded silently. The two pipper advised Briggs that he would be better occupied thinking about the welfare of his family than plumbing the depths of the appeals system. Briggs said nothing but was also unsure whether this could happen or not.

Briggs checked with one of the incarcerated barristers and was told that this could be the case, but only in really special cases. Briggs paid the barrister with two ounces of tobacco and smiled to himself, tobacco was probably the most unusual fee that the brief had ever received. Briggs mulled over the situation for a few days, finally deciding that it wasn't worth it now so near the end of his sentence. Clearly the establishment were ensuring that the Security Services were to be accommodated in their desire to keep the whole affair under wraps. Briggs finally decided to abandon his appeal. He didn't feel happy about this situation, but didn't see what else he could do. He wasn't a member of any minority group of either ethnic or sexual proclivity and, therefore, would excite neither the media nor the verbose left wing righters of injustice. On the other hand, he could see that it would not be beyond the realms of possibility that they would cause problems for his family and delay his release from prison.

About a week after he had decided to abandon his appeal, but before he had gone public, he was visited by a Detective Chief Inspector and his bag carrier, a Detective Sergeant, both of whom Briggs had served with. They were very chary about where they were posted. Briggs suspected they were both from Complaints Investigation. The Chief Inspector was very jolly. "How are you going Tel?" lots of smiles but sadly little sincerity.

"I'm okay, but being inside cramps your style, know what I mean?" Briggs not feeling very helpful, but waiting to find the reason for this visit, knowing full well that these two would not cross the road to spit on him. "Anyway you haven't come all this way to find out how I am, what do you want?"

The Chief Inspector settled himself deeper into his chair. "Tel, it's about your pension, a word has been put in for you. You can have your pension whichever way you want, draw it now, or leave it for later on, whichever." The Chief Inspector beamed the snake-like smile which some senior officers effect almost naturally. Briggs was completely puzzled. He knew that none of the others serving time with him had been offered their pensions, including the Assistant Chief Constable.

"Why me?" he asked. The Chief Inspector simply shrugged his shoulders, whilst the skipper looked aimlessly out of the window. Perhaps the skipper was related to Ron Jones, as he certainly reminded Briggs of him. "And what is required of me to keep, or get my pension?" The Chief Inspector studied the table top as though the very secret of life was inscribed there. "Nothing really Tel, just be reasonable, no rocking the boat, understood?" Briggs nodded, he knew exactly what was required of him.

The Chief Inspector placed his briefcase on the table and got some forms out. "Complete these and providing you continue to be a good boy, your pension will be there when you want it." Briggs took the forms and put them in his jeans pocket for later examination.

"That it?" said Briggs deadpan and aggressive and, in truth, becoming angrier by the second.

The Chief Inspector tried to mollify Briggs. "Now, Tel don't be that way, they're trying to do you a favour." Briggs' head went back and he laughed.

"Only because they have to." The Sergeant felt the need to inject his character on the proceedings. "Oi, Briggsy, behave or we might have to..." Briggs stared at the bag carrier and knew from previous experience that this was a lower form of life.

"Or what? What are you really going to do, kiss his dick?" indicating the Chief Inspector, "Have a wank or what?" The screw became alive as if by magic.

"Be polite to official visitors Briggs." Briggs stared at the screw for a moment.

"Fuck off." Briggs made a sudden move towards the sergeant who shrank back out of harm's way. Briggs grinned at him, "Wanker," telling the truth. The screw thumped the panic button and three screws came in and hustled Briggs out of the interview room and across the square to the punishment block.

Briggs sat in his bare cell and contemplated his future at Wandsworth. In his solitary cell and in a calmer mood, Briggs studied the pension forms closely. They appeared to state that he had left the Police Force under normal circumstances and was therefore entitled to his pension. Briggs put them back in his pocket for later. They deserved more careful consideration.

As it came close to last bell, there was a tap tap at his cell window and Briggs climbed on to the bunk and peered through the bars into the yard. There was the ex hut leader standing on a box holding a plate and a mug of something hot and steaming in his hand. Mugsy, one of his mates from the hut, kept cavey. "Here Sarge cop hold." The screw is turning a blind eye, he owes me a favour." He passed the plate and the mug onto the sill and Briggs wrestled it down onto his bed.

"Cheers Hero," he called to his departing friend. He sat on his bed and devoured his supper, after which he settled down and made his bed, climbed into it and before falling asleep, wondered over the day's events. One month to serve and here he was a police pensioner, if he wanted it. Did he want it? He was confused. He was probably going to lose his remission or best part of it when he came up in front of the Governor in the morning and that would be hard to take. Why couldn't he just keep his temper for once? Briggs sighed and fell asleep.

He slept soundly in spite of his thoughts. In the morning he was treated to a solitary breakfast which had been described to him as 'shit on toast'. Briggs waded through the toasted offering and gulped down the tea, only too aware that he was hungry. He cleaned himself as best he could. The screw gave him a razor blade for the antiquated safety razor, with a perfunctory, "Don't cut yer throat, or if you do, give me that blade back first." Briggs scraped as much stubble from his chin as he could without being able to see in a mirror. He sat down and contemplated the wall opposite, reading the graffiti with interest. One particularly caught his attention. It was a London Underground sign. Underneath it stated "Wandsworth next stop."

"Ain't that the truth" thought Briggs.

An hour later the cell door swung open. "Briggs out, now." The slimy screw who advised him to drop his appeal was on duty. "Done it up in big heaps this time Briggsy, we'll see how hard you are when the lads at Wandsworth get hold of you."

Briggs was marched across the square and, strangely enough, out of the prison into the admin area where he stood with the slimy screw outside the Governor's office. As he stood there he almost heard Regimental Sergeant Major Ted Smith bellow, "Prisoner and escort shun, left turn double march." Briggs sighed with sentimental longing for those far off days when things were so simple.

406

"Right then, in you go, keep your hands by your side, do not step over the mark, you've already done that." The chief screw laughed at his own joke. "And call the guvnor sir." The chief screw ushered him into the presence of the Governor, somebody who was rarely seen in the prison proper and whom Briggs had taken care to avoid at all costs. But here he was, yet another scrape to put down to his temper.

"Yes, Briggs isn't it?" The unmistakable officer accent. Briggs wondered which service he had been in. Briggs studied him closely, and decided it must be the navy, but was by no means certain. "Now what have you been up to? Ah yes being rude and threatening to official visitors. Anything to say on the matter?" Briggs knew the score, he had been taught at great length in the army.

"No sir nothing to say."

The Governor nodded, and turned to the chief screw. "Has he been in any trouble since he has been with us chief?"

The chief officer braced himself to attention and said, "No trouble sir, he's been a model prisoner."

The Governor closed the file. "I see. Under the circumstances, I shall admonish the prisoner, it would be a shame to take away his remission at this stage." Briggs was astounded, so was the chief officer, who ushered Briggs out of the presence.

"Right then Briggs." The chief stumbled over the next sentence. "Er, what does admonish mean, do you know Briggs?" Briggs allowed himself a smile.

"It means I have been told off, nothing more."

The chief straightened himself, "I see, well lucky you, now back to the laundry before the Governor changes his mind, he's obviously feeling very lenient today." Briggs marched away before they changed their minds and sent him to Wandsworth. Briggs found out later from the Governor's trusty that the visiting police officers had refused to give evidence or a statement of any kind. Therefore, had he pleaded 'not guilty', he might not even have been admonished, but his prison record was hardly high on his agenda of priorities.

Briggs felt his last month dragging along. He kept studying the date on the calendar, as though he could will it into tomorrow. His prison kit had been claimed by the other prisoners, things that he had in turn been given by other leaving cons. Books, pens, personal kit were all allocated to the various claimants. His denims and shirts particularly were in high demand, because Briggs, working in the laundry, had ample chance to improve the quality of his personal kit by exchanging it with some of that passing through from other prisons.

Eventually the day arrived. After thinking his photographs had been stolen and then realising he was on the out today, he sat on his bed and mulled over the tortuous course that had led to him being here. "Stand by your beds," the morning call to head count. It was slimy screw on duty, it just had to be. Briggs waited and the screw counted. Briggs stood with the mug of tea in his hand. "My last chance to be rude to you Briggsy, on the out this morning are we?" The bantering tone of the screw made Briggs shudder. He could feel himself getting annoyed.

"That's right, your last chance." Briggs said it slowly and, he hoped, heavy with menace. The slimy screw must have misunderstood him, for he threw his head back and roared with laughter. Briggs was non-plussed but didn't feel the need to say anything extra. The bell rang for breakfast and they all dressed and trooped over to the mess hall. On the way Briggs was ragged by the other prisoners. He felt great the trial was over at last, this morning he was going home. He would no longer have to bear his youngster's tears in the visiting hall.

He got his breakfast. This morning there was a choice, 'meat or cheese filth'. This was a sort of potato and something pie with a roasted crust on the top made up from yesterday's left over potatoes. He went over to the 'old bill's table', and as he did so, they all rose and began clapping. Briggs felt a lump in his throat; it seemed they all wanted to shake his hand. Derek said very little. It was obvious he was going to miss his mate. Briggs finished his breakfast quickly, anxious to be away, on the out. He rose and got his gear together. "See you later chaps, look me up when you get out." He squeezed Derek's shoulder and walked away quickly.

Briggs collected his remaining bits and pieces and left his bedspace. Mugsy and hero (the pseudo SAS man) were there. "Cheers Sarge" they said in unison and Briggs thought he detected a bit of sentimentality from Mugsy. He left the billet and walked towards reception. Loads of prisoners were waiting alongside the path and Briggs thought they were waiting for parade. He noticed that all the teams were there, including the poofs. They were all cheering and taking the piss. As he walked by, they reached forward and patted his shoulder. Briggs was surprised, he didn't think he was that popular. As he got close to the reception, he saw Derek talking to the other 'ticket of leave' men. Derek grinned. "Well done mate, they haven't broken you."

Briggs was surprised his incarceration could be seen in such terms. He had concentrated on survival, nothing else. "Here, do us a favour swop watches, yours is more reliable than mine." Briggs nodded and took off his watch and gave it to Derek in exchange for his. Briggs shook hands with Derek and went into the reception hut and waited to be processed as the teams dispersed to parade.

A Transit mini bus pulled up outside and they signed their dockets and went outside and into the mini bus. The slimy screw got in and drove them to the car park which was about fifty yards away. Briggs could see Maggie and the kids in the car park and the bus stopped to let them all out. Briggs took his cardboard boxes and went towards his beaten up old Ford Escort and waiting family, but before he had moved two yards he was grabbed by David, Sally and Tom. They were all laughing. Maggie stood by the car amused and pleased by this performance. After Briggs had kissed them all he managed to get round to Maggie. "Great to see you love, thanks for everything." They kissed and hugged, the kids threw his boxes into the boot. Briggs got into the passenger seat where Rennie the spaniel was waiting in the footwell. Briggs stroked him, "Good boy" he said and Rennie bit him. "Shit that hurt, a fine welcome home." They all roared their amusement at the old man's pain, and drove home singing the silly songs they always sang when out in the car. Tom sat on his Dad's lap and cuddled close.

After a while the boy asked, "You're not going back in there are you Dad? Briggs hugged his son. "No Tom that's all done, no more away for me. I shall be a permanent fixture now, moaning about untidy bedrooms and who can't get up in the mornings." The two in the back blew raspberries. Everything was back to normal.